THE UNCROWNED KING

A pale, silver-blue glow was emanating from the Stone where Wallace's fingers rested. The glow spread up Wallace's hands and arms until his whole body was enwrapped in a soft nimbus of pure light. A fragrance like incense permeated the air, unearthly in its sweetness. To Arnault, the perfume had the quality of angelic sanctity. Wallace's eyes lifted in wonder to something only he could see.

Arnault said softly, "We have just witnessed the calling of William Wallace to the service of the Stone of Destiny . . ."

✝ ✝ ✝ ✝ ✝ ✝

"This seamless combination of historical novel and fantasy offers rich background and . . . substantial suspense and adventure."
—*Publishers Weekly*

"A full, rich novel that I could not put down . . . unforgettable. Anyone interested in legends of chivalry should rush to read this."
—*Explorations*

Also available from Warner Aspect
Edited by Katherine Kurtz

Tales of the Knights Templar

On Crusade: More Tales of the Knights Templar

ATTENTION: SCHOOLS AND CORPORATIONS
WARNER books are available at quantity discounts with bulk purchase for educational, business, or sales promotional use. For information, please write to: SPECIAL SALES DEPARTMENT, WARNER BOOKS, 1271 AVENUE OF THE AMERICAS, NEW YORK, N.Y. 10020

The TEMPLE AND THE STONE

KATHERINE KURTZ AND DEBORAH TURNER HARRIS

A Time Warner Company

If you purchase this book without a cover you should be aware that this book may have been stolen property and reported as "unsold and destroyed" to the publisher. In such case neither the author nor the publisher has received any payment for this "stripped book."

WARNER BOOKS EDITION

Copyright © 1998 by Katherine Kurtz and Deborah Turner Harris
All rights reserved.

Aspect® name and logo are registered trademarks of Warner Books, Inc.

Cover design by Don Puckey
Cover illustration by Greg Call
Handlettering by Carl Dellacroce

Warner Books, Inc.
1271 Avenue of the Americas
New York, NY 10020

Visit our Web site at
www.warnerbooks.com

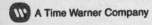 A Time Warner Company

Printed in the United States of America

Originally published in hardcover by Warner Books.
First Paperback Printing: September 1999

10 9 8 7 6 5 4 3 2 1

For Richard Bruce McMillan,
"Mr. History,"
whose name recalls
one of Scotland's most illustrious kings.
Without doubt, teaching our young
about their past is one of the most noble
of human occupations.

The TEMPLE And The STONE

it upon himself to break it.

PROLOGUE

ON A STORMY, SNOW-DRIVEN NIGHT IN MARCH OF 1286, fulfilling a prophecy of Thomas the Rhymer, Alexander III of Scotland met his death untimely when his horse plunged over a cliff near Kinghorn, across the firth from Edinburgh, as he hurried to rejoin his young bride of less than a year. No children had come of this union, and all three children of his previous marriage had predeceased him, both sons dying without issue. His daughter, married to King Eric Magnusson of Norway, had died giving birth to her only child: a princess called Margaret like herself, to be known as the Maid of Norway. Upon this solitary grandchild of Alexander III now devolved all the hopes of the noble house of Canmore, whose royal line had ruled Scotland for more than two centuries.

But de jure succession to the Scottish throne and de facto accession to it might be entirely different propositions, for the new Queen of Scots was a child of less than three years, and King Edward of England had been casting acquisitive eyes at his northern neighbor for nearly two decades. Knowing that Edward must be appeased, Margaret's father and selected representatives of the Scottish nobility declared a regency in her name and began immediately to explore ways and means by which the child might take up her birthright. Four years of careful negotiation concluded in an agreement whereby Margaret would be wed to Edward's eldest son, Edward of Caernarvon, their issue eventually to rule Scotland and England under one crown, thereby achieving by diplomacy what the English king had feared he must win by force—though that specter remained a veiled threat that was never far from the minds of the Scots nobility.

So confident was Edward in his aspirations that, even before the marriage treaty was drawn up at Birgham in July of 1290, he had dispatched an English ship to fetch his son's child-bride home, its hold laden with gingerbread, sugar loaves, and toys for the little Maid.

But Margaret's father returned it empty and without her, preferring to entrust his daughter to a ship of his own choosing . . .

Part I

Part 1

Chapter One

IN MID-SEPTEMBER OF 1290, UNDER CLEAR SKIES AND WITH a brisk following breeze, a stout Norse-built cog set sail from the Norwegian port of Bergen, carrying to her wedding with England the seven-year-old Margaret Queen of Scots, known as the Maid of Norway.

The marriage had been arranged, in part, through the offices of the bearded, white-cloaked man standing at the taffrail of the Maid's ship. Frère Arnault de Saint Clair, Knight of the Temple of Jerusalem, had been among a number of outside negotiators whose assistance had facilitated the Treaty of Birgham; for the Temple's reputation for impartial arbitration was recognized universally, and the fortunes both of Scotland and of England were of great interest to all of Europe.

A singular array of qualifications commended Frère Arnault to his present assignment. Though a veteran of nearly twenty years' service as a Knight Templar, much of it in and around the Holy Land, he had been based for most of the past decade at the Order's Paris Temple, where he was regularly entrusted with sensitive financial and diplomatic missions on behalf of the Visitor of France, who was second only to the Grand Master, and the highest ranking Templar in Europe.

Landless youngest son of a prosperous Breton knight, facile in a handful of languages besides his native French, Arnault moved with equal ease among courtiers and churchmen as on the battlefield, as glib of tongue as he was quick of wit and fleet of sword. Coupled with the fortunes of his birth, an accompanying spiritual inclination might have led him to a rich sinecure as clerkly chancellor of some great house or even an eventual mitre; but a parallel excellence in the knightly pursuits at which his elder brothers excelled had directed him instead to a vocation as a Knight Templar.

These circumstances, along with an awareness of Scottish affairs—by dint of collateral cousins in Scotland—had earned him an appointment to the Birgham delegation beside Frère Brian de Jay, the English-born Preceptor of Scotland, who had knowledge of both English and Scottish law. The two had not met prior to their present assignment, and Arnault could not say that he had warmed to Jay in the months they had spent at the negotiating table; but the English knight did seem to know his business where the law was concerned. Having seen the treaty signed and sealed, the two men were now accompanying the little princess to Scotland, where she would be met by a suitable escort of her Scottish nobles. From there, she would travel south to London, where a new life and a new home awaited her.

The wind freshened, shifting a few degrees to the north, and Arnault breathed deeply of the brisk sea air, always welcome after the years spent in the deserts of Outremer. Unarmored here at sea, though his sword was girt always at his side, he wore beneath his mantle the formal white habit of Templar monastic profession, emblazoned on the breast with the splayed, eight-pointed red cross of the Order. His dark hair was barbered close to his head, as required by the Rule, but he had leave to keep his beard neatly trimmed, out of deference to the more fastidious circles in which his diplomatic duties obliged him to move.

He allowed himself a contented sigh as he swept his gaze around him. The royal ship was threading her way along the last of the deep fjords leading out to sea. The rigging was bright with pennons in the colors of Norway and Scotland, lifting gaily on the wind, and the princess's half-dozen Norwegian attendants made a colorful gathering around her on the deck below.

Margaret herself was almost lost in the midst of them: a diminutive, flaxen-haired doll muffled in furs, sheltering in the grandfatherly embrace of Bishop Narve of Bergen. To Arnault's discerning gaze, watching from the machicolated platform of the ship's stern castle, she appeared somewhat frail and not entirely well, her small face pinched and white under its rich coif of silk and gold netting.

Less than reassured at the sight, Arnault found himself uneasily aware how the welfare of the entire Scottish nation was now dependent on the indifferent health of this one small girl. Even as that thought crossed his mind, he was joined at the rail by his Templar companion, who nodded somewhat distractedly.

Somewhat older than Arnault, Brian de Jay was a big, muscled man with short-cropped blond hair, a white-toothed grin within his curly blond beard, and eyes of a glacial blue. Leaning indolently on the railing, he cast a sour glance upward toward the ship's rigging, where the freshening wind was fretting at the reefs in the ship's great square sail.

"I would have preferred the English ship that King Edward sent," he remarked. "Even more, I would have preferred to sail six weeks ago. I like not these fickle seas in the north."

Arnault shrugged. "No doubt King Eric preferred to entrust his daughter to a ship of Norse crafting."

"The king will have been affronted at the snub," Jay replied. "It makes for a less than auspicious beginning to the alliance."

"The Norse shipwrights take great pride in their work," Arnault said neutrally, surprised at this somewhat partisan statement regarding the English king. "King Eric evidently felt that a Norwegian-built vessel would prove the more seaworthy in the event of a storm."

"Well, the delay makes storms more likely," Jay said with a grimace. "I hope he doesn't have cause to regret his decision. Aside from the political repercussions, I'd hate to see all our efforts wasted—especially when we could have been putting our energies to better effect in defense of our domains."

He was referring, Arnault knew, to the Templar strongholds of the East: Acre and Tripoli, Tyre and Sidon, Athlit and Haifa—all that now remained of the former crusader Kingdom of Outremer. Since the fall of Jerusalem, over a century before, the great crusading Orders of the Temple and the Hospital had managed—just—to retain those strongholds, bolstered by sporadic infusions of aid from the West; but their position in recent years had become increasingly perilous.

"Look at us," Jay continued disparagingly. "We are meant to be men of war. Surely our place is in the Holy Land, where the danger is—not trailing like lapdogs about the skirts of these diplomats! Our proper vocation is fighting—not matchmaking on behalf of young children."

Arnault gazed out to sea, reflecting that these militant sentiments might have carried more weight if Jay had been speaking from previous experience in the East. As it was, the Preceptor of Scotland owed his present position of eminence to the favor of the Master of England, who had groomed him for administrative function and then sent him north to oversee the Scottish houses of the Order. Unlike Arnault, who had seen active service in the Holy Land and carried the scars to prove it, Jay had yet to match words with deeds on the field of battle.

"We go where we're ordered, and do as we're told," Arnault said mildly. "And don't underestimate the value of what has been achieved by the Treaty of Birgham. If this marriage succeeds, it could bring us a step closer to redeeming the Kingdom of Outremer."

Not that the auguries were good for such an outcome. Only a few months before, the delicate balance in Acre—most crucial of the Order's remaining holdings in the East—had nearly come unstuck when a band of peasant levies newly arrived from Tuscany went on a rampage and massacred a number of Muslim merchants in an unprovoked attack. The Mameluke Sultan Qalawun had been justifiably incensed by the incident, and only some frantic last-minute negotiations on behalf of the Franks had averted an outbreak of full-scale reprisals. A fragile truce was holding thus far, but the threat of war remained ever present. The Order's military strategists hoped that if hostilities could be kept at bay long enough, the sovereign powers of Christendom might be more readily persuaded to lend their aid to the defense and eventual reclamation of the Frankish Kingdom.

"I suppose the marriage *might* pry loose some support from King Edward," Jay replied. His expression turned speculative at the prospect of a new crusade. "He certainly knows the Holy Land from the pilgrim campaigns of his youth. Given the part we have played in securing this Scottish alliance, perhaps he will show his gratitude by returning to Acre at the head of another army. I'll wager the Mamelukes would find him a formidable opponent."

Arnault merely nodded his agreement. At his best, Edward Plantagenet was a strong leader, shrewd in his judgments and farsighted in his aspirations. But he was also capable of being unconscionably vindictive; and his appetite for power, once roused, was insatiable. Having set his sights on Scotland, he would stop at nothing now to acquire it. If

this marriage compact were to fail—for whatever reason—
Edward's next recourse might well be invasion.

The weather held, despite Jay's uneasiness. Princess Margaret, her female attendants, and the bishop and his clerk were quartered beneath the stern castle, where partitioning had been installed to create cramped shelter for sleeping. The princess's military escort, including the two Knights Templar, slept out on deck with most of the crew, under the sheltering lee of the forward castle.

Some time after midnight during their second night out from Bergen, Arnault awoke to an awareness that the ship's momentum had changed. Casting off his blanket, he rose quietly to investigate, bracing himself against the rail. They had emerged from the shelter of the Norwegian coast shortly before sunset. The stars had vanished behind a thick pall of cloud. Light from the ship's lanterns showed whitecaps building on top of the waves. The captain was up on the forecastle in close consultation with the ship's weatherman.

Making his way forward against the pitch and roll of the deck, Arnault clambered up the ship's ladder to join them. When he inquired about the ship's status, the captain's response was blunt.

"I don't like the signs. There's a storm moving in from the northwest. The currents in these waters prohibit trying to outrun it. We can only hold our course and hope to ride it out."

"How bad is it likely to get?" Arnault asked.

"I can't say," the weatherman replied. "The signs might be worse. But we will see rough winds and high seas not long after first light."

The weatherman's predictions were borne out within the next few hours. Darkness yielded to an uncertain dawn, under ominously lowering skies. The ship's crew went grimly to work, dousing the lanterns and lashing down everything on deck that was not already secure. When the sail had been trimmed and the hatches closed, the captain and the helmsmen took to their stations fore and aft and braced themselves for the coming gale.

With the arrival of the first squall, the little Princess Margaret succumbed to retching seasickness and had to be confined to her bed while the ship plunged and rolled. By midday, most of her personal attendants were similarly affected, as well as a few of the crew. Bishop Narve and the young canon who served as his secretary were among the few to be spared, and set themselves to caring for those who were not. Meanwhile, the ship's helmsman fought to keep her headed into the waves, in the teeth of a blustering wind and a day that never really got light.

Arnault had been to sea often enough to be accustomed to stormy weather. When Brian de Jay proved equally resilient in keeping his sea legs and the contents of his stomach, the two Templars joined the crew in helping keep the ship battened down against the storm, which continued throughout that day and all through the night without any sign of abating.

By morning, the state of the ship's passengers was one of abject misery. Every roll of the vessel drew groans from those lying prostrate on their pallets. The air trapped in the makeshift sleeping accommodations smelled sourly of sickness as Arnault made his staggering way to the little princess's curtained alcove.

Here he found Bishop Narve and Freu Ingabritt, the little Maid's favorite lady-in-waiting, attempting to ease the child's sufferings with infusions of herbs and other folk remedies. The elderly prelate was cradling the little girl in his arms with a grandfather's tenderness, singing softly to her in the Norse tongue. The simple rhymes and melodies were those of folksong and lullabye.

"How is she?" Arnault asked from the entryway.

The bishop looked up, his expression grave. "Not well, Frère Arnault. So young a child is too delicate for rigors such as these. If this storm does not soon abate, I fear she may not survive the journey."

All that day and the next, the ship rode the storm like a leaf in a millrace, making but little headway. Towering waves tossed the ship like a toy, often crashing over the prow and sending sheets of foam racing the length of the deck. Crew and passengers alike spent their fifth night at sea without heat or comfort. On the morning of the sixth day, the ship's timbers began to crack, and the hull began letting in water. As most of the able-bodied were set to bailing, others helped move Princess Margaret and her attendants out onto the deck, in case the ship should founder and they be trapped inside.

Oilskins and blankets were rigged to create a berth for them under the forecastle, but this was poor shelter at best. The little Maid herself seemed wholly insensible to her surroundings, and lay white and motionless in Bishop Narve's arms, with only the merest flutter of a pulse to show that she still lived. Arnault and Jay took their turns in the bucket brigade with the rest of those who were still on their feet, working in relays in a ceaseless effort to keep the hold from filling with water, but Jay clearly was unhappy with the arrangement.

"This is no fit occupation for a knight," he grumbled, as he and Arnault labored alongside the crew and the military escort.

Arnault was fighting the temptation to inquire whether Jay would prefer the alternative, when there came a sudden shout from the masthead lookout.

"Land ho! Land ahead, off the port bow!"

Abandoning their labors, the two Templar knights made their way forward. Peering hard through the rain and sea spray, Arnault was just able to make out a rocky headland jutting from the waves at the outermost limits of visibility. The deck shuddered underfoot as the ship came about, its prow bearing hard on this newfound landmark. Catching sight of the captain on the forecastle, Arnault clambered swiftly up the ladder to join him.

"Have you any idea where we are?" he asked, pitching his voice loud above the roar of the wind and waves.

The captain gave a tentative bob of the head, not taking his eyes from that speck of land. "By my reckoning, we've reached the Orkneys. I would guess this to be one of the outlying islands. There should be settlements, if we can make it to shore."

The land loomed closer. A ragged cheer went up from the crew as the ship cleared the headland and the fury of the storm somewhat abated, though rain continued to fall. Beyond, sheltered by a ridge of high ground, lay a stretch of calmer water fronting a beach of pebbly shingle. Even more welcome was the sight of a plume of smoke trickling skyward from what appeared to be a substantial farmstead, perched on the grassy slope overlooking the lagoon.

Details became clearer as they drew nearer the shore. Built Norse-fashion with walls of turf and roofs of slate, the compound encompassed several barns and a number of outbuildings, all clustered around a central dwelling, the source of the rising smoke, vented off by holes in the roof slates. Encouraged by these clear signs of habitation, the captain drew as near to the shore as he dared before ordering the anchor dropped and the ship's boat put over the side. While preparations were made to ferry the little princess and the sickest of the other passengers ashore, a delegation was sent ahead to commandeer assistance from the farm.

By the time the boat could return to the ship and bring the little princess and the bishop ashore, the farm owner and some of his household had gathered on the shore with oilskins and warm blankets and even a cart for those too ill to walk the short distance to the farmhouse. The little Maid herself was swaddled in furs and tenderly carried to the farmhouse by the bishop's canon, with Bishop Narve trailing anxiously beside them.

The two Templars were among the last of the ship's company to arrive. Gratefully accepting a bowl of hot broth from one of the maids, and changing his sodden mantle for a dry blanket, Arnault shifted his attention to the other end of the long, smoky room, where the farmwife and two girls he judged to be her daughters were clucking anxiously over a small, white-faced form bundled into a bed before the roaring fire. From their tight-lipped expressions, he inferred that there was little sign of improvement in the Maid's condition.

Bishop Narve and his canon joined the women a moment later. Arnault was taken aback to see that the old man had donned a white vestment and stole over his sober clerical array; the canon bore a lighted candle and several other items. The bishop made the sign of the cross over the child's frail, unconscious form and laid his hand on her brow as his own head bowed in prayer. From the snatches of Latin that reached his ears, Arnault realized that the old man was administering the viaticum, the Communion rite reserved by the Church for those at the point of death.

"If I were a vassal of the house of Canmore," Jay remarked in an undertone, "I would be on my knees in prayer."

"God may yet vouchsafe a miracle," Arnault murmured.

Sick at heart, he drank down his broth and withdrew to an adjoining room of the house with others of the company to await further developments. Jay followed, but joined one of the men of the princess's military escort miserably warming his hands over a brazier of hot coals. Having no desire for his own comfort, Arnault made his way numbly to the opposite side of the room, where an alcove heaped with sheepskins suddenly beckoned with an insistence that, after so long without proper rest, would not be denied.

He folded to his knees like a man sinking into quicksand, but he made himself shift to sit with his back against the wall as his heavy eyelids closed, stubbornly dragging his exhausted mind toward something approaching a suitable composure for prayer—or would appear to be prayer, or sleep, to anyone observing him.

Thus blind to his surroundings, he could still feel the wayward motion of the ship, tugging him insistently toward the sleep his body craved, but he applied long familiar disciplines to turn his focus inward, drawing a deep breath as he sought the still point at the center of his being and then conjured an image of the little princess before his mind's eye: not the frail, colorless doll barely breathing before the fire in the next room but the solemn, wide-eyed child for whom he had developed a distant fondness while he waited for her ship to sail from Bergen.

With body and mind now bending to the will of soul, he slowly found himself apparently drifting with disembodied lightness back to the threshold of the central hearth chamber where the little Maid was being tended. The sensation of being in two places at once was one he had encountered before, a state over which he had some control. Conscious of having temporarily left his physical body behind, he willed his consciousness closer toward the ailing princess. The area surrounding the child's bed was like an island of light in the midst of softly muted shadows.

He caught his breath slightly as he sensed that the source of the brightness was the little Maid herself—not the fragile, wasted shell of her physical body, but the shimmering angelform of the virginal soul softly overlaying that body. Joining the two was a silvery cord as finely spun as spider silk.

A faint flutter of relief briefly suffused him, for he knew that as long as that link remained unbroken, there was reason to hope for the little girl's recovery. But even as he allowed himself to hope, he became conscious of a chill descending suddenly upon the room, not at all related to the rain and storm outside.

All the lights in the room guttered and shrank as a shade of moving darkness seemed to permeate the room. Cold as Arctic winter, a darker core of it billowed toward the little

Maid. Even as her spiritual aspect recoiled, flickering faintly brighter, the shadow-entity struck out at the fragile silver lifeline linking body and soul.

Horrified, Arnault tried to interpose himself in spirit, but to no avail. An icy buffet dashed him aside even as the little Maid's lifeline snapped. Though her soul broke free in a flash of silvery light, the shadow swooped to engulf it. Defensive instincts flaring, Arnault surged between them in spirit, deflecting an almost overwhelming wave of sheer malice as he called on the Light to aid him. But this time his intervention was enough, if only barely.

Arrested in mid-flight, the shadow briefly turned on him, furious to be kept at bay. At the same time, the roof beams of the house seemed to melt away, simultaneously opening the way to the vault of the heavens.

Fast as summer lightning, the little Maid's child-spirit soared upward. Living stars dropped out of the sky to meet her, surrounding her with a host of bright companions to guide her safely on her homeward flight.

The shadow again attempted to follow, but again Arnault surged upward in spirit to block and restrain it. The shadow at last wrenched free with a violent twist, but too late to pursue its quarry. Flinging a parting blast of hatred in Arnault's direction, it disappeared into the night. The violence of its departure snapped Arnault back into his body with a dizzying spin of images that left him gasping for breath, heart pounding, momentarily too giddy to move.

Groggily, hardly able to see, he pulled himself unsteadily to his feet, catching his balance against the wall of turf, momentarily uncertain whether he possibly could have been dreaming. In the same moment, he felt a heavy hand on his shoulder, as Brian de Jay asked, "What's the matter? You look as pale as death—as if you'd just seen a ghost."

Before Arnault could frame any kind of response beyond a blank blink, a sudden doleful cry went up from the next room. Shaking himself loose, Arnault rushed to the doorway—and halted on the threshold in time to see Freu Ingabritt drawing breath for another wail. Beside her, Bishop Narve had tenderly gathered the little princess to his breast, his lined face contorted in a soundless grimace of grief. Around them, the little princess's other ladies-in-waiting were clinging to one another and weeping, their shoulders shaking with muffled sobs.

As Jay murmured something unintelligible at Arnault's shoulder, the farmwife came mournfully toward them and the others crowding close behind, dabbing at her eyes with a corner of her ample apron and the sorrow of a mother who has lost children of her own.

"Poor, wee lamb," she managed to whisper. "May our Lord and His dear Lady Mother receive her kindly."

Arnault drew a short, sharp breath and drew back, stunned, letting the others mill past him as he attempted to comprehend the enormity of what had just occurred. Mingled with the stark political implications of the Maid's death was his sinking certainty that his own experience had been no mere foray into dreams. The shadow he had glimpsed, and with which he had sparred, was no gentle angel of death, bringing welcome release from suffering, but rather, some malevolent entity come to destroy the innocent.

All at once he felt the need for fresh air. Closing his ears to the sounds of grieving, he wrapped himself in his blanket and stumbled outside. The rain had ceased, but the sky was still stormy, the wind still tossing at the ship anchored just offshore, now become a funeral barge instead of a wedding ship. Mercifully, Jay had stayed within.

This was not the first time Arnault had encountered evil in spiritual form. But such entities rarely entered the world of men save in response to human summoning—which meant that the attack on the little Maid had been no chance occurrence, but deliberately contrived as murder. Arnault did not doubt the testimony of his inner senses; but when he tried to imagine who could have compassed such a deed, and in such a manner and for what purpose, his thoughts reeled back on themselves in bewilderment.

He turned his face to the wind while he asked himself once again whether what he had witnessed could have been his own fantasy. But he knew with a sinking feeling in the pit of his stomach that there was no question of that.

He dared not confide in anyone in the present party; certainly not the brash and insensitive Jay. But he would certainly convey his suspicions to the appropriate superiors at the earliest opportunity.

The closest of those superiors, and one who might be strategically placed to ascertain who most might have benefited from the Maid's death, was currently assigned to the principal Scottish preceptory at Balantrodoch, just south of Edinburgh, where Brian de Jay was Master. Arnault had orders to return to Paris for reassignment after concluding his escort duties to the now dead Queen of Scots; and news of the tragedy would have to be carried abroad in any event. But since transport back to France could be arranged most expeditiously from farther south, he decided that traveling with Jay as far as Balantrodoch could be easily justified. In fact, certain of his superiors in Paris would expect it.

One thing was certain: If the little Maid's death had been compassed by agents of the Dark, Arnault's assistance eventually would be called upon to counter their intentions.

Chapter Two

THE DEATH OF THE LITTLE MAID OF NORWAY WAS OVER-shadowed in the following year by two closely connected events that shook the foundations of Christendom and utterly claimed the attention of Frère Arnault's Templar superiors at all levels. The first was the sacking of the Christian city of Tripoli, at the instigation of the Sultan Qalawun. The second was the destruction of the city of Acre by the armies of Qalawun's successor, Al-Ashraf. The Mameluke conquest of these two cities left the Latin West bereft of their last bastions in the Holy Lands of the East. All that now remained of the Frankish Kingdom of Outremer was the island fortress of Ruad, two miles off the coast.

Those most immediately affected by the loss were the Military Orders, who for nearly two centuries had vied with one another in upholding the fervor of the Crusades. Subsequently, the knights who survived the fall of Acre became wholly preoccupied with plans for a campaign of reconquest. While some returned to Europe to recruit new members, others remained in the East, based at Cyprus, to monitor the movements of the enemy.

On the last day of June 1292, a Templar galley entered the Cypriot port of Larnaca and dropped anchor within sight of the town. The first boat ashore carried two disheveled and disreputable-looking passengers in tattered desert robes, who immediately set out on foot along one of the cobbled streets adjoining the waterfront. A brisk ten minutes' walk brought them to a walled town house on a terrace overlooking the bay. The keystone of the gate arch bore the distinctive inscription of a cross *pattée,* proclaiming the house to be a dependent preceptory of the Knights Templar.

The warden at the gate was a grizzled, bull-chested serjeant with a patch over one eye. As soon as he caught sight of the two travelers his scarred face lit up in an incredulous grin.

"Frère Arnault! And Frère Torquil!" he exclaimed, quickly swinging the gate wide to admit them. "Praise be to God, then you made it to Ruad! It's been nine weeks. I feared we would never see you again, this side of heaven."

Arnault de Saint Clair produced a smile that flashed startlingly white in his black beard and dirty, sun-bronzed face. "You may laugh to hear it, Ruggiero, but our old friend Eliphas ben Ephraim said much the same thing when we met up with him in Beirut."

The Milanese serjeant's jaw dropped. "Beirut? You did well to get that far!"

Arnault's long-limbed companion, some fifteen years his junior, swept back his hood and Arab headdress and ran a big-boned hand through shaggy black hair. The afternoon sun picked up glints of copper at the roots, where a disguising application of dye was beginning to fade.

"Och, we didn't stop there," the younger man stated cheerfully. "Frère Arnault had arranged for the galley to pick us up at Caesarea. Of course, we did have a few—ah—unexpected side jaunts. But nothing we couldn't handle."

Arnault chuckled and merely shook his head at the youngster's ebullience, cocksure with the confidence of youth. Torquil Lennox had come a long way from his native Scotland to fight beside Arnault and their brother-knights on the walls of Acre thirteen months before—and the younger man's promise had been emerging steadily during the months of their association.

On previous assignments in Palestine, Arnault had established an extensive network of informants and friends of the Order among its indigenous neighbors. Following the withdrawal of the Order to Cyprus, his prior successes had earned him the dangerous job of venturing ashore north of Tripoli to gather information about the strength of the Mameluke occupation forces. By then Torquil had proven himself upon the walls of Acre. Blessed with youth, a strong fighting arm, an iron constitution, and the tongue of a born linguist, the young Scot had been Arnault's first choice of companions for the venture.

Mentally calculating the distance the two knights had traveled through what was now very hostile territory, Serjeant Ruggiero whistled softly through his teeth.

"I cannot believe that Al-Ashraf's hounds didn't sniff you out. What did you do, use some kind of magic to put them off the scent?"

"Hardly," Arnault said, with an amused side glance at his Scottish brother. "We merely adopted the example of Saint Simeon Salus."

Ruggiero screwed up his face. "Salus" was the Syriac word for "crazy." The saint bearing that appendage to his name had been a sixth-century mystic and teacher in the Syrian town of Emesa, where he had gone about in the guise of a fool in order to minister to the community's outcasts.

"You don't mean to tell me that the two of you went about posing as madmen?" the serjeant said doubtfully.

Arnault chuckled. "As far as the Mameluke authorities were concerned, we were just a pair of vagrant lunatics."

"It's true," Torquil chimed in, mossy-green eyes showing a glint of amusement at the memory. "So long as we didn't get in the way of their horses, they never deigned to notice our existence. If we get back to Nicosia in time for the blessed Simeon's feast day, I intend to light a candle in his honor!"

"I'll do the same," Ruggiero promised, as he closed the gate behind them. He glanced about, then asked softly, "Forgive me if I presume, Frère Arnault, but—what are things like now in Outremer?"

A shadow crossed Arnault's face. "Different from what they were," he allowed. "More than that, I am forbidden to say, until the Grand Master himself gives me leave."

"Fair enough," the serjeant agreed. "I won't delay you, then."

With a genial nod, the visitors continued on across the courtyard and inside. Once they had paid their respects to the preceptor of the house and apprised him of their needs, they were quickly supplied with proper habit to replace their desert garb and a pair of good horses. It being noontime, they joined the resident community for the office of Sext and the Mass that followed—for Knights of the Temple were monks as well as warriors—then stayed for the midday meal in the refectory before setting out on the road that led north toward Nicosia.

For over a hundred years, since the crusading days of Richard Coeur de Lion, Nicosia had been the jewel in the crown of Cyprus. Throughout that time, its Lusignac kings had played gracious host to countless pilgrims, prelates, and warriors bound for the Holy Land. But the wrath of Al-Ashraf had stemmed that tide, transforming Nicosia into a haven for refugees. In token thereof, the noble women of the city had taken to veiling themselves head to foot in long black cloaks, as a sign of mourning for those who had been left behind.

The battle-weary core of the Templar high command—

what remained of it—had adopted the preceptory at Nicosia as their new headquarters. It was late afternoon of the following day when Arnault and Torquil rode into the shadow of the preceptory's castellated walls. The young knight who met them at the gate was a new recruit whose white habit had yet to show the rigors of life in the East, and who spoke Norman French with a strong German accent. After Arnault and Torquil had identified themselves and their mission, the man looked down his long nose and informed them that the Grand Master was most probably to be found in his personal quarters.

"But he does not welcome interruptions," the man declared with a somewhat officious air. "He is busy laying plans for a new crusade. Perhaps I should send a serjeant ahead to announce your arrival."

"Thank you, that won't be necessary," Arnault said, already heading in that direction. "The information that Brother Torquil and I have to impart is directly relevant to the Master's designs."

The Grand Master and his household staff were lodged in a tall stone tower in the northwest corner of the preceptory *enceinte*, set apart from the other residential buildings by a cobbled courtyard. Arnault and Torquil were admitted by a deferential lay servant, who conducted them to a set of chambers on the upper floor, which served as both living and working quarters for the present incumbent, Frère Jacques de Molay.

A knight of the old school, the Grand Master was far more inclined to sword than to pen, though he could read well enough to understand dispatches, and was competent at basic ciphering. When Arnault and Torquil were ushered into Molay's office, they found him dictating notes to one scribal brother while a second read aloud from a scroll bearing several pendant seals. At the sight of his visitors, Molay signaled a halt to his secretaries' labors.

"Leave us," he told them curtly. "I will speak with these brothers in private."

The two clerks quickly retired from the room. As the door closed behind them, Molay pulled himself erect in his chair and surveyed his two subordinates across a table piled high with maps, dispatches, and requisition orders.

"Welcome back to Nicosia, brothers," he greeted them. "Since you have returned, and appear relatively unscathed, I trust that your recent labors have been fruitful. While we are detained here in exile, away from the fray, the image of the Order is being besmirched by scandal."

From among the clutter of documents in front of him he plucked a small, thick volume bound in scarlet calfskin. This he passed across to Arnault, who turned it over in his hands. The cover page bore the title *Historia de Desolacione*, ascribed to someone styling himself Thaddeus de Napoli.

"This was sent to me by one of our brethren at the papal court in Rome," Molay said. "It purports to be a historical account of the fall of Acre, but seldom have I been confronted with a stronger example of the evils that can be wrought on the basis of a little learning. You were there; you know what really happened. Sit, sit," he instructed, gesturing toward the stools his secretaries had vacated.

Arnault leafed through the book as he and Torquil sat, letting his eyes rove over the text. While claiming to be accurate in reporting the events, the author of the work was harshly critical of the defenders themselves, many of whom were accused of cowardice and self-interest.

"Those who put their faith in words are all too easily deceived by them," Molay said grimly, as Arnault looked up. "Our deeds have always spoken for us, and they shall do so again. I, for one, will not rest until we have returned to Outremer and reclaimed every foot of holy ground that once was ours."

The look that accompanied this observation was intended as a prompt, to which Arnault responded immediately.

"We gathered as much information as we could, Reverend Master," he said. "I must warn you, however, that Al-Ashraf has vowed never to permit the Franks to return in force to the Holy Land, and has taken strong measures to make sure that they never will."

"Then our own measures must be even stronger," Molay replied. "Proceed with your report."

Arnault drew a deep breath. "The Mamelukes have laid waste to all the lands along the coast from Tortosa to Athlit. The orchards have been cut down; the wells and irrigation systems have been dismantled; farms, even whole villages, have been razed. We have seen the devastation for ourselves: The countryside has been stripped to the bare earth. Brother Torquil has prepared a written account of the details," he finished bleakly, "but the salient fact is that there is now nothing to sustain an invading army between one town and the next."

"Then we will need to arrange for supplies to be brought in by sea," the Grand Master said. "Now, tell me about the sultan's troop deployments."

Arnault, too, had kept careful notes of all that he and Torquil had observed during their travels. It was both records to which he now referred, in reciting the statistics that the Grand Master required. Molay listened impassively, now and again interrupting one or the other of them to request that some particular point be repeated or clarified.

"You have done well," he said when Arnault had finished, nodding to both men. "Leave your reports with my secretary so that they may be copied for the benefit of my senior advisors. The two of you may retire until Vespers. If I require further clarification, I will send for you."

As he and Torquil took their leave, Arnault was left with private misgivings. Jacques de Molay might officially be the head of the Order, but he was not privy to all its secrets. At very least, his irrational mistrust of formal learning barred him from being taken into the confidence of those brothers who shared a deeper understanding of the purposes for which the Knights Templar had been ordained. It would never have occurred to Molay to imagine that the pilgrim routes the Order was appointed to guard were not only those that led to the earthly shrines of Palestine.

As it was, Molay's determination to reestablish the Kingdom of Outremer was so firmly fixed that he was all but blind to the obstacles that now lay in his way. And there was no telling how this blindness might affect the future well-being of the Order, or undermine its less obvious long-range objectives. Arnault could only hope that others would be found to carry on the hidden work that the founders of the Order had begun. Most of those who joined the Order did so out of admiration for the worldly renown the Templars had won through valor at arms—or perhaps seeking the spiritual purification that might come of accepting the rigors and sacrifice of the battlefield, in Christ's name. Though the pursuit of holy war had its virtues, only the rare individual evinced the potential to be more than a brave fighting man and perhaps a martyr.

Just such a rarity like Arnault himself, was Torquil Lennox, whose deeper qualities of heart, mind, and soul had commended him to Arnault's notice from the moment of their first meeting—or at least from the time when his confrère at Balantrodoch, Luc de Brabant, had pointed him out. Then very junior among the Scottish knights, Torquil had been among those present when Arnault and Brian de Jay reported the death of the little Maid of Norway, at the first chapter meeting following their return to the Scottish preceptory. Arnault himself had been preoccupied at the time, with the darker aspects of that mystery, but before he left to travel on to Paris, Luc had made a point of introducing the younger man.

Very shortly, their superiors had arranged to have the Scottish knight assigned to Arnault's direct supervision, the better to observe and encourage the qualities Frère Luc had noted—little though Torquil himself realized that he was being groomed for anything out of the ordinary. The events surrounding the little Maid's death now seemed hazy and remote, the shadowy aspects yet unaccounted for, in light of all that had happened since; but Torquil's presence continued to remind Arnault that not all the Temple's wars were to be fought on the battlefield.

He was given further reminder of that hidden mission when the two of them emerged from the Grand Master's quarters. Waiting for them in the shade of an adjoining cloister walk was a Templar priest whom Arnault had not expected to see here in Nicosia.

Father Bertrand de Cavaillon was normally resident at the Paris Temple. He rose as they approached: a clean-shaven man perhaps a decade older than Arnault, with a sensitively molded face and smooth fair hair forming a dense fringe around his tonsure, only slightly above middle height. After a cordial exchange of greetings that included Torquil, he turned to Arnault with a more somber expression.

"I know you've a hard journey behind you, my friend, but if you can bear the thought of another conference, Frère Gaspar would be grateful if you could join us in the south tower."

Arnault raised an eyebrow, but there was no question of ignoring the summons, even phrased as a request.

"Of course," he said, as they began heading in that direction. "I hadn't expected that he would still be here. Have you any idea what might be on his mind?"

"Oh, more than an idea," Bertrand replied, with an apparently casual glance at Torquil. "As you will have gathered from the fact that Brother Gaspar hasn't yet left and that I am here, preparations are still being made to ship a substantial portion of the treasury on to Paris. During your absence, we were ordered to prepare a new inventory of all books, relics, and other objects of value which were previously held by the preceptories of the Kingdom of Jerusalem."

"By—?"

"By the Reverend Master, of course. Since you were actively involved in the transport of these treasures, Brother Gaspar requests that you be present to confirm the provenance of certain items."

Arnault's thoughts flashed back to the final days of the siege. When it became clear that Acre would fall, the Order's treasurer, Theobald Gaudin, had been prevailed upon to have the contents of the treasury vaults loaded aboard a waiting galley. Arnault had been placed in charge of escorting the treasure safely to Sidon, with leave to select a small number of knights to assist him.

He had weighed that selection very carefully, not only because those left behind were likely to perish, and had included Torquil not only out of personal affection. For among the items held in the Order's treasury at Acre was a small collection of very special artifacts whose value was beyond price. Each object in this collection possessed some unique attribute or affinity that marked it as an object of supernatural power. These Treasures, and the lore associated with them, lay at the heart of some of the Order's deepest, most closely guarded mysteries, watched over by an elite cadre of handpicked and uniquely talented individuals known as *le Cercle*. Though Torquil was not yet an initiate in such matters, or even aware of these hidden dimensions of the Order's work, Arnault had no doubt that one day the younger man's dormant talents would earn him a place in the ranks of this inner circle.

Meanwhile, counting Bertrand and Arnault himself, that meant that at least three members of *le Cercle* were now present at Nicosia, Gaspar des Macquelines being senior of them. Formerly an assistant to the treasurer at Acre, it was hardly surprising that Gaspar should have responsibility for safeguarding the special secrets of the treasury. What *was* surprising was that, just before Arnault and Torquil left on their just-completed mission, word had arrived at Nicosia of

Gaspar's appointment as a deputy treasurer of the Paris Temple.

That was the reason Arnault had expected the older knight to have departed for France by now—which meant that the delay, as well as this present gathering, was likely to touch on matters of extreme urgency as well as confidentiality.

Summoning a stiff smile, he turned to Torquil.

"It appears I'm to be a juggler of lists. I'm sure you can think of something better to do with your time—like catch up on your sleep, if nothing else. Why don't you go on to the barracks? I'll be along to join you, once we've got this business sorted out."

Chapter Three

THE YOUNGER KNIGHT ACCEPTED THE DISMISSAL WITH GOOD grace. Following his departure, Arnault and Father Bertrand set out across the exercise ground that divided the residential buildings of the preceptory from the stables, byres, and granaries.

Skirting the chapel at the northeastern end of the Templar church, the two made their way along a covered cloister to the entrance to the presbytery. Once inside the presbytery, Bertrand led the way upstairs to a briefing room situated at the eastern end of the building.

The chamber itself was plainly furnished, whitewashed and airy, with windows looking east over a pleasant vista of cultivated terraces and citrus groves. A tall, white-habited figure was standing at the left-hand window, and two more knight-brothers and a second Templar priest were already seated at the trestle table, all initiates of *le Cercle*—which placed in Nicosia not three but six members of that elite Order within an Order. Arnault had the sudden, fleeting thought that he did not want to know why, but he was reassured as the man at the window turned to greet him. The hawklike profile and thick chestnut hair and beard belonged to Gaspar des Macquelines himself.

"Welcome back, Brother Arnault," Gaspar said with a smile. "My compliments on your safe return."

"Brother Gaspar," Arnault returned. "I expected that you would be gone by now. And what is this—?" he added, gesturing toward the others at table.

Gaspar gave a shrug. "As you will have gathered, there is more at stake here than the mere transport of treasures, no matter how precious. I apologize for forcing this meeting upon you so shortly after your arrival, but this may be the last time so many of us will be able to meet together as a group for quite some time to come. Given the present state of the Order's affairs, I wanted you with us for the sake of any insights you may be able to contribute regarding the shape of future events."

With these words, he invited Arnault and Bertrand to stools at the table, himself taking the chair at its head.

"The outward circumstances are these: Having asked us to prepare an inventory of the Order's worldly possessions, the Grand Master now requests that we provide him with a secondary list of items from the main inventory which may be sold off. From the sale of these material assets, he proposes to finance yet another attempt to reconquer our former territories in the Holy Land. He believes, as you know, that the Order has no home outside of Outremer, and that we must return there if the Temple is to survive. Before I can make any recommendations regarding the Order's property, however, we must carefully weigh up its present vicissitudes against *all* the objectives it was ordained to achieve."

He paused to let the import of this statement sink in, glancing from one to the other of them, inviting comment. First to respond was Geoffrey de St. Brieuc, a grizzled knight from Gascony.

"It seems to me," he said, "that since the days of Hugues de Payens, the Knights Templar have had only one manifest goal: to defend the Kingdom of Jerusalem. The fact that we have not succeeded in retaining a foothold there has damaged the good repute our predecessors won for us. Now the world stands ready to accuse us of a host of failures and transgressions. Perhaps the only way for the Order to justify its existence *is* by leading a new crusade, whatever the cost."

"Except that the signs are anything but favorable," said Arnault. "I submit that if we go to war merely to salvage our pride, then we commit the presumption of putting God to the test. I can testify firsthand that the Mameluke hold on Syria is stronger now than it was a year ago. If the late Holy Father could not rally sufficient support amongst the monarchies of Europe to sustain our foothold in Acre, I doubt that Jacques de Molay has the gifts of persuasion necessary to convince them to embark on a full-scale war of reconquest."

There was a murmur of troubled assent. Pope Nicholas IV had died on Good Friday of the present year, and the college of cardinals in Rome was still no closer than it had been three months ago to choosing a successor. Thus divided against itself, the papacy was like a ship adrift amid the rocks and whirlpools of an uncertain future. Until the Church found its way again, there would be no voices raised in the Holy See to second Jacques de Molay's calls for another holy war.

"The true cause at stake here has less to do with deeds than with works," said Father Bertrand's quiet voice. "If we do not return to Jerusalem, how are we to rebuild the Temple? And if the Temple is not rebuilt, where are we to house the Treasures so that they will be safe for those who come after us?"

"I agree," said his counterpart, Father Anselmo. "Others may bear, in part, the blame for the loss of Outremer. But the failure to restore the Temple is ours alone."

A silence followed this observation. At last Arnault took it upon himself to break it.

"If we have failed in anything," he said slowly, "perhaps the fault lies not in our actions, but in our perceptions."

When all other eyes had turned to him, he went on. "Hitherto, we have always conceived of the Order's mission largely in territorial terms. But perhaps that conception was shortsighted. Perhaps our tenure in the Holy Land was never intended to be permanent. Perhaps we have been exiled from Outremer, not because we didn't accomplish enough while we were there, but because our work there is now finished, and we have more important tasks to perform elsewhere."

"Now that," said Gaspar, after a thoughtful pause, "is a very interesting suggestion." As attention shifted his way, he continued. "No one with any knowledge of spiritual principles would venture to suggest that the heavenly Jerusalem must be physically equated with the earthly city of the same name. It is worth considering that the Temple we have been instructed to build as an ark for the Treasures may also have its foundations elsewhere."

Glances flew around the table, coming to rest on Father Bertrand, who was nodding tentatively.

"There is no harm in putting the supposition to the test," he said. "But for all their supernatural associations, the Treasures themselves are material objects, and must be housed in a material setting. If not in the Temple of Jerusalem, then where?"

"Here at Nicosia?" ventured Father Anselmo.

"I doubt it," Gaspar said with a frown. "Nicosia is, at best, a temporary haven. The political stability of this island is less than certain, and its ruling nobles are already unhappy about the presence of the Military Orders in their midst."

Geoffrey de St. Brieuc shook his head. "That situation soon will change. The Teutonic Knights have already begun transferring their attentions to the Baltic, and we have indications that the Hospitallers are actively looking for accommodation elsewhere in the Mediterranean."

"Even so," said Gaspar, "we still represent too much military might to be welcomed as long-term guests by the Cypriots."

"What about France, then?" suggested Christoph de Clairvaux, a tall, fair knight with the serene profile of an ancient Roman emperor. "The Order already has a strong presence there. It would be easy to adopt the Paris Temple as our new commandery-in-chief."

"Easy, yes. But the Paris Temple is too close to the hub of Capetian affairs," said Gaspar. "One of the larger provincial houses would be a preferable alternative."

"That much is certainly true," said Arnault, "but to tell the truth, I have strong reservations about any location under the rule of Philip IV. He has no great love for the Order, apart from coveting its assets. The fact that he has placed his own fortune in the keeping of the Paris Temple merely affords his agents with an ever-ready excuse to pry into our affairs. I think it would be extremely dangerous for us to put anything of irreplaceable value within the reach of his grasping hands."

This statement was greeted with sober murmurs of agreement. King Philip IV of France had a well-earned reputation for being cold and acquisitive. His one consuming passion was his desire for power, and his one consuming need was for money: money to buy land, money to buy allies, money to buy legal support. His agents were always searching for new sources of revenue, and not even the institutions of the Church were immune to being plundered by every means at the king's disposal.

"What about somewhere in the Languedoc, then?" Father Bertrand suggested.

"To establish a secure position there," said Gaspar, "we would first have to expand our holdings. And that, unfortunately, would put us in direct competition with Philip, who has a proprietary interest in the area. He has already made significant land acquisitions there by right of purchase, and has installed a number of his own officials in key positions of authority. That isn't to say we couldn't make up for lost ground. However, given the fact that we already have our share of enemies, we might be advised to avoid making any more if we can possibly avoid it."

The city-states of Italy were already too rife with internecine rivalries to merit any serious discussion.

"Could England be a possibility, then?" Christoph de Clairvaux asked. "King Edward was, after all, a crusader in his youth, and shares with us the memory of Acre. Would he not welcome us to his shores as we once welcomed him?"

"Now, there's a thought, indeed," Gaspar mused. "Tradition would have it that Joseph of Arimathea journeyed to England after the Resurrection, and founded the community of Glastonbury at a site which our Lord Himself once visited as a boy. If there is any truth in legend, Glastonbury would certainly be a fitting place to build a new Temple, in fulfillment of prophecy."

"That would depend," said Arnault, "on what kind of man Edward Plantagenet has become in twenty years' time."

"He has proven himself to be a strong and able king," said Geoffrey.

"True—but the exercise of power can corrupt even the most virtuous of men," Arnault replied. His thoughts turned to Scotland. The question of the Scottish succession had been referred to Edward for arbitration, but there was clear evidence that the English king meant to exploit that situation to his own territorial advantage, as he had done when negotiating the marriage between his son and the ill-fated Maid.

"By all accounts," he continued, "Edward does not lightly tolerate anything which might pose a challenge to his authority. The danger is that, having granted the Order sanctuary, he might well attempt to bend it to his will. Failing this, he would certainly try to destroy it. Knowing what the stakes are," he concluded, "can we afford to put Edward's good will to the test without some clear indication that this really is our best choice?"

This question provoked another round of debate. Further discussion, however, brought no resolution.

"All we're doing is chasing our tails around in a circle," Geoffrey growled. "The only thing we can say for certain is that all the choices before us seem equally doubtful."

"Well, we have to do something," Father Anselmo pointed out.

"I agree," said Geoffrey, "even if it means making the best of a bad lot."

After a long pause, Gaspar finally spoke. "Logic is no guide here. What we require is a sign. The safety of the Treasures is too important to be ventured on the strength of a guess. When we act, it must be because we are sure. And the only way to be sure is to seek guidance from a higher authority—by a means more direct than prayer."

Father Anselmo looked alarmed. "What are you suggesting?"

A glint appeared in Gaspar's dark eyes. "Amongst the artifacts in our custody are objects which possess oracular virtues. I propose that we choose the one which is most closely aligned with our own affinities and avail ourselves of its powers of divination."

An uncomfortable silence deepened as all eyes darted to the two priests.

"This is a dangerous proposition," Father Bertrand warned. "We hold these objects in trust for the good of the world. To utilize one purely for our own benefit would be a serious breach of our vocation."

"I would suggest that this is not a personal matter," Gaspar said confidently. "An error in our judgment now could result in the Treasures being lost—or worse, falling into the wrong hands. We cannot afford to make a mistake that would put the welfare of future generations at risk. Under the circumstances, I think we are fully justified in availing ourselves of the means at hand."

The silence that followed was still uncertain. As the silence drew itself out, Arnault ventured to speak.

"When it comes to discerning the workings of the Spirit," he observed quietly, "we are like blind men stumbling along the edge of a precipice. Surely it is no crime for a blind man to use a stick to help him find his way? By the same token, surely it is no crime for us to use one of the tools in our keeping to help us avoid falling into the abyss. Gaspar has rightly interpreted the gravity of our situation. I recommend that we act on his advice."

He flashed a look around the table, and was relieved to encounter nods of acceptance.

"My thanks for your support in this matter," Gaspar said. "For as God Himself is my witness, I truly believe that there is no other way."

He went on to lay before them the procedure he had in mind. The adoption of the plan was confirmed by a further vote. Having named himself and Father Bertrand as two of the three participants needed for the work, Gaspar turned lastly to Arnault.

"I appreciate that you have just returned from an arduous mission, but of all of us, you possess the greatest aptitude for what I have proposed," he observed gravely. "You have also worked with the artifact before. Will you consent to serve as the medium for the exercise in divination?"

Arnault inclined his head in assent, for whatever the cost, whether physical or psychic, there could be no question of refusing—not when the request came from Gaspar, who had been his mentor, had brought him into *le Cercle* when hardly older than Torquil.

"Such gifts as I have, I place at the service of the Temple and of God," he said, then smiled faintly. "But if you intend me to do this tonight, may I have a few hours' sleep first?"

"Of course," Gaspar replied, with a faint smile of his own. "And I do think we dare not delay." He cast his gaze over the rest of the company.

"I have already advised the Grand Master that it will take a few days to prepare the inventory he requires, and to separate out those treasures designated to be sold. But our other work will proceed tonight. The sooner we know where we stand, the better equipped we will be to face the future."

Chapter Four

WHEN ARNAULT FAILED TO APPEAR AT VESPERS, TORQUIL Lennox was mildly curious but not unduly concerned. When he failed to show up for supper, however, the Scottish knight began to wonder what could have happened to detain him.

In general, a brother of the Order was allowed to absent himself from meals and sacred offices only if he was engaged in some practical endeavor that could not readily be interrupted, such as shoeing a horse or working metal at a forge. Otherwise, his absence required special permission from a superior—which Gaspar des Macquelines, as a senior treasurer of the Order, was certainly qualified to grant. If the Rule of the Order had not forbidden talking at meals, Torquil might have been tempted to make a few casual inquiries as to his mentor's whereabouts. As it was, he was obliged to ponder the riddle in silence, amid the gentle drone of a scripture passage being read from the pulpit above the hall.

Casting his gaze around the refectory, Torquil noted that Father Bertrand was likewise nowhere to be seen among the company at table. This discovery suggested that the summons from Brother Gaspar might have involved more than a mere confirmation of lists of lading—but surely nothing to be a cause for worry. Torquil knew that Arnault was privy to matters of great confidentiality concerning the Order—matters that were really no concern of a relatively junior knight such as himself, regardless of the confidence Arnault had always shown in him personally.

At the conclusion of the meal, the brothers rose collectively and began making their way toward the chapel, as custom dictated. Torquil dutifully joined in the assembly, but found it hard to keep his attention focused on his devotions. Twice he lost track of his tally of paternosters and had to begin again. He was relieved when the communal prayers came to an end, leaving the brethren free to disperse.

Arnault was waiting in the shadows when his protégé emerged from the chapel. As Torquil moved past him, he reached out and laid a sinewy hand on the younger man's shoulder. Torquil started round, his own right hand flying to the hilt of his sword. Arnault stepped back a pace.

"Pax! It's only me!" he exclaimed softly.

Torquil relaxed, lightly shaking his head. "Sweet Jesu, you startled me. Was there some problem?"

"We had a great deal to discuss," Arnault said cryptically. He cast a look around them and, seeing no one else within earshot, continued in a lower voice. "Have you been detailed to any particular duties just now?"

"No, why?"

"I have a rather particular assignment for you, if you're willing."

A note of calculation showed briefly in Torquil's eyes. "What kind of assignment did you have in mind?"

"An item of sentry duty," Arnault said. "Brother Gaspar and I have one remaining piece of business to resolve. Father Bertrand will be present. For the moment, suffice it to say that completing this work will involve our doing something a trifle . . . unorthodox. It—would not go well with us if we were disturbed."

"This sounds serious," Torquil ventured.

"It is *very* serious," Arnault said. "The very future of the Order is at stake—and with it, the future welfare of generations yet to come. I mayn't give you any of the details, other than to pledge you my solemn word that we intend nothing blasphemous or irreverent. Nevertheless, there are some, including our esteemed Grand Master, who would condemn our actions. Discovery could mean expulsion from the Order—or worse. I will not think any less of you if you decide that you prefer not to get involved."

Torquil inclined his head cautiously. "You would not ask this if it were not important," he said quietly. "Nor have I ever known any ill to come of taking instruction from you. What is it you wish me to do?"

Arnault smiled faintly. "Good man! I regret that I cannot give you a fuller explanation just now. But if you keep faith with me, I promise you that one day, all shall be revealed."

Beckoning Torquil to follow him, he set out across the courtyard that separated the chapel from the barracks. From there, the two men made their way along the exercise green toward the square, thick-walled keep that dominated the west corner of the preceptory *enceinte*. The serjeants posted at the entry port admitted them without demur when Arnault delivered the watchword. Once beyond the guardroom, he and Torquil set out for the west tower.

Skirting the gallery overlooking the great hall, they descended a steep flight of steps leading to a narrow passageway. A door at the far end of the passageway admitted them to a square office chamber dominated by a heavy oak table with a door behind it. Writing at the table was a big-boned man with chestnut hair and gray-streaked beard who set aside his quill as the pair entered: Gaspar des Macquelines himself. Torquil did not know him well, but he had met the treasurer before their flight from Acre.

Rising, Gaspar greeted Arnault with a warmth that dispensed with distinctions in rank. When Torquil advanced to pay his respects in turn, the older knight subjected him to keen scrutiny.

"Our brother gives you the tongue of good report," he observed with a faint smile, then turned to Arnault. "Does he understand what is required of him?"

"In general, yes. And he is prepared to trust us," Arnault replied.

"In faith, young Lennox?" Gaspar said to Torquil.

Torquil drew himself to attention, sensing that this was a test. "On my honor, sir."

"Then on your honor, I am prepared to accept your services," Gaspar said, inclining his head. "Be faithful in small things, Brother Torquil, and greater things will follow. If you learn nothing else tonight, remember this."

With this injunction, he bent briefly to lift a smallish, oblong casket from the floor to the table. It was made of pale wood, smoothly polished to the luster of satin, banded with silver. The sight of it jolted Torquil's memory back to that last, dark night in Acre, mere hours before the collapse of the Templars' great citadel by the sea. With almost uncanny clarity, he recalled seeing a larger chest very like this one being loaded aboard a waiting galley, under the direct supervision of Theobald Gaudin, the treasurer of the Order. That chest might have slipped Torquil's notice in the confusion of the withdrawal from Acre, had he not been seized by the sudden, overwhelming impression that it contained something far more precious than mere diamonds or gold.

As the young Scot gazed now at the smaller chest before him, his earlier impression returned with an intensity that was almost palpable, like a wave of heat. He had to tighten his jaw to keep from blurting out the sudden torrent of questions that came to his lips. Only with difficulty did he succeed in wrenching his gaze away.

Apparently oblivious to this inner turmoil, Gaspar tucked the chest securely under one arm and half turned toward the door behind the table, opening it upon a torchlit landing.

"Come with me," he instructed. "Father Bertrand has prepared a working place for us. We should not keep him waiting."

Stairs spiraled upward and downward into darkness, apparently spanning the height of the tower's interior. Not looking to see whether his companions followed, Gaspar began to climb. Arnault followed, Torquil close behind him, feeling their way with booted toes and hands on newel post where the torchlight did not penetrate. A second torch lit the next landing, washing the stone flags with wavering light, but they kept climbing. At the second landing, as Gaspar continued upward, Arnault paused and turned toward Torquil.

"The rooms on this level are chambers of record, with no direct connection with any other part of the donjon," he said. "You will keep watch here. From now until Brother Gaspar and I return, no one else is to pass beyond this point. *No one.*"

Torquil squared his shoulders and nodded, setting his hands on his sword belt. "I understand."

"This part, perhaps," Arnault said with a faint smile. "There is one thing more: No matter what you may hear or see, you must *not* make any attempt to enter the room above, in which we are working."

Wary apprehension flickered in the younger man's eyes. "What you will do—is it dangerous, of itself?"

"Not so long as we all respect the rules which bind us," Arnault answered. "As I am bound, will you also be bound by the instructions I have given you, on your knightly honor?"

Torquil gave him a tight-jawed nod of acceptance. "I have pledged you that already," he said. "I shall not interfere."

"Please understand that I was required to confirm it," Arnault said with a faint smile of apology.

Turning, he carried on up the steps toward the door before the single room that crowned the tower's summit. Father Bertrand was waiting for him on the threshold. Gaspar had already disappeared within. When Arnault had passed inside, the Templar priest shut the door and carefully secured the bolt. A lingering fragrance of incense and a subtle tension in the air confirmed that the premises had been carefully prepared.

"I believe you will find everything in readiness," Father Bertrand reported, indicating the contents of the room with a sweep of his arm. "We can begin as soon as you have prepared yourself."

So saying, he moved his hand before the door in a finalizing ritual gesture, then leaned expectantly against the wall beside it. Arnault cast a look around him. The chamber was round, like the tower that contained it, with narrow window slits piercing the thick walls at each of the four cardinal points of the compass. Suspended on a chain from the center of the ceiling, a lamp of pierced brass cast a dappled pattern over the linen cloth covering a rectangular trestle table set immediately beneath it. A seven-branched candlestick made from burnished bronze adorned either end, mounted with fine beeswax candles, as yet unlit.

Several wooden chests were set around the perimeter of the room, pushed against the walls—containing, Arnault knew, Treasures of the Temple not included in the official reckonings shown on the inventories. Gaspar had set his casket on one of these, and was opening it with a small brass key on a fine chain around his neck. On another of the chests lay the vestments Arnault would wear for what must be done—a lightweight tunic of checkered linen, a mantle of violet silk, its border trimmed with golden bells and pomegranates, the priestly ephod with its golden chains—raiment recalling the vestments worn by the high priests of Israel.

And what Gaspar now revealed, as he opened the smaller casket, had also been sacred to those high priests, and was sacred to their successors—one of the Treasures brought out of Acre. Inside was a smaller receptacle made of silver, in the form of a reliquary. The light from the lamp overhead picked out fluid traceries of Hebrew inscriptions on the lid, just before Gaspar turned it back to reveal a weighty packet wrapped in fine white silk and secured with leather bindings. Seven wax seals secured the bindings, each bearing a Hebrew sigil.

With a solemnity approaching reverence, Gaspar broke the seals and undid the bindings, parting the silk. Within lay a flat, square object of creamy linen over some stiffening material, the size of a small book, adorned with twelve large jewels in four rows of three, their gold bezels stitched to a backing of quilted linen and catching the light in a profusion of rich color.

Arnault caught his breath, for the antiquity and sheer beauty of the object never failed to move him, especially coupled with the undoubted aura of potency it exuded. The relic had come into the hands of the Templars early in their tenure of the Temple of Jerusalem, but it was older than the Temple by fifteen hundred years and more. The specifications of its design were believed to have been divinely dictated to Moses on the Mount of Sinai, and Aaron the brother of Moses thereafter had worn it as an integral part of his regalia as High Priest of Israel.

Often thought to have been lost or destroyed, the High Priest's Breastplate had survived intact through the turbulent centuries, always finding its way into the safekeeping of a worthy guardian. And in all that time, it had never lost the virtue ascribed to it by the associated presence of the *Urim* and *Thummin,* the Lights and Perfections, whose oracular powers remained a matter of deepest mystery. Though rarely exposed to view, Arnault knew that the two stones manifesting the physical vehicle of the *Urim* and *Thummin* were contained in a pocket on the back of the Breastplate. But they would not use the stones tonight—at least not directly.

For a moment, Arnault merely gazed at the Breastplate in mingled awe and fascination, well aware that their present Grand Master would have had strong reservations about the Order's retaining custody of such a potent Jewish artifact as this, even though it was part of the common heritage that Jews and Christians and even Muslims shared. Molay would regard the use of such an object as an act of vilest apostasy. And there were others, less narrow-minded than Molay, who nevertheless would condemn any endeavor to visualize the future as a presumptuous attempt to meddle in the workings of Divine Providence.

As Arnault reverently kissed his fingertips, then touched them to one of the stones on the Breastplate, he reflected that, in fact, he and his companions were striving not to interfere with Providence, but rather to interpret Providence correctly—to the greater glory of God. *Non nobis, Domine, non nobis sed Nomini Tuo da gloriam*—Not to us, Lord, not to us but to Thy Name give the glory—the motto of the Order of the Temple. And never had such insight been more necessary than now. The Order stood dispossessed and beleaguered, its duties unfulfilled, with a dark future hanging over all the world if he and his companions should fail in their trust.

Left alone on the landing to keep vigil, Torquil could only speculate about what might be taking place in the room above him—and whatever it was, it also involved Gaspar des Macquelines and the priest, Father Bertrand. Not for the first time, Arnault's assurances had raised more questions than they answered—as had Gaspar's. Strangely, Torquil did not find himself alarmed by any of this.

Perhaps it came of his many months spent working

closely with Arnault, often in life-and-death situations—a spillover of the serenity and focus that seemed to accompany Arnault wherever he went. Even Torquil's own assignment to work with Arnault seemed hardly coincidental: to be posted to the Holy Land from distant Scotland, to work with the aristocratic French knight. He could only suppose that Arnault had asked for him specifically.

But from the beginning, there had been that about Arnault that was kept quietly discreet—not furtive; simply not for all eyes and ears. Tonight, having seen the casket Brother Gaspar had taken to that room above, Torquil was convinced that whatever they were doing, it somehow connected with what he had felt that night in Acre, as he and Arnault prepared to embark with the Temple's treasures. But what any of it was about, he had no idea.

At times, there was a . . . stillness about Arnault, when he thought no one was watching; as if he were listening to something no one else could hear. At first, Torquil had ascribed it to mere piety, a habitual turning to prayer; but over the months of their close association, interspersed with hard physical testing and the perils of their military duties, he had come to feel that it was something more—though he had never dared to ask about it.

He still dared not ask—though both Arnault and Gaspar had hinted that more would be revealed to him, in due time. If waiting for that time did not particularly bring him contentment, still, his faith in Arnault gave him reluctant patience. Time enough, when Arnault felt him ready. But while he was quite prepared to believe that the Order had arrived at a critical point in its history, what Arnault and his companions could do by themselves to amend the situation defied his imagination.

Thus thwarted in his speculations about the immediate situation, Torquil found his thoughts turning to the more distant but comprehensible concerns of his native Scotland. Having stood alertly on the landing for several minutes, he decided that he could keep watch just as easily if he sat on the topmost step on the stairwell.

The fate of the Scottish people, like the fate of the Knights Templar, seemed to be hanging in the balance. The death of the Maid of Norway two years before had extinguished the royal house of Canmore and left the Scottish kingdom with an empty throne sought by more than a dozen claimants. Fearing civil war, the Guardians of the Realm of Scotland had reluctantly approached Edward of England to arbitrate among the various rivals.

It was an offer not without cost. Before he would agree, Edward Plantagenet had first demanded that the magnates of Scotland acknowledge his feudal superiority as Lord Paramount. Having obtained this concession under duress, he had then set out to make real his pretense by manipulating the Scottish succession to his own advantage.

Of the thirteen contenders, some four could be said to have a serious claim, and of those, only two had emerged as strong candidates: John Balliol of Barnard Castle and Robert Bruce of Annandale. But neither could obtain the crown except at the hand of the English king—and to accept it under his terms would be to accept English domination. So far, Edward had been content to use diplomatic subterfuge and the complexities of feudal law to delay a decision while he strengthened his hold over Scotland. However, if these measures should ultimately fail to bring the Scottish monarchy under his control, there remained the threat of a full-scale invasion. One way or another, Edward meant to make himself overlord of Scotland. It remained to be seen if there was anything the Scottish people could do to retain their independence.

On a personal level, for Torquil himself, the fate of Scotland was a question made no easier by his present situation. In pledging himself to the Order of the Temple, he had in effect renounced all other earthly bonds of fealty. Nevertheless, he could not help but retain an interest in the affairs of his homeland. For the sake of the family and friends he had left behind, he could only hope that some agency of Providence might yet intercede to thwart Edward Plantagenet's territorial ambitions.

Even as that thought crossed his mind, he became abruptly aware of a change in the air. The still, stone-smelling atmosphere of the tower's interior seemed all at once quickened by a subtle stir. A curious expectancy niggled at his senses. In the same instant, he thought he felt something waft past him, unseen but palpable, like the brush of an invisible robe.

He eased to his feet, hand on the hilt of his sword, all his senses straining to catch some intimation of that passing presence. It was like trying to apprehend a sound too pure for mere hearing to register—and yet he was aware of its resonance, like an echo of distant music. As he caught his breath to listen, he knew with a certainty stronger than mere faith that all was well: That whatever it was, neither he nor those he guarded had anything to fear while under the mantle of protection that the Presence cast over them by virtue of its coming. Though still vigilant for less celestial stirrings, he surrendered himself to a gladness that, for all its intensity, was as familiar as coming home, and was content to rest in speechless joy.

Up in the tower room, sunk to his knees on a cushion set before the altar table, Arnault likewise became aware of an immanent Presence, suddenly filling the room to overflowing. Gaspar and Father Bertrand had helped him don the requisite vestments over his white Templar habit: the tunic, the mantle, the priestly ephod upon his chest, its golden chains securing the Breastplate, with its twelve mystical stones.

Now, abruptly overwhelmed, closed fists pressed tight against his chest—and the Breastplate—Arnault would have prostrated himself, had not that Presence taken him in its embrace. The divine touch both ravished and harrowed him, piercing him to the heart with a flaming arrow of enlightenment. Consuming as refiner's fire, that flame ignited his mind and soul in a blaze of revelation.

In that instant, it seemed that he was surveying the whole of creation from the throne of heaven. All around him, far flung to the very limits of the cosmos, stretched a wondrous city of crystal and gold, whose myriad towers shimmered like jewels against a radiant firmament of stars. Far below, across a chasm of midnight air, lay the fallen earth, a sullen orb half swallowed in shadow. He would have given it up for lost, had he not seen that it was anchored yet to the throne by the thinnest of silver chains.

The chains made a ladder spanning the gulf between heaven and earth. Luminous winged forms moved up and down the ladder in progressions as stately as dance. As he gazed at them in awe, one of these angelic beings separated itself from the others and came to meet him. Trembling, Arnault bowed his head in mute salute, gasping as a voice whispered to his soul, mingling fire and music in its unearthly purity.

Have no fear, Knight of the Temple. Thy desires are known. To build the Fifth Temple, a cornerstone has been prepared. Behold and see.

In the blink of an eye, Arnault found himself standing at the ladder's head. The angel took him by the hand, and suddenly they were descending.

The earth rose to meet them, wreathed in veils of cloud. The ladder of angels became a rainbow bridge suspended between the sunlight and the rain. Where it touched the ground, its base was shrouded in shining mist. At the heart of the mist lay a strange, dark stone charged with the meteoric resonances of a fallen star.

Thus saith the Lord of Hosts, blessed be His name; Behold the pillow where slept Jacob, son of Isaac—legacy of the house of Israel. Follow in the footsteps of Holy Columba, and thou shalt surely find it: hallow of saints and high seat of kings. Build thee thy Temple upon this foundation, and it shall not fail.

At this pronouncement, a sudden radiance burst from the stone like a lightning flash. It leapt from the heart of the stone to the jewels of the Breastplate on Arnault's chest, kindling a surge of raw power so fierce that it all but took his breath away.

Arnault doubled forward with a choked exclamation of dismay, arms closed over the Breastplate as he sank back on his hunkers. His sudden collapse drew Gaspar and Father Bertrand closer, but they were loath to interfere, for the gems affixed to the Breastplate were blazing with colored fire, casting their rainbow light all about the room.

"Should we end it?" the Templar priest whispered, poised to move.

"Not yet, I think," Gaspar breathed. "Let the vision run its course."

Before Father Bertrand could question further, the fiery emanance died back as abruptly as it had come on, the jewels again only jewels. Shuddering, Arnault drew a short, sharp breath and slowly let his arms sink to his sides, his eyelids quivering. After a moment, he shakily drew himself upright and opened his eyes.

"Arnault?" the priest whispered.

Reeling a little, still light-headed, Arnault lifted trembling fingers to the Breastplate on his chest and brushed one of the stones in gingerly caress, focusing only with difficulty. The linen was unmarred, the stones only stones.

"I am—not harmed," he murmured.

Still a little dazed, he let them help him to his feet and guide him to a seat on one of the chests, let them divest him of the Breastplate and other regalia, assured them that his physical reaction had come of fatigue, not the working itself. With many a pause he recounted the details of his vision, still caught up in wonder. While they worked, throughout the recitation, Bertrand and Gaspar exchanged troubled glances.

"What you have described is consistent with biblical accounts of true vision," Gaspar noted, sitting on another of the chests as his shrewd gaze continued to assess Arnault. "The question is, have you any idea what it means?"

Slowly shaking his head, Arnault once again found himself recalling a very different vision two years ago, on a remote island in the Orkneys, and was suddenly struck by the unassailable certainty that both were part of a larger picture, somehow linking the death of the little Maid with the dilemma now facing the Templar Order. He could not see how the two could possibly be connected. And yet . . .

"Perhaps I do," he said, frowning. "An intimation—nothing more. I . . . think—though I'm by no means certain—that the vision may have been pointing us toward Scotland as the site for the new Temple."

"Scotland?" Father Bertrand repeated.

"What brings you to that conclusion?" Gaspar asked.

"Give me a moment," Arnault whispered.

Dropping his head into his arms, he tried to make sense of what was coming to mind—more difficult than it would have been, because of his physical fatigue. While he was thus occupied, Gaspar and Bertrand busied themselves restoring the room to its usual appearance, locking away the ritual accoutrements they had assembled. By the time they were finished, Arnault was prepared to offer more coherent speculations about his earlier statements.

"You will recall that I have distant kin in Scotland, so I am somewhat familiar with what I am about to tell you," he said, straightening to stretch his kinked neck, rubbing it with a callused hand. "And exposure to young Lennox has given me further insights in this regard. It becomes clear to me that the stone I was shown in my vision may very well have been the one known among the Scots as the Stone of Destiny, which has been used as the inaugural seat of all the Scottish kings since the days of Kenneth MacAlpin. As I recall, it is kept by Augustinian brothers at Scone Abbey, not far from Perth."

Gaspar looked thoughtful, but Father Bertrand cast them a dubious glance.

"I have heard mention of such stones," he said tentatively.

Arnault gave a distracted nod. "Tradition has it that the Scottish Stone was brought from Ireland by Saint Columba—who, you may recall, was of the royal lineage of the kings of Leinster. Irish legend claims that the Stone came originally from Israel by way of Egypt. It figures there as the legacy of a Hebrew princess, the exiled daughter of King Zedekiah, who married an Irish king and gave her name to the Irish hallow called Tara. I know of no other stone which answers so closely to the conditions revealed to me by the angel."

"I will concede that the elements would seem to fit," Gaspar allowed. "The injunction to walk in the footsteps of Saint Columba can be read as a clear instruction in that regard."

"All the same," Father Bertrand said, "even if your interpretation is correct, I do not see how we can act upon this vision until the issue of the Scottish succession is settled for good or ill."

"I agree," Arnault said. "That being true, I think it prudent that someone of our number go to Scotland and investigate the matter further. I would seem to be the obvious choice—and I would suggest that Brother Torquil be assigned to accompany me."

Gaspar nodded. "I agree—though the final decision does not rest with me, of course. But as soon as I return to Paris, I shall render a full report of this night's work. Assuming that *le Maître* agrees with our assessment, you can expect to receive a change of orders before the end of autumn."

"Are you satisfied that Brother Torquil is ready for such an assignment?" Father Bertrand asked Gaspar.

Gaspar nodded as he rose. "We shall find out, soon enough. At very least, he is a Scot. And from what you have said of his progress thus far, Arnault, it seems to me that this might be a fitting time to further test his mettle."

Chapter Five

MUCH THOUGH IT PLEASED HIM, BEING SENT BACK TO Scotland was the last thing Torquil Lennox had expected, either for himself or for Arnault de Saint Clair. Riding now with Arnault across a broad expanse of bracken, swept by an October wind, less than a day's ride from Edinburgh, he fancied he could taste the savor of distant heather on the air as he reflected on the somewhat unlikely circumstances surrounding their return.

It was common knowledge that the Grand Master intended to launch a new crusade as soon as the Order could rebuild its strength. Every effort was being made to enlist a host of new knights to replace those who had been killed in the defense of Acre and its environs. Surviving veterans like Arnault and Torquil were sorely needed in Cyprus to help train these raw recruits in the arts of desert warfare. Even so, the two of them had been recalled to Paris in late August, and now were en route to their newest assignment, detouring first by way of the Templar preceptory at Balantrodoch.

Their orders had been issued at the instigation of Gaspar des Macquelines, after taking up an appointment as a deputy treasurer at the Paris Temple. This, by itself, was enough to make Torquil wonder whether their present mission might be somehow connected with whatever mysterious work Gaspar and Arnault had undertaken four months ago, back in Nicosia. His own recollections from that night remained strangely beclouded, at once luminous and obscure. More than once, he had considered mentioning his experience to Arnault, but the dream—if dream it was—was so unlike anything else he had ever experienced that he was uncertain how to put it into words.

Their current assignment, by contrast, seemed reasonably straightforward. After nearly two years of debates and delays, the judicial proceedings surrounding the Scottish succession were at last drawing to a close. It was expected that Edward Plantagenet would award the Scottish crown before the end of the year. A Templar delegation, to include Arnault and Torquil, was to proceed to Berwick, there to observe the final deliberations of the court of claims and witness the installation of the new King of Scots—whoever he might be.

Carrying orders to that effect, signed by the Visitor of France, the pair of them had set out from Paris via Calais, traveling first to London and there reporting to Guy de Foresta, the Master of England. Armed with the appropriate safe conducts for their passage north and authority to procure provisioning and fresh horses along the way, they headed then for Scotland by way of the long North Road once called Ermine Street by the Romans, then through Ancaster, Lincoln, and York, across Hadrian's Wall at Corbridge, and on past the border abbey of Jedburgh. Nearly a fortnight after leaving Paris, they began to spot familiar landmarks, and expected to reach the gates of Balantrodoch well before nightfall.

Vaguely restless, Torquil pushed back his hood and briskly rubbed at his hair and beard, now neatly trimmed for diplomatic duties and nearly grown out to their proper copper hue. It had been raining intermittently since daybreak, and the copses flanking the trail on either hand were heavy with trembling droplets. The misty autumn landscape seemed strangely blurred after the sun-drenched vistas of Syria and Cyprus, but the air had a keen, cold bite that quickened his blood.

This homecoming would have been the sweeter had he not been all too aware that his country's continuing independence was far from assured. And he still was uncertain about aspects of their present assignment, having always thought that tiny Scotland figured but little in the grand schemes of the powerful Temple. Arnault, he knew, was sympathetic to the Scottish cause, but those sentiments set him apart from most of their fellow Templars—including the Master of the Scottish Temple. Torquil could understand, if only grudgingly, why an English-born knight like Brian de Jay might favor the union of Scotland with England. What he could not fathom was why Gaspar des Macquelines should be taking so keen an interest in Scottish affairs, when his own responsibilities were bound up with the concerns of the Paris treasury.

He had considered asking Arnault about it; but something in the other's manner had made him hesitate. Given Gaspar's involvement in whatever had happened back in Nicosia, and because of Arnault's none too subtle allusions to the danger, if they had been discovered—not to mention his cryptic references regarding not only the future of the Order, but of future generations—Torquil had feared even to mention that night, though he had considered it more than once. Glancing again at his mentor, apparently half dozing in the saddle, he decided again not to do so, only ranging his gaze off toward the ragged outline of the hills to their left, blurred by a veil of drifting cloud.

Arnault, meanwhile, was well aware that his younger companion was harboring a growing number of questions.

Such answers as he had to give, however, would have to wait a while longer—at least until after they reached Balantrodoch.

He was by no means certain what kind of reception they would receive when they got there. Though Brian de Jay had proven competent enough in his duties regarding the Maid of Norway, his was an awkward personality, not likely to have been improved by acquisition of the additional authority carried by his present rank as Master of Scotland. Nor had he been happy to have Torquil seconded to service in Palestine. Arnault had mentioned his misgivings both to Gaspar and to the Visitor of France when the orders were being drawn; but it was perfectly correct that the Master of Scotland should lead the Berwick delegation.

His misgivings had been echoed by Torquil during the course of their long ride north. Though normally the soul of charity and tact, the younger man had made it clear that, while delighted to be returning to his native Scotland, he was far less sanguine about having to answer, in any way, to Scotland's Master. When pressed, he had told Arnault something of Jay's notion of military discipline, from his own experiences as a new recruit when first he entered the Temple. On reflection, Arnault suspected that the reality might have far exceeded the tactics of mere condescension and occasional intimidation to which Torquil had alluded—which meant that both of them would have to tread carefully in the weeks to come.

Fortunately, they would have at least one ally when they reached Balantrodoch. Secure in the upper echelons of the principal Templar command in the north, following twenty years of active service in the Holy Land, Luc de Brabant had been the eyes and ears of *le Cercle* in Scotland for more than a decade, far predating the arrival of Jay, with hidden talents that far outweighed the more visible skills that had secured him his current office as the preceptory's treasurer. Arnault's friendship with Luc went back to his own entry into the

Temple, and his gradual recruitment to *le Cercle*, in the decade that followed; and it was to Luc that Arnault had entrusted his private observations regarding the death of the little Maid. He remained confident that if anyone could penetrate the heart of that unresolved mystery, Luc was the man most likely to succeed.

Arnault caught his horse on the bit as the animal stumbled on an exposed root, the sudden lurch jolting him from his reverie. They had entered a wooded valley flanked on both sides by higher ground. The trail was little more than a ribbon of mud, winding back and forth through tangled brakes of elder and rowan. From somewhere off to their left he could hear the gurgling rush of running water. He was about to ask Torquil if the stream had a name when he caught a glimpse of something white moving among the trees up ahead.

Torquil noticed it, too, his green eyes narrowing sharply and then relaxing as the flash of white gradually became another horseman, white-mantled like themselves and white-hooded against the drizzle, weaving his way toward them between the trees at a leisurely pace. Sighting them in turn, the newcomer reined in behind a fallen log and raised a hand in greeting as they came into hailing distance, then pulled back his hood to reveal a backswept shock of silver hair above sparkling gray eyes, an aquiline nose, and a full silver beard.

"Luc de Brabant, as I live and breathe!" Arnault exclaimed, gigging his horse forward with Torquil only a half length behind.

Sensing their intention, the older knight skillfully backed his mount out of their path, grinning as the two jumped their horses over the log and wheeled around to rein in on either side of him.

"Well met, my brothers!" he said with a laugh, gentling his snorting mount as it sniffed noses with the two newcomers, and the three animals quickly sorted out the niceties of equine precedence.

"Well met, indeed!" Arnault agreed heartily. "But, what on earth are you doing here?"

The treasurer's gray eyes were twinkling. "Why, looking for you, of course. I had an inkling you'd be coming this way."

It was entirely possible that London or even Paris had sent a message on ahead of them, alerting the Balantrodoch community to their impending arrival. But it was also true that Luc de Brabant had his own methods for finding things out. Either way, Arnault was glad of the older knight's presence, for they must needs be circumspect once they reached Balantrodoch. Luc, meanwhile, had transferred his attention to Torquil, reaching across to punch him lightly on the upper arm.

"Brother Torquil, how *are* you? Tell me, Arnault, can this *gentil chevalier* possibly be the same boisterous wolf cub who followed you off to the wars in Outremer?"

Torquil had the grace to blush.

"The very same, I fear," Arnault confirmed with a droll grin. "And you'd scarcely credit the breadth of his accomplishments since."

"Then he's a credit to his training," Luc replied easily. "I've been looking forward to swapping tales with the pair of you ever since we received word that you were coming."

"Who told you? London, or Paris?" Arnault asked.

"Oh, Paris, to be sure," Luc replied easily. "Come. The preceptory's less than an hour's ride from here, as Brother Torquil will recall. You can tell me all about matters in Outremer and on the Continent."

Together the three men set out northward along the rutted track, Torquil falling in behind his elders when the trail got too narrow for three abreast. Under cover of passing along the latest military gossip, Arnault took note of the small changes that the past two years had wrought in his friend's appearance. Luc's hair was more white now than gray, and despite his present jaunty manner, there were indications of strain to be read in the deepening lines of his face. As conversation shifted to the local situation, the causes for Luc's anxiety began to emerge.

"The signs are already in the wind that Edward intends to award the crown to John Balliol," he informed his companions, as the three of them paused to let their horses pull at grassy tussocks already burned by the first frosts. "The Balliol connection with the royal house of Canmore comes by way of an elder daughter of David, Earl of Huntingdon, while Robert Bruce of Annandale is descended from a younger daughter of the same line. Of the two dynastic claims, Balliol's is generally acknowledged to be the stronger."

"Only in accordance with the English laws of primogeniture," Torquil chimed in. "The Scottish tradition of tanistry allows for much greater freedom of selection."

He fell silent as Arnault raised an eyebrow at him in question, but Luc nodded for him to continue.

"By tanistry, the important thing is not who stands closest in blood kinship to the late monarch," Torquil explained, "but rather, who among the eligible candidates is best suited to wield the power that goes along with the crown."

"That is my understanding," Luc agreed, taking up the thread. "The difficulty, of course, lies in getting the various contenders to reach an agreement without recourse to civil war—which is why the Scots let themselves be bullied into accepting Edward's claim as Lord Paramount. Now that he's nearing a decision, the piper will have to be paid, and the new king will be forced to pay homage to England's king."

Arnault scowled. "Can nothing be done to stop it?"

Luc shook his head. "The present situation has advanced too far to be reversed. It must now be allowed to run its course. The chance for a change will come after the award of the crown has been made. And then it will depend largely on the character of the man who ascends the Scottish throne."

"You say that's likely to be Balliol," Arnault said. "Will he prove little more than an English puppet, or does he have sufficient strength to assert his own independence—and Scotland's?"

Luc considered briefly. "He has considerable support among the older baronial families of Scotland, not least that of the Comyns of Buchan and Badenoch. The latter is married to Balliol's sister."

He paused, looking vaguely troubled, and Arnault cocked his head.

"You don't sound very sure about the Balliol contingent," he said.

"Indeed, I am not," Luc said grimly. "Balliol himself is hardly inspiring, and the Comyns are a calculating lot. If they're supporting Balliol's bid for the kingship, you can be sure it's entirely to suit their own purposes."

"Was this what you wanted to discuss before we arrived at Balantrodoch?" Arnault asked quietly.

"Actually," said Luc, "my greater worry strikes rather closer at home."

Arnault looked at him sharply, unaccountably thinking at once of Brian de Jay. "If this is some confidential matter touching the Order, I think you may rely on Brother Torquil as readily as you would me."

"Very well," Luc said, tossing a brief glance across the meadow around them—a gesture not lost on Arnault. "This is going to sound outlandish—which is, indeed, why I didn't want to discuss it back at the preceptory—but it was sparked by something you and I discussed the last time you were in Scotland."

"Go on," Arnault said.

"You asked me to look into the possibility that someone in a position of eminence might be using—shall we say—illegitimate means to influence the course of Scottish affairs."

Torquil looked at them curiously, but Luc continued in a low voice.

"After you left, I did as you requested, but as you know, my investigations came to naught. Since the beginning of this year, however, something has come to light that started me wondering again. Torquil is a Scot, and knows this area, as well as the local lore, so I'm happy to have his impressions on this."

He drew a deep breath and went on.

"Back in March, one of our tenants was clearing some land at the edge of his property when he stumbled across a very old pagan burial site—and a stone coffin, with the contents still astonishingly intact. The discovery so frightened him that he wouldn't even rebury the remains. He told the factor in charge of the estate, who sent word to the preceptory, requesting that someone come to examine the relics and determine how they should be dealt with. The porter on duty at the gate referred the message to me, with the result that I was the one who rode out to the site with our priest to make the necessary assessment."

Torquil was listening intently, his face betraying nothing. Arnault merely nodded for Luc to continue.

"The remains were those of a tall man, apparently a shaman-priest of some Pictish tradition," the treasurer went on. "The bones were still clad in the rags of a Druid-style white robe, with a wreath of dried leaves that crumbled to dust when disturbed. He'd also had Roman coins covering his eyes—probably pre-Christian, I later decided, though I think the grave was not so old as that. Among the grave offerings buried with him were a bronze amulet inscribed with the head of a bull, face-on, and a small ivory chest containing a bundle of rune-staves, of the sort used for divination. The—ah—characters inscribed on the staves were of a kind I had never seen before, and the general feel was—well, not clean, if you catch my drift. Rather than risk having anyone else tamper with the grave items, I had them taken back to one of our underground vaults for safekeeping, until I could study them more closely."

Arnault's interest was thoroughly aroused, both by the information itself and by Luc's somewhat coded description, in light of Torquil's presence. The younger knight looked both intrigued and repelled.

"Have you been able to learn anything from the items?" Arnault asked.

"No," Luc replied, "and that's the stranger half of the tale. I had kept out the coins, in hopes of establishing some kind of time frame or association for the original burial, but it occurred to me that if I were going to attempt translating the runic inscriptions, it might be easier—and safer—to work from transcriptions, rather than from the rune-staves themselves. With this object in mind, I went down to the vault two days later, only to discover that the artifacts were gone."

"Gone?" Torquil blurted. "Do you mean to say that someone stole them?"

A fleeting scowl crossed Luc's sharply defined features. "I'm not sure 'stole' is the right word," he said. "When I questioned others with access to the vault, I was informed that all the artifacts—the bones and the grave goods together—had been taken away and disposed of by order of Brian de Jay."

It was Arnault's turn to look askance. "Were you able to find out why?"

"After a fashion," Luc said neutrally. "Having viewed the artifacts for himself, the good Frère Brian—so I was told—pronounced them to be the product of pagan sorcery and an abomination to the house. Two senior knights, actual brothers named John and Robert de Sautre, were charged with getting rid of the objects. When I questioned them in turn, they told me that, at Jay's orders, they had loaded everything into a chest and thrown the chest itself into the waters of a lake several miles from here. Of course," he finished, "I have only their word for it that this is what they did."

"But—what else would they have done?" Torquil said blankly.

"I don't know," Luc said, "and that's what bothers me."

Arnault gazed off across the mist beginning to rise off the meadow, both thoughtful and troubled. The implication that Jay might be cultivating an interest in arcane objects was not one he liked to think about, especially given Jay's presence when the forces of Shadow had attempted to snatch the soul of the little Maid. That the Master of Scotland might be trying to build up a collection of such objects was a prospect even more disturbing. The further possibility, that he might intend to attempt unlocking their potential, was worst of all.

Or, he reminded himself, Jay could be as prejudiced as the Grand Master himself, when it came to dealing with objects of non-Christian origin—in which case, the pagan relics and the bones of their former owner probably *were* now at the bottom of the nameless lake where the de Sautre brothers claimed to have tossed them.

"I suggest that we all keep our eyes and ears open, and say nothing of this except among ourselves," he observed aloud, gathering his reins and glancing at the sky, beginning to dim toward twilight. "Even if all three of them have acted only from the most pious of motives, this may not be the last we have heard of this affair."

Chapter Six

THE BLEAK AUTUMNAL TWILIGHT WAS CLOSING IN BY THE time the three of them rode through the gates of Balantrodoch. They had scarcely dismounted when a bell began to ring, calling the community to Vespers. Surrendering their mounts to a pair of lay brothers, the three fell in among the other white-mantled figures converging on the chapel from various parts of the compound.

Torches in sturdy cressets beckoned from either side of the chapel's entrance, more torches strategically placed to chase the shadows from before the other buildings fronting the cobbled yard. Arnault found himself noting many changes since his last visit—and saw that Torquil was noticing them, too. The south range had been extended by the addition of several new outbuildings, and the encircling bawn wall had been strengthened by the erection of a guard tower at the salient corner of the south and west parapets—ambitious and expensive propositions, all.

Domestic changes had been made as well. As they mounted the chapel steps, Arnault looked twice at the new tympanum that had been erected over the porch, lavishly decorated with panels depicting the Last Judgment. Likewise, the stout and plain oak doors he remembered from his earlier visit had been replaced by new ones enriched with carvings illustrating scenes from Scripture. The expense involved would not have been negligible, and Arnault found himself wondering where the money could have come from to pay for these amenities.

It cost him conscious effort to lay these speculations aside while he turned his thoughts to the prayers of Vespers. Afterward, instructed to report to Brian de Jay, he and Torquil repaired to the Master's lodge—enlarged since his last visit, Arnault noted, and its previously unglazed windows on the upper floor fitted with panels of leaded glass.

Sleek and well muscled as a tomcat, Jay received them with the smug air of a man who has good reason to be pleased with himself. Arnault, for his part, was prepared to accord Jay the outward tokens of respect if this would lessen any resentment of the orders he was about to deliver and make it easier to carry out their mission. It was with measured courtesy, therefore, that he gave appropriate salute and presented the Master of Scotland with the sealed documents he had been issued in Paris by Hugues de Paraud, the Visitor of France. Torquil tried to appear equally deferential, but apparently did not entirely succeed. Jay favored him with a hard look.

"A junior knight has no place in the counsels of his betters, Brother Torquil," he told the younger man brusquely. "You will withdraw to the corridor and wait there until Brother Arnault and I are finished."

Arnault had no doubt that the condescending dismissal set Torquil's teeth on edge, but the younger man bowed himself out with a becoming display of humility. Only then did Jay venture to break the seals. Arnault remained standing at easy attention while the other man read over the enclosed orders. After reading them again, Jay looked up at him coolly.

"Are you familiar with the contents of this missive?" he asked.

In fact, Arnault was intimately acquainted with Jay's orders, but he knew better than to admit as much.

"My role is principally that of courier," he said diplomatically. "It is for you to decide, on the basis of your own instructions, whether or not it is appropriate to tell me anything more."

This response earned him a look of calculating scrutiny, but Arnault kept his face expressionless. After a moment, the Master of Scotland grudgingly yielded to logical necessity.

"With regard to the Scottish succession," he informed Arnault, "it has been deemed desirable that the Order should bear fair and honorable witness to the proceedings of the court of claims. As Master of Scotland, I am directed to assemble a delegation of suitable observers and proceed to Berwick, there to take note of all that transpires.

"That my own presence should be required is perfectly reasonable," he went on, leaning back in his chair with a somewhat supercilious smirk. "It would be an insult to the dignity of the King of England to send anyone other than the Master of Scotland to head such a delegation. You, as the Visitor's agent, are likewise an appropriate choice, especially since the pair of us were instrumental in negotiating the ill-fated Treaty of Birgham. What I do not understand," he finished with a sour grimace, "is why I find myself specifically enjoined to include Brother Torquil in the delegation. Furthermore, he appears to have been taken permanently from under my command."

Arnault was careful to keep his response both neutral and noncommittal. "I am given to understand," he said, "that the Visitor has been quite satisfied with his work over the past two years—due in part, I have no doubt, to the excellent preparation he received before leaving Balantrodoch," he added, in oblique compliment to Jay. "In addition, since Brother Torquil is a Scot, I believe it is hoped that he may be able to provide a native's insight at the court."

Jay was clearly less than pleased, but he accepted the logic of this explanation without further demur. "Very well. It appears that decisions have been made by those superior to both of us. I hope you're prepared to earn your keep in the meantime," he remarked with an affected jocularity that made no secret of his true feelings. "Scotland may be a long way from Outremer, but we still make a point of keeping up military standards of behavior and performance. You may go."

Both Arnault and Torquil had been aware that the Master of Scotland would be given leave to make his own selections in filling out the complement for the Berwick delegation. The return to Balantrodoch after a two-year absence had convinced Torquil that any close associate of Jay's was likely to prove tedious at best; but that hypothetical aggravation gained a more worrisome aspect at the next morning's chapter meeting, when Jay announced the names of the remaining appointees: A Yorkshire knight called Thomas Helmsley and the younger of the two de Sautre brothers, Robert, whose involvement in the disappearance of the Pictish grave goods had already given Luc cause for concern. The elder, John, would assume command at Balantrodoch during Jay's absence.

The de Sautres, like Jay himself, were of Anglo-Norman descent, new to the Scottish preceptory since Torquil's departure two years before. Both were black-haired and dark-eyed, but beyond that, they were so dissimilar that had they not shared a surname, no one would have guessed that the two were closely related. John, the elder of the pair, was raw-boned and taciturn, with a sparse beard, sallow skin, and a lantern-jawed scowl that occasionally turned calculating. His brother, by contrast, was plump and fresh-faced as an overgrown choirboy, with an officiously busy manner and full red lips that pouted within the bush of his black beard when he was not smiling somewhat inanely.

John was inclined to keep to himself; Robert was sociable to the point of being intrusive. Later on the day of their appointment, the latter seemed to make a point of seeking out Torquil during one of the leisure periods provided by the Rule among the offices and duties of the day. Torquil was sitting on a bench outside the common hall, methodically cleaning and polishing his sword while he enjoyed the Scottish air, when his rubicund counterpart came sauntering over and sat down uninvited beside him.

"Since we're to be riding together on this Berwick junket," he told Torquil breezily, by way of greeting, "I thought we might as well get better acquainted. Where are you from, and what made you decide to join the Order?"

Strictures of knightly courtesy forbade Torquil to utter the first words that sprang to mind. Perhaps primed by Luc's remarks of the previous day, he had taken an instant dislike for both de Sautre brothers.

"My family holds a manor in the earldom of Lennox," he told the younger de Sautre. "I have an elder brother who is the heir, so I chose to follow the way of the cross."

Robert de Sautre flashed one of his fleeting, facile smiles. "You needn't have joined the Order to fight in the Holy Land."

"True enough," Torquil agreed, and added reluctantly, "The Abbot of St. Kenneth's, near my home, was the one who suggested I should seek knight service among the Templars, and his advice seemed worth taking."

Abbot Machar had been a crusader in his youth, serving with distinction in one of the many defenses of Jerusalem. Torquil had no intention of telling de Sautre how raptly he had listened to the old man's tales of desert patrols and siege engagements. He was even less inclined to discuss his reasons for becoming a Templar.

That decision had been prompted by a dream he had had some five years ago. On the night in question, he awoke—or thought he had awakened—to find himself being observed from the foot of his bed by a luminous apparition he now believed to have been the Archangel Michael, flaming sword in hand and girt about in armor that shone like the sun. Obeying the being's gesture to rise, he had been lifted up as though on fiery wings, to a wondrous edifice of spires, buttresses, and campaniles suspended in a crystal sphere between earth and sky.

In a voice of unearthly melody, his heavenly companion had declared, *"Behold the Temple of the Lord!"*

The sight of the temple had filled Torquil with longing and rapture, but even as he gazed at it, from out of the depths arose a hideous host of demon-creatures. The creatures hurled themselves at the shining sphere, and began hammering at it with weapons of shadow. Through the rising din, Torquil heard the angelic voice again, asking, *"Who will defend the Temple against the armies of Darkness?"*

To which Torquil had found himself answering, "I will go! Send me!"

Smiling, the Archangel had set a burning coal in the palm of his right hand. The coal blossomed into a fiery sword. Swallowing his fear, Torquil strode forward to meet the enemy. Even as he braced himself to strike the first blow, he had awakened with a start, and found himself once more in the familiar confines of his chamber.

So vivid and compelling was the dream that he had turned to Father Machar for counsel. The abbot had seconded Torquil's own conclusion that he was being called to defend the city of Jerusalem—and as a Knight Templar, by the dream's temple imagery. But he had never mentioned the dream to another soul besides Father Machar.

"If you're from the Earldom of Lennox," said Robert de

Sautre, breaking in on these reminiscences, "you'll no doubt be hoping to see the Scottish crown be awarded to the Bruces of Annandale."

True it was that the Earl of Lennox himself was a supporter of Robert Bruce and his family. That issue, however, was so far removed from Torquil's immediate reflections that he was caught off guard. Mentally giving himself a shake, he said stiffly, "I'm not sure I follow you."

De Sautre's white teeth flashed another disarming grin. "Then let me put it another way: If it were up to you to choose, who would you nominate to occupy the Scottish throne?"

Torquil was not about to let himself be drawn, even on a point of speculation. "I would give it to the man who could prove he had the best right to it."

"Ah, but what sort of proofs would it take to convince you?" de Sautre said with a chuckle.

"I'm not the one who needs to be convinced," Torquil pointed out bluntly. "If you're interested in the finer points of legal debate, I suggest you go and ask a law-monger."

"Oh, I expect we'll hear quite enough from *them*, when we get to Berwick," de Sautre said, refusing to be put off. "But I don't suppose you can have kept much abreast of local affairs, off in Outremer. No matter. Tell me, what was it like out there? We have few recent veterans here at Balantrodoch."

Relieved to be able to change the subject, Torquil reluctantly began a terse recital of some of the more usual sights and experiences of campaigning in the Holy Land, gradually gathering a growing audience of listeners, wondering whether it was Jay who had sent the younger de Sautre to sound him out.

Arnault, meanwhile, was with Luc de Brabant down in the treasury vault where the pagan grave artifacts had been stored prior to their disappearance.

"This is the last place I saw the items," Luc said in a low voice, holding a torch aloft as he pointed to a spot on the floor in the left-hand corner. "I regret that I didn't make a point of copying out some of the runic inscriptions at the very outset. Had I done so, we might now have a better idea what we're dealing with."

"And then again, we might not," Arnault said. "You can hardly blame yourself for not anticipating that Jay might have the artifacts removed."

Stooping down, he ran a hand lightly over the stones where Luc had indicated. A faint but repugnant sensation registered in his fingertips, like a residue of slug slime. He straightened up with a grimace of distaste, rubbing his thumb against his fingertips.

"Did you try touching the floor here?" he asked.

"Yes, but that isn't my talent," Luc replied with a wry smile.

"At times like this, I wish it weren't mine, either. Something has left its mark here, right enough. I would guess that it might have been the rune-staves—and I think it's safe to speculate that they referred to something more sinister than tallies of hides or cattle."

"I just wish I knew for certain what's become of them," Luc muttered.

"Have you any proof that the chest *isn't* at the bottom of the lake where Jay's men are supposed to have put it?" Arnault asked.

"No. That is to say, I've tried more than once to visualize its whereabouts, but the results have all been inconclusive. For all the success I've had, the chest might as well have been magically translated *awa' wi' the faeries.*"

Arnault restrained a flicker of a smile at the fastidious Luc's adoption of imagery from local folklore, for the implications were all too sobering.

"I doubt that the wee folk had anything to do with it," he said, "but there are many veils, both dark and light, which divide the Seen from the Unseen. It would seem to be a darker veil that obscures what has happened here. I wonder, though . . . Perhaps, together, we can discover some glimpse of what we're really dealing with."

"I was hoping you would say that," Luc replied. "That's why I wanted you to look around the vault. I do have the Roman coins I took off the body," he said, displaying them on his palm. "I thought we might try to use them as a link. Shall we give it a try?"

"I don't see why not," Arnault said, with a glance at the closed door. "Are we likely to be interrupted?"

"Not at this hour. This part of the undercroft is all devoted to stores—and treasury vaults, of course. Most of the brothers are well aware that I'm apt to have them shifting heavy chests and sacks, if they're around when I'm doing inventories—which I've made a point of doing a lot of, since this all began."

"Let's have a look, then," Arnault said, taking one of the coins to examine it in the torchlight. "The worst that can happen is that nothing will happen."

After dragging another chest nearer the corner where the artifacts had previously been stored, the two men sat shoulder to shoulder on it, each with one of the coins closed in his hand.

"Now tell me, very particularly, what it is we're looking for," Arnault said. "You mentioned the ivory casket with the rune-staves. What about the bones and other grave goods?"

"Everything but the casket was put into a leather sack to bring them here," Luc replied.

"Then, that's what we're looking for—the remains of the man whose eyes were covered by these coins. Let's begin."

Closing their eyes, both men took a moment to steady themselves, measuring their breathing as each sought the tabernacle of stillness at the core of his being. As minds and bodies came to rest, Arnault prefaced their entry into the realms of the spirit by softly whispering the motto of their Order as a prayer of invocation, Luc's voice quietly joining his:

"Non nobis, Domine, non nobis sed Nomini Tuo da gloriam."

The murmur of their combined voices dwindled into the profound hush of interior silence. Casting forth with the vision of soul, not of body, aware of Luc's shadow-shape beside him, Arnault turned his focus to the coin in his hand and found himself drifting amid a ghosting whisper of silvery fog, not limited by time or space. The visionary ground that stretched away beneath them was pale and smooth, as featureless as sand. As he sought some sign by which to orient himself, the mists before them curdled and swirled, affording a fleeting glimpse of something moving away from them in the gloom.

He could accord it very little shape, but it seemed roughly the height of a man. He knew that Luc saw it, too. They set off after it with purpose, only to have it melt into the fog before they could catch a better look. Baffled, renewing his focus through the coin, Arnault scanned above and below, to left and right, wondering which way it might have gone— and was drawn by another ghostly flit of movement off to his left.

Again he started forward, this time sending Luc off to the right with a flick of shadow-thought. A glimpse of something again melted away before him, dematerializing into the fog whence it had come. A moment later he sighted it again, this time a short distance away and to his left. When he altered course to keep pace with it, it faded from view, as elusive as a shade.

There commenced a game of hide and seek. To Arnault, the suggestion of shapes that lured him on seemed to alter form with each new manifestation. At first it seemed that he was chasing a naked youth with streaming golden hair, then a white-robed and white-bearded shaman, then again a wolf running on all fours, tongue lolling amid savage-looking jaws. The fog itself seemed part of the game, now opening to offer a clear path, then closing in again to baffle his pursuit.

But always, the beckoning images remained tantalizingly out of focus. The longer the game went on, the more convinced Arnault became that he was being deliberately baited. After repeated failures, he signed for Luc to give it up. This tacit acknowledgment of defeat was greeted by a faraway screech of derision, like the echo of a raven's caw.

Or a specter's malignant laughter. Abandoning the hunt, and suppressing a sudden shiver of premonition that penetrated to the bone, Arnault set about withdrawing from his trance. Luc roused a heartbeat behind him, and the two men turned to look at one another uneasily.

"Did you hear anything?" Arnault asked.

Luc nodded. His lined face was very pale beneath his silvery beard.

"Have you ever heard anything like it before?" Arnault persisted.

"No," said Luc, and added soberly, "I think we must have gotten close, though—either to the man buried with these coins or to some less than savory entity associated with him."

He took the other coin from Arnault and examined it and his own yet again.

"Whatever he or it was, it was quick to get our measure," Arnault agreed. "Pictish, you said. It certainly had the feel of old power." He thought a moment. "I wonder if your farmer perhaps stumbled on the burial place of some pagan sorcerer."

Luc slowly nodded. "It's possible. Celtic legend abounds with accounts of magicians and priests of ancient times. Some of them had rather spectacular clashes with the early saints who came to Christianize these lands—and they do seem to have had access to real power." He paused a beat. "I hope you aren't suggesting that our fellow with the rune-staves is one of those, and that his power somehow is still potent?"

"I don't know what I'm suggesting," Arnault replied, casting another glance around the chamber. "But I do think it might be a good idea not to do anything else with those coins until we've had a chance to consider the situation further—certainly not before Torquil and I return from Berwick."

"Then perhaps it might be best to lock them away in a place where such an entity cannot possibly use them as a link to this world—say, hidden in a back corner of the tabernacle of the Blessed Sacrament," Luc said grimly.

"An excellent precaution," Arnault agreed. "Meanwhile, there's still the question of what actually happened to the relics of the coin's owner—which may or may not have actually ended up at the bottom of a lake. I think you should keep your eyes and ears open, and see whether you can find out where, specifically, the de Sautre brothers might have dumped that chest."

Chapter Seven

THE TEMPLAR DELEGATION SET OFF FOR BERWICK THE NEXT morning under bleak October skies: the Master of Scotland, attended by Brothers Thomas of Helmsley and Robert de Sautre, and Arnault and Torquil, on behalf of the Visitor of France. Brother Thomas, though utterly correct in every aspect of military deportment and pious decorum, proved to be a man of little affability and fewer words, as were the three serjeants who accompanied them to care for their horses and equipment, each with a pack pony on a lead. Accordingly, Arnault and Torquil found themselves obliged to affect amusement at the ongoing byplay of sycophance and bluster between Robert de Sautre and Brian de Jay. The strain made the three-day ride to Berwick seem like a week.

The royal burgh of Berwick-upon-Tweed was perched on a jutting headland at the mouth of the River Tweed. The thriving center for Scotland's wool trade with the Low Countries, its prosperity was proclaimed by the size and quality of the houses that lined its busy thoroughfares. The market square at the head of the High Street commanded a view of the harbor, whose gray waters were dotted with fishing boats. Two Flemish cogs were moored at the quayside, where bales of raw wool and stacks of hides were waiting to be loaded aboard in exchange for grain and fine-dyed cloth shipped in from Bruges.

Dominating the town itself was Berwick Castle, a strongly fortified shell-keep enclosed within a stout curtain wall. But as they rode beneath its gates, the Scots-born Torquil stifled a snort of indignation at the crimson flutter of England's three lions flying arrogantly above the keep's topmost tower, ostentatiously proclaiming to all comers that Edward Plantagenet, King of England, had taken possession of this and all other royal Scottish castles pending his judgment with regard to the Scottish crown. Nor, by this symbol, did Edward scruple to remind all concerned that his was the sole royal power in Scotland until such time as he chose to relinquish it on his own terms.

Not unexpectedly, Berwick's narrow cobbled streets were packed, bustling with courtiers and clerics, servants and serjeants, merchants and adventurers. Augmenting the town's resident population of nearly three thousand were several hundred visitors from both sides of the border, some of long standing, some but newly arrived, in anticipation of Edward's forthcoming announcement, all competing fiercely with one another for hospitality and lodging. Among those fortunate enough to own property in the burgh itself were the hereditary officers of the Scottish crown—the constable, chamberlain, chancellor, and steward. All other comers had to make the best of the available resources, according to their rank and means.

The castle, of course, had been taken over by Edward and his household and officers. In the town below, all the usual accommodations were long ago spoken for. The religious houses within the burgh itself were full to capacity. The local inns, likewise, had nary a bed or pallet to spare. Across the River Tweed, in the English settlement of Spittal, the town's hospital and almshouse had been converted into a hostel for the duration. Those unable to find shelter in one of the friaries, nunneries, public houses, or private homes on either side of the Tweed were obliged to live under canvas, encamped on the common lands that extended out into the surrounding countryside.

The more eminent members of the English clergy were quartered a few miles downriver at Norham Castle, the administrative seat of Anthony Bek, the Bishop of Durham, who was King Edward's principal advisor on matters of policy. More soldier than priest, Bishop Bek was more distinguished for his military expertise than for his pastoral achievements. The Scottish prelates, including William Fraser of St. Andrews and Robert Wishart of Glasgow, had chosen to take up residence at Coldingham Abbey on the Scottish side of the border, a few hours away. On hearing of this arrangement, the night before their arrival in Berwick, Torquil had remarked to Arnault that it was probably native prudence, as much as a desire for civilized comfort, that had prompted the Scottish prelates to put some distance between themselves and Bek's well-armed following.

"Bek may be a bishop," Torquil muttered, "but he's English, and I dinna trust him."

The Templars' destination was a substantial two-story house in the Flemish quarter of the city, gifted to the Order by the family of a knight-brother who had been killed at the siege of Tripoli. Though it had since been leased out to a prosperous Flemish wool merchant and his family, the merchant, one Johan Lindsay, had readily agreed to provide accommodation, in exchange for a remittance on his rent.

The early dusk of late October was settling as the Templars rode into Lindsay's prosperous yard. Within an hour, they were sitting down to meat with Lindsay and his two strapping sons, his wife and a teenage daughter having absented themselves out of deference to the Templar Rule that forbade contact with women. At Arnault's urging, Lindsay ventured to offer his Templar guests a local assessment of how the court of claims was progressing.

"Quite frankly, the folk of Berwick would like nothing better than to see this dispute settled by the end of the year," Lindsay informed his listeners. "Some few may be doing well enough, out of the increase in local trade, but the resources of the town are being strained beyond their limits. The drains are backed up, the streets are ankle-deep with rubbish, the local courts have been disrupted, and the incidence of thievery has doubled from what it was a year ago. Speaking as a merchant, most folk in these parts don't really care who gets the crown; all they want to do is to get back to business as usual."

Arnault was not surprised by this disclosure. From discussions with Torquil and Luc, he knew that the Guardians of Scotland had done their best to govern the country during the interregnum, but their powers were circumscribed. Only a duly enthroned monarch could hold full parliamentary assemblies, confirm and grant charters, or treat authoritatively with another foreign sovereign. Until such time as Scotland once again had a king to sit upon her throne, royal burghs such as Berwick would continue to suffer from disruptions to trade and industry.

The various claims to the Scottish throne were being examined in detail by two separate juries, one Scottish and one English. The English jury of twenty-four had been chosen from among Edward's English barons; the Scottish jurors numbered eighty, half chosen by Balliol and half by Bruce, who were considered the principal contenders. At Edward's behest, these juries were conducting their deliberations behind closed doors in the upper levels of the castle keep. The respective reports of the two juries were relayed to the English king and his advisors in the castle's great hall, in the presence of the Scottish competitors, their auditors, and various eminent witnesses, both secular and religious. These reports were then turned over to Edward's own team of legal experts for a final review, by dint of whose deliberations the claim of Count Florence of Holland had recently been disallowed, leaving only John Balliol and Robert Bruce as increasingly bitter contenders.

"We understand that Balliol is generally acknowledged to have the stronger legal case," Arnault said.

"So he does," Lindsay said with a grimace. "And more's the pity."

"Why do you say that?" Jay asked sharply.

Lindsay shrugged. "Mind you, I am a Fleming, not a Scot, but if the Scots are to emerge from this business as a free and independent people, their new king, whoever he is, will have to face up to Edward's demands to be recognized as Scotland's feudal overlord. That is going to take more steel, I fear, than Balliol has in him."

"And you think the Bruces might be better fitted for such resistance?" Robert de Sautre asked, with the affected laugh that habitually characterized his manner.

"Aye, that I do," Lindsay answered bluntly. "The Bruces are no man's lackeys. Whatever the grandsire starts, the grandson will surely finish."

The following morning, Jay led the Templar delegation on horseback up to the castle. Here they were received by Sir William Latimer, one of the senior knights of Edward's royal household, to whom Jay made formal petition that the Templar party be allowed to observe the proceedings of the court at first hand.

"Such a request is certainly in order," Latimer told Jay, when the latter had finished, "provided that you and your brother-knights are prepared to swear that you will commit no breach of privilege by openly discussing the proceedings of the court outside the confines of the session chamber."

Such oaths were an accepted formality, and Jay agreed without demur. When each of the Templar knights had submitted his oath in turn, Latimer conducted them to a door-

way that gave access to the minstrels' gallery at the lower
end of the castle's great hall. Here, they took their places
among a number of other observers, who included representatives from several religious orders, a Norwegian emissary,
and a legate from the papal court. From this vantage point,
it was possible to hear and see everything that was going on
in the hall below—and for most of those in the Templar delegation, it provided their first actual glimpse of the English
king.

Edward Plantagenet was seated on a dais at the far end of
the hall, flanked by a handful of personal advisors, long-
limbed and yellow-haired, with hard, pale features and eyes
as icy and unfathomable as a winter lake. He followed the
speeches of the jurors in heavy-lidded silence, one long-fin-
gered hand resting idle on his knee. The other was clasped
with casual firmness around a golden pendant hanging from
a rich chain about his neck, perhaps in echo of his obvious
intent to keep a similar hold on the realm of Scotland.

"Isn't *he* the one?" Torquil muttered under his breath, so
that only Arnault could hear him.

Arnault, less personally affronted, was more intent on
weighing up the two chief competitors, Bruce and Balliol,
who were also present in the hall, together with a select following of adherents. John Balliol of Barnard Castle was a
lean, hatchet-faced man in his middle fifties, whose darting,
close-set eyes held an acquisitive gleam. Robert Bruce of
Annandale, by sharp contrast, was burly and truculent as a
badger, still fiercely bellicose despite his seventy-two years.
Arnault thought it likely that the old man had bequeathed
more than his name to the grandson who stood at his shoulder: a fiery-looking youth of eighteen, with more than a hint
of his grandsire's indomitable spirit in his keen gray eyes.

Standing at Balliol's right hand was his brother-in-law,
Black John Comyn of Badenoch, accompanied by a clever-
looking young man of much the same age as Torquil—
surely Comyn's son—with restless dark eyes and a

predatory excitement in his manner that put Arnault in mind
of a hunting cat. Though Comyn figured publicly as Balliol's staunchest supporter, Arnault was struck by the curious impression that he, and not Balliol, was the one in
authority. That impression prompted him to consider Comyn
and his son more closely.

Outwardly, there was nothing to hint that the Comyns
were anything other than they appeared: a wealthy, influential nobleman and his promising young heir. But as Arnault
continued to study them, his vision seemed gradually obscured by a curious darkening of the air in their vicinity, as
if someone had cast about them a transparent veil of shadow.

He stiffened slightly and rubbed his eyes. With his next
blink, the shadow was gone, leaving him to wonder whether
it had been merely a curious trick of the light. His air of per-
plexity prompted Torquil to look at him askance, leaning
slightly closer.

"What is it?" he whispered.

By no means certain of what he might—or might not—
have seen, Arnault merely shook his head, summoning a
fleeting smile.

"Nothing of import," he murmured back, hoping he was
speaking the truth. "Just a momentary lapse in concentration."

But his deeper instincts, once roused, warned him that the
Comyns would bear watching in the future.

All of them came away from that first day at the court of
claims with heads in a daze over the conflicting complexities of various compendia of law. More debates followed
during the days and weeks that followed, as October gave
way to November. Hackles continued to bristle among the
rival parties as their respective legal experts continued to
trade arguments and rebuttals.

Then on the night of the sixteenth of November, after the
court of claims had been adjourned for the day, the spokes-
men for the two jury parties came together in King Edward's

presence to deliver their final assessment. Edward heard them out in private. When they had finished, he gave orders calling for a general assembly to meet outside the castle on the morning of the seventeenth, there to hear the public proclamation of his verdict.

That night the folk of Berwick retired to their beds amid a storm of flying rumors. Up at the castle, lamps burned late in the stables as heralds made ready to carry the news abroad to the outlying corners of the land. Servants and clerks of the privy chamber stayed awake into the small hours of the morning, making preparations to commemorate the occasion with all due ceremony. Knights of the king's household put their arrays in order so as to do credit to their lord when he stepped forth into the sunlight to make his long-awaited proclamation.

The next morning, the Templar delegation was among the excited throng that gathered outside the castle walls. Nor were they long kept waiting. As the late autumn sun climbed in a cold gray sky, a flourish of trumpets heralded the appearance of Edward of England on the battlement, resplendent in his royal robes of ermine and cloth-of-gold and with a golden crown upon his head. With him, at the fore of the English king's retinue, was John Balliol of Barnard Castle.

Bruce of Annandale was nowhere to be seen. The significance of his absence was not lost on the crowd below. Though a second flourish of trumpets served as prelude to the official proclamation, the crowd gathered on the green were already cheering: "Long live John Balliol! Long live King John!"

There followed a ceremonial procession from the gates of the castle to the open field that adjoined the castle embankments. Here in the open air, with banners snapping all around in the cold, bright wind, Balliol was invited to come forward and place his hands between those of the King of England. In a ringing voice, Edward Plantagenet professed that he was now handing over the kingdom of Scotland to her rightfully appointed monarch. Arnault, however, could not help noticing the feudal significance of the gesture, which tacitly presented Balliol in the role of a vassal submitting to an acknowledged overlord.

Lending reinforcement to the impression that Balliol's sovereignty was already compromised, the newly nominated King of Scots shortly proceeded to offer formal homage to the King of England. Balliol's oath was carefully worded to emphasize that he was acknowledging Edward's lordship only with respect to the lands that Edward had granted him in England, but Arnault doubted that Edward would notice—or heed—the technical distinction.

As this part of the ceremony was drawing to a close, the Bruces of Annandale arrived, without fanfare. With them was the English Earl of Gloucester, who had allied himself to the Bruce family by means of marriage. Their faces were hard, and they carried themselves with an air of grim purpose. Anticipating the possibility of violence, the crowds hastily opened the way before them as the Bruce contingent advanced on the dais where Balliol stood poised to receive the homage of his supporters.

The Comyns and their followers tensed, hands hovering near to weapons. Before they or anyone else could offer challenge, the Earl of Gloucester reached out as he walked and gripped the senior Robert Bruce by one gauntleted hand. Thus joined, the two men continued forward to confront King Edward, halting before the dais. With all eyes turned to them, the Earl of Gloucester addressed himself to Edward in ringing tones.

"Take heed, Your Majesty, of the kind of judgment you have given today," he warned loudly. "And remember that you must be judged at the Last Judgment!"

This admonition drew a suppressed gasp from the surrounding crowd, but before King Edward could summon more than a frigid glare, Robert Bruce of Annandale took up the veiled challenge.

"My noble lords, I shall be brief," he declared. "My family have fought long and hard to defend our right to the Scottish crown. Since the adjudicators have ruled against us, I feel it only fitting that I should henceforth absent myself from the Scottish court. To that end, I hereby renounce my title as Earl of Carrick in favor of the son who bears my name. Let him do what is required here today, and let me retire with such honor as my services to the community of the realm have merited."

Following this dramatic resignation, the eldest Bruce of Annandale and his ally Gloucester bowed themselves out of King Edward's presence and retired from the field. Their departure was attended by a storm of speculative murmurs, and it was several minutes before the king's officers could restore order to the assembly. As the confusion subsided, the new king's brother-in-law strode forward decisively, to drop down on one knee at Balliol's feet.

"I, John Comyn, Lord of Badenoch, do hereby acknowledge King John Balliol to be my liege lord," he cried loudly, "in token of which fealty I present to him my sword, together with my right arm and the strength of my following, to defend the ancient kingdom of our ancestors and the honor of the Scottish crown!"

This ringing endorsement drew cheers from the crowd. The cheers redoubled as a Comyn cousin, the Earl of Buchan, came forward to do homage in his turn. This example was copied by the earls and other nobles who had supported Balliol's claim throughout the long, drawn-out court battle. When these had all fulfilled their feudal obligations, all eyes turned once again to the two remaining representatives of the Bruce family.

There was a moment's bristling silence. Then the new Earl of Carrick advanced to the edge of the dais and knelt, as custom required, to pledge his support to the new king. His face in profile wore an expression of grim resignation. Several members of the Comyn faction were openly smirking at his discomfiture, but Arnault wondered if it had perhaps escaped their attention that by sacrificing his own honor, the new earl was effectively preserving intact the honor of both his father and his son.

Following the solemn presentation of homages, a general celebration ensued, which would last over several days. When it became clear that no outright hostilities were likely to erupt over the day's developments—at least not in the immediate aftermath—Brian de Jay authorized procurement of a keg of ale for himself and his knights and gave leave for private indulgence within the privacy of Johan Lindsay's hall, himself giving reinforcement to the oft-quoted simile, "to drink like a Templar." Torquil, however, though obliged to join in Jay's gesture of magnanimity, could find little reason to take pleasure in the reason for the indulgence.

"But I think perhaps this *is* an occasion to get quietly drunk," he told Arnault bleakly, as the two nursed leather tankards of tasteless ale, a little apart from the others.

For no amount of revelry could alter the fact that John Balliol had won the crown at the expense of Scotland's independence. Edward of England had established himself as Scotland's suzerain; and with Balliol under his thumb, there was nothing to prevent him from further pressing his intention to eventually absorb Scotland into his own kingdom.

Chapter Eight

WITH THE ELECTION OF JOHN BALLIOL TO THE SCOTTISH throne, the duties of Brian de Jay's Templar delegation now were to shift to those of peacekeepers as well as neutral observers; for the process begun in Berwick would culminate at the abbey of Scone, near Perth, once the capital of the ancient Pictish Kingdom of Dalriada, where Balliol's accession must be validated by enthronement upon the kingdom's sacred inaugural stone—the so-called Stone of Destiny.

It was to this place that the magnates of Scotland were summoned to appear on Saint Andrew's Day, the thirtieth of November, to witness the new king's formal inauguration. With a full fortnight allowed to move the court to Scone, Brian de Jay announced his intention to make the journey via Balantrodoch.

"I will wish to pick up an additional escort before proceeding to Scone," he told his fellow Templars, as they broached his keg of ale in Johan Lindsay's hall, "but the detour will not delay us overlong. We leave at first light."

Accordingly, while the folk of Berwick were still at their revels and Jay and his knights made short work of the allotted keg of ale, the lowlier serjeants set about making preparations to leave Berwick in the morning. Much later, when all had retired to their pallets laid out in the darkened Lindsay hall, Arnault sat hunched over the trestle table by the kitchen hearth, pen in hand and parchment and inkhorn before him, and put the finishing touches on his report of the day's proceedings, while the details were still fresh in his mind.

Troubled by Torquil's misgivings, that the election of John Balliol was only prelude to further disputes with Edward of England, Arnault tried to keep his report concise and objective. The flickering light of the fire and a cobbler's lamp cast a dappled, hypnotic pattern of shadows on the wall as he wrote; and before he was aware of it, he lapsed into a dreamlike doze between trance and sleep, pen slipping slack from his fingers.

His sleep was broken some time later by a sudden bellowing crash, like the roar of a cannon. He roused with a start, to the sounds of screams and wails and the harsh clang of warring weaponry—nearly in darkness, for the lamp had gone out and the fire had died down almost to embers. As if slowed by thick treacle, as his hand closed around the hilt of his sword and his leg muscles bunched to launch him to his feet, he seemed simultaneously to find himself bolting toward the door to the yard, wrenching at its bars to fling it wide and race to the street beyond.

The sounds of chaos doubly assailed him: The treble shrieking of women and children mingled with hoarse battle cries and the din of repeating explosions. The street outside seemed a hellish theater of fire and shadow, with armed and armored men clambering through clouds of roiling smoke with weapons brandished. As a family of three came bursting from a nearby pend, hotly pursued by two hard-eyed men-at-arms, the father turned to fend them off and the soldiers hacked him down, turning then on the mother and child, with bloody weapons raised.

Horrified, Arnault would have raced to their defense, but then—between one heartbeat and the next—the chaos vanished, leaving him still in the process of rising from his stool before the fire, fingers white-knuckled around the hilt of his sword and only silence around him.

Heart pounding, gently easing his sword from its scabbard, he made his way quietly around the sleeping bodies of his brother Templars and opened the door in fact, slipping out into the still, frosty yard to cross silently to the wicket gate that led into the street. The night was dark and peaceful, the houses all tight-shuttered against the mid-November chill, with only faint snatches of song and laughter drifting on the darkness from a tavern in a neighboring street—and no fire, no smoke, no marauding soldiery, no murdered corpses in the gutter.

Only a dream, then—but its implications were so startling and horrendous that it refused simply to be put out of mind as a mere nightmare.

Drawing a deep, shuddering breath to calm his still racing pulse, Arnault returned his sword to its scabbard and made his way quietly back into the house, where he rebarred the door. Before settling back on his stool, he built up the fire again, considering whether such a dream might merely have been sparked by remarks Torquil had made—product of his disappointment and uneasiness about John Balliol's election. But the dream's images retained such immediacy that Arnault very much feared it might have been prophetic— Edward's soldiers running amok in a frenzy of mayhem, perhaps in response to an all-out invasion of Scotland.

Troubled on something of a personal level, for he had grown somewhat fond of the honest and pragmatic Johan Lindsay and his family during their weeks in Berwick, Arnault turned his thoughts to whether there was anything he might do to mitigate such a fate, at least for them. If and when his dream came to pass, it was all too likely that the wool merchant's little enclave would be caught up in the midst of it—and the house, at least, *was* Templar property.

Refreshing his quill from his inkhorn, he found a clean scrap of parchment and thought a moment before he began to write, his words brief and to the point:

This is to signify that the bearer and those of his household are under the protection of the Order of the Temple of Jerusalem. Let no man presume to do them injury, on pain of peril to his soul.

Arnault had no personal authority to issue such a writ, but he concluded this simple statement with his signature as a Knight of the Temple, to which he added an additional signatory flourish. That final element was, in fact, a potent symbol of blessing, transforming the document into an amulet of protection. He could do little else. When the ink was dry, he rolled the parchment tight and secured it with a twist of leather thonging from out of his scrip, with the heartfelt prayer that their host could be sufficiently persuaded of its virtues to keep it by him in the days that were to come.

He found opportunity to deliver it early the following morning, while horses were being saddled and Jay and his two attendant knights were busy satisfying themselves that the serjeants had not forgotten any of their equipment.

"Please take this," Arnault told Johan Lindsay, drawing him casually aside. "I want you and your family to have it."

Lindsay raised a quizzical eyebrow. "What is it?"

"A token of our esteem," Arnault said. "Or, if you prefer, a writ of indemnity against future misfortune."

Looking more quizzical still, Lindsay slid the leather thong off the little scroll and read the brief message inside. Raising his eyes to meet Arnault's, he said, "I appreciate the gesture, Frère Arnault, but—what makes you think we might need this?"

Arnault chose his next few words with care.

"A simple precaution; nothing more. From what we have observed over the past several weeks, it seems to me that Scotland's troubles are far from over. Having arbitrated the Scottish succession, King Edward may now feel that he has the right to dictate the course of Scottish affairs. You said when we first arrived that you had misgivings about John Balliol's ability to resist Edward. I fear that I share those misgivings." He gestured toward the writ. "If war should come of it, I hope you'll not hesitate to claim the protection of the Order, which must be recognized by both sides as a neutral authority."

Lindsay refurled the scroll and wound the leather thonging back around it.

"It's good of you to make the offer," he told Arnault with a crooked grin. "Thank you. It never hurts to know where to find a port in a storm."

Three days later, amid a light flurry of snow, the Templars' party rode back through the gates of Balantrodoch. On hand to greet them in the yard was John de Sautre, left in charge of the preceptory in the absence of Brian de Jay. Once the party's horses and equipment had been seen to, Jay summoned the entire community to the chapel to announce the news from Berwick and the plans for a Templar contingent to attend the forthcoming investiture at Scone. Prayers were offered for the newly appointed king at the service of Vespers that followed, but even as he spoke the responses, Torquil kneeling at his side, Arnault found himself remembering glimpses of his vision with misgivings.

Supper that evening was the most informal that Arnault had experienced under Jay's authority, with the Rule being relaxed to allow mealtime discussion of what had been announced prior to Vespers. Following Compline, as the community made preparations to retire, Arnault took Torquil with him for a quick private word with Luc, in the latter's tiny accounting office off the western cloister range.

Careful of his phrasing—though it no doubt was time to begin exposing Torquil to a little of what he and Luc did, and he doubted Torquil would take alarm, given his matter-of-fact acceptance of Luc's account of the purloined grave goods—Arnault told Luc about his Berwick vision, also mindful of how Torquil would react.

"If there *is* such a thing as prophetic vision," he concluded, knowing Luc would fathom his reason for qualifying the statement, "and the Scriptures certainly tell us that there is—this must surely be its curse: to perhaps be given such a glimpse, presumably in warning, but with no inkling of when such a disaster might actually occur, or how to prevent it.

"But perhaps it was all sparked by hearing Torquil wax pessimistic about Balliol's election," he added with a faint smile, conceding that very real possibility as he glanced at the younger man. "You know, you were poor company that night, Brother Torquil, with your dour Scots intimations regarding your new king's prospects."

Torquil snorted, apparently not at all dismayed.

"You'll not be telling a Scot about catching glimpses of the future," he said. "In the Highlands, we call it the Second Sight. My Da has it—though he doesn't usually know for sure until after something's happened."

"Isn't that called 'hindsight'?" Luc said, with a droll but not unkindly smile.

"Gently, Luc," Arnault said lightly. "I am quite prepared to believe that Brother Torquil's family are folk of special talents. How else could he work so well with men of such peculiar vocation as you and me?"

"That is certainly true," Luc allowed, well aware that Arnault was speaking on several levels. "Regarding prophetic vision, however, it seems to me that the greater question, even beyond the truth or falsehood of such visions, is whether the images themselves are part of a pattern already laid out, or whether they are simply mutable reflections of possibility."

"Surely we must believe that it's the latter," Torquil said promptly, then fell abruptly silent as both his elders looked at him in faint surprise.

"Please continue," Luc said. "I quite agree, but I should like to hear your reasons for thinking so."

"Well, if men are to have free will at all," Torquil went on, "then it seems to me that the future must always be fluid. Otherwise, what reason have we to hope? Surely Brother Arnault has done the best he could, to preserve at least a few of the innocents in Berwick. Now all of us must trust in—"

He broke off at a sudden loud crash from somewhere outside Luc's office, farther along the western cloister range. All of them started, and Luc glanced in the direction of the sound in some alarm.

"What, in God's name?" he murmured. "There shouldn't be anyone abroad in this part of the compound at this hour . . ."

Taking up the lamp, he got to his feet and started for the door. He was unarmed save for a dagger at his waist, but Arnault and Torquil followed with hands on sword hilts, exchanging puzzled glances. As they left the room, another crash like the sound of splintering wood sounded at the far end of the corridor to their left, and all of them broke into a trot, Luc leading the way.

Only silence met them as they halted outside one of several doors at that end of the range. Passing the lamp to Arnault, the treasurer swiftly selected a key from the ring at his belt and used it to open the door.

The room beyond was dark and windowless—and empty.

Leaving that door ajar, Luc moved on to the next one, the correct key already in his hand. As he tripped the lock and gave the door a shove, a breath of freezing air blew out the lamp, plunging them into near-darkness. Jerking back with a muttered oath, Luc bade his two armed companions guard the open doorway while he retreated far enough back up the corridor to relight the lamp from a wall torch. Meanwhile, though nothing could be seen inside save a feeble swath of moonlight shining through a high, narrow window, both men quietly drew their swords.

When Luc returned, also carrying the torch, he passed it to Torquil before signing for Arnault to enter the room ahead of them. Arnault did so, easing around the left of the door frame with his back against the wall as Luc thrust his lamp into the room: modest enough in size, its far wall lined with long wooden shutters behind a writing desk and a stool situated to give light from behind the sitter when the shutters were open. As Torquil, too, entered the room, the added illumination brought the room to life around them—and revealed a large, leather-bound book lying open and face down in front of the writing table, with other leaves of parchment scattered around the room like fallen leaves.

With a wordless exclamation of dismay, Luc darted over to the book and crouched to set down his lantern, picking up the splayed volume with a little crooning sound of regret. Arnault followed more cautiously, casting his wary glance into the shadows of the room and signaling uneasily for Torquil to close the door as he, too, hunkered down beside the older man, sword across his knees. Something about the room . . .

"Who could have done such a thing!" Luc muttered, as he turned the volume to assess the damage. "This *was* a rather fine copy of Adamnan's *Life of Saint Columba,*" he added indignantly.

He fingered the book's broken spine, where several pages toward the middle had been ripped out. These were lying close by, crumpled and ink-smudged, some of them torn, and Luc gave another murmur of dismay as he gathered them up, cradling them to his breast as though he were handling a wounded bird.

Glancing beyond Luc, Arnault saw more leaves of parchment lying scattered at the feet of the stool behind the writing table, with the contents of an inkhorn spilled wide across the pages, still shiny-wet. Finding a candle stub amid the debris, he lit it from Luc's lantern and bent closer to pluck one of the pages from the mess, its delicate calligraphy all but obliterated by a spidery black stain.

"Well, this has to have happened when we heard the noise," he said, "though I can't imagine how the culprit got away without us seeing him. This ink is fresh. And this page doesn't look like it's part of that book," he said to Luc, noting the untrimmed edges of the parchment. "Have you any idea what it might have been?"

Laying aside the copy of Adamnan and its torn pages, Luc came to take the parchment from Arnault, *tsk*ing as he shook his head.

"What a pity," he said. "Unfortunately, I do. This is Brother Colman's work. He's been making a copy of the Adamnan text in his spare time. That isn't a usual pursuit of our houses, as you know—and he's but a lay brother, with little formal education—but he had too much talent not to let him develop it."

He cast another glance around the room, shaking his head bleakly.

"I gave him this little room for a scriptorium, some years ago. When Jay came, he wanted to take it back—you'll have gathered how he feels about men getting ideas above their station—but by then, Brother Colman's work had gained a modest local following. I managed to persuade Jay that the work should be allowed to continue, as it would only add to the prestige of this house. The trade-out was that Brother Colman must not let his scrivening activities interfere with his domestic duties; and of course, it does produce extra income for the preceptory."

"That *would* make a difference to Jay," Arnault replied. He spotted what looked to be the book's brass-banded carrying case against a wall and went to retrieve it. "That still doesn't answer who might have done this—or why."

"I couldn't even hazard a guess," Luc replied, returning to his inspection of the damaged volume and nodding permission for Torquil to join him, showing him what had been done. "It may be possible to repair at least some of the damage, but the book's value has been significantly reduced. Jay is sure to demand an explanation, and I haven't the faintest idea what I'm going to tell him."

Arnault sheathed his sword before bending to pick up the wooden case meant to house the book, one corner of which was badly shattered by impact with the wall. As he lifted it, a blast of glacial cold momentarily turned his blood to ice as he recoiled before a sickly charnel stench, simultaneously sweet and rotten, as memorable as it was revolting—and last encountered in a farmhouse in the far Orkney Islands.

The implication struck him almost like a physical blow, and he reeled back with a gasp. The box slipped from his grasp with a hollow clatter as he caught at his balance against the wall, trying desperately to reconnect with the impression—but it was gone.

"Arnault?" Luc had called softly, at the clattering sound. Both he and Torquil hurried over when Arnault did not immediately respond.

A little dazed, Arnault shook his head, cautiously fumbling to pick up the box again; but now it was only a box with a splintered corner. Nonetheless, a multitude of unsavory conjectures were tumbling through his mind, premier among them the unshakable impression that whatever had run amok here in Brother Colman's scriptorium had also been responsible for the death of a little Norwegian princess and the extinction of the royal Canmore line.

"I'm all right," he muttered to Luc, not yet ready to voice his growing conviction—and aware that he must be careful what he said in front of Torquil. "I am suddenly minded to consider whether what happened here was more than just a random act of destruction. How many others have a key to this room?"

"Myself," Luc said promptly. "Brother Colman, of course—but he would never destroy his own work, much less a book like the Adamnan—"

"Anyone else?" Arnault broke in impatiently.

"Jay, of course; a few others. But everyone else is abed, or nearly so. And it only happened when we heard the noise, I feel certain. You yourself said it: The ink is still wet. But no one could have made their escape so quickly, and from a locked room—and as you can see, the shutters are intact, the only other window too high and small for access."

"Those were my observations," Arnault agreed. "Perhaps, then, the pages themselves may hold the answer."

Carrying the box over to where the light was strongest, he directed Luc and Torquil to gather up all the damaged pages, both Brother Colman's copies and those from the damaged Adamnan, and to lay them out in order. All of them were either ink-stained or badly torn, but comparing the two versions, Arnault was able to point out two consecutive chapter headings, still readable by combining parts of both copies.

"Now, *that* is very interesting," he noted. "Both these chapters mention a pagan magician by the name of Briochan: Here at chapter thirty-three—*De Briochana mago*—and *De beati viri contra Briochanum refragatione*, at chapter thirty-four."

Torquil sagely echoed Luc's nod of agreement and pushed a little closer to see better, apparently better acquainted with the Celtic lore of his heritage than either of them had realized.

"Och, aye, this second reference is a celebrated passage," he pointed out, before Luc could speak, stabbing one finger toward a line of text. "Abbot Machar drummed it into our heads when my brothers and I were pupils at St. Kenneth's. Briochan was arch-druid to King Brude at the time Columba visited the king at Urquhart, and a very serious threat in his time. But Columba, as it says here, 'bested Briochan in various trials of power,' rather in the way Moses was able to outdo Pharaoh's sorcerers."

"Indeed," Arnault murmured, according Torquil a glance of respect. "I—ah—I don't suppose you know what became of this Briochan—where he might have died?"

Torquil only shook his head, and Luc shrugged as Arnault directed the same question to him with a glance; but a calculating flicker in the latter's expression told Arnault that the older man had made the connection he himself was trying to avoid—and had discarded it.

Arnault then remarked on the whiff of charnel smell he had detected as he retrieved the box made to house the book telling of Briochan's deeds, knowing that Luc would remember the account of his impressions surrounding the death of the little Maid of Norway, two years before.

"But, what possible connection—?"

"I don't know!" Arnault said sharply. "Or rather, I *am* almost certain that there *is* a connection; I just haven't figured out why or how. I also haven't figured out why I should be suspecting that your missing pagan grave goods are somehow linked with all of this—but that's what I think."

"You're suggesting that the grave was that of Briochan?" Luc whispered—then glanced in concern at Torquil, who was listening in tight-lipped and increasingly wide-eyed silence. Arnault caught the glance and also turned his attention to the younger knight—now, it seemed, rather sooner than planned, about to be further tested as to his suitability for eventual service with *le Cercle.*

"Brother Torquil," he said in a very low voice, "what you are about to hear goes no further than the three of us—not even a confessor. Do you understand?" At Torquil's solemn nod, he went on. "I can tell you that this is akin to what you assisted with in Nicosia. I promise to explain later, as and when I can. Do you agree?"

"My oath on it!" Torquil whispered fervently, crossing himself and then kissing his thumbnail.

That resolved, so far as Arnault was concerned, he swung his focus back to Luc.

"Now, as to that grave," he said, without missing a beat. "Whether or not it was Briochan's, I am saying that, almost certainly, it was the grave of *some* pagan sorcerer, whose remains were here at Balantrodoch for a time. I think the rune-staves you described make that clear. And we don't know for certain what happened to them."

"Go on," Luc murmured, rubbing at his beard.

"And I am saying that who or whatever caused *this*"— Arnault gestured toward the tattered and ink-marred pages—"seems to have taken particular exception to—or notice of—references to Briochan." He drew a deep breath before continuing.

"I am also saying that what I smelled, when I picked up the box from which the Adamnan was wrenched"—he tapped the damaged book box with a forefinger—"was, without doubt, what I smelled on the day the little Maid died. Now: You tell *me* whether any of these things connect."

Utter silence answered Arnault as he sensed both his listeners mulling what he had told them—Luc with cool if troubled detachment, Torquil still struggling to regain his equilibrium in the wake of his mentor's disclosure, though his bearing betokened mere bewilderment, not fear or hostility. But then, before either one of them could speak, came the echo of booted feet approaching in the corridor outside—several pairs.

Instantly on alert, Luc laid a finger vertically across his lips, giving them both an urgent glance, then whisked the ruined pages back onto the floor with a sweep of his arm and picked up the damaged book, moving back into the center of the room with it as he began exclaiming again over its condition. Following his cue, Arnault and Torquil at once joined in, starting to pick up and examine damaged pages, so that

by the time the door opened, all three of them appeared to
be well engaged in assessing a scene of apparent vandalism.

"Brother Luc, what on earth!" Brian de Jay said sharply,
torch in hand and flanked by the two de Sautre brothers.
"And Brother Arnault, Brother Torquil . . ." His tone turned
more calculating. "What, pray tell, are you doing?"

Luc looked around mildly, the damaged Adamnan in his
hands, his face reflecting his earlier reaction of consternation and regret.

"We were in my office; we heard a sound and came at
once. Look what someone has done: ruined months of
Brother Colman's work, and damaged our copy of
Adamnan! Can you fathom it?"

Glancing around the room, Jay went a little pale, but he
quickly recovered his composure. The de Sautre brothers
likewise looked vaguely uneasy.

"How can this have happened?" Jay murmured, though
something in his eyes gave Arnault pause.

"That's a good question," the latter said, indicating the
closed shutters. "As you can see, the room was properly secured."

"Obviously, not secured enough!" Jay blustered. "I'll
have some answers, by God! Whoever has done this has
stolen from the Order, by destroying the Order's property.
He'll wish he had never been born! Brother John, call out
the garrison, every last knight and serjeant and lay brother.
Light the torches in the yard. I want every man questioned,
beginning with Brother Colman."

The ensuing flurry of muster and interrogation enabled
Arnault, Luc, and Torquil to sidestep much further inquiry
regarding their own proximity to what had occurred—by the
speculation of Brian de Jay, surely a spiteful act of defiance
by some disgruntled member of the community. Brother
Colman was quickly cleared of any possibility of involvement, but spent the next hour weeping over his ruined manuscript. Under subsequent interrogation, the bewildered men

who lined up in the preceptory yard betrayed nary a flicker of preknowledge of the deed.

By the time the brethren were dismissed to return to their beds, several hours later, Arnault still had not managed to make sense of it, and had no opportunity that night to discuss the matter further with Luc or Torquil. Rolling up in his blankets, he lay staring up at the dormitory ceiling for some time, by the soft flicker of the night lamps kept always burning there, examining and recombining the various elements of the mystery developing here at Balantrodoch.

He told himself first that it surely was unlikely that tonight's attack could have been the result of interference by some spirit-entity—unable though he was to explain how any human agent could have carried out the attack on Brother Colman's scriptorium without being caught.

And *why* would anyone perpetrate such an attack? Though it was conceivable that the ongoing harshness of Brian de Jay's command style could, indeed, have sparked some such mutinous display—as Jay himself had posited— that was not likely either, given the Temple's expectation of unquestioning obedience to its military discipline, and the known severity of punishment for infractions of the Rule. And with Jay having been absent from Balantrodoch for the better part of a month, it seemed unlikely that his return would have sparked such an immediate display of resentment. Nor did it explain how a mere man might have done it.

Unable to make further progress on *that* tack, Arnault reluctantly returned to the original notion of nonhuman intervention—which was the only remaining explanation, if no human could have done it. He even had a name for the entity—though surely it was asking too much of coincidence to suggest that the spirit of Briochan, a sixth-century Pictish magician, might somehow have found reason to invade a Christian religious establishment and attack writings mentioning his name—though Arnault could not deny that references to Saint Columba's old adversary did seem to have been the focus for the attack.

Then, there was the matter of the charnel smell, and its association with the premature death of the little Maid. And though reasonably certain that no connection existed between that death and the coincidence that Brian de Jay had also been part of that failed mission, Arnault found himself still vaguely troubled by Jay's previous involvement in the disappearance of the grave goods that Luc had briefly examined.

As he finally drifted into sleep, it occurred to him to wonder whether the disturbed pagan grave conceivably might have been that of Briochan himself, but by then his speculations were becoming sufficiently far-fetched that he put all of them out of mind and at last surrendered himself to slumber.

Chapter Nine

BECAUSE OF THE STATUS OF ARNAULT AND TORQUIL AS REPresentatives of the Visitor of France, there had never been any question that they would be part of the delegation traveling on to Scone to witness the inauguration of the new King of Scots. But when, as the first item of business at the next morning's chapter meeting, Luc de Brabant was named to command the advance party, to leave immediately following morning Mass, Arnault could not help wondering whether this speedy banishment from Balantrodoch had anything to do with the events of the previous night—though Jay said not a word of the incident.

"You will make your way north with all speed and begin surveying the security requirements at Scone," Brian de Jay announced, speaking from the Master's chair of carved stone in the vaulted chapter house. "I am directed to await the arrival of a party of English knights riding up from the London Temple. We shall follow in a few days' time, with an additional half-dozen men from this preceptory."

Far more precipitously than might have been expected, however, those designated for the advance party found themselves making hasty preparations to depart, having barely been allowed to break their fast following Mass.

"One might almost suspect he was in a hurry to get all three of us away from here," Luc muttered under his breath to Arnault, from between their horses, while adjusting his cinch before mounting up to ride out. "And God knows what Flannan Fraser may have done to merit being banished to our company."

His glance directed Arnault's attention to the redheaded knight mounting up beside Torquil—another Scot of about Arnault's age and, by his easy banter, apparently known and liked by the younger man from his previous sojourn at the Scottish preceptory.

"He isn't one of Jay's minions, being sent to keep an eye on us?" Arnault said quietly, some doubt in his voice.

"No, he's straight and honest—as are most of the men of this house. It's Jay and his de Sautre shadows who make me a little nervous."

Their precipitous banishment from Balantrodoch also made both men wonder whether Jay might somehow suspect that the three of them were more than they seemed. Arnault's trust of the Scottish Master was waning by the day; and the gradual accumulation of circumstantial uncertainties was beginning to suggest that Jay might be developing some agenda of his own, perhaps at odds with that of *le Cercle*.

Of course, it could merely be Jay's growing resentment of their status—in his bailiwick, but not really under his command—coupled with more purely pedestrian motives of furthering his own pecuniary ambitions . . .

But just now, it was more important that *le Cercle* have a presence at Scone, for John Balliol's inauguration—and whatever schemes Jay was up to, they could have little to do with the Scottish succession. Meanwhile, the ride north, out from under Jay's scrutiny, would give Arnault and Luc time to ponder further on the various pieces of the puzzle; and perhaps the observations of the Scottish-born Brother Flannan would provide fresh insights regarding the immediate Scottish questions.

They rode toward Edinburgh amid a mild drizzle, guesting that night with the monks of Holyrood Abbey in the city. The next morning, under glowering skies, they engaged a boatman to convey them across the Firth of Forth from Queensferry. During the crossing, unsolicited, Flannan Fraser alluded to that ill-fated night, now six years past, when Alexander III, grandfather of the little Maid of Norway, had attempted this same journey.

"He shouldna have tried it—they say the rain was lashing something fierce, an' the wind was a-blowing—but he made it safe across the firth," Flannan said, as their boat neared the shore near the royal salt pans at Inverkeithing. "Well I remember the night, because we had a lot of slates come down at Balantrodoch. Water was pourin' through the dormitory ceiling."

Luc gave a bemused snort as he nodded vigorously. "I could hardly forget *that* night! My bed was right under one of the holes!"

"What, exactly, happened to Alexander?" Arnault asked Flannan, curious to hear his perspective on the death of the last Canmore king.

"No one really knows," Flannan replied. "He was riding on toward Kinghorn when his horse misstepped, God rest him, at a place since called King's Crag." He crossed himself in pious remembrance of the dead king. "They say he was eager to join his new young wife. He was desperate keen for a new male heir."

"A pity he was not so fated," Arnault replied, also crossing himself as the others did the same. "Do you think John Balliol will prove worthy of the succession?"

Flannan glanced at him in brief appraisal, then shrugged, venturing a faint smile. "As a Templar—and since ye be the

Visitor's man—I'm obliged to answer that it isn't our place to express opinions on such matters, since we answer to a higher Overlord than Balliol or England's king. But since I was a Scot before I was a Templar," he added with a wink, "and since I hail frae Bruce territory, like Brother Torquil, I suppose I would have to admit that I would have preferred the Bruces. Still, we serve as we are sent, don't we?"

Both Arnault and Luc agreed that this was so, echoing Torquil's nod of agreement, and Arnault marked the Scots knight as a man they could probably count on, if they needed allies in the Scottish preceptory.

They obtained fresh horses at Inverkeithing and headed north into Perthshire, conversation tending mainly to speculation about the probable unfolding of events at Scone. Over the next three days, Flannan proved an agreeable travel companion and a ready resource on both politics and local history.

"Did ye know, Brother Arnault, that Perth is sometimes called Saint John's Town?" Flannan asked, as they emerged from the ford across the Tay, bypassing Perth Town to push on toward Scone Abbey.

"No, why is that?" Arnault said genially.

"I can answer that," Luc interjected. "The writings of Saint John the Evangelist are said to have provided a great deal of inspiration to Saint Columba and his followers."

"Columba was active in this part of Scotland, then?" Arnault asked.

"Here and in the west," Luc replied. "But many of his relics ended up at Scone Abbey—which was built and endowed by King Kenneth MacAlpin, wasn't it, Torquil? That's how it also became a repository for so many of the Honours of Scotland, in addition to the inaugural Stone."

"I can see that Brother Luc has been using his time to good effect, since I went off with you to the Holy Land," Torquil said to Arnault with a grin. "When I first came to Balantrodoch, he was as vague about our Scottish history as most of you Frenchmen—though I must say, both of you have certainly made it your business to become better informed. Don't you agree, Brother Flannan?"

Flannan only nodded affably as Torquil glanced out across the gently rolling hills before them under a watery sun.

"By our dear, sweet Lady, what a bonnie, bonnie land it is," he said with a contented sigh. "And glad I am, that the Order should see fit to let me come back here, to carry out its work."

Arnault said nothing as they continued to ride northward, only exchanging a tiny smile with Luc before indicating a stretch of road suitable for a gallop to vary their pace.

They reached Scone late in the afternoon, as the early dusk was lowering. Remembering the crowded conditions at Berwick, Arnault and Torquil were half prepared to find themselves sleeping under canvas on the lands adjoining the abbey. But Luc clearly had other arrangements in mind.

"I'll have a word with Abbot Henry," he explained matter-of-factly, as they drew within sight of the abbey gates. "Brother Flannan has met him. I brought Brother Colman to his attention, when he needed a manuscript copied and had no one available, and we've been on friendly terms ever since. I sent word as soon as I knew that the Order would be sending a delegation to attend the inaugural ceremonies— though I didn't know I'd be in the party. The abbey's resources aren't limitless, but I think he'll have been able to find us better billeting than a tent. You'll both like him; he's a good man."

Abbot Henry himself was not immediately available, but thanks to his goodwill, the four Templars subsequently found themselves shown to a modest stone cottage tucked away in a wooded corner of the abbey's demesne, originally built as a private retreat for one of the abbey's patrons. The wooden floors of its two small rooms were swept and scrubbed, the larger of the rooms furnished with a trestle table and a few stools near the hearth, which was laid ready for a fire to be lit. Against one end of the building was a byre suitable for the stabling of their horses, well stocked with good hay.

"It wasn't deemed suitable for any of our other noble visitors, on account of the roof being in want of repair," Brother Mungo explained, with a broad wink that gave this tale the lie. "But since you'll be used to campaigning in all weathers, Father Abbot hopes you won't find the situation too intolerable. He invites you to take your meals with our community, and to join in our devotions."

"We will be honored to do so," Luc assured the monk. "Please convey our sincere thanks to Abbot Henry, and assure him that we have only the highest regard for the hospitality of this house."

After caring for their horses and unpacking their bedding and sparse belongings in the smaller of the two rooms, the four Templars joined the rest of the monastic community for supper in the refectory, as invited. Compline was afterward recited in the abbey church. As they entered, Luc quietly pointed out the side chapel to the north of the sanctuary.

"That's where the Stone of Destiny is kept," he whispered.

They could not see the Stone from where they stood with other abbey visitors in the nave, but Arnault resolved to take a closer look at it at his earliest opportunity.

The following morning, following the office of Prime, the four Knights Templar were invited to join Abbot Henry for the abbey's daily chapter.

"The circumstances attending this inauguration represent a significant departure from all previous precedent," Abbot Henry told his assembled community, to explain the presence of Templars at the meeting. "Many of those who challenged Balliol's claim to the throne will be here in force, and as host for these coming proceedings, I would be both derelict in duty and less than prudent if I did not take every precaution to forestall any outbreaks of violence during these proceedings.

"Many of you know Brother Luc," the abbot went on. "I have asked him and his brethren to join us this morning because the Order of the Temple has a well-deserved reputation for acting as impartial mediators in potentially volatile situations. They will be joined by additional knights of their Order before the arrival of the principals for the ceremonies. Brothers Luc, Flannan, Arnault, and Torquil are prepared to assist us in determining how best to keep the peace during the week that lies before us."

During the long ride north, Luc had commended that selfsame question to their combined consideration. In anticipation of the discussion, Flannan had been already prepared to present an immediate array of recommendations tested in the past and tailored to the unique conditions of the Scottish situation, further refinements of which had been offered by Arnault. These Luc now presented to the abbey chapter.

Precedent had been set at Berwick for all prospective attendees to swear a formal oath of good conduct. This oath was to be reinforced by a ban on all weaponry within the boundaries of the abbey. Earls and clan chiefs were to be made responsible for keeping their own followers in order, and a punitive list of fines was drawn up to be imposed on offenders. While these measures could not guarantee the peace outside the abbey grounds, the Templars hoped that they would discourage the most hotheaded elements from acting on rash impulse.

Abbot Henry was quick to approve these suggestions, and delegated the four Templar knights to begin putting them into effect. One of their first tasks was to liaise with the abbey's guest master and the comptroller of the royal household, to make certain that all rival factions were housed separately from one another. When John Balliol arrived, as befitted his status as king-elect, he was given exclusive use of the abbey guest house for himself and his following, which included the Comyns of Badenoch and Bishop William Fraser of St. Andrews. Less fiercely partisan magnates like Earl Malise of Strathearn and Lord Soules of Liddesdale were allocated places in the monks' residence, with those of lesser eminence being billeted wherever space could be found for them elsewhere on the abbey grounds.

The Bruce delegation was among those who chose voluntarily to take lodgings in the nearby burgh of Perth. This choice was seconded by Bishop Wishart of Glasgow, who likewise seemed inclined to keep clear of the abbey, with its incursion of English clergy.

By the time Brian de Jay arrived with his escort and the contingent of English Templars—a total of eight, including three serjeants—most of the hard work was already done. Finding no fault with his subordinates' arrangements, Jay left them to finish what they had begun while he and Robert de Sautre set off to mingle with the other abbey guests in a spirit of conviviality. The serjeants set about securing the sleeping arrangements for the new arrivals, in the larger of the cottage's two rooms, and the English Templars went to report to King Edward's representatives. Since the cottage was intended only to provide billeting space, the arrangement did not look likely to cause undue friction.

Preparations continued apace. Arnault made it his personal business to secure the agreement of the Bruce contingent regarding the oath of good conduct. Two days before the scheduled inaugural ceremony, in the company of a Templar serjeant, he sought them out in the town house they had hired on the banks of the Tay. He was received courteously, if not warmly, by the newly designated Earl of Carrick and his son, who listened without comment while Arnault explained the purpose of the visit.

"I am prepared to believe that this request is being made in good faith," the earl told Arnault, after studied reflection. "Show me the writ, and let me read in so many words what is to be required of me."

The document Arnault had helped draft already bore a number of seals and signatures. The Earl of Carrick took note of these, as well as the text itself, and lifted it for his son's perusal as he returned his attention to his visitor.

"I will take this oath, for the sake of expediency," he declared, "but if anyone else breaks faith with this agreement, be advised that I also will no longer consider myself bound by it."

When the earl had added his seal and signature to those already in place, Arnault took leave of him with thanks. The youngest Robert Bruce accompanied him from the room. Taking note of the young man's taut, hawklike profile, Arnault sensed that he had something more to add to what his father had already said. As they approached the outer door, young Bruce stepped ahead to lay his hand on the latch, turning to regard Arnault appraisingly.

"Make no mistake about us, Templar," he warned, in a voice of implacable calm. "Oaths notwithstanding, my family's loyalty is pledged to Scotland and our own house, not to that puppet Balliol or any other pawn it pleases Edward of England to settle on the Scottish throne."

This stark declaration was backed by a force of personality that Arnault had rarely encountered in anyone so young, but that strength had yet to be tempered by either hardship or self-discipline. Both might come in time, but in this present moment there was only raw energy, yet unbridled by maturity of judgment.

"What makes you so sure that Balliol is not his own man?" he asked.

Young Bruce's lip curled. "Because he was dancing to John Comyn's piping long before he ever lent his ear to an English jig," he said bitterly. "Now Edward Plantagenet plays the tune, our new king will have to learn to step lively, else we shall have English soldiers marching north over the border to teach us all how to keep in time!"

Startled, Arnault wondered if this was speculation or insight. Aloud, he said, "You sound as if you were already at war."

"We are," young Bruce said grimly. "Only, Balliol doesn't know it yet."

Visitors continued to arrive at Scone and its environs over the next two days. While Luc, Flannan, and Arnault were being kept busy elsewhere, Torquil, as junior of the knights, found himself cast in the role of general factotum for the Templar delegation. Though all the menial household chores remained the province of the Templar serjeants, Brian de Jay seemed to take pleasure in finding duties that warranted the particular attention of a knight-brother.

The result was that Torquil spent the next few days relaying requisition orders, supervising the delivery of supplies, and carrying endless streams of messages back and forth between the Master of Scotland and his fellow dignitaries. His encounters with Luc and Arnault were limited to mealtimes and those periods of the day set aside for devotions, neither of which permitted conversation—an arrangement Torquil began to suspect was Jay's way of ensuring the three did not exchange any news of which he was not also aware.

King Edward had retired from Berwick to Newcastle, leaving Bishop Anthony Bek of Durham to attend the enthronement in his stead. On the evening of November the twenty-ninth, the Templars received an invitation from Bek, asking them to come and dine with him at the abbot's house, in the company of all the other senior clerics who had come to Scone for the ceremony. In continued demonstration of the dislike Jay appeared to have conceived for Torquil since his return with Arnault, the Scottish Master accepted the invitation on behalf of himself and selected members of his entourage. Of the knights, Torquil alone was excluded, on the stated grounds that someone of knightly rank needed to maintain an ongoing patrol of the abbey grounds to be sure that all was secure for the events of the following day.

Far from resenting the slight, Torquil was relieved to be excused. Aside from his own growing antipathy for Jay, his instinct as a Scot was to regard the very English Bek as an enemy, and he was by no means sure that he could have concealed this animosity from the gimlet gaze of the English prelate. Once Jay and the others had departed for their evening's engagement, he took two of the three serjeants with him on the required inspection round. Satisfied to find everything in order, he instructed his auxiliaries to continue their patrol, rotating off with the third of their number, who was taking his shift of sleep, then headed off for a visit to the abbey church, there to say a last prayer for the future well-being of his homeland and to steal a brief close-up look at the fabled Stone of Destiny.

The church was empty, lit only by the red-shielded Presence lamp within the sanctuary and a spill of golden candle-light illuminating the arch of the north transept. Feeling more than a little self-conscious, Torquil made his way diffidently up the nave to the crossing and paused briefly to genuflect before the Presence on the altar. Then he moved into the doorway of the side chapel where he had caught his first glimpse of the Stone several days before. In the morning, it would be moved outside for the inauguration.

The Stone was standing uncovered in the middle of the floor, directly under the chapel vault, flickeringly lit by an array of vigil lights lined up across the front of the chapel's altar. Seen by candlelight, it was a large block of dense black rock the size and shape of a low chair, its contours rounded rather than angular. Its surface had the grainy finish of roughly forged iron, rather than the vitreous sheen of polished stone, and parts of it seemed to be carved, though he could make out no shapes in the dim light.

Set far apart into the Stone's front surface was a pair of down-turned, crook-shaped hooks apparently meant for taking a carrying pole; Torquil assumed there would be a second set of hooks on the back. The suggestion that it was meant to be a seat was enhanced by the presence of a shallow depression in its uppermost face.

Torquil ventured a step closer, a part of him half expecting that simply to be in the Stone's presence would impart some frisson of mystical kinship with his beloved Scotland—but the Stone registered inert as a lump of brick. Scowling slightly, he put out a tentative hand to touch the Stone's dark surface, bracing himself to snatch it back, but his fingertips met only the leaden roughness of dead rock.

He withdrew his hand and retreated a pace. Only then did it occur to him that he had been hoping for something like what he had experienced back in Cyprus—some flicker of numinosity to make truth out of all the old legends that spoke of this Stone as something marvelous and unearthly. To have felt nothing at all was profoundly disappointing. If the so-called Stone of Destiny was nothing more than a lifeless rock, then the ritual of enthronement was nothing more than empty ceremony.

"I used to think the Stone had merely fallen asleep," said a voice from the shadows at his back. "But lately I've begun to wonder if it might be dead."

Torquil controlled a start and turned around. Standing a few paces off was the old monk, Brother Mungo, who had greeted them upon their arrival at Scone and shown them to their lodgings. His lined face, so jovial at that first meeting, was overcast now with regret as he gazed at the Stone with faded blue eyes.

"What makes you think it was ever alive in the first place?" Torquil asked.

His words rang sharper than he intended, but the old monk seemed to take no notice. He said softly, "Had you been present beside me, lad, to see the enthronement of Alexander III, you would find no need to ask that question."

Something in the old monk's tone of voice caused Torquil's heart to give a sudden queer lurch. "What was it like?" he murmured.

A wistful smile touched Brother Mungo's wrinkled lips as he came and laid a hand on the Stone. It was a moment before he spoke, and Torquil sensed that he was groping for words to convey an experience that did not readily lend itself to description.

"It was like—magic," he said at last. "Magic of the most wonderful kind. It was as if the Stone was a great drum, ready to vibrate at the stroke of a hammer. When the king took his seat, the drum began to beat of its own accord, throbbing and booming like the tide against the seashore. There was nothing you could see, or even hear with mortal ears, but you could feel the power emanating from it in great pounding waves, like the heartbeat of the land."

He paused, shifting his gaze to meet Torquil's.

"Saint Columba himself initiated this ceremony at the enthronement of King Aidan. The angel of the Lord decreed that when the rightful king should sit upon the Stone, he would receive power to serve the land, according to his measure. In the old days, the power was always there, always making its presence felt in the way that a hidden spring constantly sends ripples to the surface of a pool. Now, it is as if the spring has dried up, and the pool with it."

He lapsed into silence. Torquil scarcely knew how to take the old monk's testimony, though it was evident that he believed it himself.

"What do you suppose could have happened to change things?" he wondered aloud.

Brother Mungo heaved a heavy sigh. "Who knows? Perhaps our people have tried the patience of God once too often. Perhaps we have lost faith in the miracles of Saint Columba. Perhaps too many of the great men of this kingdom now see the Stone of Destiny not as a strong support to Scotland's sovereignty, but as an obstacle standing in the way of their own ambitions."

Torquil's thoughts reverted to Berwick. Many of the magnates there, not least the Comyns of Badenoch, had been less interested in upholding the commonweal of Scotland than they had been in securing their own lands and privileges. Still, it seemed to him unfair that the self-interest of a few should outweigh the welfare of the many.

"The throne has been vacant for nearly six years," he noted thoughtfully. "Small wonder that the power of the Stone should have waned in that time. Perhaps all that is necessary to revive it is the return of a Scottish monarchy."

The old monk nodded. "I pray that this may be so. Tomorrow will tell; I certainly cannot. God grant you sleep's blessing, my young friend."

The conversation troubled Torquil as he continued on his rounds, checking in with the serjeants on patrol and then heading back to the cottage for the brief spell of sleep his duties would permit before the crucial ceremonies of the morrow. On his way, he was moved to wonder whether Abbot Henry had observed any changes in the Stone since the death of Alexander III.

He would have liked to discuss Brother Mungo's remarks with Arnault and Luc upon their return; but once again the intrusive presence of Brian de Jay and Robert de Sautre made him shy away from mentioning such a subject. The report that he tendered to Jay was limited to purely routine matters. Bottling up his more speculative observations until a more propitious moment, he sought permission to retire.

His rest, however, was far from peaceful. The darkness that surrounded him was like an unwanted blanket, hampering his limbs and interfering with his breathing. For a long time, he tossed and turned, trying vainly to find a comfortable position. When he finally did fall asleep, his dreams were even darker than the room.

The darkness was full of noise—a tempestuous rushing like the bluster of gale-force winds, paired with a roar like the crashing of sea waves against a rocky cliff. The sounds of storm and thunder were shot through with shrieks of wind that, at times, seemed to verge into demented laughter. The sound of it was so unnerving that he clapped his hands to his ears and turned blindly to flee.

With his first stride, he slammed into something unyielding. He recoiled with a blink and discovered that he was thrashing on his side in a tangle of bedding, his back against one of the walls of the cottage. The log on the nearby hearth had burned down to mere embers, telling him that it must be nearly morning. Only belatedly did it register that he must have rudely awakened from a dream—or nightmare.

The room was cold. He shivered and moved to retrieve his blankets. As he did so, a familiar figure materialized noiselessly beside his pallet and dropped to one knee beside him.

"What is it?" Arnault inquired in a whisper.

Before Torquil could respond, there came a rustle of movement a few yards away as Robert de Sautre poked his head up out of a nest of blankets and peered blearily over at them.

"What's going on? he muttered thickly. "What time is it?"

"It's time to be up and moving," said Brian de Jay, from the doorway leading to the adjacent room. "We have perhaps twenty minutes to spare before Matins. After that, we all have work to do."

Chapter Ten

THE ENTHRONEMENT OF JOHN BALLIOL AS KING OF SCOTS was to take place at mid-morning following a High Mass in the abbey church. Unlike the sacring accorded English sovereigns, who were crowned in a religious rite having kinship with the ordination of priests, it would be a purely secular ceremony, reflecting ancient Celtic custom—not only because Scotland possessed her own traditions for inaugurating her kings but because Scottish kings had yet to win the right from Rome to be anointed.

After joining the monks for the first office of the day, the Templars dispersed to their assigned positions to watch against any breaking of the peace, armed and mailed beneath their white habits and mantles but bareheaded under a wan wintry sun. As the magnates of Scotland and concerned guests began to assemble for the day's proceedings, Brian de Jay drew slightly apart with the Master of England and several of King Edward's men, idly watching for any sign of impending disruption.

Nominally Jay's second-in-command for the operation, Luc de Brabant remained near the abbey church to see the Stone transported safely up to the Moot Hill, beyond the burying ground that lay to the east of the church. Arnault and Torquil repaired to the hill itself with Flannan Fraser, to survey final preparations at the investiture site.

The hill was crowned by a circle of wind-flattened grass, faintly yellowed from the season's first frosts, only partly sheltered on three sides by a curving wall of ancient trees. The framework for a baldachin had been erected the day before, at the spot in the center where the Stone of Destiny was to stand. This morning, workmen were adorning it with a canopy and drapings of heavy silk, others pounding holes into the ground to receive a series of gilded staves that would support a festoon of purple silk cord to define the ceremonial area.

Back in the direction of the abbey church, a small procession of monks began moving ponderously toward the hill, bearing the Stone by means of stout carrying poles supported on their shoulders. Behind them, gentlemen from several of the premier Scottish houses were bringing along an elaborate gilded chair resembling a throne, curiously wrought with a movable seat and side panels, devised as a setting to contain and surround the Stone. This being significantly more portable than the Stone itself, its bearers had it in position on the hilltop well before the monks arrived with the Stone.

Conveying the Stone was heavy work. The two Scottish Templars watched in some trepidation as the monks approached the summit of the Moot Hill, half fearing lest the Stone be dropped. The men who had brought the chair lent their muscle as, with much grunting and not a little muttered swearing, the Stone was jockeyed into position in the chair atop the mound. After a weather look at the sky, a chamberlain directed rich cloths of silk brocade to be draped over both.

With his own glance at the sun—for time rather than weather—Arnault signaled Brother Flannan and one of the Templar serjeants to remain with the men who would stay to attend the Stone while everyone else was occupied at Mass. Flannan had requested the privilege, and Arnault was glad to be able to grant it.

"We'd best get back to the church," he murmured to Torquil. "If there's trouble today, it will likely be where there are Comyns and Bruces in the same place. The Stone is safe for now."

Torquil nodded, but he cast a last look at the Stone before they started back for the abbey.

The pale winter sun was halfway to its zenith as the magnates of the realm began assembling in the small abbey church, filling it to capacity. Accorded status with the more eminent visiting clergy, as warrior-monks, the Templars detailed to attend Mass had been allocated space in the choir, well back from the sanctuary but not far from part of the royal household. Craning to see past the sea of heads in front of him, Torquil had a reasonably good view of the royal party assembled closer to the high altar. He noticed that Bishop Anthony Bek was prominently placed at the new king's right hand, his demeanor outwardly gracious and unruffled—but Torquil was reminded, nonetheless, of a gaoler mounting guard over a valuable prisoner.

A choir of monks began the entrance antiphon, on this, the feast day of Scotland's patron saint. Since the abbey of Scone belonged to the See of Dunkeld, its bishop, Matthew Crambeth, had claimed his due right to preside at the Mass. Supporting him were Bishops Wishart of Glasgow, Fraser of St. Andrews, and Cheyne of Aberdeen. Though previously divided over the question of the Scottish succession, the four senior Scots prelates presented all appearances of unity as they processed into the abbey church and the Mass commenced, with a traditional collect in honor of Saint Andrew and amid fervent prayers for the future well-being of the realm.

The first reading was taken from the twelfth chapter of the first Book of Kings, read by Bishop Wishart of Glasgow. The earlier passages in the chapter gave details of a period of internecine strife between Israel and the tribe of Judah. The later passages, however, chronicled the resolution of that conflict as required of King Rehoboam, in response to a divine edict:

"Haec dicit Dominus: Non ascendetis neque bellabitis contra fratres vestros filios Israel . . ." Thus saith the Lord: Ye shall not go up to make war on your kinsmen the Israelites. Return every man to his house; for this is my will . . .

It was not the usual reading appointed for the feast day of Saint Andrew, but Torquil had no doubt that it was intended to serve as an oblique recommendation to all present to put aside their differences and keep the peace.

The psalm prescribed for the feast had likewise been set aside in favor of a passage more appropriate to the occasion, read by the Bishop of St. Andrews in a shaky voice:

"Sedes tua, Deus, in saeculum saeculi . . ." Thy throne, O God, is for ever and ever; the scepter of Thy kingdom is a right scepter. Thou lovest righteousness and hatest wickedness . . .

The Gospel text was Saint Matthew's account of how Saint Andrew and Saint Peter were first called to be disciples. While Bishop Crambeth launched into his attendant homily, discoursing at length on the theme of vocations and linking this to the vocation of kings, Torquil glanced at Balliol. The new king's gaze had strayed from the pulpit toward a painted fresco on the wall beyond, of Christ stilling the storm at sea. Contrary to what might have been expected, Balliol wore an expression best described as indifferent—as if the impending ratification of his kingship were of little enough consequence. But perhaps that was because of the presence of Edward of England's bishop at his side.

The distraction of thinking about this kept Torquil from minding the homily as much as he ought, but as the Mass advanced toward the consecration and the elevation of the Host, he at last found his meditations uplifted of their own accord to a contemplation of higher things. When he recalled himself to his earthly surroundings, he discovered that the bishops were commencing to administer Communion.

Balliol and his immediate attendants were the first to receive. They were followed, in turn, by the officers of the royal household. The greater magnates were next to approach the sanctuary. Torquil was faintly surprised to see the Bruces precede the Comyns, but any real examination of this development was precluded when Jay began moving forward with the English Templars, glancing for his subordinates to follow.

Hastily composing himself to worthily receive the sacrament, Torquil made his way forward in the wake of his superiors, just behind Arnault. He was just mounting the steps into the choir when he encountered John Comyn and his son, who were just retiring from the sanctuary. Both Comyns wore the bland, faintly distracted expressions typical of those around them; but as the two shouldered past him, Torquil caught a fleeting gesture suggesting that the elder Comyn had surreptitiously slipped something small and white into a sleeve pocket of his velvet robe.

Comyn carried on with measured tread, as though nothing whatever out of the ordinary had occurred, but Torquil half turned to stare after him—and got a gently admonitory nudge from the elderly canon who was following on his heels. He mended his pace with an apologetic nod, but his thoughts had gone racing off in shocked speculation. He was almost, but not quite sure that he had just seen the Lord of

Badenoch hide away a Communion wafer, rather than consuming it.

As he shuffled forward with the others to receive in his turn, Torquil tried to rehearse what he had seen, only just refocusing his own thoughts to a properly prayerful state as he came before Bishop Fraser and stuck out his tongue. But as he made his way back to his place, only faintly fortified by his own Communion, his mind resumed clamoring with questions. If Comyn *had* palmed and hidden away a consecrated Host, it could only be construed as an act of rankest blasphemy. Further reflection only strengthened Torquil's impression that he had seen what he had seen.

The mystery gnawed at him throughout the remainder of the Mass, so that he hardly heard or heeded the concluding prayers and intercessions. Attempting to justify Comyn's actions—and applying the most benign possible motives—Torquil had to suppose that, whether through a recent fall from grace or from mere failure to avail himself of confession and absolution in a timely fashion, the Lord of Badenoch had judged himself unprepared to properly receive the sacrament. And yet, as near kin to the new king, he had found himself obliged to go forward for Communion with the rest of the king's household—for failure to go forward might have been to cast a possible shadow on the character of the new king.

A conflict of morality and political expedience, to be sure—but if Comyn was one of those for whom the Mass held no meaning beyond social expectation, there was nothing to prevent him from taking Communion for the sake of maintaining appearances. Torquil was well aware that the faith of many so-called Christians was only nominal; not all shared his own religious dedication, or that of Arnault and others of his acquaintance. As it was, to have spat out the consecrated Host betokened a man in serious peril of his soul, acting either from fear of the spiritual consequences of ingesting Christ's most sacred Body and Blood while in a state of sin, or else from contempt for this most holy of Christian sacraments.

Torquil cast a furtive glance at Arnault, longing to communicate his observation and subsequent uneasiness and be reassured that his reasoning was faulty, his fears unjustified; but the elder Templar's regard was fixed on the sanctuary, where the Bishop of Aberdeen was reading the final Gospel:

"In principio erat Verbum . . ." In the beginning was the Word, and the Word was with God, and the Word was God . . .

Telling himself that perhaps he had not *really* seen what he thought he had seen, Torquil schooled himself to resigned forbearance and promised himself he would tell Arnault about Comyn's strange behavior at the first available opportunity—and tried to find reassurance in the familiar reading and then the final blessing.

The officiating clergy retreated to the sacristy and the magnates left the church in an order determined by precedence. While this exodus was in progress, Balliol and the great officers of state also retired to the sacristy, there to make final preparations for the inaugural procession. As previously agreed, the Knights Templar, both Scottish and English, inserted themselves at strategic intervals amid those proceeding to the Moot Hill, their white mantles serving as stark and visible reminders of the peace to which all were bound by their oaths, and which the Templars would enforce, if need be.

Out on the hilltop, banners of the great houses had been hung from the branches of the trees ringing the lower reaches of the grassy mound—mostly evergreens. As the great men of the kingdom arrived at the summit, each took his place, together with his retainers, under his own banner. To Arnault and Torquil fell a post to the east of the ceremonial area, with Luc not far away. The remaining Templars had occupied similar positions of vantage, mostly dispersed among the Scottish contingents.

Even just past noon, the wintry sun cast chill tree shadows across one side of the ceremonial area, beginning to encroach on the brocade-draped chair and Stone. Shivering, Torquil drew his mantle more tightly against the blustering wind and fidgeted on aching feet as they waited for the ceremony to begin, still wondering about what he thought he had seen Comyn do—and impelled by the presence of the Stone to wonder what Arnault would think of what Brother Mungo had told him the night before, about the Stone having lost its power. But surrounded by others, he dared not share either concern with Arnault yet.

The rising drone of bagpipes signaled the commencement of the procession. Heads turned as a stir at the church side door heralded the emergence of three pipers, followed by the new king. John Balliol now was robed in a rich swath of crimson velvet, trimmed with ermine and laced with gold. On his head he wore a red velvet bonnet turned up with ermine, adorned with a spray of osprey feathers held in place by a ruby brooch. Somehow, the trappings of regality seemed almost incongruous on the tall, lanky form.

He was flanked on the left by Abbot Henry and on the right by Sir John de St. John, who was standing in for the infant Earl of Fife. Behind them were assembled the royal officers, led by Gilbert de la Hay, the hereditary Constable of Scotland, all of them also arrayed in rich raiment of red and gold. The items belonging to the royal regalia had been shared out among the members of the procession—the crown, the sword, the scepter, the white wand—and the weakening sun picked out random gleams of their gold and jewel tones under the pale winter sky.

The party started up the hill to the wail and drone of the pipes. When they reached the summit, Sir John de St. John led Balliol over to the rich canopy that now sheltered the chair and the Stone. Bonneted heads craned to watch as Sir James the Stewart folded back the layers of drapery covering the seat of the chair to expose the Stone itself. Silence settled on the hill as he turned to address the assembled company, Balliol standing between him and John de St. John.

"Most noble lords of Scotland," Sir James declared in a loud voice, "we are here assembled, on this day and in this hour, to bear witness to the enthronement of John Balliol, late of Barnard Castle, as King of Scots. May he live long and rule well, wisely administering the laws and customs of the community of this, our sovereign realm!"

An expectant murmur whispered through the company as the king's chamberlain came forward and presented the royal mantle of state to Sir John de St. John—who, without comment, laid it around Balliol's angular shoulders. Acting then for the infant Earl of Fife, whose line had the hereditary right to seat the king upon his throne, Sir John took the king by the hand and formally assisted him to his proper place upon the Stone. Oddly, to Torquil's thinking, Balliol looked preoccupied and even distracted as he settled within the arms of the stately chair.

A *seannachie* now advanced to declaim the new king's royal lineage according to custom: a wizened old graybeard attached to the household of the lords of Badenoch, leaning on a shepherd's staff topped with a crook of carved antler.

"*Slàinte, Ard-rìgh Albainn!*" he cried. "*Iain Balliol, mac Devorguilla, nic Mairearad, nic Dairbidh . . .*" We hail as King of Scots this John Balliol, son of Devorguilla, daughter of Margaret, daughter of David, Earl of Huntingdon, son of Henry, son of David I of the house of Canmore . . .

The bardic cadence of the recitation unfolded Balliol's personal descent back through recorded history and into the misty realms of legend. Bred to such Highland tradition, Torquil found himself all but mesmerized by the litany of names that rolled from the old man's tongue.

And yet Balliol himself seemed curiously unconnected with this heroic list of predecessors. The atmosphere atop the Moot Hill was charged with excitement, but to Torquil it seemed almost as if the witnessing crowd were all waiting for someone else who had yet to appear. That was something else he must mention to Arnault.

The recitation came at last to an end. When the *seannachie* had retired, the Constable of Scotland came forward and delivered into Balliol's hands, by turn, the sword, the scepter, the white wand, each with words to accompany it, each given back to make way for the next item of regalia. The Lord Marischal followed, briefly kneeling to present an ancient-looking gold and crimson banner depicting the royal arms of Scotland, long borne by Balliol's Canmore predecessors—the golden field with its red lion rampant surrounded by a red double tressure. The embroidered silk stirred and lifted on the breeze, teasing at the edges of some memory or perception just beyond the intrigued Torquil's ability to retrieve it, as the marischal then retreated to stand with it behind the throne. He was there joined by the elder John Comyn, who set his hand upon the staff above the marischal's with almost proprietary assurance.

But now came the moment set in most men's minds as truly signifying kingship, whether or not the Scots inaugural gave greater weight to enthronement than to crowning, as was done in other realms. Approaching from behind, the king's chamberlain respectfully removed the cap from the head of John Balliol, then yielded his place to Abbot Henry, whose status as guardian of the Stone likewise had made him the designated bearer of the crown. A whisper of expectation shivered through the assembled company as the abbot held this final token of kingship suspended for a moment in the sight of all.

"John, son of Devorguilla, daughter of Margaret," he declared, "receive the crown of Scotland as its right and lawful king!"

And with these words, set the crown on Balliol's head.

The wind snapped the lion banner behind the king at that instant, wrenching at Torquil's perceptions. His stomach

turned queasy, and his vision blurred. In the space between
two heartbeats, he seemed to find himself transported to another place: looking down upon a lofty hall, whose walls
were hung with tapestries and lit by a profusion of smoky
torches.

Before him, lounging in a tall chair set before the hearth,
a lean, dark-haired man in a fur-lined robe was gazing into
the blazing fire, a horn cup in one hand and with a pair of
wolfhounds dozing at his feet. Above the chimney breast
hung the silken banner but lately given over to John Balliol.
The Scottish lion seemed almost to take life in the shimmer
of firelight and warmth-born drafts. With a certainty borne
only of such psychic visitations, Torquil knew without question that the man before the hearth was none other than
Alexander III, grandfather of the little Maid of Norway and
last reigning monarch of the house of Canmore.

The open and closing of a distant door briefly bracketed
the sound of a wintry gale blowing outside the hall, and
Torquil could feel icy drafts flitting like ghosts around the
outer corners of the room. Instinct bade him closer to the
fireside, but he could not seem to move.

A door to his left swung open, admitting a bonneted man
wrapped in heavy, sleet-sparkled tweeds. At the king's gesture to approach, the man offered him a scroll of parchment,
tightly rolled. The king accepted it, dismissing the man with
a wave of thanks, and broke the wax lozenge sealing the
scroll. Torquil found himself drifting closer as the king un-
furled it to read the message inside—close enough to see
that the two lines of text were written not in the crabbed
court hand of Latin or French or even the uncials of Gaelic,
but angular characters he somehow knew were runes. The
runes were accompanied by a single sigil, carefully executed
in a substance the color of dried blood. The device was that
of a bull.

The king's features went slack as he gazed at it. The
parchment slipped from his lax fingers and burst into flame.

In the same instant, Torquil's frame of vision was once again wrenched askew.

An icy blast swept him off his feet and plunged him into a dark maelstrom, spilling him onto a sleet-scoured stretch of frozen ground, where a howling storm wrenched at hair and garments. Pulling himself up, he recoiled with a gasp to find himself at the very brink of a sheer cliff.

White-capped waves pounded the rocks below, sending sheets of icy rime exploding upward to mingle with snow and hail. Instinct drove him scuttling back from the edge, one arm shielding his eyes from the driving wind as he sought shelter in the lee of a nest of boulders. Only belatedly did he glimpse the distant cluster of torches bobbing toward him like will-o'-the-wisps along the path that hugged the cliff's edge.

Through the fury of the storm, he could just make out four horsemen in the party. The one in front had dismounted and was leading his steed by the bridle rein, holding his guttering torch aloft in a futile attempt to light the way ahead. The rider following immediately behind was lean and dark-haired—the king he had seen in the hall.

In the same heartbeat, something even colder and darker than the storm surged out from the rocks at Torquil's back. Borne skyward on the beat of dark-pinioned wings, it peaked, then plummeted directly toward king and steed. Its downward plunge killed the torches. Out of the darkness, in quick succession, came a frantic scrambling of hooves on stone, a hoarse outcry, and then a panicked equine squeal, abruptly cut short.

Alarmed, dismayed, Torquil staggered upright and made for the sound—and recoiled, appalled, at the sight of the king's stricken horse on its knees, the king himself struggling in the grip of a monstrous hag-creature with hair like streaming kelp.

It was clinging to the horse's crupper with bare, leprous thighs, its sinewy arms twined tight around the king's chest in a throttling embrace. As its lambent eyes flared green in the darkness, an agonized scream burst from the king's lips—just before the creature dragged horse and rider over the edge of the cliff, in a surging peal of demonic laughter. Torquil, too, tried to cry out, but the storm itself seemed to seize him by the throat, so that the sound that burst from his lips was little more than a strangled cough.

Even so, it drew Arnault's attention—and even more, he saw the younger man's face go suddenly white and blank as the face of a corpse, just before his knees started to buckle. He caught Torquil under one elbow, hissing for Luc to assist him, and together they managed to keep the Scottish knight on his feet and begin easing him back from the crowd. The incident drew little notice, for the clearing was reverberating with cheers for the newly crowned king, but the movement of three white mantles was enough to make Jay look their way and glare at them. Assessing the situation at a glance, he curtly signaled them to withdraw.

Taking Torquil's weight between them, half carrying and half dragging their charge, Arnault and Luc together managed to manhandle him into the shelter of the trees without arousing much further notice. Finding there a dry upcropping of rock, they eased him to a sitting position and urged his head between his knees.

By then, Torquil had started regaining control of his legs, and was taking urgent, gasping breaths, shaking his head as if to clear it. After a few minutes, with Arnault murmuring, "Easy, easy, just give yourself a moment, and keep your head down for a bit," he raised his head experimentally, bleary eyes reflecting bewilderment and a lingering ache behind his eyes.

"What the devil happened?" he muttered hoarsely.

Arnault traded swift glances with Luc, who moved to support Torquil from behind. "Suppose you tell me."

A painful frown furrowed Torquil's brow. "I—don't know. Some kind of . . . vision?"

"Close your eyes and relax for another minute or two," Arnault advised quietly, glancing again at Luc. "There's no one about just now. They're all still back at the Moot Hill."

Torquil obediently closed his eyes, breathing in and out gustily at Arnault's further direction. Signing for Luc to keep a lookout, Arnault sank down on his hunkers and flexed his right hand, readying himself to draw on his inner faculties. Focusing on the stillness that formed at the center of his being, he then lightly closed his hand around Torquil's nearest wrist.

"Take another deep breath—now another. Are things getting clearer now?" he asked, nodding at Torquil's nod. "That's good. Now tell us about this vision of yours. Keep your eyes closed."

Haltingly at first, then with greater fluency, Torquil described what he had seen. It soon became clear to both his listeners that the experience had shaken the younger man far worse than any of the physical dangers he had ever faced in battle. His face had regained its normal color by the time he finished his narrative, but he still looked more than a little unnerved.

Glancing over his head at Luc, who was well aware of his previous misgivings regarding the extinction of the Canmore royal line, Arnault wondered whether Torquil understood the implication of what he had told them—that Alexander Canmore had met his "accidental" death by means of sorcery.

"May I—open my eyes now?" Torquil asked, when Arnault said nothing immediately.

"Of course." Arnault released Torquil's wrist and eased down on the rock beside him, considering the more immediate implications for Torquil himself. Both he and Luc had been anticipating and hoping that the younger man would prove to have talents such as they themselves wielded on behalf of *le Cercle* and the greater Temple, but the time and place of manifestation were hardly what either would have wished—and far overshadowed by the import of what the younger knight apparently had seen.

"You may have provided us with very valuable information," he said quietly, aware that they must return to their duties before they aroused unwelcome interest in what, for now, could probably be explained as a momentary lightheadedness on Torquil's part, perhaps brought on by too little sleep and food. "But this is not a good time to discuss it—and do *not* mention it to Jay or any of the others, even if they should ask."

"But—I would never—"

"I'm sure you wouldn't, son," Luc cut in quietly. "You neglected to break your fast sufficiently this morning, and watching your Scottish king crowned was a very emotional moment," he went on, only nodding deliberately as Torquil looked at him askance. "You started to feel faint, and we took you aside until you could recover, so you wouldn't disgrace the Order by keeling over. That's all you need to say."

"Well, I certainly wouldn't tell anyone else what I really saw," Torquil muttered, then pulled a sour grimace. "But Jay will certainly make as much of this as he can. He's constantly looking for ways to belittle me, make me look the fool."

"*Humilité,* my young friend," Arnault said with a faint smile, clapping him on the shoulder and urging him to his feet. "We'll discuss this at a more appropriate time and place. You and I have skirted around such subjects before, but I think perhaps you're ready for some solid answers."

"I *need* some solid answers," Torquil muttered. "There's more I need to tell you: something about the Stone, that Brother Mungo told me last night, and something I saw at Mass earlier—"

"Later," Arnault warned, with a speaking glance at Luc. "We haven't time right now. Your new king will have started receiving the homage of his magnates—and the ever diligent Master of Scotland has ordered me to take note of all those present who swear fealty."

And up on the hill, awaiting his turn to pledge his fealty, the Lord of Badenoch surreptitiously retrieved what he had secreted in his sleeve and, as he briefly crouched—ostensibly to free the hem of his robe from one roweled spur—at the same time deposited a whitish, coin-sized object amid a scattering of manure. This he trod purposefully under the heel of one steel-shod boot as he rose, befouling and obliterating what had been offered as a visible manifestation of purity and profound faith, before moving forward to offer his sword to the new king.

Chapter Eleven

THE INAUGURATION OF THE NEW KING OF SCOTS WAS TO BE followed by a celebratory feast, lasting well into the night. Given the expected consumption of wine, the Knights Templar were requested to maintain a quiet but visible presence. Accordingly, it was not until much later that evening that Arnault and Luc could withdraw to confer privately regarding the day's developments.

By then, the implications of those developments had been rendered even more disturbing by additional information that Torquil passed on to Arnault later in the afternoon, while ostensibly reporting a minor breach of the peace. For, though obliged to be both brief and somewhat cryptic, Torquil had contrived not only to summarize his previous night's conversation with Brother Mungo regarding fears about the Stone, but also to convey some of his shock at what he thought he had seen the Black Comyn do.

This startling new information, coupled with the earlier intimations of Torquil's vision, forced Arnault to reexamine his assumptions on several levels, and made it imperative that he seek out Luc's counsel. Though unable to arrange a meeting until later that night, and only able to mention, in passing, that Torquil had supplied several additional items of information having possible bearing on recent developments, he knew that Luc took his meaning.

Accordingly, while the magnates of Scotland were toasting the health of their new king—and were unlikely to notice that the number of Templars in and about the hall had been reduced by two—first Luc and then Arnault slipped out of the dining hall and made their way across the dark cloister yard to the now-silent precincts of the abbey church.

The opening creak of the door seemed preternaturally loud as Arnault entered, but the church was deserted, as he had hoped. Compline was long past, and the monks had retired to their beds, unlikely to return until time for the office of Matins, still several hours away. The glow of the Presence lamp before the high altar was seconded by the many votive candles that had been set burning throughout the church in honor of the day.

With this light to guide him, Arnault skirted quietly along the north aisle and into the side chapel of the north transept, where the Stone had been restored to its accustomed place. At once Luc stepped into the light of its attendant vigil lamps, beckoning Arnault to join him.

"Now, what's all this about Torquil?" Luc asked, as they took position against a far wall, where they would see anyone entering the church long before being seen themselves. They spoke in whispers, ever mindful lest someone overhear.

"Our young friend has given me two more rather intriguing pieces of our growing puzzle," Arnault replied. "In light of what he claims to have seen earlier this afternoon, we have a number of new and startling permutations possibly pertinent to what has been happening."

Briefly he reviewed Torquil's observations regarding the

Stone, and also the senior Comyn's startling action. Luc listened in growing incredulity, his unfocused gaze fixed on the squat, dark silhouette of Scotland's palladium—now, it appeared, perhaps but an empty shell.

"Let's put aside the question of Comyn, for the moment," Luc said, when Arnault finally wound down. "If he *does* intend some improper use of a consecrated Host, I see no immediate connection to anything else presently concerning us—and he *might* simply have wanted it as a protective talisman. Poor theology, but it could be put to far worse use."

"That's true enough," Arnault agreed.

"As for the Stone possibly having lost its potency—that strikes me as far less significant, in the immediate sense, than the implication of what Torquil says he saw in his vision—mainly, because that tends to corroborate what *you* saw, when the Maid of Norway died."

Arnault only nodded.

"Incidentally, how do you feel about the vision itself?" Luc asked. "Do you think he has true sight?"

"For its content, I very much wish I could say no," Arnault returned. "And of course, what it *means* may be another story entirely. But your own instincts were squarely on the mark when you spotted his initial potential—and he did tell us that his father has the Second Sight. Since you passed him into my supervision, he's only continued to advance— as the last day's developments clearly show. It may be that coming back to Scotland has somehow triggered his next additional growth. In fact, it strikes me that his awakening, at this time, might well be bound up with what's happening here in Scotland."

"I wouldn't argue that," Luc replied. "What concerns me is that his vision regarding Alexander's 'accident' links rather alarmingly with your own fears regarding the death of Alexander's granddaughter. That raises the possibility that not one but *two* Canmore sovereigns somehow were murdered by means of sorcerous intervention."

"I've been doing my best to avoid that notion," Arnault said uneasily. "The extinction of the Canmore line has had dire enough consequences, even attributing it to mere fate."

"I agree," Luc said. "But if that extinction was deliberate, rather than the result of random accident—and by the means that you and Torquil suggest—then it bespeaks the involvement of some human agency: someone who would benefit from it and also had the wherewithal to enlist demonic assistance. We should also remember," he added chillingly, "that demons do not lend their aid without a price—and moreover, are not normally inclined to intervene in the affairs of humans without ample incentive."

Arnault allowed himself a shiver—no difficult thing in the cold church.

"That's hardly comforting. What you're posing is the existence, presumably somewhere here in Scotland, of a black magician—or maybe several of them—with sufficient power and influence to bring about the end of the Canmore royal line." He glanced at Luc, suddenly struck with a notion even more chilling than the night. "You don't suppose this could link with what happened back at Balantrodoch, do you?"

Luc cocked his head. "You mean, the attack on Brother Colman's scriptorium?"

"*And* the disappearance of those pagan grave goods," Arnault replied. "You yourself said that the rune-staves had the feel of dark power."

"Mere coincidence?" Luc said doubtfully.

"I little believe in coincidence," Arnault replied. "Not in the matters that *we* are appointed to deal with—not when considering whether someone perhaps has used dark powers to topple a dynasty. And now I can't help wondering whether the arrogant and grasping Brother Brian de Jay might somehow be connected with what's going on."

"Surely not," Luc said flatly. "His ambitions lie within the Order; he'd have no reason for meddling in the Scottish succession, even if he had the ability. And as for what you're suggesting—well, I should never have credited him with the self-discipline needed to master even gray magical arts, much less black ones."

"Maybe we've greatly underestimated him," Arnault said. "He was nearby when the Maid died, and he certainly was involved in the disappearance of the missing grave goods—whether he actually appropriated them or merely dumped them in a lake as he claims. There's also no doubt that he was nearby when Brother Colman's manuscripts were attacked."

"He *was* rather in a hurry to see us away from there," Luc conceded.

"Yes, he was," Arnault went on. "And if you're looking for a motive, you needn't look outside the Order. You yourself said that he's ambitious. In former times, he could have expected to be posted off to the Holy Land to fight Saracens, and perhaps covered himself in glory and gained promotions, if he survived it—but the Order has lost its mission in the Holy Land. Nonetheless, he's managed to get himself named Master of Scotland—helped along, I have no doubt, by the way he's ingratiated himself with the English court—"

"He *is* English," Luc pointed out. "And it was the Master of England who received him, as I recall."

"Yes—well, that part of his ascendance could be merely political," Arnault conceded. "God knows, secular political leverage is not unknown within the Order.

"But what if Jay *has* somehow gotten himself involved in esoteric matters? We of *le Cercle* are not the only ones to have stumbled onto such things in the Holy Land—and even though he hasn't been there, others have—maybe down in the London Temple. This is all conjecture, of course, but— well, given the circumstances surrounding the disappearance of those relics of Briochan—not to mention the scriptorium incident—I don't think I much like the direction my thoughts are taking—whether or not Jay is directly involved."

Luc slowly nodded.

"I, too, find myself coming back to those relics. We still don't know what really became of them. Nor can we assume that they were necessarily those of Briochan. But we *can* surmise, from what happened that last night at Balantrodoch, that *something* connected with Briochan has certainly been stirred up.

"But, why?" He rubbed at his beard as he stared into one of the votive candles on the altar, thinking out loud. "Briochan was an adversary of Saint Columba, resisting the replacement of ancient Pictish religious forms with those of Celtic Christianity. By overcoming Briochan, Columba succeeded in securing the primacy of Christianity in Scotland and establishing a Celtic Christian monarchy, supplanting the older Pictish customs."

As Arnault nodded, following his narrative, Luc went on.

"If we postulate that the deaths of Alexander III and his granddaughter were brought about deliberately—and both Torquil's vision and your own impressions at the Maid's death suggest such a possibility—then it follows that someone—or some*thing*—may be at work to undo what Columba accomplished. Eradicating the Canmore line would certainly be a step in that direction. And given the coincidental discovery of Briochan's relics—and then, their entirely too fortuitous disappearance—we perhaps must consider whether there is some connection. Some attempt, perhaps, to revive Briochan's cult, to reawaken him and use his power to further present dynastic aims."

"Here's a possible connection," Arnault said thoughtfully, "though I can't say I like it better than any of the others. It occurs to me to wonder whether any of this has an impact on the greater mission of the Temple—to rebuild the Fifth Temple here in Scotland."

"Now, *there's* a chilling thought," Luc said. "We know, or

at least believe, that the Stone on which the Canmores were inaugurated is also linked with the restoration of the Temple." He cast his gaze over the Stone again. "Which brings us back to Torquil's claim—or rather, Brother Mungo's—that the Stone is ailing; that it has lost or is losing its power—power that both the Temple and the sovereigns of Scotland need badly, in order to accomplish their respective missions."

A taut silence descended between the two of them, until Arnault said, "If the Stone *has* become deficient in some way—whether or not there has been interference in the Scottish succession—we have an entirely different and more serious problem, as from today. Because even though John Balliol was duly enthroned upon the Stone, that means little without its empowerment."

Luc slowly nodded. "I see where this is leading. The Stone has been mystically linked with the Scottish monarchy since the time of Columba himself—the vessel by which divine grace has been transmitted to the Canmore kings. That vessel is like a well, fed by the fount of grace which is the Arch-Sovereign—except that, in this case, the well has been—clogged, or damaged, so that it cannot fill—or what fills it cannot be contained."

"An apt image," Arnault agreed. "And whichever is the case, we must find out how to undo it, to unclog the well or repair it, else John Balliol wears an empty crown." He paused a beat. "I think it's time I had a closer look at our so-called Stone of Destiny."

"You'll want wards set, then, and someone to keep watch," Luc said—and added wryly, "Since Brian de Jay became Master of Balantrodoch, I find I've become something of an expert at this sort of thing."

"Which may, in itself, say something," Arnault replied, indicating his acceptance of the offer with a gesture to proceed.

Luc withdrew to the arch that joined the chapel to the north transept, standing with his back against the wall, and turned his gaze out to the darkened nave. Leaving him to set in place the needed protections, Arnault moved before the Stone itself, kneeling down on its western side and laying both hands on the indented top surface. With a murmured prayer of invocation, he closed his eyes and bowed his head, pausing to collect himself.

Like a flock of scattered birds, his thoughts and fears came lightly to rest and the outer world receded, fading into the profound hush that marked the boundary between waking and trance. Turning inward in spirit, he sought the shimmering jewel that lay at the center of his being, pulsing with the heartbeat of the cosmos, then cast his senses outward into the world of spirit.

Lifting his gaze, then, to the altar beyond the Stone, lit by votive candles and luminous with a brightness of spiritual virtue, by reason of the countless Masses celebrated upon it, he could sense the holiness of Presence imbuing altar and surrounds with sheer holiness. But when he turned his gaze downward to what lay beneath his hands, the dark Stone lay inert and apparently lifeless.

He spread his fingers and sought deeper, thinking that surely he must be mistaken; but it was as if he knelt at the brink of a vast, empty hole into nothingness. Only far into infinity could he sense the faintest glimmer to suggest that what usually was resident within the Stone might yet return to it.

Troubled, he turned his focus inward, seeking clarification, framing a call to those angelic masters whose counsel he sought in times of need. After a moment, a hint of vision came—but only the image of a rich cup overturned atop a small, round table of marble the color of the Stone, bloodred wine spilling across the polished surface. The table was set beneath an airy pavilion whose canopy was like a silver cloud raised up on twelve pillars of alabaster, these forming a circle of brightness around a standing column of pure white light. Three marble steps led the way up onto the floor of the pavilion.

Not presuming to mount those steps, Arnault bowed himself in spirit and lifted open hands in a gesture of appeal. The air grew still brighter around him, as though a number of lamps had been uncovered, and Arnault dared to frame a wordless plea for insight.

A light gust of wind seemed to stir the pure air of the hallow, prompting him to lift his gaze. The pavilion itself had vanished, its pillars now become twelve shining, winged beings armored in light, each with the scarlet cross of the Order burning on its breast. In their midst stood yet another such being, though vested after the manner of a Grand Master of the Order, with wings and beard and eyes all of flame. Before Arnault could bend again in wordless, awed salute, the being came to clasp his hands between its own—acknowledgment of homage due, but also the greeting of a brother warrior of the Light—and bent to seal the exchange with a fraternal kiss of peace.

The holy and transcendent rapture of that angelic kiss all but made Arnault swoon, igniting remembrance of the vision granted him in the tower at Cyprus. Though newly reassured that the Stone beneath his hands was meant to be the cornerstone of a Fifth Temple, there was that about the Stone itself that yet seemed—wrong. As, in appeal, he turned physical vision to the altar beyond the Stone, he focused his present need in a scarcely whispered prayer, his inner sight still ensnared by the fiery eyes of the angel, hands still clasped in prayer between those mighty hands.

"Show me . . ." he breathed, with all the fervor he could summon. *"Give me a sign . . ."*

For an eternal instant the angel's eyes seemed to draw him into their fire. Then he felt the floor seem to melt away from under him, leaving him briefly weightless before he began a precipitant downward plunge. Strong winds rushed past him, like a tempest trapped in a tunnel. Then, all at once, he grounded with a bone-setting jolt, still on his knees.

Recovering himself with an effort, he tried to force his eyes to focus. He was kneeling once more in the chapel at Scone Abbey, still confronting the Stone of Destiny, but now he was seeing everything around him with new eyes. The objects near at hand were visible not as fixed and solid substance, but as fluid patterns of energy. The altar before him was a tablet of shifting rainbows; the lamps that burned before it were silhouettes of variegated fire. But under his hands, the Stone of Destiny lay dark and lifeless as a tomb slab, its cold sucking the warmth from his hands. Then a wash of red seemed to draw across his vision like a curtain.

He gasped—and blinked—and all the images blurred and whirled, dissolving away. Once again he felt like he was falling, his fingers even grabbing at the Stone to steady himself.

Then, abruptly, he was back in his body again, reeling with dizziness. Trying to push himself back up on his knees—for he had sunk back on his hunkers during the vision—he wobbled and then sat back onto the floor with a faint clashing of the mail beneath his robe. Luc at once turned to look at him, then sketched a sign of dismissal in the air before the entrance to the chapel and came to join him, setting a hand on his shoulder in concern as he crouched beside him.

Arnault took a deep breath and let it out gustily, shaking his head at Luc's look of inquiry and letting the older man help him to his feet.

"Well, *that* was an interesting exercise," he murmured. "If my vision was clear, then Torquil and Brother Mungo were right: Something is seriously wrong with the Stone. I had the sense that it *can* be made right—but I have no idea where we begin to find out how."

He swayed and almost stumbled. Not speaking, Luc took him by the arm and guided him to a seat on a stone bench set against the back wall of the little chapel, where Arnault haltingly described what he had seen.

"So the Stone is dead—or at least ailing," Arnault concluded, his eyes, like Luc's, fixed on the dark bulk of the Stone, "and the Canmore line has been extinguished. Could it be that someone has been interfering with the Stone *and* stirring up whatever power Briochan wielded, to thwart both missions?"

"Who could do that, or would want to?" Luc whispered. "Jay certainly doesn't fit those parameters."

"I shouldn't think so—but you know him better than I," Arnault said. "But if not Jay, then who? Some remnant, perhaps, of the cult that followed Briochan, back in Columba's time?"

"I suppose it's possible," Luc allowed. "This is an ancient land, with ancient gods, who did not bow willingly to Christ or to Columba."

"Precisely my point. And what if votaries of those old gods are now attempting to obliterate all that Columba achieved, including Scotland's Christian monarchy?"

"What, indeed?" Luc said. "And it's certainly possible that disturbing the bones of their patron might have drawn unwelcome attention to the Temple."

Arnault nodded grimly. "I'd thought of that. It could well be that what now unfolds in Scotland is bound up with the larger crisis looming over the Temple—and, indeed, the whole of civilization. We see the old order of things being disrupted at every turn, and a flood of random hazard let loose on the world. The loss of the Christian East was our first warning of that danger, and now the signs are everywhere. What nations and institutions may rise out of this chaos, only the events of the next several years will tell. But you and I, and all the Inner Circle, will have to make our choices very carefully, if the Temple is to survive the fire and fulfill the role to which it is appointed by Providence."

"A sobering prospect," Luc agreed. "What do you propose we do?"

"For the immediate future, continue to watch and listen. In particular, Jay must be watched. My work here is mostly done for now, with the new King of Scots now crowned—though only time will tell what that is worth, given the condition of the Stone. I shall take counsel of our superiors when Torquil and I return to Paris."

"They must be aware of all of this," Luc agreed.

"There is one thing more," Arnault went on, after a slight hesitation. "Given Torquil's part in recent events, I intend to speak with Gaspar about him, There can be no doubt that the potentials you first noted have begun to surface, and to specific intent. He should be initiated. Unless Gaspar forbids it, I shall submit Torquil's name to *le Maître*."

Luc's brow furrowed, his gray eyes troubled. "Are you certain he's ready, my friend? You know what is required. If he is not sufficiently prepared—"

"I know what will happen," Arnault said steadily. "And I'm prepared to stake my life—or rather, *his* life—that he will come through it.

"We need him, Luc; and it appears that Scotland needs him as well."

Chapter Twelve

THE FOLLOWING MORNING, THE NEW KING OF SCOTS AND his party headed south for Edinburgh and the remaining guests at Scone Abbey began to disperse. The Templar contingent rode with them, providing a discreet rear guard for the royal party. Arnault and Torquil traveled in their company, intending to continue on with the English Templars as far as London; but when Arnault's horse took a bad fall in driving rain just outside Edinburgh, leaving Arnault with a badly bruised shoulder and arm—and temporarily unable to wield a sword—he decided to capitalize on the flexibility of his orders from Paris and to winter at the Scottish preceptory. While it would delay furthering Torquil's advancement until the spring, Luc rightly pointed out that it also afforded them an opportunity to observe, from closer hand, the beginning of John Balliol's reign—and Brian de Jay.

Not unexpectedly, the Master of Scotland was less than pleased at the prospect of having two more mouths to feed through the winter, not to mention two more horses, and clearly resented the ongoing presence of two "spies" from the Visitor of France—under his roof but not really under his command for the duration—but he could hardly insist that Arnault ride on when unfit to fight; and winter was already setting in with a vengeance. By the time the English Templars continued on to London, after several days' delay at Balantrodoch to wait out an early winter storm, they carried with them, among routine reports and documents intended for the Paris Temple, Jay's official report of John Balliol's investiture and also, coded in what appeared to be a routine report to the Paris treasury, a somewhat expanded account, prepared by Arnault and Luc, which would find its way to superiors of which the Master of Scotland was not aware.

In the ensuing four months of bitter cold and inactivity, no further incident touched the community at Balantrodoch that could be construed as uncanny; nor could subtle inquiry uncover any further clue as to the fate of the missing grave goods. Nonetheless, Arnault and Luc continued to harbor serious misgivings about the affinities and intentions of Brian de Jay, both esoteric and political. Both at Berwick and at Scone, Jay had taken every opportunity to ingratiate himself with Bishop Bek and other senior servants of the English crown assigned to carry out King Edward's intentions in Scotland. Soon after their return to Balantrodoch, as it became apparent that Edward was not backing down from his ongoing goal to bring Scotland firmly under his control, Torquil pointed out how Jay's active support of this policy might eventually create a split within the ranks of the Templar Order.

In the meantime, signs of dissension were already beginning to reappear among the Scottish nobility. John Balliol, against the advice of his more farsighted ministers, journeyed south to Newcastle shortly before Christmas, there to do homage to King Edward of England on the feast of Saint Stephen. In a contrasting show of independence, Robert Bruce of Annandale, the second of that name, renounced his position as Earl of Carrick rather than swear fealty to Balliol upon his return.

These ostentatiously evasive tactics on behalf of the Bruces only served to underline the limitations of Balliol's authority—a weakness that Arnault made no effort to disguise in the further report that he and Torquil made to the Visitor of France when they returned to Paris at the beginning of March.

The stranger elements of the Scottish situation Arnault reserved for the exclusive attention of Gaspar des Macquelines, delivered privily after their arrival, at a meeting deep in the bowels of the Paris treasury. At Arnault's suggestion, Torquil had been sent off to the preceptory at Prunay, a day's ride from Paris, on the pretext of delivering a letter from Gaspar to the provincial treasurer. The senior knight listened intently as Arnault acquainted him with all the new permutations of the information that he and Luc had assembled, together with their further speculations concerning same, though he made no emphasis of Torquil's part in the proceedings at that time.

"We can only conclude that someone, somehow, has contrived to eradicate the Canmore dynasty," he declared by way of a summation, "and our evidence points to black magic being the vehicle. We strongly suspect the involvement of a cult of apostates who want to set aside the Christian traditions of Saint Columba in favor of a return to paganism. We *may* be dealing with devotees of a particular adversary of Columba called Briochan. Luc is pressing on with the investigation. He'll send word to us here, as soon as there's anything further worth reporting."

"That could prove a dangerous job for one man on his own, even someone of Luc's capabilities," Gaspar said with a frown. "I'm surprised you didn't leave young Lennox behind to help him."

It was the opening Arnault had been waiting for, now that the groundwork had been laid.

"I thought about that," he said. "And Luc does have a good man there, who can be trusted in the ordinary things: another

Scot, called Flannan Fraser. But I have an urgent request to make on behalf of Brother Torquil—and it wasn't something I dared delay or that I wanted to entrust to writing."

Gaspar only inclined his head, giving permission for Arnault to continue. With a slowly indrawn breath, Arnault prepared to take the plunge.

"You are well aware of my satisfaction with Brother Torquil's work on all levels," he said. "By now, you will have gathered that his contributions to our esoteric work have begun to take on significant dimensions. His vision regarding the death of Alexander III helped validate my own insights and suspicions regarding the death of the Maid of Norway. And his levelheaded handling of subsequent observations has only convinced me further that he shares in those affinities by which our Inner Circle is served.

"In view of this development, I should like to propose that he be received, without delay, into the ranks of *le Cercle*."

Gaspar raised one bushy eyebrow. "That is a singularly audacious request, my friend, quite apart from the risks to which you would subject him."

"I know that."

"Do you? Understand that I have never doubted this young man's potential—believe me, I have not—but when you and I last spoke, his inner talents were only just beginning to manifest. Would you really have me believe that he has achieved, in only a few short months, what normally takes years—if, indeed, it is even attainable?"

"He is still achieving—and that is a lifelong process for all of us—but, yes," Arnault said steadily. "What prompts my request is not only the speed with which he has progressed, but also the quality of that progression. I believe that this sudden blossoming of his mystical gifts has been divinely instigated in response to the crisis now facing us. That's the reason I brought him back with me—in the hope that you and *le Maître* would assent to his immediate initiation into our company."

This pronouncement reduced Gaspar to thoughtful silence. When at last he spoke, his tone was carefully measured.

"Putting aside the danger to Brother Torquil—you do realize that what you're asking is wholly unprecedented?"

"So is our present situation," Arnault replied. "Did we, in our wisdom, ever foresee that the Order would be driven from the shores of Outremer? Did we ever foresee that we would one day find ourselves without a homeland? Who are we to refuse to change our ways, when everything else around us is in a state of flux?"

"We are the guardians of sacred tradition," Gaspar said. "It is upon those traditions that our strength depends."

"And what will become of those traditions, if the Order fails in its mission to rebuild the Temple?" Arnault countered. "We claim to be believers in signs and miracles. We presume to take guidance from sources that, if it were even suspected we had access to them, would instill such fear in those who do not comprehend, as could bring about our deaths and the end of our holy Order. If we accept the validity of a vision which instructs that the Temple should be rebuilt on Scottish soil, then surely we must admit the possibility that a native-born Scot might have been granted particular gifts for the sake of accomplishing this task."

Seeing his superior still silent, Arnault persisted.

"At least consider my request, Gaspar. I am not asking this as an overly fond parent pleading a favor on behalf of a precocious child. I am asking because I am convinced that Torquil has a part to play in this work, which cannot be fully realized until he knows consciously what is at stake. Will you at least speak to *Maître* Jean?"

Gaspar shifted in his chair, troubled eyes searching Arnault's. "You know what the initiation entails. If your young protégé isn't ready—if you've misread the situation—"

"I'm aware of what could happen," Arnault said. "But I'm sure he won't fail."

"A visionary pronouncement?"

"No, a statement of faith. Have any of us any more to go on, in the work we have undertaken?"

"No," Gaspar said softly.

"Then, will you speak to *Maître* Jean?" Arnault asked again.

"Very well, since you ask it in faith," Gaspar said heavily. "But I hope none of us will have cause to regret this."

It was well after dark when Torquil returned from his excursion to Prunay, weary and chilled to the bone. He had scarcely finished stabling his horse when a serjeant approached him with a message that Arnault wished a word with him. The message directed him to report immediately to one of the upper chambers of the treasury tower. Sighing inwardly, for he had not eaten since midday, Torquil dismissed the serjeant with a word of thanks and went off to answer the summons.

The designated chamber occupied one of the turrets on the northwest rampart of the citadel. Using the watchwords supplied by Arnault before his departure that morning, for the treasury tower was guarded even within the Temple complex, Torquil made his way past several intermediary guard posts and eventually arrived before the appointed door, where he slipped his dagger from his belt and gave the door's lock a brisk double rap with the pommel. At the muffled word of query from within, he announced himself and sheathed the dagger as he waited for the door to open.

It was Arnault who admitted him, stepping back with a nod and a gesture to enter. He looked uncharacteristically sober, making Torquil wonder whether he had done anything to displease.

"Please come in," Arnault said quietly. "There is someone I wish you to meet."

As Torquil shifted past him, his mentor shot the bolt to secure the chamber from within. Out of the corner of his eye, the young Scot noticed that Arnault made a curious gesture with his right hand before taking charge to guide him farther into the room.

Seated behind a cluttered writing table before the far wall was a venerable figure of a man whom Torquil had never seen before. His snow-white hair and beard glistened like hoarfrost against the pristine whiteness of his robes as he looked up, laying aside a quill pen, his patrician features sternly delineated in the lamplight. The impact of his dark gaze arrested Torquil in his tracks, as if he had come up against an invisible wall.

"*Maître* Jean, this is Brother Torquil Lennox, of whom we have spoken," Arnault said, on a note of quiet deference. "You have heard my account of his merits. It now remains for you to examine him, and judge for yourself whether or not he is fit to receive further instruction."

The man Arnault had addressed as Master gave only the slightest inclination of his frost-white head by way of acknowledgment. His dark eyes remained locked on Torquil's. At the same time, the irresistible force of their regard seemed to strip his subject's spirit bare of all defenses, imparting a fleeting impression of being naked and unarmed as a prisoner in a hostile camp.

One startled, gibbering part of Torquil yearned to run and hide, but honor and his own inherent courage demanded that he stand his ground, no matter his personal fear. Though that fear persisted, the Master's gaze held him and continued to probe, imparting the certainty that every petty sin and secret failing was being exposed and examined with the relentless focus of a surgeon exploring a deep-seated wound. A faint gasp escaped Torquil's lips, and a part of him flinched from the scrutiny, but it never even occurred to him to plead for mercy.

This silent probing seemed to last for an eternity. Then, abruptly, the Master's gaze released him. Torquil swayed briefly on his feet, blinking with astonishment as he realized that whatever had happened was over. As he steadied himself, *Maître* Jean transferred his attention to Arnault, speaking aloud for the first time.

"I commend your discernment, Brother Arnault: You see with clear vision. But the outcome of any final decision must rest with an authority greater than mine."

His dark gaze shifted back to the younger knight. "Brother Torquil, on the strength of Brother Arnault's commendation, I propose to reveal to you certain knowledge that is not shared with the rest of our brethren. Should you ever betray the trust that admits you to this knowledge, the price will be more terrible than you can possibly contemplate." He paused for just a beat. "Do you wish me to proceed?"

Still focused utterly on the mysterious and somewhat daunting Master, Torquil yet was peripherally aware of Arnault, standing silent at his side. Suddenly missing, however, was the sense of constant and reassuring rapport that he only now realized had been part of his mentor's presence almost from the beginning. That bolstering rapport had become so natural to him, during the two years of their partnership, that its absence made him feel suddenly abandoned.

But that feeling of abandonment yielded almost at once to the intuitive certainty that it was only temporary: that Arnault had withdrawn whatever spiritual bond they shared only to leave him greater freedom to make his own choices—and that his mentor trusted him enough to be finally revealing some glimpse of the secret work to which he sometimes had made veiled references, but about which Torquil had never dared to ask.

This realization brought with it a strange sense of detachment, of being curiously at peace. Now that the tension of the Master's first scrutiny was behind him, Torquil's awareness seemed to have settled at a point above and beyond the reach of fear or even apprehension, so that whatever might happen next, it was as if that higher part of himself had already perceived and accepted the outcome.

He became aware that *Maître* Jean was still awaiting his response, and found his voice only after swallowing with difficulty.

"Yes, sir," he said huskily. "I do wish you to proceed."

The elder knight accepted this declaration with a grave nod.

"Glad am I to hear it—and I assure you, on my immortal soul and my hopes of the life to come, that this knowledge and the service I would ask of you are of the Light. However, I must also caution you that even His Holiness the Pope could not save you, were you to reveal it beyond the sacred circle to which we propose to offer you access. If you are willing to accept both the burden and the joy of this knowledge, I will require your solemn oath upon a holy relic more sacred than you can imagine—and that oath will be tested by a trial certain to cause your death, if you swear not with all your heart and soul and mind, without reservation or equivocation. Are you prepared to abide by these conditions?"

The Master's words suggested secrets far beyond anything Torquil might have conceived on his own. Yet it occurred to him, in a passing flash, that he had already seen remote glimmerings of such secrets reflected in some of Arnault's own deeds and words. He could recall any number of times in the past when the other's behavior had suggested an adherence to some mysterious higher purpose, which eluded the understanding or even the awareness of those around him.

To share in that work would be to repay, if only in part, the debt of gratitude he felt for Arnault's friendship and teaching—and to join him in the great work to which both he and the mysterious *Maître* Jean clearly were dedicated—work that clearly went far beyond the work he himself initially had set out to do when he joined the Temple, defending the faith in the Holy Land. Also in mind was the steadfast certainty that Arnault would not have exposed him to the danger of an ordeal likely to kill him, if he were not equipped to survive it.

"I am prepared," he said aloud.

"I rejoice in your acceptance," *Maître* Jean said mildly. "Had you declined, even your knowledge of this offer would have required that Brother Arnault take your life to ensure your silence."

A firm hand came to rest on Torquil's left shoulder from behind, but he half turned his head to the right, where Arnault stood, not flinching from the caress of steel laid across his throat as his gaze flicked briefly downward to a glimpse of Arnault's fist closed around the hilt of a dagger. No fear remained as he lifted his gaze to his mentor's.

"Do what you must, but there is no need for that," he said with utter conviction. "Your secrets will be safe with me."

Maître Jean nodded, and Arnault withdrew the blade. Though the latter gave no outward sign of emotion, Torquil had the distinct impression of relief. But before he could refine that impression, the Master's voice recalled his attention.

"Your peril is not past, Brother Torquil. On the contrary, it is only just beginning. Now I must take you to another place for a final testing. This test may not be refused. From this point onward, any resistance on your part will cost you your life."

Torquil's gaze again sought Arnault's.

"I am entirely in your hands—and in God's," he said quietly.

And knew that it was true. If anyone else but Arnault had placed him in such a situation, he would have fought to the death rather than submit. But he and Arnault had faced many dangers side by side, and he owed the older knight his life many times over. It would take more than anything the mysterious *Maître* Jean might say or do to break the trust that lay between them.

The Master rose from his chair. Arming himself with a lamp, he turned to open a door to the right behind him. The door gave access to a narrow spiral stairway, plunging into a well of shadows below. Starting downward, he did not look to see whether Arnault and Torquil followed.

"Your silence is required from this moment onward," Torquil heard his mentor murmur, as a tug at his elbow urged him forward. "All will be made clear in the fullness of time."

Lit by the Master's light, the three of them descended the steps in single file. The stair took them four flights down, well below ground level, ending at a stout oak door banded with iron. This *Maître* Jean unlocked with one of a set of keys that he carried on a ring attached to his belt. Entering behind the Master, Torquil found himself in a barrel-vaulted chamber with the dimensions and decor of a small, stark chapel.

Against the east end of the room stood a red marble table arrayed with pristine altar linens, with a large crucifix above it and a frontal cloth depicting the scarlet cross of the Order, with its eight points for the eight Beatitudes. Bronze lamp stands stood at either end. Built into the wall to the left of the altar were two aumbries of unusual size, both with substantial-looking locks—more like safes than like cupboards intended to house the usual Mass vessels associated with such a chapel.

Torquil gave them a curious glance, wondering what lay inside, as *Maître* Jean set his lamp on one of the stands and wordlessly directed Arnault to secure the door behind them. The Master then produced from under his habit a neck chain dangling three finely wrought silver keys. One of these he used to unlock the left-hand cupboard.

The cupboard yielded up a pair of silver candlesticks, an incense boat, and a thurible charged with charcoal, which he placed upon the altar with the candles bracketing the thurible. Arnault, meanwhile, had come to join him, and used a taper to light the candles and the charcoal from the flame of the lamp. As the shadows receded amid a fragrant waft of incense smoke, the Master used a second key to unlock the second of the aumbries, from which he brought out a stoppered flask of alabaster and a miniature silver chalice.

These he carried over to the altar, placing them reverently in the center before sinking to his knees, hands joined as his head bowed in prayer. As Arnault did the same, Torquil followed their example. He could hear the Master softly start to speak, though none of the words were quite distinct—and Arnault offering murmured responses—but Torquil somehow understood that the pair were offering up prayers for purity and enlightenment, and turned his own thoughts to the same, also commending himself to the protection of Divine Providence.

When the two had completed their litany, both signed themselves with the cross. His heartbeat quickening, Torquil copied the gesture. A moment later, the two rose and turned to face him. Arnault signaled Torquil to rise as well.

"In the Holy Scriptures it is written," the Master said, "that the priest shall hold in his hand the bitter water, the water of contention which brings forth the truth. The moment of that truth is now upon you, Brother Torquil Lennox. I charge you now to prepare yourself to taste of the bitter water. It is the trial which separates truth from falsehood, as by a two-edged sword; and that sword shall smite the faithless and those found unworthy, who fear to open utterly to God's outpouring of grace. Do you, of your own free will, accept this challenge?"

Far from sparking any fear, the Master's words dispelled any remaining apprehension in Torquil's mind, leaving him calm and clearheaded.

"I accept it willingly," he said softly. "May God Himself bear witness to my choice, for I am His."

"So be it," the Master replied. "Come forward now, before His altar."

As Torquil obeyed, the Master picked up the flask and drew the stopper, turning then to Arnault, who lifted the tiny chalice and held it steady as the elder knight tipped a measure of clear fluid into the cup. With another murmured prayer, the Master sketched an intricate sign above the mouth of the chalice. The first part looked like a cross, but Torquil could not identify the rest.

"This cup represents both life and death in a single draft," the Master said, taking it from Arnault and holding it before Torquil. "If any evil or falsehood taints your heart, that evil will turn to poison in your belly, and strike you down in the fullness of your pride. But if you have no reason to fear the judgment and mercy of the Lord, take and drink. For if your heart is truly pure, no harm will come to you."

Torquil took the cup. The liquid it contained had no discernible odor or color. Silently commending himself to the intercession of the angels, he briefly closed his eyes and raised the cup to his lips, drinking it down in a single swallow.

His first taste was, indeed, bitter. That bitterness, however, evaporated swiftly on his tongue, to be replaced by a pervading numbness that filled the inside of his mouth. He ventured to speak, but found his lips sealed, his jaws frozen. Someone took the little chalice from him, guided both his hands to rest lightly on the edge of the altar.

One by one, his other sensibilities abandoned him. The fragrance of the incense faded from his nostrils and his ears went deaf. A deadness laid hold of his extremities and spread throughout his body. A shadow darkened his vision, so that he could no longer see.

The loss of all outward sensation left him floating in a void. Even so, he remained curiously unafraid. The surrounding emptiness was charged with expectancy, like the darkness of the abyss awaiting a divine act of creation. And he himself was at one with that abyss, a virgin soul waiting to be born into a new world.

With new-made eyes, he watched the dawning of the world's first day. Shining images sprang up around him, brought to life by the coming of the Light, and he found himself at once standing on a mountainside in the midst of a circle of peaks. Flanking him were figures he vaguely sensed were Arnault and *Maître* Jean, clad in robes of astonishing whiteness.

A breath of wind swept across them. As it enveloped Torquil, his deaf ears were quickened by the sound of a voice singing, seeming to come from the cloud-wreathed mountaintop that towered above them.

Enraptured, he began to climb, seeking the source of the singing. Close behind him he could sense Arnault and the

Master following. When they reached the lower fringes of the cloud, Torquil began to catch the subtle scent of roses. The fragrance grew stronger as he continued upward through an enveloping mist. When he emerged above it, he espied before him a shining pillar of fire atop the mountain's summit.

Here, too, the air smelled of roses, burning sweet and pure. Heedless of the heat, drawn by the sweetness, Torquil let his feet carry him closer to the flames. The scent was intoxicating. Without pausing to think, he stepped forward into the heart of the blaze.

The fire enfolded him in a shimmering, roseate embrace. In that instant he was swept aloft. The flames that bore him upward had tongues of melody, lifting his soul in sheer delight. Then the perfumed tide receded, leaving him kneeling before the entrance of a great temple.

Arnault and *Maître* Jean were there beside him. Looking down at himself, Torquil saw that he now was clothed in white robes like theirs. Advancing to the doors, Arnault laid his palms flat against the paneling. At his spoken Word, the doors swung inward to the chamber beyond.

At the far end of the chamber stood an enormous tabernacle veiled in crimson silk. Together the three of them approached it to kneel in homage. Certain beyond doubt that he was in the presence of holiness, Torquil kept his gaze averted as Arnault's voice echoed amid the aery vaults above their heads, speaking from beside him with merely human lips, but also resounding on some higher plane.

"Glorious Michael, Captain of the Hosts of Heaven, we here present one whom we would admit to the fellowship of the Sacred Circle, that he may better serve the Lord our God. May he be found worthy."

A stir of movement whispered through the hall, bringing with it a sense of nearing presence, unearthly and yet not wholly unfamiliar. Daring to lift his eyes, Torquil beheld the curtains drawing back from the tabernacle, revealing the presence of a mighty throne.

The throne was sculptured out of ruby fire, studded with blazing orbs like peacock eyes. But more glorious than the throne itself was the princely Presence who presided there, royally mantled—or winged—with a sweep of blazing peacock feathers; with hair like living flame and eyes like twin, newborn suns, and shining armor that reflected the swirling galaxies. The eyes burned deep into Torquil's soul, holding him transfixed. A voice made itself heard, mingling harmony and unity in a single utterance.

"Torquil Lennox, be touched by the benison of that Name that is above all other names. What gifts dost thou bring to the Temple of the Lord?"

Stunned that he was known by name, Torquil pondered the question, but his heart was too enraptured to reply. A part of him sensed and accepted that the Master was serving as vehicle for the words, but his soul wept with joy at the angelic blessing.

Leaning forward, the Archangel plucked a coal of fire out of the surrounding air and touched it to Torquil's lips. The flame unlocked his tongue, and he was able to speak again. But the only words that came to him seemed poor and uncouth.

"Nought have I to offer but myself," he said to the Archangel in all humility. "All that I am, however, I pledge with all my heart!"

He bowed his head, bereft of further words, but his silence was abruptly broken by a peal of music, like the clear ringing of crystal chimes. Astonished, he realized that it was the sound of angelic laughter.

That laughter filled the hall with a joyful brightness. Through a haze of radiance, Torquil heard the angel's voice again—but no longer filtered through the human medium of either of the men standing beside him.

"No man could offer more, Torquil Lennox. Such was the gift of God's own Son unto the world. When thou lookest upon His likeness, be forever sealed unto the fellowship of His eternal Light."

The tabernacle and its furnishings melted away in a blinding shimmer of incandescence. When Torquil's vision returned, he was standing once more in the underground chapel, flanked by Arnault and *Maître* Jean, dazed and all but overcome. He managed to make his dry throat swallow as the Master turned to him.

"Now stand with awe and trembling, and cleanse your heart and mind of all worldly reflections," the Master said, "for what is about to be revealed to you is precious beyond any earthly comprehension: an object worthy of our most profound veneration—and one which your own efforts assisted in bringing safely out of Acre. Its presence in our keeping is a closely guarded secret—a secret which you must now swear upon your life to protect and preserve.

"Let all the angels and saints and all the company of heaven bear witness to the oath you are about to take. And may that oath be to you ever afterward a light unto your feet, a shield upon your arm, and a guard upon your soul."

With these solemn words, the Master turned to open the right-hand aumbry again. Reaching deep within it, he slid back a panel to reveal a secondary recess cunningly concealed behind the first, using his remaining key to unlock this secret safe.

Torquil felt a sudden prickling of excitement at the back of his neck as the older man reverently lifted out a flat, rectangular object wrapped in white silk, perhaps twice as long as a man's forearm and half as wide. The shallow box that was revealed as he unwrapped it was less than a hand's breadth in thickness, clad in gold and studded with gems along its edges—clearly, a reliquary of astounding worth, whatever it might contain.

What it did contain, Torquil could not have conceived in his most sweeping flight of imagination. All at once, the chapel seemed flooded with a lively brightness, as if the sun itself had come into their midst, though it was not light in any earthly sense. As *Maître* Jean bent to kiss the reliquary, then lifted it to prop oblong against his left shoulder, Torquil could see that the lid of the golden box had been fashioned with an openwork of latticed grille. And behind that grille, imprinted on a yellowed linen cloth, was the image of a man's face, battered and bloody, but serenely triumphant.

"Dear Lord . . ."

The words whispered from Torquil's lips even as he realized what he was saying. As Arnault bent reverently to brush it with his lips, then turned to Torquil, the younger man understood that he was being invited to do the same. The prospect set his knees quaking so that he could hardly hold himself upright, but he obeyed. The touch of his lips to one of the jewels studding the edge of the reliquary was part shock, part ecstasy, threatened to bring him to his knees, and only Arnault's strong grasp under his elbow kept him from collapsing under the weight of emotion.

"Place your hand upon this relic of Christ's most holy Shroud," *Maître* Jean said quietly, waiting until Torquil had brought himself to rest his fingertips to the outermost rim of the grille revealing that Face.

"By the authority of Saint Michael himself, you have been deemed fit to join the ranks of our company, the inner brotherhood of *le Cercle Sacré*," he said. "Here before God, I require you now to pledge your unswerving allegiance to that fellowship, binding yourself by all things holy in heaven and on earth to give faithful service unto our Lord, even unto death. Do you so swear?"

Torquil's voice was the merest thread of sound. "I so swear."

"And do you likewise swear to honor and obey those who are set in authority over you?"

"I so swear."

"And do you swear to serve only that Light which is Christ, now and forever?"

"I so swear."

At this declaration, the Master's solemn expression yielded unexpectedly to a smile that was almost luminous in its wakening joy.

"Torquil Lennox, I am privileged to accept this triple oath of yours in the name of the Father, and of the Son, and of the Holy Spirit. May God prosper that good work which you have begun in Him today, and keep you ever in His loving protection."

Reverently he turned to replace the relic of the holy Shroud on the altar.

"I greet you as a brother of *le Cercle* and salute you with a holy kiss, which binds us in fraternal love, one to another."

He leaned forward and touched his lips lightly to Torquil's in a chaste and holy kiss of peace. It was the last thing the young Scottish knight remembered before, overcome at last, he sank into a swoon.

Arnault caught him as he crumpled and eased him gently to the floor. *Maître* Jean reverently rewrapped the reliquary and returned it to its hiding place before crouching beside them. Arnault's face was drawn with weariness, but his expression was one of profound satisfaction.

"I told you he was ready," he murmured, smiling over Torquil's slack form in his arms.

"He still has much to learn," the Master said. "Now his training must begin in earnest—and to do that, I must take him from you for a while."

"Is it not your will, then, that he should return to Scotland?" Arnault asked.

Maître Jean shook his head. "In time, but not yet. For now, I wish him to remain here in France. Only here may he receive the instruction he requires, if he is truly to fulfill the destiny which has been laid on him."

Part II

Part II

Chapter Thirteen

DURING THE CHILDHOOD OF THE YOUNGER JOHN COMYN, his father had thrilled him with many a tale of the ancient times: tales of the lost pagan kingdom that once had flourished here, centered on their own lands of Badenoch. Those tales of valiant battles and terrible gods had enthralled him as a boy; but as he grew to manhood and the world's realities, he had sadly decided that those days were little likely to return.

Now, however, as father and son rode toward the ancient fortress of Burghead, the younger Comyn could see soldiers manning the weather-beaten ramparts, and banners aflutter in the cold north wind, defiantly declaring that here, at least, a vestige of that past still survived. Whether it could, in fact, be restored, as was his father's dream, remained to be seen, but if ever that was to happen, John Comyn had to admit that this seemed a fitting place.

He had come to Burghead only twice before. Though he had no recollection of his first visit, his father claimed to have brought him as an infant, to dedicate him to the service of the old gods. He did have memories of his second visit, not long after his thirteenth birthday—disjointed images of a fearsome, tumbled ruin, haunted by shadows and strange whispers—but in the decade since then, Burghead clearly had undergone a radical transformation.

Naturally defended on three sides by the cold North Sea, the landward approach had once been fortified by two broad ditches and a gated rampart wall. The ditches had been filled in long before young John first came, but the wall still towered twice as high as a man, its lichen-studded facade showing patches of new stonework. Seeing it now, through the eyes of a man, the younger Comyn found himself half believing that perhaps they *could* succeed.

And if they did, it was likely to be through the sheer force of will of the dour man riding at his side. Holder of half a dozen lordships in addition to Badenoch, and brother-in-law to the king, the man known as the Black Comyn was the single most powerful nobleman in all Scotland, though his actual exercise of that power had yet to match his aspirations. Today, however, he was bringing his son and heir for initiation into the greater mysteries of their shared heritage—and into that destiny, which, one day, might grant to the son the glories long yearned for by the sire.

A sudden gust of wind brought the tang of the sea beyond, frisking the horses, and Comyn laughed aloud as he and his son let the animals have their heads. Briefly, as they galloped through a shallow dip in the grassy track, the tumbled ruins of a former church obscured the view of the distant fort. The Black Comyn spat his contempt as they skirted past it—leveled by distant ancestors for the impudence of having been built so close to a place where the old gods still held sway.

They continued on to the crest of the next hill, where both Comyns reined in at the elder's signal to survey this new aspect, which spread itself before them in the broadening morning light. The Black Comyn's eyes lit with pride and pleasure as he swept a gauntleted hand before him.

"Behold, the last stronghold of the Pictish kingdom," he declared, exercising the prerogative of a patriarch to reinforce old lessons for a neophyte's instruction. "When Norse raiders attacked the coastal settlements of Dalriada, in the west, the Scots who lived there fled eastward into Pictland, seeking safe haven among the domains of our forebears.

"But the Scots brought with them the accursed religion of Columba and the White Christ, and these new beliefs weakened the warrior resolve of our ancestors. Those who accepted the new faith betrayed the ancient bargains they had made with the old gods, by which they had prospered in these lands. These treacherous Scots undermined the Pictish throne by intermarriage and bribery—and when they had accomplished all that they could by guile, they crushed out the last embers of resistance by force of arms."

As he spoke, his gaze roved the ramparts of the distant citadel. His voice held a note of brisk immediacy, as if he were recalling events he had witnessed in person, rather than repeating accounts passed down through generations.

"It was here at Burghead that a loyal remnant of Pictish nobles made their stand," he went on, though the younger Comyn well knew the story. "But Malcolm Canmore's army of Scots overran these ramparts, and thought to slay the last of the royal bloodline, intending that no Pictish king should ever again challenge the Canmore claim to Alba's throne. A few, however, escaped that slaughter, and have since kept to the old ways, awaiting the day when they would be strong enough to return in force."

He exhaled on an anticipatory sigh and leaned his elbows on the high pommel of his saddle. "That day now is nearly upon us, my son. In our veins flows the blood of those ancient kings, and in their veins flowed the blood of the gods who gave birth to our race. That blood is the pact which binds the two together, gods and men. With the last of the

Canmores now nearly seven years in her grave, we have it in ourselves to invoke the pact and bring freedom back to our land."

John heard his father out in silence. He had been bred on such tales extolling their family's pagan past. Always before, however, he had assumed such sentiments to be mere nostalgic yearning for the glories of bygone days. But now it seemed that the elder Comyn was speaking of the present—and the future—wholly in earnest.

"I shall do my best to be worthy," he said dutifully. "Not of our king, John Balliol, but of you, Father."

Comyn gave his heir a pleased and approving look and rubbed at his grizzled beard. In a few days' time, the younger John Comyn would be riding south to join the Scottish earls mustering an army near Carlisle—but only incidentally in support of the craven John Balliol.

Since his election four years before, Balliol had been bullied and humiliated repeatedly by Edward of England, undermined at every turn, treated as vassal, not as fellow king, his resistance beaten down as much by Edward's ferocious words as by any actual force. When, the previous year, Philip of France had attacked Edward's possessions in Aquitaine, the English king had prepared for war, commanding Balliol and the Scots to provide troops for his army.

Once again failing to provide the bold leadership the Scots had hoped for, Balliol had made a mealymouthed acquiescence; but the Scots nobility had delayed following Edward's instructions with every excuse they could think of, until finally, goaded beyond endurance at last, they had formed a Council of Twelve to take charge of the nation as Balliol had failed to do.

The Black Comyn was prominent among those Twelve, and had been instrumental in forming an alliance with France. As part of this agreement with Philip, the Scots were now preparing to march against Edward themselves—and in doing so, hoped to pay him back for the insults and injustices the nation had suffered at his hands.

"Balliol," Comyn muttered, almost making of the name an epithet. "Better him, I suppose, than any of the Bruces. And when I married your mother, to bind him to me, I knew he was malleable.

"That is why I lent him our family's support—so that he could be bent to our cause! Certainly Edward had to be appeased in the beginning, until he lent his weight to a final judgment of all claims; we dared not risk civil war, by any after-dispute about the succession. Little did I dream that Balliol would prove so much a man of straw that he would continue to bend the knee to Edward, like a dog running to his master's whistle!"

He spat aside, as though the recollection of those humiliations had left a vile taste in his mouth.

"But it will profit him little," he went on. "Now that Edward is beset with war in France, we have bypassed this supposed king of ours, and will make our own war on England. Let the weak Balliol fall where he will, if he cannot play both king and warrior.

"Then shall we vanquish our foes, and pave the way for the restoration of that ancient kingdom that once was ours! Our long-neglected gods will rise from their resting places in the lochs and caverns to sit once more upon their mountain thrones, dispensing both justice and vengeance to mortal men. And we, my son, will be at their side—kings of this land by their favor!"

"First we must claim the victory," John reminded him pragmatically, "and that we surely must do by force of arms."

"Such a victory is easily won, and easily thrown away by those who give no credit to their gods," Comyn retorted. His eyes once again roved the ramparts of distant Burghead, as if seeking glimpses of earlier times.

"In ages past, we denied the gods of Rome and, in doing so, drove their armies from our borders, with the Dark

Mother before us and her arch-priest Briochan at our side. So fierce were we then in the ways of war that the Romans built a mighty wall to keep us back, and cowered behind its ramparts like frightened mice. This was the northern bastion of the ancient gods, their stronghold against all invasion.

"But now they are long abandoned, and in consequence do we face the domination of a foreign king. If compelled to bow before his throne, we likewise will be forced to share his faith, unless we cast aside all such weakness and clasp once more the ways of old, that hurled back the legions of Rome's emperors!"

"Those were brave times, Father," John agreed, shortening his rein to keep his horse from straying toward a tempting tuft of grass.

"You do not yet truly believe," the elder Comyn noted evenly. "But that is because you have not seen. Today that will change, for you shall receive the blessing of the Dark Mother, to guard you in the battles to come."

So saying, he spurred his horse forward and started down the hillside toward the fort, not looking back. John followed with somewhat less alacrity, sourly wondering what forgotten rituals his father had prepared to impress him this time. Having but little patience for any faith, and eager to join his counterparts mustering in the south, he could conjure little enthusiasm for this particular passion of his father's. But there was no denying the Black Comyn; and his eagerness to include his heir in his intrigues was as irresistible as the tide beating upon the rocky promontory beyond.

When they reached the newly reconstructed gateway, the guards saluted their arrival and opened the port to admit them. The sky above was overcast, and the steely light bathing the far ramparts gave John Comyn the fleeting sense that he was passing out of the world he knew and into a realm where time had been arrested, even reversed, and ancient days had risen anew in defiance of the centuries.

The gates closed behind them as they dismounted within

the first yard, handing their horses into the care of a man in a blacksmith's leather apron. Elsewhere in the yard, he could see half a dozen other workmen at various tasks. The air was redolent of salt brine, peat smoke, and the pungent aroma of horse droppings, and seemed to conjure up images of bare-legged warriors making battle preparations.

"Come," his father said.

Now grave of mien and even a little tense-looking, the Black Comyn led his son through a secondary gateway, passing into the fort's inner ward. Before them lay the citadel, dark against the sky, atop a man-made mound of earth. Nearer at hand, guarding the approach to the fortress, two immense standing stones overshadowed everything else in the yard.

"These I had brought here from far to the north, where they had lain neglected for five long centuries," Comyn declared, with no little satisfaction.

The younger Comyn halted to stare up at the monoliths in some wonder. The massive slabs of sparkling gray rock reared more than twice as high as a man, frowning across the western wall like grim sentinels. On one had been carved the powerful, stylized image of a charging bull, prominent genitals declaring its virility. The other stone bore the more primitive likeness of a female form rising out of the sea, hair like writhing serpents, broad of hip and heavy of thigh, with what looked like a skull suspended between her swollen breasts.

Painted around both figures, in vivid, garish colors, were abstract symbols indicative of elemental invocations—complex patterns of spirals and rods, zigzags and circles, very like those adorning other Pictish stones to be seen dotted all over this part of the country.

"Siohnie and Gruagagh, the gods of our land," Comyn said, indicating the Bull and the Woman respectively. "In scarcely a handful of places all across Scotland are their names even remembered—and we have been paying the price for that negligence, both in Canmore dominance and now, under the yoke of England's slavery."

While his father was speaking, John became aware of a sibilant murmur in his right ear—like someone standing at his shoulder, whispering seductively. He glanced around sharply, but there was no one to be seen. Instead, he found his eyes drawn to a stone stairway descending into a black slot in the earth. He realized at the same time that he and his father were alone in this second courtyard.

"Ah, you have heard Gruagagh calling you," Comyn said with some satisfaction, noting his son's reaction. "That is good, but it is not yet time." He set a hand on John's shoulder. "Let us proceed."

Somewhat taken aback, for he told himself he did not believe in any of this, John allowed himself to be guided on past the monoliths toward the entrance to the citadel, hurriedly reexamining his previous assumptions. He knew, from his father's stories, that this was where the last of the Pictish rebels had been burned to death by King Malcolm Canmore's men, calling upon their gods for vengeance as they perished in the flames. The elder Comyn more than once had made vague allusion to the extinction of the Canmore line as a long-awaited act of retribution: blood for blood, almost as if he had played some part in it.

Wondering whether it could possibly be so—and he found a part of him hoping that it *was*—John suppressed a shudder for the fates of his ill-starred forebears. Very briefly, as he and his father continued on toward the citadel, a final intimation of the latter refused to be put by. His mouth went dry as he became aware of a ghostly crackling in his ears, like the distant roar of a bonfire. A spectral gust of heat swept past him, bringing with it the stench of burning flesh—imagination, surely . . .

Shaking his head to banish such echoes of the past, he turned his gaze to the present. Like the outer ramparts, the walls of the ruined citadel had been partially repaired. Embedded here and there among the plain building stones and rubble were other blocks inscribed with figures of charging bulls—fragments of structures long ago tumbled to ruin in the wake of the White Christ's triumph over the gods of the Picts.

Well did John remember the night his father had been instructed to restore it thus. Only just coming into his beard, at last permitted to sit with the men at table, he had listened enthralled at his father's side as the man called Torgon, purporting to be a priest of the old gods, had declaimed the past glories of his ancient deities with an eloquence and fervor rivaling that of the White Christ's devotees, calling upon the true sons of Alba to rebuild the ancient holy places for her native gods. In specific, Torgon had instructed that stone fragments bearing images or sigils of bulls should be inserted into the restored walls. So sited, the array of bulls would present simultaneously a defensive barrier and an invocation of indomitable strength.

And it clearly had been done, according to Torgon's instructions!

The younger Comyn roughly recalled himself to the present as his father's voice intruded on his amazement, speaking to one of his lieutenants, a powerful bearded battle veteran called Seward, who had appeared within the open doorway to the citadel. The man's bare arms were painted with runic symbols traced out in blue, and upon his forehead he bore the blue-traced head of a bull, the long horns extending to the temples.

"Has all been prepared in accordance with my instructions?" Comyn demanded.

Seward inclined his head. "It has, my lord."

"Away with you, then, and see that the men remain withdrawn from this ward," Comyn ordered. "I will brook no intrusion or interruption of the proceedings."

With a parting salute, Seward loped off down the hill to carry out his orders, leaving the Comyns to enter the citadel unattended. The enclosure was roofless, and the dull day-light did little to dispel the deep shadows oozing along its walls. Within the circuit of those walls had been erected a broad altar stone, its low sides carved with runic inscriptions that John knew were intended to invoke the intercession of the old gods, who demanded blood in tribute and to whom captured enemies were sacrificed by drowning.

Both had been offered on the occasion of the younger Comyn's last visit to Burghead, though he had seen only the sacrifice of a bull like the one tethered just behind the altar, whose blood had been smeared on his face and hands in mark of his coming of age; and he had understood what would be the fate of the trembling youth, no older than himself, whom the high priest Torgon led down into that dark stairwell, out beside the monoliths, nude save for a crown of mistletoe and rowan, and with wrists bound behind his back. Only Torgon had come out. On the ride back home, his father had assured him that the boy was from without the land of Alba, taken in a raid across the borders far to the south, and therefore of little consequence.

He therefore was not surprised to see another bull today—and vaguely wondered whether another captive would be drowned. But behind the bull were ranged only a pair of soldiers to tend it, the bull sigil upon their foreheads and garlands of rowan and mistletoe wound around their left arms to show that they had been inducted into the mysteries; and to either side of them, the white-robed forms of Torgon and a younger assistant, both of them bearded and tonsured ear to ear in the Celtic manner, the remaining hair plaited in greasy braids to either side of their heads, both marked with the bull sigil and crowned with leafy garlands. Torgon had around his neck a golden torc denoting his rank, and iron bracelets upon his forearms, and in one hand a staff of gnarled black wood. The younger priest was holding the tether of the bull, letting it nose among a few sparse tufts of grass springing from between uneven flagstones surrounding the altar.

Comyn raised his hand in salute, and the priests bowed their heads in acknowledgment. At a sign from Torgon, his priestly companion helped the soldiers heave the bullock up onto the altar slab—so placid, John suspected it had been drugged—while Torgon himself took up a bowl with a leafy aspergillum and began circling the altar widdershins, sprinkling it and the bull with aspersions of water infused with mistletoe berries.

While this was taking place, the Black Comyn disarmed himself and stripped off to the waist, gesturing for his son to do the same, letting the younger priest paint the bull sigil upon his brow. As the younger Comyn also submitted to the ritual marking and joined his father in kneeling before the altar, he felt the gooseflesh rising on his arms, not alone because of the chill and damp, this near the sea.

Lifting his hands, the elder Comyn now began an invocation in the Pictish tongue—words he had recently taught his son in preparation for this day, and in which the younger Comyn haltingly joined. When the prayer ended, Torgon thrust his staff over the bullock in a gesture of bidding and began a long, keening chant of his own, which sent chills up young Comyn's spine.

The younger priest and the soldiers had bowed their heads, but still held the bullock's legs from kicking. John Comyn could comprehend only a little of what was said, but he clearly heard Torgon calling upon the names of Siohnie and Gruagagh, then of Briochan, their priest: first vanquished by the Christian Saint Columba, then banished from the court of his lord, the Pictish King Brude, who had been converted to the new faith. Briochan had died in exile somewhere in the Scottish borders, his resting place unknown. But his name continued to be a talisman and touchstone for those struggling to preserve the old faith; and it was

Briochan's service to his gods that Torgon invoked upon himself in closing, before laying aside his staff.

Without further ado, the shaman-priest then detached a bronze hand sickle from the cincture at his waist and set its blade to the bullock's throat, abruptly jerking it toward him in a single swift stroke. Young Comyn flinched as blood gushed from the wound like ale bursting from a spiked barrel, spurting over the front of Torgon's robe and down the side of the altar as the victim thrashed in its death throes and gave a gurgling groan.

Impassive, Torgon put aside his bloodied sickle and held a stone bowl beneath the stream, filling it almost to the brim. Hands still reeking with the blood, he then carried the bowl before the Comyns, sire and son, signing each with bloody sigils upon cheeks and palms before placing the bowl in the elder Comyn's hands.

Comyn inclined his head in a stiff gesture and let Torgon help him to his feet, allowing the younger priest to lay a crimson cloak around his shoulders—a mark of the authority of the Pictish kings, which Comyn believed was his by right. Thus arrayed, holding the bloody bowl like a precious treasure, he turned to his son, who only now dared to rise.

"Follow me now, boy," he commanded, "for I bring you now into the presence of our gods."

Preceded by Torgon, he moved toward the doorway back to the yard where stood the monoliths—and that dark slit in the earth—not looking to see whether his son followed. The cool dispassion of his tone sparked a queasy pang of apprehension in the younger Comyn's belly, but he followed resolutely, knowing that he must see this through before riding south to seek more tangible glory on the battlefield. His uneasiness increased as they reached the stairwell and Torgon stepped aside, clearly not intending to accompany them.

Without hesitation the Black Comyn began his descent, each probing step downward a measure only of his care that he not spill even a drop of the bowl's precious contents. The younger Comyn cast a last look over his shoulder before reluctantly following his sire into increasing darkness.

The stair took a dogleg turn—and then another—cutting them off from what little light penetrated the narrow shaft. The younger Comyn had caught a fold of his father's red cloak when they first started down, mainly so he would not tread upon it, but now it became his lifeline in the darkness. As they continued downward, a dank chill seemed to curl itself around his ankles and slither ever higher up his body, wrapping him in dread, threatening to turn his bowels to water. Though reason told him his father would not bring him into peril of his life, he could not shake the impression that this was surely an entrance to the underworld, where mortal men were foolish to tread.

Another turn of the stair gave access to a level passageway where, beyond his father's broad shoulders, he could see a faint glow ahead. The passage gave way at last to a cavernous room—whether natural or dug out of the solid rock, he could not tell—lit by a single smoking torch fixed to a bracket on the opposite wall, and surely kindled by one of the priests, for no one else willingly would have ventured down here.

Not hesitating, the elder Comyn bore his bowl of blood into the chamber like a precious talisman, his son still close behind him, straining to see in the dimness. Directly before them, like a gaping wound in the center of the floor, lay a pool or well of still, black water, as wide as the span of a man's two arms and contained by a raised lip of stone.

Opaque and impenetrable, the water reflected not the faintest glimmer of torchlight—as if the meager glow were being swallowed and extinguished by that smothering darkness. Craning for a better look, John tried to dispel the illusion, but the pool appeared bottomless; and softly stirring upward from its depths, more felt in the bowels than heard, came a remote booming sound, like the clashing waves of a sunless, subterranean sea.

"Hold your tongue, and neither do nor say anything unless it is asked of you," the elder Comyn said softly, casting an admonitory glance at his son and then moving hard against the stone curbing, signing for John to do the same.

John nervously obeyed. His father's jaw was grimly set, his eyes reflecting red from the flickering torchlight. The torch itself guttered and wavered as though starving for air. Should it go out, John feared he might go mad in the smothering darkness.

Lifting the bowl of blood above the pool in a gesture of oblation, the Black Comyn began to chant softly in the Pictish tongue: the ancient words of another pagan prayer that rustled sibilantly amid the shadows, sending back echoing whispers that rose like an eerie chorus. As the last of the whispers faded away, Comyn reverted to the common tongue.

"Therefore, Mother Gruagagh, accept this blood of your lover Siohnie, to mark the communion of heaving sea and fertile earth! Accept his seed in your watery womb, and open for us the gateway of ages past and ages yet to come!"

So saying, he tipped the bowl. With seeming sluggishness, the blood snaked downward into that midnight blackness, thick and viscous, tendrils of paler darkness blossoming outward to stir the inky water into uneasy motion, spinning the tendrils in a pattern of shifting whorls and spirals suggestive of the monoliths above ground.

Tiny bubbles began to break the surface in the center of the pool—small ones at first, but quickly growing larger. The water churned and roiled like a witch's cauldron. The temperature dropped, and John instinctively hugged bare arms across bare chest in shivering embrace until his father's hiss called him sharply to order.

Eyes fixed apprehensively on the bubbling water, John began to fancy he could see a baleful point of cold green light awakening in the depths of the pool, now rising swiftly toward the surface, growing brighter and more virulent as it came. The patterns on the water dispersed as the emerald glare spread throughout the chamber, reducing the torchlight to a puny flicker. The bumps and cracks that seamed the surrounding walls took on the aspect of leering faces, like the visages of the dead. A gust of icy air swirled around the chamber with force enough nearly to kill the torch—earthy and wormy, like freshly turned soil.

With it came the noxious stench of rotted flesh and stale blood, like the stink of an open grave. John Comyn's first whiff of it caused his stomach to heave, but his second breath fired his blood with a strange intoxication, like a draft of strong whisky.

At the same time, the roiling waters began to calm, permitting glimpses of some vague but repulsive form beginning to take shape beneath the murky surface, limned in green flame. John flinched from it in instinct, a gasp filling his lungs a third time, but his father at once seized his arms and checked any would-be retreat.

"Stand your ground!" the elder Comyn warned through gritted teeth. His grip on his son's biceps was strong enough to bruise as he began to chant:

"Death and decay lend life to the earth.
The serpent's tooth and the beast's sharp horn
Give worship to thee, O Gruagagh,
With blood and the fruits of the sea."

In answer, the churning waters were burst asunder by the upper half of a giant, loathsome figure whose head nearly touched the chamber's curved ceiling, its emergence sloshing an icy wave over the stone curbing.

Female it was, with pendulous breasts and wild hair streaming over raw-boned shoulders to float like rotting tangles of seaweed and kelp on the water surrounding it. The cold eyes smoldered with a muted green phosphorescence; the sharp-planed face was wrinkled and ravaged, the mouth contorted by a gleaming pair of boar's tusks. And yet, the being had a transparency about it, as if it occupied no physical space in fact. The voice that spoke was like a winter's gale ripping the bare branches from dead trees.

"Aye, doom and decay shall come to thee, mortal, unless thou worship me and feed my blood-thirst again!"

"Enough blood for now, Mother," the Black Comyn answered, in a voice as steady as a rock. "When all the kingdom falls once more at your feet, then shall you drink your fill."

Astonished at his sire's fearlessness in the face of such an apparition, young Comyn drew himself up, determined not to be put to shame by the older man's example. He could sense his father's approval as his arm was released—but in the next instant, the creature turned her dreadful gaze upon him, and her fearsome lips curled in contempt.

"And what is this whelp thou hast brought before me?" she rasped. *"Fresh sacrifice, to be drowned in my sacred waters?"*

"This is my son, John," Comyn told her. "He is setting out for war, to win back what was ours of old, and seeks your blessing to protect him in battle."

"Will he worship me as I desire, and bend himself to be my tool?"

"He knows his duty," the Black Comyn replied.

The figure's grotesque features contorted in a hideous semblance of a smile.

"Then let him drink from the water of my plenty, and savor the sweetness of his goddessss," she hissed.

Her breath was like an arctic blast, fetid and revolting, but John stood his ground. Though his heart was pounding like a hammer on an anvil, he met the lambent eyes without flinching.

Comyn handed his son the empty bowl and motioned him to fill it from the pool. Hardly daring to think, for fear of losing his nerve—still half convinced that the figure must be some illusion—John took the bowl and hunkered down at the lip of the pool. A strange sense of fatalism took hold of him as he dipped the bowl and brought it out again brimming, tainted with the skim of blood still clotted on the rough stone. Cupping the bowl in both his hands, he raised it to his lips and boldly drank.

Icy liquid gushed into his throat, both sour and cloying, but he made himself gag it down, not daring to do otherwise, increasingly convinced that any failure to comply might cost him his life. Only when the bowl was empty did he dare to lower it, setting it gingerly on the pool's stone curbing.

Almost at once, a clap of force seemed to strike him hard between the eyes, reverberating in his head like the tolling of a massive bell. Aghast, he sat back hard on the stone floor, senses reeling, arms only barely catching him from bowling over backward. For an interminable instant, the chamber seemed to expand and contract with the heaving of his own lungs, like being a part of the breathing of some fearful leviathan.

Then the dizziness abruptly subsided, and he found that his earlier fear and revulsion had vanished, leaving him faintly giddy but steady enough to take the hand his father offered and scramble self-consciously to his feet, strangely purged of all human weakness.

"Has he not drunk bravely from your well, O goddess?" the Black Comyn declared proudly. "Has he not proved himself worthy of a warrior's blessing?"

In answer, their loathsome familiar moved suddenly closer, sloshing another wave over the edge of the pool, the taloned fingers of one grasping hand flexing as they stretched toward young John's widely staring eyes. Only minutes earlier, he would have drawn back in alarm, thrown up his arms to shield himself, but now he felt no inclination to do so—not through any confidence that she would not harm him, but rather an acceptance of her right to do so if she wished.

The fingers hovered a few inches before his awestruck gaze, describing a complex pattern with their movement—compelling, seductive—then tapped once between his eyes with a taloned forefinger before she pulled back into the pool.

"*It is done,*" came the rasping declaration. "*Any blood he spills belongs to me, and his trophies of war must be hung in my honor.*"

"And will you grant us victory," the Black Comyn asked, "that we may once more raise your temples under the sun, and chant your name in the streets of cities?"

"*Will I grant victory?*" she repeated, the lambent eyes flashing. "*That lies yet in the days to come, and will have its cost. Ye shall seek my servant Briochan to be thy guide in the ways of my power, so that my worship may spread and my armies may cover the land, laying waste to the unbelievers and those who have defiled what was once my kingdom. I must call him forth! Briochannnnn . . .*"

Her cry shook her hair like the branches of a great tree beaten by the wind, and her face convulsed in a rictus of longing. The atmosphere grew thicker, and soon both Comyns found it difficult to breathe.

A sensation of great weight pounded at the air, like the thunder of a thousand hooves trampling over the land with untamable force. The strength of the bull and the ferocity of the boar, which once had shaken the mountain heights and echoed through the depths of the sea, became focused in the chamber as the goddess stretched her perception across the land and past the gulf of death itself.

Then suddenly the close space was riven by a clamorous shriek.

"*Briochan?*" she cried. "*Briochan, beloved, come to my call, and lead my servants along the paths they must walk!*"

Then she howled like a hound caught in a trap. The sound was rending. Young Comyn gasped aloud and clapped his hands to his ears. His father bit his lips and clenched his fists tight to withstand the torment of the goddess's desolation.

"*He lies no longer in the earth!*" she keened. "*His bones, his lore, and all his potency—all locked in thrall by servants of the lost temple, the white-robed ones—they who bear the hated symbol of the murdered god!"*

She tore at her hair, her glowing eyes lending a sickly pallor to the torchlight as her lament took on the cadence of a dirge.

"They seek, as well, that thing by which reigned the heirs of Ceann Mor—thrice-cursed palladium from far across the sea. And soon comes the reign of the Uncrowned King—he who can give renewal to that which our ancient foe brought to this land—that by which may founder all thy desires."

The heaviness of the air was almost suffocating, and the words made little sense to the young John Comyn. The beating pressure of her fury came close to forcing him to his knees, and only his pride kept him upright.

"Faithless mortals—it must not be!" she cried. *"Briochan must be freed—and before the seven years have passed, the Uncrowned King must be untimely slain. Do this or seek no more my favor!"*

On this demand, she quickly withdrew into the depths of the pool, hair writhing around her like a nest of serpents before she vanished from sight. The light from the pool faded to nothing, and young John found himself suddenly drained of strength. He teetered before the lip of the pool, and only his father's firm grasp kept him from falling in.

"Do not falter *now*," the Black Comyn said dazedly. "You did well, my son. You bore yourself like a man. But there is more than courage needed yet, if we are to win through."

"But—what did it *mean*?" young Comyn whispered.

The elder Comyn's bearded face was pale. For the first time he appeared shaken. When he spoke again, it was more to himself than to his son.

"The die is already cast," he murmured. "The Scottish host is gathering in the south, ready to spring on the backs of the English as the wolf slaughters sheep. We cannot go back. We must ponder the meaning of what we have heard, but with or without the favor of our patroness, we must go on, trusting in our own valor to carry the day. And always, in the heat of battle, we must seek out those whom our goddess has named as her offenders. When they are found and slain, then we shall stand doubly in her favor."

John's head was still swimming, so that he found it difficult to follow his father's words.

"I don't understand," he said weakly. "What was she talking about? What was all that about Briochan? He's been dead for centuries!"

His father drew a deep breath and gustily exhaled. "Death is a barrier only to the weak," he declared. "Briochan's spirit has always lived on to guide us in the faith that he gave us, but his physical legacy—the means by which he may return to us in fact—have been seized by those not of our blood. And the goddess has told us by whom."

"By the servants of the lost temple?" John said doubtfully. "Does she mean the Knights Templar?"

"Aye, the white-robed ones, who bear the symbol of the murdered god, the White Christ," the elder Comyn said fiercely. "At least a few of them have power that I fear. But for Templar intervention, the innocence of the last Canmore heir would have been offered to appease the ancient gods—not merely severed from earthly life. And it was because of Templar presence when John Balliol was crowned that I made a point to spurn their Christian sacrament. Little did they know how that act leached at the potency of what they tried to guard."

"Surely the fact that they serve the English is reason enough to scorn them," John said, again uncertain what his father meant.

"They serve the Temple—and that is far greater cause to beware of them," the Black Comyn returned. "But now we know the face of our true enemies—may it be long before they realize that we are *theirs*—and if we are to prevail, then the Templars first must die!"

Chapter Fourteen

IN THE SPRING OF 1296, IN RESPONSE TO AN INCREASING number of reports of Scottish defiance, and English troops massing for a punitive march northward, Frère Arnault de Saint Clair at last found himself aboard a ship bound for Scotland, for the first time in three years—for the Temple's time was reckoned in decades and even centuries, not in mere months and years.

Up in the bow of the sleek Templar galley, hunkered down behind the forward railings, he could see Torquil Lennox squinting happily against the salt-spray, eager to be going home, a sharp North Sea wind whipping at his white mantle and coppery hair. It bellied the ship's square sail, painted with the eight-pointed red cross of the Order, driving them westward at a spanking pace. Behind them lay the lowlands of Holland, recently disaffected from a long-standing alliance with England. Ahead, obscured by a chilly haze of spring mist, lay the coast of Scotland—a nation equally determined to shake loose from England's leading-strings.

Arnault made his way forward, nodding amiably to members of the crew, and came to join Torquil in the bow, one gloved hand holding his white mantle closed over quilted gambeson and mail hauberk.

"Trying to see into the future?" he asked.

Torquil pulled a face. "If only I could. Unfortunately, my hindsight is far clearer than my foresight."

"You are not alone in *that*," Arnault replied, with a grimace of his own as he sank down beside the younger man in companionable silence.

In his own case, it was tantamount to a confession of helplessness. Since their departure from Scotland, in the spring following John Balliol's enthronement, he had found himself increasingly distracted from the use of his gifts of discernment by the onslaught of growing turmoil threatening to overtake the whole of Christendom.

Even at Balantrodoch, they had seen the warning signs. Now the coming storm was imminent, and he could only stake his faith blindly to the revelation vouchsafed to him at Cyprus: that the underlying order of the world at large was somehow inextricably intertwined with the political order of Scotland.

It was not a bright picture at present. Edward of England and Philip IV of France had gone to war over possession of the Duchy of Gascony. The merchant states of Italy and the provinces of Germany were likewise mired in conflicts over influence and sovereignty. The papacy had been flung into turmoil by the abdication of Celestine V—a condition not improved by the election of Boniface VIII. Only the nations on the outer fringes of Europe could claim any degree of tranquillity, and now even they were being pulled into the net of conflicting alliances that threatened to ensnare and strangle the Frankish West.

This dark tapestry of recent events, however, was threaded here and there with strands of light: threads that shone out all the brighter in contrast to their setting. One such triumph, in Arnault's view, was Torquil Lennox's continuing achievements as a working member of *le Cercle*. The three years since his initiation had seen him stretched and tempered by the finest instruction that the Temple had to offer, both in the conventional work of the Order and on levels not dreamed of by the Order at large.

The physical signs of Torquil's maturity were readily apparent to anyone who had known him before. Outwardly, he was more powerful and less restless, the result of having learned to harness his energies to support the work of his inner faculties. More subtle were the signs by which his spirit evinced its acquired strength. But to Arnault they were clearly visible, the proofs that vindicated his initial belief in Torquil's promise.

Realizing that promise had been no simple matter. Following his initiation, while Arnault carried out diplomatic missions of increasing complexity on behalf of the Order and *le Cercle,* the young Scottish knight had been sent away to a remote preceptory in the mountains of Tuscany, where he had spent six months in prayer and meditation to fortify himself for further instruction.

Thereafter he had gone to Rome in the entourage of the Grand Master, amid the turmoil of Celestine's abdication and the long delay in electing a new pope, there remaining for another six months to broaden his knowledge of arts and languages from the master scholars gathered about the papal court. Upon his subsequent return to Paris, interspersed with occasional forays into the world of financial services and merchant banking—for which Gaspar des Macquelines declared him also to possess a marked aptitude—he had received careful, graded instruction in the esoteric disciplines practiced by those elite few who guarded the Temple's greatest treasures, with Arnault as but one of his teachers.

But having nurtured his pupil's strengths, Arnault still was unable to predict what, in the greater work of the Order, Torquil's ultimate purpose and test was likely to be. All he and the others of *le Cercle* knew for certain was that Torquil's role seemed intrinsically bound up with the mysterious direction handed down in Cyprus: that the Fifth Temple, whether physical or spiritual or both, was to be established in Scotland as a permanent reliquarium for the secret treasures of ages past, a bridge between the Seen and the Unseen.

Unfortunately, the prevailing turmoil of Scottish affairs since John Balliol's inauguration had precluded *le Cercle* laying any groundwork, physical or otherwise, for that intention. This latest insurrection by the Scottish barons seemed headed for doom, and Balliol with it. With conditions in Scotland deteriorating by the day, Arnault and Torquil had been authorized by their superiors of *le Cercle* to take whatever action was necessary to resolve the situation in favor of *le Cercle*'s greater mission—and had routine dispatches to deliver, as cover for their presence back in Scotland. But much would depend upon what they could accomplish in the days and months to come, with Edward apparently once more poised to crush the Scots.

A warning outcry from the watch up in the fighting castle drew the attention of both Templars astern and to starboard, where a broad-beamed carrack was bearing down on them from the north. As the crew hurriedly manned their stations, and the vessel drew gradually close enough for her colors to be read, Torquil eased slowly to his feet and hissed, *"Sassenach,"* almost unheard, though few other ships would have been bold enough to venture into these waters.

Closer scrutiny of the lines of her hull and the set of her rigging only reinforced his assertion that the ship was English; and her machicolated castle decks fore and aft proclaimed her to be a warship, without doubt. This declaration of English belligerence was confirmed a moment later when a shout from the other vessel ordered them to heave to, on the authority of Edward, King of England.

While unlikely to be more than a mere formality—for a

vessel belonging to the Order of the Temple could justifiably claim neutrality, as could Templars traveling aboard her— the challenge came as no surprise to anyone on board. Following the outbreak of hostilities between England and France, Edward Plantagenet had taken steps to impose controls on all maritime activity in the Channel and the North Sea. The number of English naval vessels patrolling Scottish waters, especially along the eastern coast, had further multiplied when it became known that Scotland's ruling Council of Twelve had entered into a formal alliance with France.

Most fortuitously, English Templars were known to be advising King Edward in the present hostilities, and Arnault had been provided with documents that gave him and Torquil legitimate cause to be entering these Scottish waters. As the galley's crew turned into the wind and gathered in the sail, the pair made their way onto the main deck, silently watching the English ship come alongside, her war ramparts bristling with archers.

Grappling lines secured the two vessels, flank to flank, and English sailors laid a bridge of planks across the gap to accommodate a boarding party of the captain and two men-at-arms. Already, the sight of two men in the full habit of Knights Templar had caused a stir on the En-glish vessel. Under the eyes of the English archers, Arnault came purposefully forward, saying nothing, Torquil at his side and the galley's captain following respectfully behind them. The captain of the English vessel was waiting a little nervously just beside the side railing, and accorded the knights a guardedly civil greeting before giving his attention to the parchment that Arnault held out to him.

"I see you are bound for Berwick," he noted grimly, as he began to scan the document.

"We are," Arnault agreed.

"Indeed. And your purpose?"

"Diplomatic," Arnault replied. "We come on orders of the Visitor of France, as you can see."

"We already have Templars with King Edward's army," the man replied. "No diplomacy is required. The king means to crush the Scottish rebellion."

"The Temple would prefer to see a lasting peace," Arnault said. "No one wants Scotland to be drawn into the net of hostilities which already threatens the people of France. My brother and I are charged to arrange a truce between the English and the Scots, as a prelude to negotiating a more lasting peace."

The English captain's jaw tightened as he refolded the document and handed it back.

"If you were hoping to stop a war before it starts," he said, "you're already too late. Three days ago, a Scottish army crossed over the border and attacked Carlisle."

"Indeed," Arnault said, with a glance at Torquil, whose eyes had narrowed. "Have you any news of the engagement?"

"Little of substance," came the response. "At last report, the folk of Carlisle were holding their own. King Edward, for his part, has sent his forces to besiege Berwick."

This new intelligence produced a queasy pang in the pit of Arnault's stomach as he recalled his vision of three years previous. Though Berwick Castle was well fortified, the town itself was defended by nothing more substantial than a ditch and a timber palisade—hardly enough to turn back a determined English assault. Recalling the Lindsay family, he could only hope that his writ of protection would serve its purpose, if events came to pass as he had envisioned them.

"But, these stubborn Scots will not stand long against King Edward's might," he heard the English captain saying. "Meanwhile, you are free to go. You may count yourselves fortunate that the Master of your Order in England has earned the king's favor by the service he has rendered in this present venture."

Replacing the travel document back in his scrip, Arnault pricked up his ears at this oblique mention of Brian de Jay, who had recently succeeded Guy de Foresta as Master of England, and also of Scotland and Ireland.

"Am I to understand that the Master of England is here in Scotland?" he asked.

"Where else?" the man countered. "He is the king's principal advisor on Scottish military affairs, having previously served your Order in Scotland. He came north with the army, as a member of the king's retinue."

The news had not been entirely unexpected, but Arnault could sense Torquil restraining bitter comment as the English captain and his men made their way back to their own ship. But once the English crew had cast off the grappling lines, and the galley's captain had gone to relay orders to proceed to Berwick, the younger man could contain himself no longer.

"What does that strutting bag of foul wind think he's doing?" he muttered in an explosive undertone. "Jay has no business favoring Edward's cause on the strength of his own authority."

"Ah, but he follows the example of his predecessor in that," Arnault replied. "Guy de Foresta was also friendly with Edward of England. In any case, you yourself have observed that Jay cares far more for prestige than he does for justice. Whatever the conflict, he will always curry favor with the side he perceives as most likely to advance his own importance."

Arnault had conveyed his suspicions regarding Jay and his motives several years before, but neither Gaspar nor *Maître* Jean nor any other member of *le Cercle* had been able to prevent Jay from being elevated to his present eminence. Arnault was driven to wonder if the same chaotic influences that had proved so disruptive to his own talents were likewise starting to undermine the function of *le Cercle* as a whole. The thought that there might be dark forces at work within the Templar Order itself was not one that made for comfortable reflection.

In the meantime, however, the situation in Berwick demanded immediate consideration. If the city fell, there would be little to stop the English forces from marching north on a mission of conquest. Even if the Scottish army were to offer pursuit, Edward would always have the advantage of being able to choose his own ground on which to meet them. And once the English king gained the upper hand, Arnault did not hold out much hope for the Scots salvaging their independence.

His worst immediate fears were confirmed when the ship drew within sight of the Scottish coast. The sea haze hanging over Berwick town was mingled with billows of greasy gray smoke. Torquil joined him at the railing, and together they watched in growing dismay as the galley approached the entrance to the harbor. Both of them had seen enough siege action in the Holy Land to recognize the signs of a disaster in the making.

The scene at the waterfront was one of panic and pandemonium, with scores of townsfolk clambering for space aboard the handful of fishing boats tied up at the quay, recalling similar hysteria attending the fall of Acre. The captain of the galley, likewise a veteran of the wars of Outremer, prudently ordered his crew to drop anchor at some distance from the quay, and posted armed guards on the upper decks to repel any attempt to take possession of the ship.

"Are you certain it's wise to try landing in the midst of all that?" he asked Arnault.

"I'm afraid we have no choice," Arnault replied. "Have a boat lowered—but I'll risk only one of your men to row us ashore."

The boat landed them well clear of the harbor front, nosing into a sandy spit for just long enough to disembark them. Helmeted and lightly armored in mail hauberks and coifs, with mantles bunched up to keep them dry, they splashed through the shallows and quickly navigated a short, rocky incline, clambering then through patches of gorse to head to-

ward the row of fishermen's cottages that marked the seaward boundary of the town. After vaulting over a stone wall
festooned with fishing nets, they made their way along a
narrow alleyway that ran westward between two rows of
houses. The streets beyond were teeming with citizens of
Berwick town, aimlessly milling like sheep without a shepherd.

One hand on the hilt of his sword, Arnault stepped into
the path of a grim-looking man towing his wife and two
young sons behind him, holding up his other hand in a halting gesture.

"What has happened?" he asked urgently.

The man recoiled, wild-eyed, his family scurrying fearfully behind him.

"Don't you know?" he gasped. "The English have broken
through the town's defenses. There's still some fighting
going on along the perimeter, but it won't be long before
they'll be running riot in the streets."

His glance flicked timorously to the broadswords the two
knights were wearing, and Torquil said, "You have nothing
to fear from us. No one but a craven makes war on innocent
civilians."

"That's not what we've heard," the woman said from over
her man's shoulder, somewhat emboldened by the sound of
Torquil's Scottish voice. "They say that King Edward has
ordered his men to slaughter anyone they meet. Please let us
go, good sirs! We must get away before the En-glish soldiers
come and murder our children before our eyes!"

Both men wordlessly stood aside, and the family fled off
down the street.

"Dear God, your vision was true!" Torquil murmured.

Arnault only nodded, heartsick. Through and above the
surrounding hubbub of babbling voices and hurrying feet, he
could make out more distant sounds that chilled his blood:
screams and wails and the harsh clangor of weaponry—
sounds that both of them had heard too many times before.

"We've got to find Jay," he told Torquil grimly. "Maybe he can persuade King Edward that mercy is the better part of conquest."

The pair set off at a lope, hands on sword hilts, making for the line of the River Tweed, which marked the battlefront. The din grew louder as they drew nearer the town's center. The smoke they had seen from the harbor was growing thicker. Here and there among the housetops could be seen the lurid glare of burning timbers.

Torquil was in the lead when they came to the cobbled crossing of two thoroughfares. The sight of a painted sign above the door of one of the nearby buildings made him stumble to a halt.

"The Lindsays!" he exclaimed to Arnault. "Dear God, their house is just along there!"

Together the two Templars charged off up the road to the right. Some of the houses were already burning. From somewhere ahead came rending sounds of breakage mingled with screams of distress. They had come almost abreast of the sounds when the door to one of the houses flew wide, disgorging two English soldiers dragging a disheveled teenage girl between them.

Two more soldiers followed with a second girl, perhaps slightly older than the first, bodice ripped asunder, one breast exposed. Both girls were white with terror, too shocked to put up much of a struggle. The drawn swords of the soldiers were red and dripping with fresh blood.

The sight of two Knights Templar brought the marauding party to a jumbled standstill. Their leader, a big man with a broken nose, gave the pair a broad leer and an elaborately drunken salute, apparently assuming that the Templars were on the same side. Before either Templar could correct that assumption, a small boy of five or six came hurtling out of the house to fling himself at the rear-most soldier, sobbing in childish fury and hammering ineffectually at the man's armored bulk. The man clouted him with the pommel of his sword and drew back for a finishing thrust as the boy collapsed to the ground.

"Strike him at your peril, Sassenach!" Torquil bellowed, and lunged forward, sword in hand.

His charge caught the leading pair of marauders off guard. They hurled their captives aside and scattered, leaving him room to attack the two in the rear. A powerful downstroke took the first of his adversaries high on the right shoulder, all but severing the man's sword arm, and he folded screeching to the ground.

The second man backed at once, suddenly dead sober—but when he tried to use his prisoner as a shield, she came suddenly to life and sank her teeth into his wrist. Bellowing curses, he wrenched his arm away and dashed her from him. A clumsy parry saved him from being skewered on Torquil's blade, but the impact made him drop his weapon and he turned to flee.

At the same time, Arnault dispatched the first of the remaining men with a close-handled thrust through a weak point in his foe's mail shirt, bursting the net links under one arm and penetrating the man's rib cage. The man collapsed choking, blood frothing from his lips, as Arnault vaulted over him to press the attack on the last ravager.

The first man's demise had given the second one time to plan his attack. The big man sprang to meet Arnault, their swords clashing in a ringing shower of sparks. Lighter on his feet than his adversary, Arnault spun on his heel, sweeping his blade upward as he did so. His opponent's lunge went wide, and Arnault used that brief advantage to bring his sword cleaving down with killing force on the other man's skull.

He wiped his blade clean on the dead man's cloak, then turned to look for the children. The three of them were cowering in the shelter of the doorway, faces averted to the wall. Ducking briefly into the house, Torquil fetched a blanket and tossed it to the girl with the torn dress.

"Their parents have been butchered," he told Arnault in a low voice. "We can't leave them."

"Then we'll have to take them with us," Arnault said. "Let's move on."

Shepherding the children between them, they carried on up the street, swords still drawn. But as they approached the familiar gateway to the yard of the Lindsay house, they knew they were too late. The gate had been torn off its hinges, and the house beyond was in flames. Of Johan Lindsay and his family there was no sign.

"There's no way to know where they may have gone," Arnault said bleakly. "And they could all be dead, in there." He gestured toward the burning house with his sword.

"Could they maybe have gone to the Red Hall?" Torquil asked.

"The Red Hall?"

"Aye, the guildhall for the Flemish cloth merchants," Torquil replied. "Didn't Johan Lindsay deal in wool?"

"Of course!" Arnault paused a beat, thinking, then gestured with his sword.

"The nuns of St. Bride have a house back that way," he said. "We'll hope that the English soldiers won't violate a religious house. Take the children there, then make for the English lines and seek out King Edward and his commanders. Use every argument at your command to try and secure clemency for the local populace. If you find Jay, see if you can flatter him into helping you."

"I'll do what I can," Torquil agreed. "Where will you be?"

"Paying a visit to the Red Hall. I gave Johan Lindsay a writ of protection when we were here before. He's a tenant of the Temple. If he's there, he may appreciate a bit of clout to back up that writ. I'll join you in the English camp as soon as I can."

Leaving Torquil to shepherd his charges back the way they had come, Arnault set off in the direction of the Red Hall. Every turn revealed increasing evidence of mass slaughter and an army running amok. The streets leading toward the town center were littered with corpses. The air rang with the hideous din of drunken laughter and rampant looting, punctuated by the roar of flames and the occasional collapse of a burning building.

By the time Arnault came within sight of the merkat cross marking the center of the town, he had encountered hardly a handful of citizens left alive. Those still capable of reason he sent off to seek sanctuary at whatever religious house lay nearest. The rest he was obliged to leave to the care of Providence, while he hurried on in the hope of perhaps preserving the lives of the Flemish guildsmen.

A strong smell of burning met him as he turned into the High Street. In front of him and to the left stood the Red Hall itself, its castellated rooftop bristling with activity. The lower levels of the hall were wreathed with dense, billowing black smoke lit by glimmers of orange flame. From out of the smoke came a hungry, crackling roar.

With a murmured word of prayer on behalf of those inside, Arnault hurried forward. Between him and the hall stood an encircling array of English soldiers, hoarsely jeering and brandishing their swords and shields. Intermittent flights of arrows came whistling down from the roof of the hall, sowing bloody damage wherever they broke through the English defenses, but the smoke was growing denser by the minute as the flames ate their way up the walls of the building, outside and in.

Making the most of his armored height and Templar livery, Arnault shouldered his way through the ranks, sword in hand, until he located the captain in command of the attacking forces.

"What's going on here?" he demanded.

His voice was steel-edged with authority. The captain swallowed a sharp retort when he got a good look at his questioner.

"There's thirty or so Flemish rats holed up in their den," the man said. "We've orders to smoke them out, or let them perish in the flames."

"Have you offered them terms for surrender?" Arnault asked.

"Aye," the captain said. "But they threw the terms back in our faces. As far as I'm concerned, their road to hell starts here."

As if in response to this unsparing declaration, there came a sudden catastrophic *boom* from inside the burning hall. Every visible window was simultaneously etched in flame. The whole building quivered on its foundations, lit up from inside like an alchemist's forge. Then, with another deafening roar, the hall collapsed, burying everything and everyone inside under a mountain of blazing rubble.

A shock wave of hot air swept the street, raining fiery cinders down on the neighboring buildings. The English soldiers turned and bolted, diving for cover into alleys and doorways. Arnault was driven into retreat along with the rest. When it was safe to look again, there was nothing remaining of the Red Hall but a raging funeral pyre.

No one could have survived that inferno. Whatever fate Providence had decreed for Johan Lindsay and his family, Arnault could only trust that they were now in God's hands, whether here on earth or in heaven. Swallowing his rage and frustration like bitter bile, he turned his back grimly on this latest atrocity and set off in search of Torquil.

With the town overrun and half its buildings on fire, the garrison of Berwick Castle put up less resistance than had the men of the Red Hall. By the time Arnault came within sight of the castle gates, the royal banners of the English king were flying high above its battlements, as they had before the election of John Balliol. Various members of Edward's household troops patrolled the perimeter and manned the gatehouse.

Sheathing his sword and doffing his helmet, Arnault presented himself to the first guard he came upon.

"A big, redheaded Templar? Aye, he was looking for an audience. You'll find him in there somewhere," the man said, gesturing inside.

Arnault's livery passed him on into the castle without further challenge. Making for the great hall, he bypassed a line of English knights with prisoners waiting to be delivered into the custody of one of the king's wardens—all, by their dress, wealthy burgesses and members of the gentry, who could be expected to pay handsomely for their lives and their freedom. The common folk, by savage contrast, had been left to suffer butchery, unless something could be done to ease their desperate plight.

The hall was teeming with anxious townsfolk and soldiers, but Arnault's arrival was noticed almost immediately by Torquil, who came shouldering through the throng to meet him, helmet under his arm.

"The children are safe with the nuns of St. Bride," he reported, "though I had to remind a band of Welsh mercenaries that religious houses are not fair plunder. The mother superior of the house asked to be escorted here so that she could beg for mercy on behalf of the townspeople. A lot of other clerics are here, too, for the same reason, but so far the king has declined to see any of us." His green eyes flicked over Arnault's taut, soot-streaked face. "Did you find Johan Lindsay?"

"Whoever was in the Red Hall, they're all dead now," Arnault said baldly. "Edward's soldiery fired the hall. By the time I got there, it was already too late."

Torquil shook his head and crossed himself, murmuring, "May they rest in peace." He sighed. "I haven't had any luck finding Jay, either, though I'm sure he's somewhere around. I caught a glimpse of Robert de Sautre as I was coming up on the castle, but he was in the middle of a troop of mounted knights and I couldn't chase them down." He drew himself up. "So what do we do now?"

Before Arnault could summon an answer, a familiar, self-satisfied voice penetrated the undercurrent of anxious murmurings that filled the room, from somewhere above their heads.

"I heard there was a Templar brother looking for me. Now I see there are two of you."

Arnault and Torquil turned and looked up. Brian de Jay was surveying them from the gallery that overlooked the chamber. When he saw their faces, his blue eyes narrowed,

"Why, Brother Arnault de Saint Clair—and the ever-faithful Brother Torquil Lennox," he noted with an affability that rang patently false. "I had no idea we were expecting such an illustrious visitation. When one of my serjeants told me that two knight-brothers had come ashore from the galley in the harbor, I chided him for spreading rumors. Now I see he was reporting the truth. Come up and join me—*now.*"

Arnault and Torquil found a wheel-stair in a corner of the hall and climbed to the next floor, where Jay received them with a curt nod and led the way to a small room on the seaward side of the citadel. Looking them over, he took a seat behind a writing table cluttered with correspondence and writing paraphernalia, but he did not invite them to sit—clearly meant as a reminder of the deference he expected as Master of England.

"You look somewhat the worse for wear," he observed. "You would have gotten a better reception, had you come ashore on the English side of the Tweed. Now, tell me what brings you to this benighted place at this most inauspicious time."

Arnault sensed Torquil tensing and flashed him a warning glance to mind his temper and his tongue.

"Paris had sent us to negotiate a truce between the English and the Scots," he informed Jay neutrally. "I regret to see we have arrived too late to accomplish our primary mission. It now becomes our duty to engage our negotiating skills to mediate some restraint in the treatment of those who haven't borne arms. Given your past record of diplomacy, I'm sure we can count on your assistance."

"What, *now*?" Jay said, on a note of incredulity.

"Now, more than ever," Arnault replied. "I am told that you stand high in King Edward's esteem. If you were to recommend clemency on behalf of the people of Berwick, surely he would listen to you."

"I very much doubt that anything can be done," Jay began.

"If I could do this myself, I would," Arnault said. "But sadly, I lack your eminence. As Master of England, and the king's confidant, you are perceived as a man capable of succeeding where others might fail. Needless to say, it would be a credit to your reputation if you could sway King Edward in favor of taking pity on those who have done him no harm."

He was relieved when Jay succumbed to this appeal to his vanity. "I'll do what I can," said the Master of England. "But as for trying to put a stop to this war, you might as well have stayed in France and saved yourself the trouble. The Scots are too stubborn for their own good, and only harsh measures will teach them otherwise."

Chapter Fifteen

AFTER MUCH FRANTIC AND IMPASSIONED PLEADING ON BE-
half of the clergy of Berwick, Edward of England at last
condescended to order an end to the general slaughter. By
then, over the space of three days, nearly three quarters of
the town's population had perished by the sword—perhaps
as many as twenty thousand souls. The streets were piled
high with corpses: men, women, and children of all ages,
slain indiscriminately. The air quickly became so poisoned
by the reek of decay that the conquerors were compelled either to throw the bodies into the sea or to bury them in
hastily dug pits outside the boundaries of the town.

"Jay's intercessions were about as much worth as a
whore's honor," Torquil grumbled, through a muffling ker-
chief tied over his nose and mouth, as he and Arnault rode
to inspect the state of the mass grave sites. It was one of the
few places where they could speak without fear of being
overheard.

"I won't dispute that," Arnault replied. "For what it's

worth, I don't think anyone could have moved Edward to re-
scind his initial decree until the worst of the damage had
been done. Clearly, he meant to make an example of
Berwick, to intimidate the Scottish people as a whole. The
spread of fear can often do more damage than any siege en-
gine, when it comes to weakening the resolve of the enemy."

"On the other hand," Torquil said grimly, "it can convince
folk that they have nothing to lose by fighting to the death."

The speed with which events were unfolding in Scotland
put a certain urgency on proceeding with their true mission.
Nearly a fortnight passed, however, before they were permitted to depart Berwick. Brian de Jay was preparing to
travel south to London and thence to Cyprus, there to deliver
the Order's annual rents and revenues to the Grand Master.
On learning that Arnault and Torquil planned to remain in
Scotland during his absence, Jay made little attempt to disguise his displeasure.

"There can be no question of negotiating a truce now," he
informed the pair, in a meeting at which Guy de Foresta, the
former Master of England, was also present—for he would
be accompanying Jay to Cyprus. "Under the circumstances,
I feel that the Order would be best served if you and Brother
Torquil were to return to France. No doubt the Visitor will
have fresh orders for you, once he has learned of the failure
of your mission."

"On the contrary, the Visitor was not unaware that war
might break out before we could arrive to prevent it," Arnault replied. "In that event, our orders stipulate that we are
to approach various influential members of the Scottish
clergy, and solicit their advice concerning how best to resolve the conflict."

"What is there to resolve?" Foresta grumbled. "Four years
ago, John Balliol did homage to King Edward, acknowledging him to be supreme suzerain of Scotland. Since then, he
has violated his feudal obligations and rebelled against his
overlord. There can be no question that Balliol has commit-

ted treason, and all those who fight in his cause are guilty of the same crime. There is no greater offense—and until they confess and make restitution for their actions, there is nothing more to be said."

"No one could refute that analysis," Arnault answered smoothly. "In this instance, however, one cannot overlook the possibility that John Balliol has fallen victim to bad counsel. Who better to sift the conscience of Scotland's king than those eminent clerics—abbots, priests, and priors—who could be expected to have the best interests of the Scottish people at heart? If Balliol has done wrongly by the community of Scotland, surely his own clergy are the ones best suited to persuade him of the error of his ways and convince him to amend his judgment."

Jay snorted. "Your faith in the impartiality of the Scottish church is singularly ill-founded. One has only to examine the careers of men like Bishop Wishart of Glasgow, to see that they are as wedded to the cause of Scottish independence as any member of Balliol's rabble."

"That is why Brother Torquil and I are instructed to look elsewhere for counsel among Scotland's religious," Arnault returned calmly. "With respect, I would urge you to let us be off about this business without further delay. The Visitor's intentions are clearly spelled out in his orders. And the longer we remain here, the greater the danger that things will deteriorate beyond anyone's ability to salvage something for the people of Scotland."

The protocols Arnault had brought from Paris had been discreetly worded to allow him and Torquil far greater freedom of movement than normally was permitted any brother of their Order. The documents bore the signature of Hugues de Paraud, second only to the Grand Master; and much as Jay would have liked to dispute the point, he could not countermand those orders without himself committing a breach of authority. In the end, he had grudgingly given them permission to depart. But Arnault was certain that the Master of

England would use every means at his disposal to keep an eye on them.

Their first destination was Balantrodoch, ostensibly to deliver documents to Luc from the Paris treasury. In truth, they required Luc's current assessment of the less obvious aspects of the Scottish situation.

Sketchy reports of the sack of Berwick had preceded them by at least a week; but the prospect of an eyewitness account was sufficient inducement for John de Sautre, now Preceptor of Scotland, to convene a second chapter meeting on the day of their arrival. The brethren listened with keen attention, bombarding the new arrivals with questions, after which discussion shifted to speculation about the direction the conflict was likely to take next.

"We are given to understand that the Scottish earls abandoned the siege at Carlisle and withdrew to Annandale," Torquil told them, presenting a Scots perspective. "Apparently, they were able to inflict only slight damage on the town's defenses. At last report, the Scottish host were said to be reassembling at Jedburgh, and are using it as a base for harrying across the border into Northumberland."

"What response has Edward made?" Flannan Fraser asked.

"So far," said Arnault, "he has declined to pursue them. When we left Berwick, Longshanks was gathering his forces in preparation to march north toward Dunbar. If he takes it, his next objective will certainly be Edinburgh. And if he isn't halted at Edinburgh, there will be nothing to prevent him from advancing across the firth and into the heart of Scotland."

Afterward, when John de Sautre made a clumsy attempt to sound out their next intentions, Arnault repeated the gist of what he had already told Jay regarding their orders to approach various Scottish clergymen, additionally revealing that they planned to go first to the Abbot of Scone—which, indeed, they did, though not for the reasons stated. A short time later, while Torquil saw their horses shod and made arrangements for an early departure on the morrow, Arnault sought out Luc de Brabant in his treasury office, to deliver the treasury documents that he did, indeed, carry.

"Torquil is not with you?" Luc asked, as he admitted Arnault and glanced into the corridor behind him before closing the door.

"He's seeing to the horses," Arnault replied. He cast a glance at Luc in pointed query as to the security of the room, but Luc only gave him a wry smile as he waved Arnault to a bench along the outside wall and sat down beside him.

"We can speak here. What news from Paris?"

"Oh, you'll find nothing to alarm you in those," Arnault replied, handing over the official dispatches. "Thanks to your able stewardship, the fiscal stability of the Scottish houses is above reproach."

"Faint praise, given the state of the rest of the country." Luc laid aside the documents without even looking at them. "I assume, since you're going on to Scone, that you've been given some direction in that regard."

"We have," Arnault agreed. "The fate of the Fifth Temple continues to generate grave concerns within the Inner Circle. Having determined that the Stone of Destiny may be a cornerstone on more than one level, they feel that certain clarification is essential before we proceed on any large scale."

Luc only nodded as Arnault went on.

"My official orders reflect the realization that the political situation in Scotland is rapidly deteriorating. Balliol's leadership is disintegrating. The Council of Twelve have been no more effective. The siege of Carlisle was doomed to failure before it began, and now the earls are set to clash with Edward's armies at Dunbar—almost certainly without any chance of standing against him. As things stand, Scotland seems likely to lose her independence within the year."

"Does the Visitor really think the clergy could make a difference?" Luc asked.

"I doubt it. They were able—eventually—to mitigate the horror at Berwick; but I very much doubt that their words will count for much where Balliol is concerned. Nonetheless, I am charged with the task of making the approach—which gives Torquil and me ample reason to travel on to Scone, to discuss such matters with Abbot Henry."

"And also, I warrant, to discuss the Stone," Luc said, nodding his understanding.

Arnault echoed his nod. "That reflects your own recommendations, over the past several years. Under the Canmores, the vitality of the Scottish monarchy was always dependent on the power vested in the Stone of Destiny. And we know that, at least from the time of Balliol's enthronement, something was not altogether right about the Stone.

"Taking all of this into account, Torquil and I have been sent to make the following determinations: Firstly, can the Stone of Destiny somehow be reempowered? And secondly, would such an infusion of power revitalize this present Scottish monarchy and thus enable it to keep Scotland free?"

"Questions I have asked myself more than once, in the intervening years."

"What about Abbot Henry?" Arnault asked. "Do you think *he* has considered such questions, as Keeper of the Stone? More to the point, is he likely to become hysterical if he learns that our investigative methods are—ah—less than orthodox?"

"Actually, I have reason to suspect that he would be quite open to such things," Luc replied thoughtfully. "Remember that the folk of these Celtic isles have always had a high regard for the mystical. Scone is an Augustinian house, but they take much of their spirituality from Columban sources; you may not be aware that many of Saint Columba's relics are housed at Dunkeld Cathedral, but a few hours north of Scone. Some of Scone's most celebrated sons had connections with the community at Iona, where Columba established his first mission. And of course, it was Saint Columba who brought the Stone to Scotland."

"I'm aware of that," Arnault replied. "And long before Columba's time, that the Stone is said to have been Jacob's pillow in the wilderness—which perhaps gives it affinities with another precious Hallow of the Holy Land, already in the keeping of the Temple—which is why I was given the loan of this."

From out of the breast of his habit he produced a flattened packet, which he had been carrying next to his heart since leaving Paris, suspended from a white silk cord around his neck. It was roughly the size and shape of a small book, wrapped in oilskin and then in several layers of silk, which, when he carefully unfolded them, revealed the precious and potent Breastplate of the High Priests of Israel. Glinting in the wan light of the room's one window, the twelve gems stitched to the stiffened linen reflected a profusion of rainbow colors.

Luc's eyes widened and his jaw dropped.

"The urgency must be even greater than I feared, if they allowed you to bring *that* here," he breathed. "You took a terrible risk!"

"But one deemed acceptable, given the circumstances." Arnault began rewrapping the relic. "Like the Stone, the Breastplate is a legacy left to the world by our Hebrew forebears, who built the first four Temples at Jerusalem. It was by means of the Breastplate that we first received the revelation that Scotland was to provide the foundation site of the Fifth Temple, with the Stone as cornerstone. Hopefully, by bringing the Breastplate and Stone together in an appropriate manner, we can discover how best to proceed."

"I regret that I cannot accompany you," Luc said gravely. "Even though I have the utmost faith in Abbot Henry, I know my presence would reassure him. But I am already regarded as the spy of Paris, within these walls. I feel certain that de Sautre has orders to keep me under close watch."

"He probably has similar orders concerning us," Arnault replied, slipping the Breastplate back into its hiding place. "He is still Jay's man."

"Oh, he is indeed!" Luc agreed. "And his toadying younger brother is Jay's right hand, down in London. What happens here, you can be sure Jay knows about within the week."

"Well, he's on his way to Cyprus with Guy de Foresta and the annual responsions from the English province, so his intelligence will be somewhat interrupted for a few months," Arnault said with some satisfaction, "but the interest of the de Sautre brothers will be inconvenient enough. I've already been grilled about the trip to Scone." He shook his head and sighed.

"And we still don't know what connection they—and Jay—had with those missing pagan relics—or maybe even with what happened that night in the scriptorium. If it weren't for the likelihood that black magic connects the deaths of Alexander III and the Maid and whatever has happened to the Stone, I might not be as concerned; the evidence that similar stirrings might be afoot here at Balantrodoch is purely circumstantial, and there's nothing I can see that connects these phenomena with the larger Scottish questions.

"But it is a measure of these sorely troubled times that we must even consider that opposition might come from within our own Order, and on this level."

"Aye," said Luc, "we must be as wily as serpents, as the Scriptures tell us. And there is another thing you may not have thought of." He gave a heavy sigh as Arnault looked at him in question.

"As precious as we hold our vows to the Order and its work, we are bound to an even higher work through our ties to *le Cercle*. And having said that, we must be prepared for the day when our fidelity to that work may even require us to go against our knightly vows to the Order at large."

Chapter Sixteen

ARNAULT AND TORQUIL LEFT BALANTRODOCH THE NEXT morning as planned. John de Sautre had nothing further to say regarding their plans, but by the time the pair were skirting the vast mound of Edinburgh Castle, Torquil was certain they were being followed.

"Are you surprised?" Arnault asked, as they rode toward the ferry that would take them across the Firth of Forth.

"No, I'm angry!" Torquil retorted, smoldering. "Who does John de Sautre think he is? You showed him our orders. They're nothing to do with him."

"He thinks he's the Preceptor of Scotland, and we're operating in his territory," Arnault said mildly. "Also, I expect that Brian de Jay has told him to keep an eye on us. Jay regards us as a threat, because we're outside his command."

"I know all that," Torquil muttered.

The sense of being shadowed persisted as they continued northward past the firth, avoiding the vast ecclesiastical complex at Dunfermline and heading on toward Kinross and

Perth. Whoever their shadowers were, they were careful not to show themselves.

"Do you think they're de Sautre's lackeys?" Torquil muttered in an undertone as he and Arnault rode along.

"That would seem the most likely assumption," Arnault replied, resisting any impulse to glance behind them.

"We could set a trap for them," Torquil said.

"To what purpose? I made no secret of the fact that we're on our way to Scone. It's simpler for everyone if our shy friends don't realize we're on to them. If they *are* de Sautre's men, all we would accomplish by confronting them would be to make him wonder why we thought we might be followed."

"What if they *aren't* de Sautre's men?" Torquil asked, with a sour glance aside.

It had already occurred to Arnault that Brian de Jay and the de Sautres might not be the only ones taking a hostile interest in their affairs.

"If they're *not* de Sautre's men," he said, "we're probably equally well advised to leave them alone, at least for the moment. If we stop this present contingent from trailing us, they might be replaced by others more adroit and more dangerous."

Their shadow companions continued to keep pace with them. By the time the two Templars came within sight of Scone Abbey, the habit of vigilance had become wearisome. It was with some relief that they heard the outer gates of the abbey grange close behind them.

Abbot Henry accorded them a cordial welcome. He had grown visibly grayer and more careworn since their last visit—which was hardly surprising, for the instability of John Balliol's kingship had so undermined the country as a whole that there was scant peace of mind to be found anywhere, even within the supposedly detached confines of a monastic community.

Sketchy news regarding the fall of Berwick had reached the abbey several days before, and the abbot was eager to hear further details. While accommodations were being readied in the guest house, he invited Arnault and Torquil to join him in his private study for a light collation. After offering a prayer of thanksgiving for the food and the safe arrival of his guests, he himself poured wine for the three of them.

"It pleases me to see both of you again," he assured them, "though I would that you brought more gladsome news. But before we speak of darker matters, first tell me how it is with my friend Brother Luc."

"He is well, Reverend Father, and sends you his warmest regards," Arnault said.

"Pleased am I, always, to receive his regard," the abbot replied. "He is a kind and gentle man. The Temple is well served by him, as is our Lord. But, tell me what brings the pair of you to Scone? Not merely to be the bearers of ill tidings, I trust."

"No, to ask your assistance."

"*My* assistance?"

"Officially," Arnault said with a faint smile, "we are sent to seek the counsel of you and others of the Scottish clergy concerning what may be done to temper John Balliol's folly with regard to Edward of England. Unfortunately, since Edward is marching north to engage a Scottish force at Dunbar, even as we speak, I very much doubt that he will be inclined to deal gently with the Scots or their king. Nor are the pleas of the clergy likely to be any more effective than they were at Berwick."

Abbot Henry's brown eyes narrowed thoughtfully as he measured both knights. "You said 'officially.' Am I to infer that there are also unofficial reasons for your visit?"

Arnault glanced at Torquil, who set aside his wine, choosing his words carefully.

"Father Abbot, you know I am a fellow Scot. When I fought in the Holy Land, it seemed to me that the aspirations of all Christendom were bound up in the quest to recover Jerusalem, the Holy City.

"That quest is a good and holy cause—but when I came back to Scotland, I came to wonder whether it was but part of a larger struggle for which Scotland itself may be a pivot point. There is a darkness abroad in this land, especially since the death of the last Canmore, being spread abroad by something—or someone—bent on swallowing up all that is good in this world. If is not contained and dispelled, such a darkness could continue to spread until it has swallowed up the whole of Christendom."

Abbot Henry's face had gone very still, and he answered only after a studied pause.

"I fear you have not spoken all that is in your heart, Brother Torquil. If the knights of your Order have some deeper knowledge of this matter than is common to the Church at large—and by my friendship with your Brother Luc, I think they may—I pray you most fervently to be plain in what you are trying to say."

Torquil glanced at Arnault, who allowed himself a faint sigh of relief.

"That is why Brother Torquil and I have come back to Scotland," he said. "For we have come to believe that both the cause and the cure of Alba's ills lie here at Scone, with the Stone of Destiny."

"The Stone?" Abbot Henry murmured.

"Aye, consider it in light of Scotland's mystic lore," Arnault went on. "Ever since the days of Columba, the Stone has been Scotland's greatest talisman of light, her palladium, the cornerstone of Scottish sovereignty. But in recent years, that light has dimmed, and likewise the power of Scotland's monarchy. If this nation is to survive the coming storm, it seems to me that we must find a way to rekindle the Stone's secret flame. Only then will the crown—and the kingdom—stand firm."

The abbot looked startled, but also somewhat relieved. "How curious it is that you should say this," he said. "Twenty years ago, I would have been quick to dismiss the notion that so holy and time-honored a relic as the Stone could ever lose its virtue. But for some time now, I have felt it in my heart that all was not as it should be."

"How long?" Torquil asked.

Abbot Henry shifted his attention to the younger knight. "I think," he said slowly, "that it was in the year that King Alexander III died, that I first noticed something amiss. But it wasn't until the day of John Balliol's enthronement that I became sure of it."

Torquil gave a little gasp, and Arnault leaned forward eagerly.

"Can you describe what you felt was wrong?"

A frown furrowed the abbot's brow as he groped to put his feelings into words. "It is akin to the sense one sometimes has of an altar long unused—or one that has been profaned. A spark may remain, but such an altar has a different feel from one used daily to offer the holy sacrifice of the Mass."

Arnault nodded, precisely aware of what the abbot was trying to describe.

"Perhaps this is a peculiarity of our Celtic race—to sense such things," Abbot Henry continued. "I have heard it said that those of great holiness can choose between a consecrated Host and mere bread—which seems to me quite likely, if one accepts that diabolical entities cannot bear the presence of the Host. Clearly, it is more than mere faith that is involved; but I cannot tell you *what* more.

"But the waning power of the Stone is akin to all of these things. And on the morning of John Balliol's enthronement, suddenly it seemed that there was nothing left but a flicker."

Arnault glanced at Torquil—clearly dying to speak—and signed his permission.

"Father Abbot," Torquil said, "on the night before John Balliol's enthronement, one of your brothers told me much the same thing—a Brother Mungo."

"Ah, Brother Mungo," the abbot said with a faint smile. "Alas, he has passed on—may God grant him rest—but he was a very dear and holy man. Odd that you should mention him just now."

"How so?" Arnault asked.

"Brother Mungo came to us from the Iona community—founded, as you may know, by the blessed Columba himself. And I count your mention of him odd because only last week, another Columban brother appeared at our gate and asked permission to spend a period of retreat with us—a Brother Ninian. Even more oddly, he has spent a large part of each day in contemplation of the Stone. I cannot think that he could have known you were coming—or why. But it occurs to me that this cannot be coincidence. I think, perhaps, that you are meant to make his acquaintance."

"I think, perhaps, we are," Arnault agreed. "Before we do, however, there is one thing more that you should know, concerning our interest in the Stone—and I choose my words with care, because I have no wish to give offense or cause for scandal."

"If we are speaking here of things Unseen," Abbot Henry replied, "I assure you that I will not take such words as scandalous, if that is your fear, Brother Arnault. Please speak freely."

"Very well. These are our perceptions. You mentioned that you first began to notice a change in the Stone after the death of Alexander III. When Brother Luc and Brother Torquil and I were last here, we came upon certain indications suggesting that black magic may have been involved both in the death of Alexander and that of the little Maid of Norway. Incidentally, I was present when the Maid died. We have yet to trace this evil back to its source. But there is every reason to believe that the disempowering of the Stone may be one of the effects linked to this cause."

Abbot Henry's face had drained of color during this recitation, and he recovered himself with a shudder.

"Dear God, why did Luc not tell me?" he whispered.

"I pray you, do not fault Luc," Arnault said. "He would not have been certain how such a claim would be received—and we have yet to establish clearer proofs. Even now, we are not in a position to name any names. In view of the present crisis, however, I think a closer examination of the Stone becomes imperative—and I think, Reverend Father, that the sooner you introduce us to Brother Ninian, the better."

"I shall send one of the serving brothers to fetch him immediately," Abbot Henry said, rising to do so. "Under the circumstances, I feel certain he will be as anxious to meet you, as you are him."

The serving brother returned a short while later, bringing with him a tallish, fine-boned figure of a man whose white robes and Celtic tonsure marked him as the Columban brother of whom Abbot Henry had spoken. As the abbot made the formal introductions, Arnault allowed himself to refine his first impressions.

Brother Ninian appeared to be on the young side of forty, clean-shaven and graceful of carriage, with flaxen hair drawn back in a tail behind his tonsure and a gray gaze the color of rain-washed agate. His hands were slender, with long, tapering fingers that bespoke a gift for artistic expression. A serene containment in his manner suggested depths of spirit rare even among those dedicated to a life of prayer and self-denial.

Brother Ninian, in his turn, was eyeing his new acquaintances with a curiosity as unaffected as it was single-minded. On an indrawn breath, his face was transfigured by a beatific smile, his eyes like sunlit wells brimming with love and compassion.

"All praise to the High God," he murmured. "You are the ones I was told to expect!"

This declaration both surprised and intrigued all three of his listeners.

"Who told you to expect us?" Arnault ventured.

"Why, *Cra-gheal* himself," Ninian answered.

"*Cra-gheal?*"

"It's the old Scots tongue," Torquil said eagerly, before Ninian could explain. "*Cra-gheal—the red-white one.* It's one of the names given to the Archangel Michael. Is it Saint Michael to whom you refer, Brother Ninian?"

"It is, indeed. Michael of the White Steeds, Michael of the Battles. *Cra-gheal* instructed me to come here and await the arrival of two warrior-monks who would be wearing his sign in token of his fellowship." He pointed to the distinctive red crosses emblazoned on the surcoats and mantles of the two Templar knights. "Do you not claim great Michael as one of the patrons of your Order?"

"We do," Arnault acknowledged.

Ninian nodded as if the matter was settled. "Then I know why you are here: to seek the renewal of the Stone of Destiny."

He turned his gaze to the room's tiny window and continued, holding his listeners spellbound.

"I was standing upon a rock by the shores of Iona," he said, "when the voice of *Cra-gheal* called to me from over the waters, bidding me rise and go to where the Stone lies sleeping. To that place would come two of his warriors here on earth, seeking the means to rekindle the Light that has come down to us from ancient times. He bade me offer you aid and counsel according to such wisdom as has been given to me."

The light in his eyes, as he shifted back to gaze at them, bore witness to the truth of his declaration, so that Arnault could not doubt that Brother Ninian had been vouchsafed a mystical revelation—or that he would accept, without question, the framework of esoteric focus by which their present mission was guided. Briefly, and without mincing words, Arnault acquainted both Ninian and Abbot Henry with the background and rationale of what he proposed to do, not failing to mention the role of the High Priest's Breastplate.

"What I am suggesting is best approached with due preparation," he said, by way of summation, "preferably over several days. Given that the Eve of May is only three days hence—which Brother Torquil tells me is also the turning of the old Scottish new year—I suggest that we agree on that day, and use the intervening time to prepare ourselves by fasting and meditation."

"An apt and auspicious choice," Ninian agreed. "It is the eve of the ancient festival of *Bealtuinn* or Beltane, when bonfires still are lighted upon the hilltops to welcome in the summer. The night is no less potent in these times in which our allegiance is given to the Son, rather than the sun."

"That is surely true," Abbot Henry declared with a solemn nod—making it unnecessary for either Arnault or Torquil to comment on this reassurance that none of them need feel constrained by conventional expressions of religious practice.

For the next two days, Brother Ninian and the two Templars immersed themselves in the abbey community's rhythm of prayer, hearing daily Mass, and reciting all the offices of the liturgical day, the knights with their mail and weapons put aside, affirming the monastic aspect of their calling. On the last night before May Eve, however, the two Templars armed themselves before Compline and remained afterward in the abbey church to keep vigil in a peculiarly chivalric devotion.

It was a practice particularly beloved of Arnault, and one that Torquil had also taken very much to heart, always yielding of refreshment of the spirit and, in Arnault's case, a source of illumination. Kneeling down at the foot of the sanctuary, before the altar of the Blessed Sacrament, he held his drawn sword before him at arm's length, hands just beneath the quillons, the point resting lightly on the floor.

He fixed his gaze first on the center of the cross formed by quillons and blade and whispered aloud the motto of the Order: *"Non nobis, Domine, non nobis sed Nomini Tuo da gloriam . . ."* Then he let the focus blur to include the candles beyond, flickering on the altar, and gave his thoughts freedom of flight, like doves seeking a resting place in the wilderness.

His mind lighted for a time on Brother Ninian, kneeling in the chapel of the Stone, as he did each night. In his quiet ways and loving respect for the whole of creation, the Columban brother reminded Arnault of the followers of Francis of Assisi, who, like Ninian, affirmed and embraced the Divine spirit in all things and celebrated God and nature in a single act of worship.

In Ninian's case, however, those attitudes and practices were an inheritance from Scotland's mystical past. In manner and appearance, the Columban brother might almost have been the living embodiment of those early times, his white habit and Celtic tonsure linking him with his inheritance of Druid spirituality, which had seen the coming of the teachings of Christ as fulfillment and extension of a Trinitarian concept long honored in their traditions.

And yet there was nothing distant or remote in Ninian's grasp of war and politics, as the Templars had discovered that first day they met him. On the contrary, it was his awareness of the spirit dwelling in all things that illuminated his understanding of Scotland's present need.

That Ninian's practices were grounded on Scottish soil was visibly demonstrated the following day, the Eve of May. As the Templars left the abbey church after Mass, at that "third hour" of the ancient world, when the Holy Spirit came down upon the Apostles, they glimpsed the Columban brother's white-clad form setting out toward the neighboring summit of the Moot Hill, where he remained for the rest of the day in fasting and in prayer. Bound to a similar regimen of observances, the two Templars did not see him again until late that night, when they and he and Abbot Henry met in the chapel of the Stone to perform the proposed rite of divination.

It was approaching midnight. The church was empty and silent, dark save for the Presence lamp above the tabernacle and the gleam of the lanterns that the party had brought to light their way. While Abbot Henry silently fetched a brace of candlesticks from the nearest aumbry and invested them with fresh beeswax candles, Arnault and Ninian moved to the rear of the chapel, where Ninian proceeded to lay out several small items from a deerskin pouch at his girdle. Arnault spent those few precious minutes with head bowed in his hands, preparing himself for the work to come.

The altar of the side chapel was dedicated to Saint Andrew. Once Abbot Henry had lit the altar candles, he extinguished the lanterns and knelt down before the altar to offer up prayers for the protection of the participants and the success of their evening's work. Torquil, for his part, drew his sword and made a sun-wise circuit of the chapel's inner perimeter, tracing out a protective circle and pausing at each of the quarters to embellish it with an additional symbol of protection. Once having closed the circle, he positioned himself just within the chapel's entrance, facing outward with his sword grounded beneath his hands, ready to defend the sacred space and its occupants against all intruders, physical and otherwise.

Arnault sensed the completion of that part of the work, and looked up to find Ninian quietly gazing at him. With a faint smile, Arnault took out the Breastplate from its resting place next to his skin. Ninian watched with grave respect as the oilskin and silken wrappings were removed, reverently kissing the fingertips of his right hand and then glancing at Arnault for permission before lightly touching one of the stones in salute.

"A precious Hallow," he breathed. "May God grant you discernment to use it wisely."

So saying, he moved back a step and bowed to Arnault, gesturing toward the Stone in sign for him to begin. Mentally commending himself to God, Arnault then sank to his knees behind the Stone, as he had knelt once before, then took a deep breath to steady himself before slipping the Breastplate's fastening chains around his neck, so that the ornament came to rest over his heart.

"Almighty God, Eternal Father of Lights," he prayed aloud, "in Whom there is no darkness, and before Whom no secrets lie hid, lift the veil from my mortal eyes and enlighten my soul, I pray, that my spirit may discern the nature of hidden truths and my heart may clearly know Thy will."

With these words, he reverted to contemplative silence, sinking back onto his hunkers. While Abbot Henry continued his own supportive intercessions, Ninian picked up a small wooden bowl he had filled from a vial of collected rainwater, stirring the contents with a sprig of flowering hawthorne, cut earlier by the light of the moon.

"I spoke to the wood," he chanted softly, "and it sang to me of the earth. I spoke to the water, and it sang to me of the sky. Blessed be wood and earth, water and sky, in token of their Creator. Let their songs be on my lips, in praise of the High God."

With these words, he used the hawthorne sprig as an aspergillum to shake water on the Stone in blessing. Pale hawthorne petals also shook loose, fragile and fragrant.

"Creature of earth," he whispered, "be blessed in the name of that One Who is above all others. Awake and know thyself for what thou art: a vessel of God's power!"

After bowing profoundly to the Stone, he set the bowl aside and sank down opposite Arnault, taking from his pouch a flat, water-smoothed gray stone the size of a hen's egg and perforated at its center by a naturally formed hole, which he laid into Arnault's up-cupped palms.

"This is called a *keekstane,* a seeing-stone," he explained. "Such objects are rare gifts of nature. The eyehole is a window on the world of hidden things. I give it to you now, as the one to whom true Vision may be revealed."

Pulse quickening, Arnault closed the *keekstane* in his two hands and prepared to engage his inner perceptions. After a moment he invoked the power of the Breastplate, and soon became aware of a growing warmth at his breast, and even an answering tingle from the *keekstane*.

Bowing his forehead to it, he began reaching for a link to join the two. Very soon he became aware of a sensation of warmth radiating from the Breastplate. The warmth quickened to a glow and spread to his chest, setting his blood racing. The act of breathing seemed to fan the flame brighter and hotter, like bellows stoking a forge. It set his heart ablaze so that it burned in his breast like a live coal.

The chamber of the Stone seemed to waver around him as he dared to lift his head, hands clasped tightly around the *keekstane*, held close before the Breastplate. With a faint sense of dizziness came the feeling that he was being lifted up to some higher plane of perception, where the firmness of the floor beneath his knees seemed the only thing keeping him anchored to the physical world. All else was being ignited and transformed by the fire in his heart.

The heat at his breast soared above the threshold of pain, but even as Arnault gave a gasp, the fire discharged itself with a sudden jolt. There came a dazzling burst of light from the center of his chest, and in that instant, all the jewels in the Breastplate came suddenly to life in a rainbow blaze of unearthly radiance.

Hands trembling, Arnault dared to lift the *keekstane* before his gaze. Seen through the *keekstane*'s window, bathed in that supernal light, the Stone of Destiny underwent a startling change. Its opaque density drained away like wine from a cup. Its remaining mass became transparent as a block of clear glass. As Arnault gazed into its vitreous depths, still peering through the *keekstane*, an arc of rainbow fire leapt from the Breastplate to the Stone.

Shimmering colors mapped its surface in crackling force lines. In the same instant, at the very heart of the Stone, there appeared an answering splinter of light. Like a seed of starfire, it blossomed outward, meeting and merging with the fire dance of colors on the surface. Then, just as swiftly, it died back, leaving only the ghost of a glimmer behind.

The waning wrenched at Arnault with an almost physical sensation—as if he were being pulled inside the Stone. At the Stone's core, he could feel a pulse of invisible energy, throbbing like the lingering heartbeat of a dying man. In a single, bleak instant, he sensed that revival might be possible—but by no means was it certain.

As if in response to that revelation, he felt a sudden, rending pain in his chest, as if his heart were being torn out. The anguish took his breath away. His body crumpled, bringing the realm of vision crashing down in ruins around him. As he slid toward the floor, the *keekstane* slipping from his fingers, a voice seemed to whisper above the fading tumult.

"The realm has fallen into the hands of an apostate!" it cried. *"Only blood may pay the ransom price. The time of the Uncrowned King draws near—the time of the warrior-victim, stalwart in battle. To him, the sacrifice; to his successors, the victory!"*

Chapter Seventeen

"THERE IS SOME LITTLE COMFORT TO BE TAKEN FROM THE fact that the Stone of Destiny still retains a spark of its former power," Abbot Henry observed heavily. "But if we cannot find the means to fan that ember back to life, I fear that the future of this land will be bleak, indeed. And as to the cost of putting things right, we have nothing more to go on than hints and riddles."

"Prophecy, I'm afraid, is nearly always obscure," Arnault said. "Still, we've been given this guidance for a reason. We must now use our human wits to hammer out a meaning."

He was speaking from a chair drawn up by the hearth in Abbot Henry's study. Though it was now morning, and he had had the benefit of several hours' sleep, he still was not fully recovered from the rigors of their previous night's work. Slouched deep in a neighboring chair, Torquil was looking similarly weary and perplexed. Only Brother Ninian, standing by the window, continued to preserve an appearance of unruffled calm.

Arnault had no recollection of anything past the point where his vision had overwhelmed him. He had awakened in a bed in the abbey's infirmary, with Brother Ninian watching over him. Very shortly, both Torquil and Abbot Henry had joined them. The Breastplate had been returned to its wrappings and was back in its accustomed hiding place, under Arnault's shirt and against his skin. On Ninian's recommendation, he had hung the *keekstane* around his neck on a thong of leather.

"Whatever the meaning," Abbot Henry said, "it behooves us to fathom it as quickly as possible. There is, indeed, a shadow on the Stone and on the land, apparently intent on plunging us into pagan darkness. The cure would seem to lie in the hands of this so-called Uncrowned King. And unless we find out who he is—and how he must empower the Stone—King Edward will overwhelm our lands, and the shadows will overwhelm our souls."

A lengthy discussion followed. Various speculations and proposals were examined, only to be discarded as untenable. Eventually the debate dwindled into frustrated silence, finally broken by Brother Ninian.

"It occurs to me," he said, "since I was sent by *Cra-gheal* to assist you, that perhaps you are meant to accompany me back to Iona. We have in our library many ancient texts and manuscripts. A few are even ascribed to the hand of Columba himself. In addition, we preserve the oral traditions of our distant past. Some of our brethren have been trained in the ways of the *seannachie,* who carry vast sums of ancient wisdom in their memories. It may be that one of them can offer the enlightenment that presently eludes us."

Both Arnault and Torquil brightened at that prospect, and Abbot Henry gave an enthusiastic nod.

"We'll come, of course," Arnault replied.

After a quick discussion of practicalities, they planned to make their departure the next morning. Torquil and Brother

Ninian began assembling provisions after the noon office, while Arnault caught a few hours' sleep.

But shortly before Vespers, when Arnault had just joined the pair in the abbey stables, inspecting the mounts available for the journey, a clatter of hooves in the yard outside at once was joined by the sound of running feet and a growing murmur of anxious voices. Arnault glanced outside, then beckoned for the others to join him, for an exhausted-looking rider on a lathered horse had just drawn up in the abbey yard, and two lay brothers were leaning hard against the horse's sides and trying to keep it from collapsing as monks began emerging from doorways all around the yard.

"The English have taken Dunbar!" the rider gasped out as he slid gracelessly down from the saddle. "At least three earls are taken as well, and many other men of rank. Next Edinburgh itself is threatened—and then the whole of Scotland!"

A general outcry of dismay greeted this announcement, along with urgent clamorings for more details, but few were forthcoming. From what the Templars could gather, grave strategic blunders had doomed the Scots defense from the outset, and King John was now retreating northward with the Comyns and others of his baronage. To Earl Warenne's cavalry had gone the honor of attacking and taking Dunbar on King Edward's behalf—and the English king and his main army were now believed to be making their way west toward Edinburgh in a leisurely fashion.

"So much for John Balliol's military acumen," Torquil muttered in an explosive undertone as he and Arnault moved off. "And what were those fool earls thinking of? They might have held Dunbar!"

"Your countrymen lack experience in the art of warfare as Edward pursues it," Arnault said. "It remains to be seen what lessons they learn from this disaster."

There was no telling how long the English would remain

in the vicinity of Dunbar before moving on. The prospect of English armies on the march gave Arnault pause for thought.

"It occurs to me," he said, "that it might be less than politic for two Templars to be moving openly in Scotland without being attached to any English contingent. I wonder if this might be a good time to drop out of sight, perhaps take up disguise."

"Oh?" Torquil said, with an arch look that spoke volumes regarding his opinion of previous disguises he and Arnault had worn.

Arnault chuckled. "Nothing too odious this time, I think. We shall be . . . pilgrims finally returned from the Holy Land—bound, I think, for a time of religious retreat and penance with the good brothers of Iona. That illusion will require leaving our armor behind, and borrowing habits from Abbot Henry, but I think that cover gives us justification for taking along our swords."

"At least that means we travel light," Torquil said, obviously relieved.

The final touch was added by Abbot Henry, who supplied them with the black habits of Augustinian brothers and two unremarkable-looking rouncys from the abbey stables to replace the blooded palfreys they had ridden north from Balantrodoch. In this guise, with packs tied behind their saddles and swords strapped under their knees—and with Brother Ninian mounted on the wiry mountain pony he had ridden from Iona—the three slipped out of the abbey gates early the next morning and headed north for the episcopal town of Dunkeld.

The road to Dunkeld was well marked. They easily covered the intervening fifteen miles in less than a day. From the fearful looks and whispers flying among the people in the streets, it was clear that news of the fall of Dunbar had preceded them. They lodged that night in a hospice adjoining the cathedral, and set out early the next morning on the trail continuing north and then westward along the River Tay.

The fickle weather of spring turned stormy, so it took the better part of a fortnight to cross the breadth of Scotland. The road following the course of the river dwindled to little more than a poorly defined pony track as it skirted the north shore of Loch Tay, periodically losing itself amid encroaching forest growth. Human settlements were few, usually consisting of a few mean huts clumped together in a rough-hewn clearing. The scattering of crofters and fisher-folk who occupied these hovels were wary of strangers and kept their distance.

The terrain grew increasingly wild as they continued westward. All sound was muffled by the thickness of the surrounding forest. Several times a day, most often toward dusk, their passage would startle small herds of red deer, that scattered in panic before them. The trail, such as it was, cut a ragged line along the floor of the long river valley, which formed a bridge between the lower reaches of Loch Tay and the upper waters of Loch Awe. The valley floor was densely forested, and they found themselves obliged to dismount more than once to clear the way ahead, until they came at last before a broad vista overlooking a spread of steel-blue water.

"I know this place," Ninian said. "This is where the River Awe feeds into the loch. Ahead lies the Pass of Brander—and beyond that, Loch Etive, and the way to the sea."

"I hope you aren't going to say we must swim across that," Torquil said.

The Columban monk shook his head and smiled faintly. "There is a fording place about a mile upstream. I'll show you the way."

A shallow strip of stony beach marked the dividing line between the forest and the loch. As the three riders emerged from the dense shadows of the trees, the primordial silence was broken by a sudden outcry from somewhere off to their right, followed by a confused outburst of other sounds. The din was sharply punctuated by the all-too-familiar clang of metal meeting metal.

With a speaking glance at Torquil, Arnault swung down from his horse, handing the reins to Brother Ninian and pulling his sword from under his saddle flap as Torquil did the same.

"Stay with the horses," he said to Ninian in a low voice.

From the shouts and grunts coming from the direction of the struggle, and the clangor of weapons, Arnault judged that there might be eight or ten combatants. He revised his estimate a moment later, when he and Torquil got a glimpse of the clearing ahead, where three burly, bare-legged High-landers were pressed back to back in the middle of the clear-ing, spears defensively lowered to keep five circling horsemen at bay.

The Highlanders spotted Arnault and Torquil before any of the horsemen were aware of their presence. As their red-haired leader noted the swords in their fists, he threw back his head and gave a bellowed shout.

"To us, if ye be of Scots blood! Otherwise, be damned to ye!"

The liveried horsemen were all in toughened leather jacks and steel caps, armed with long cavalry lances as well as swords. As the captain jerked his mount around to confront the newcomers, his eyes narrowed at the sight of two addi-tional would-be adversaries. A barked command brought two of his subordinates wheeling to charge at them, not waiting to see for whom they declared. The two Templar knights struck defensive positions, for the riders had the reach of them with the long lances.

"Timing," Arnault muttered aside to Torquil through clenched teeth, as the two horsemen spurred forward, split-ting left and right as they closed.

Bracing his sword in both hands, Arnault waited till the last possible instant to shift and, as the tip of his opponent's lance whizzed narrowly past his chest, swung his blade downward, hacking down on the shaft with all his strength.

The lance shattered with a splintering crack, and its owner reeled in the saddle. Casting aside the useless weapon, the man heaved himself upright with a curse and brought his mount sharply about, reining in long enough to rearm himself with the mace he was carrying slung from his saddletree.

Back where the Highlanders were holding off the other three, out of the corner of his eye Arnault saw the sudden flurry of the riders' captain tumbling backward from the saddle with a well-thrown dagger protruding from the socket of one eye. Torquil was still on his feet after evading the first charge of *his* attacker, and as both their adversaries came around for second passes, he dived under a lance and seized the horse by the bit, wrenching it off stride. The animal reared back, spilling its rider to the ground.

The thunder of approaching hooves warned Arnault of his own peril. As Torquil leaped in to grapple with his fallen opponent, Arnault could see and hear the heavy mace swinging toward him, but he ducked and sidestepped nimbly and came up under the blow, his thrust sliding between the joins of the man's leather jack and piercing him to the heart. As the man toppled from the saddle, wrenching away Arnault's weapon as he did so, the two remaining riders abruptly broke off the engagement.

Scrambling to retrieve his sword, Arnault rolled aside to avoid being trampled as the two horsemen spurred past him, but they fled into the trees and quickly disappeared from sight, leaving the disguised Templars in the company of the three Highlanders and three dead bodies. The big red-haired leader paused long enough to shout a Gaelic taunt after their departing foes, brandishing a fist in defiance, then came over to raise a hand in greeting to Arnault and Torquil.

"The blessings of Michael be upon ye for most welcome assistance," he said. "All the more, since ye have the look of strangers—and I dinna think ye learned *that* in any monastery." He nodded toward the swords the pair were cleaning on the cloaks of two of the fallen men. "I am called Euan MacDougall, of the following of Alexander Mac-Dougall, Earl of Lorn. Who might ye be, and what brings ye to these parts?"

Arnault flicked an expectant gaze toward Torquil, who nodded amiably to their questioner.

"We've come but lately from the Holy Land," he said in a deliberate Scots accent, only slightly stretching the truth. "We are making pilgrimage to the holy monks at Iona. Who were these?" He gestured toward the bodies littering the clearing. "Nae Hieland men."

Their new acquaintance curled his lip. "Och, no. Nor Sassenach, either. Irish hobelars sent by Longshanks. Yon laddies were just a scouting party. The main force sailed up Loch Fyne and made landfall a few days ago, near Inveraray. We watched 'em start offloading troops, then hied ourselves north to report what we'd seen—but it seems *we'd* been seen. This lot overtook us just before ye arrived, thinking tae silence our tongues."

He broke off as a crackling in the underbrush heralded the arrival of Brother Ninian on his pony, leading a stray horse by the bridle rein, in addition to their own two mounts. The Columban brother's anxious expression faded when he saw his travel companions alive and unhurt.

"This is Brother Ninian from Iona," Torquil told the Mac-Dougall clansmen. "I am called Brother Andrew, in honor of Scotland's saint, but I hie from Lennox country. Brother Michael here is French, so he doesna have the Gaelic."

Euan MacDougall accepted these introductions without demur, according all three of them a broad grin.

"Weel, we canna hold *that* against him. It's no every man lucky enough to be born a Scot. But if ye care to ride with us from here, I can offer ye shelter at Dunstaffnage, in thanks for the help ye gave us—an' from there, mayhap ye can get a boat as far as Mull. We'll tarry long enough tae bury the dead; but then we're awa', to tell his lordship what we've seen."

"Brother *Michael*?" Arnault whispered under his breath to Torquil later, as they helped dig three shallow graves. "You've given me a name with high aspirations."

"But fitting," Brother Ninian returned, "since we are about *Cra-gheal*'s business."

Riding with the MacDougall men, nightfall overtook them before they reached the other side of the Pass of Brander. They camped within sight of the peak of Ben Cruachan and pressed on early the next morning, hoping to make the castle at Dunstaffnage before dark. At the western end of the pass, near the headwaters of Loch Etive, they encountered a much larger contingent of mounted MacDougall men who, after a rapid exchange in Gaelic, rode off south to pick up the trail of the Irish mercenary force. The three pilgrims and their MacDougall escort continued on toward the castle under skies that promised more than a hint of rain.

The Earl of Lorn was not at home, having ridden south to investigate reports of English warships off Seil. In his absence, the three travelers were received by the captain of the castle garrison, who saw to it that they were suitably lodged among MacDougall's chief retainers. When Torquil inquired about sea transport to Mull, he was told that the captain of a galley anchored under the lee of the castle might be willing to accept their hire. The captain in question proved sufficiently contemptuous of English seamanship to accept the gold Torquil offered him, and it was agreed that they would set out the next day on the first outbound tide. Since the vessel was unfit for horse transport, Euan made arrangements for their mounts to be stabled at the castle until they returned.

"An' if ye shouldna come back," he said cheerily, before they retired for the night, "the beasts are worth more than they'll eat."

As the three of them lay down to sleep that night, their one remaining worry was the weather.

That anxiety proved well founded when a storm blew in during the night, bringing with it heavy squalls of hard rain. By first light, the clouds had cleared, but the waters out in the Firth of Lorn were wild, whipped into foamy peaks by strong winds from the west.

"I think we may be in for a rough passage," Arnault remarked with misgivings as they made their way down to the shore, provisioned with bread and cheese and several stone bottles of ale for their journey, and both knights carrying their swords.

The galley was still secured at her moorings, but the captain and several of his crew were pacing the beach with dour expressions on their faces. As soon as he caught sight of his three passengers, the captain came to meet them.

"We canna sail until the wind changes," he told Torquil. "Nae for gold or sil'er. Even rowin' with all our might, we couldna fight this gale."

Torquil exchanged sour glances with Arnault and Brother Ninian.

"How long do you reckon this will last?" he asked.

The captain shrugged. "I canna say. The wind and the sea have their own ways. Only a fool tries to fight them."

Arnault suppressed a vexed sigh. "I suppose we've no choice, then, but to wait until the weather takes a better turn," he said quietly.

"Not necessarily," Ninian said. "This errand of ours is no light matter. Perhaps there is something to be gained by asking aid of a higher authority." He turned to the ship's captain. "Stay by your vessel," he instructed. "I think you will have your fair wind before much longer."

"Do you know something that we don't?" Torquil asked curiously, when the captain had departed with a shrug.

"Columba has brought us this far," Ninian said calmly. "By his favor, we shall complete this journey in good time."

Beckoning the pair to accompany him, he set off along the beach. Sensing that there was more than caprice in the Columban brother's actions, Arnault signed for Torquil not to speak as they followed after him. Ninian strolled along the shoreline in what seemed a leisurely fashion, stooping now and again to pick up and examine some of the pebbles that strewed the sand. In a little while, he had collected four smooth stones of sea-polished quartz and a stick of driftwood peeled white by the surf.

Taking these items with him, he led the way to a flat, firm stretch of sand at the edge of the tide line. The Templars watched in silence from a few feet away as he squatted down and used the stick of driftwood to draw a circle in the sand, little larger than a man's head. To this he added two intersecting lines, quartering the circle with the sign of the cross.

Signing himself with the same symbol, he then struck a casual posture of supplication, face uplifted, open palms turned to the sky.

"O great Columba," he said quietly, "is it truly your will that we should be stranded here on this shore, when our hearts are longing for the counsel of your house? Surely it is no hard thing for you to obtain for us God's favor, so that He send us fair winds to speed us on our way."

The Templars were startled to hear Ninian address his spiritual patron in such familiar, almost reproachful terms. At the same time, however, such informality bespoke the close personal affinities that evidently existed between Ninian and the saint of his house, in defiance of time or space. Exchanging glances, they waited with interest to see how he planned to proceed from here.

Humming to himself, the Columban brother next took the four smooth stones he had gathered and placed one at each of the cardinal points of the circle he had drawn. Having done this, he again turned his palms upward in supplication and raised his eyes heavenward, intoning softly:

"Bless to me, O God, the four elements.
Bless to me, O God, the four quarters of the sky.
Bless to me, O God, the four winds.
Bid those that hinder me be still,
And those that favor me awake."

With these words, he reached out and transposed the stones resting at the east and west points of the circle.

"As the world turns, so turns the wheel of the sky," he murmured. "As the sky turns, so turn the winds under the sky."

He remained crouching there with head bowed and eyes closed, in an attitude of prayerful repose. Amid the ceaseless roll of the waves and the screech of wheeling gulls, a stillness slowly built, during which everything around them seemed to hold its breath.

Then, after what seemed a long, drawn-out wait, Arnault realized that the strong winds out of the west were starting to abate. Each successive gust was lighter than the last, until even the last breeze subsided into gentle stillness. As that calm settled over the beach, the waves smoothed themselves out until the sea was bright and level as a mirror reflecting the sky.

Then, just as gently, as Arnault glanced at Torquil in wonder, a new wind arose out of the east. The first they felt of it was like a feather brush past their cheeks. The breeze gathered strength, bringing with it the scent of heather and gorse from the surrounding cliff tops.

As it continued to build, Ninian lifted his head and opened his arms wide in a gesture embracing the sea and the sky, his eyes alight with praise and pleasure. Then, lowering his arms, he began to remove the stones from their settings, each with an accompanying phrase of thanksgiving.

"Thanks be to thee, Michael of the Angels, and thanks be to thee, Bride of the blessings. Thanks be to thee, Mary mild, and thanks be to thee, Columba of the rock. Thanks be to thee, in heaven above and earth below, for thy words in the ear of the Shepherd of my heart."

When all of the stones had been removed from their ceremonial alignment and tossed, one by one, back into the sea, the Columban brother rose jerkily from his crouch and clapped his hands three times, scuttling backward then as the next wave rolled high enough to smooth away the lines in the sand. He seemed quite oblivious to the looks of wonder on the faces of his companions as he rejoined them.

"We'd best get back to the boat," he said. "Our captain will be eager to sail, and our crossing now should be swift and sure."

Chapter Eighteen

I<small>N LESS THAN THREE HOURS' TIME, THE SHIP WAS NOSING THE</small> shingled beach on the south shore of Mull. As its three passengers waded ashore, after first helping turn the bow back to sea, Arnault was still marveling at the turn of nature wrought in response to Ninian's prayerful appeal. Such eloquent demonstrations of Columba's provident care for his flock encouraged Arnault to believe that the saint of Iona would not be deaf to their own petitions. He looked forward more keenly than ever to meeting Ninian's superior, Abbot Fingon.

First, however, the three of them must cross the width of the island's south end on foot. Ninian had already warned them that the terrain between here and Iona itself was as rugged as any they had encountered so far. The only habitation nearby was a handful of crofters' huts. The only farm beasts to be seen were a motley scattering of sheep, a few scraggy cows, and one swaybacked plow pony.

"It's been a while since we last had to carry our gear on our backs," Torquil observed, hefting his share of the provisions under his cloak, behind his sword.

"Just be glad we left the armor back at Scone," Arnault replied. He slid his own sword between his back and the pack he already wore, shifting the weight more comfortably as he glanced at Brother Ninian. "Which way?"

Ninian gestured behind him, where a thin track no wider than a game trail disappeared amid spring-green vistas of bracken and gorse.

"As you see. We have perhaps three or four hours of daylight left."

"Then I suggest," said Arnault, "that we see how much of the trail we can put behind us before nightfall."

The trail in question was little more than a rugged footpath. During their first afternoon's march, they saw no other living creatures save for a pair of hawks on the hunt and a scattering of wild sheep roaming over the gorse hills that flanked them on either hand. They camped in the open that night, eating sparsely of their travel fare and rolling up in their cloaks by the side of a shallow, peat-bottomed burn. Early next morning they set off again, hoping to reach the halfway point of their journey before the end of the day.

The trail they were following cut a crooked swath through several interconnected valleys. Their packs seemed to grow heavier as they trudged through the bracken. Toward the middle of the afternoon, they caught sight of two fat ponies with wicker panniers across their backs, browsing lazily on a patch of sparse, wind-flattened grass. Beyond the ponies stretched a brown slash of peat bog, where two white-clad men with tonsures like Ninian's were industriously cutting peat with long-handled implements, robes kilted up between their legs.

"Ah, now *there's* happy happenstance," Ninian said, waving an arm to attract their attention. *"Se do bheatha!"* he called out.

The two monks looked up, faces splitting in delighted grins at the sight of Ninian.

"Go mbeannai Dia dhut!" one of them called back.

Tossing their cutting tools onto the embankment, they scrambled up to hurry toward the new arrivals. One of them was dark-haired and wiry, the other a match for Torquil in height and build, but fairer haired. Their legs and arms were muddy, their habits also sporting peaty smears, but there could be no doubt that they were brethren of Ninian's community, as confirmed by their Gaelic chatter and the hearty embraces the three exchanged before Ninian shifted to Latin to make mutual introductions.

"This is Brother Fionn, and this is Brother Ciaran," he declared, indicating first the dark-haired brother, then his fair, big-boned companion. "They came across to Mull two days ago to gather fuel. If we help them load up the ponies, we can all travel back to Iona together."

The prospect of company and an end to their journey more than made up for the prospect of a few hours spent cutting and stacking peat turfs. Shedding their cloaks and packs, the two knights set to work contentedly beside Ninian and the other two monks. Long before dusk, the ponies' panniers were full to capacity.

"There's a bothy about a mile west of here," Brother Fionn announced, as they washed off the worst of the mud in a narrow rivulet feeding into a burn downhill. "We can sleep there tonight under cover, then move on to Iona in the morning."

The bothy was only a rough freestone structure, but it provided welcome shelter from the chill winds that blew up with the setting of the sun. Once the ponies had been watered and turned out to graze, and a fire had been lit, initial conversation between Ninian and his fellow monks was concerned primarily with news of their little community. Cooking oat porridge over the fire in a leather bag, speaking of such small matters as the taking of fish and the herding of flocks, the Columban brothers seemed blessedly far removed from the dark complexities of war and politics.

And yet, it soon became clear that they were not so isolated as they seemed, when Brother Fionn moved on from a disquisition on the making of parchment to ask for news of John Balliol's war against Edward of England. Surprisingly, the monks of Iona had even heard reports of the fate of Berwick, and were anxious on behalf of the people of the other east coast burghs. When Torquil described the inglorious defeat of the Scottish host at Dunbar, Brother Ciaran shook his shaggy blond head in dismay.

"We Scots have not studied war as the English have done," he remarked. "If Scotland is to retain her independence, our people will have to make up in faith and fervor what we lack in experience."

"Then you are not opposed to the idea of fighting?" Arnault asked.

"Not if the cause is just," said Brother Fionn. "In slaughtering the people of Berwick, Edward has proved himself a tyrant without conscience. To allow an evil man to continue to do evil at the cost of innocent blood is a thing which cannot be allowed."

"Indeed," Ciaran put in. "As our Lord's servants on earth, we must be ready to defend the lives of others as faithfully as we must be willing to sacrifice our own."

The mention of sacrifice reminded Arnault once again of the mysterious Uncrowned King of the prophecy, and it seemed to him increasingly likely that, in the end, this capacity for self-sacrifice might well be the measure between victory and defeat.

Their little party made good speed the next day, coming into sight of Iona under the rose-gold skies of dusk. The half-mile ribbon of water that separated Columba's isle from the Isle of Mull was calm as a lake, softly reflecting the low, gray cluster of monastic buildings nestled against the island's gentle hills. When Brother Fionn went down to the waterside and shouted, his voice seemed to reverberate like the peal of a bell across the distance. Very shortly, a flat-bottomed boat could be seen putting out from the opposite shore, trailing a V of ripples, two white-robed figures at its oars.

In the time it took to unload the ponies and turn them loose to graze, the little boat had made the crossing. Leaving Brothers Fionn and Ciaran to stack the newly cut peat turfs under a lean-to for drying, Ninian and his strong-backed Templar companions made short work of loading several panniers of previously dried peat into the boat for the first trip back. When the three of them had also climbed aboard, Ninian and Torquil taking the oars as they started back across, Arnault was struck by the feeling that they were leaving the material world behind, in favor of a place where time held no sway. The impression was only illusory, he knew; yet there was something strangely durable about the simple cluster of buildings growing larger against the shoreline, as if the stones themselves had been endowed with some measure of the spirit of the community's founder.

The little ferry grounded smoothly on pebbly shingle, to be taken in hand by a pair of fresh-faced novices, neither of them above twenty. As the three passengers splashed ashore, carrying their belongings, a further gaggle of novices joined the first two and began offloading the cargo of turf, some of them cheerfully vying for the privilege of taking the ferry back for its second run while others cast curious but friendly glances at the two sword-bearing men in Augustinian habit who had come with Ninian.

Up the slope from the pebbly beach, a waist-high free-stone wall encompassed the monastic buildings, also including a burial ground adjacent to the church, where lay many of the ancient kings of Alba. In the fields beyond the enclosure, sheep and cattle were placidly grazing in the gathering dusk. As Ninian began leading his companions up toward the abbey complex, there came the chiming of a hand bell from before the abbey church, calling the community to evening prayer.

From conversations of the past week, the Templars had gathered that the full Iona community numbered about a score, with twelve fully vowed brothers like Ninian, who made up the seniors of the order, and nearly that many novices in various stages of formation, all under the governance of Abbot Fingon, their superior. Most of them seemed to be congregating before the abbey church as Ninian led his companions toward the sound of the bell. The church beyond was gracefully proportioned, without any of the costly embellishments that Jay had lavished on the chapel at Balantrodoch.

The abbot himself proved to be the ringer of the bell, and handed it off to another smiling, white-robed brother before coming forward to greet them. He was a spare, white-haired figure of a man with a broad, chiseled brow and far-seeing blue eyes. Though his lean frame was slightly stooped with age and years of study, his voice still had the ringing clarity of youth as he and Ninian exchanged an embrace and the monastic kiss of peace.

"Welcome back, my son!" he exclaimed warmly. "We have been praying every day for your safe return. Have you been successful in your quest?"

Ninian inclined his head, indicating his black-cloaked companions with the sweep of an arm.

"I have, Father Abbot. Despite their misleading attire, these are knights of *Cra-gheal*: Frère Arnault de Saint Clair and Frère Torquil Lennox, Knights of the Temple. They have news of grave concern regarding the Stone of Destiny—and questions that need to be answered."

Abbot Fingon bestowed his greeting on the two Templars, in their turn, keenly surveying their faces as he took their hands in his.

"You are most welcome to this house, my brothers. Clearly, we have much to say to one another. Our first duty, however, is to our Lord. It is the hour of Vespers. If the two of you would be pleased to join us, I promise there will be ample time later for us to speak of our common concerns. Please. Come."

Turning to enter the church, they passed close beside a ringed stone cross, nearly twice the height of a man, and exquisitely carved. The upper portion of the cross bore a scene from the Last Supper, while the longer lower portion depicted Jesus stilling the storm at sea; the arms to either side were decorated with an intricate knotwork design that put Arnault in mind of Irish manuscripts he had seen in the library of an abbey in Brittany.

Inside the church, the air smelled not of incense but of delicate floral offerings, underlaid with the scent of beeswax. Garlands of greenery were swagged across the upper reaches of the simple Rood screen that stood before the choir, and the white-draped altar beyond the screen was lit by stubby candles of a pale, creamy gold, which gave off the mingled fragrances of heather and thyme and honey as they burned and gave the church the air of an ancient shrine.

As Arnault and Torquil took places amid the other members of the community, to either side of Ninian, Abbot Fingon moved into the center of the choir. Lifting his hands in an attitude of praise, he all but sang a graceful bidding antiphon in Gaelic that Torquil clearly understood, then shifted into the Latin versicles of the opening litany without missing a beat. The answering harmony of the monks' sung responses was arresting in its beauty.

The office proceeded along lines that were generally familiar to the two Templars, but the Columban brothers tended to revert to the Gaelic for their hymns, and sometimes even the prayers were interwoven with poignant invocations from Celtic tradition, recalling Ninian's prayer that had calmed the wind.

But the transitions from Latin to the Gaelic and back again were virtually seamless, their versatility finally underscored yet again as the monks segued into the ancient and hauntingly beautiful *Phos hilarion,* praising God in the setting of the sun and the gracious radiance of the Vesper light, which symbolized God's abiding presence through the night to come. In the interweaving of these many strands of spiritual tradition, as vivid as the knotwork adorning many a page of precious psalter or Gospel illuminated by the great abbey scriptoria of the Celtic lands, Arnault found himself profoundly moved, the harmonies awakening answering resonances from the depth of his own spirit.

The simple evening meal that followed in the abbey's refectory was eaten in contemplative silence. The prevailing mood was one of tranquillity and abiding joy. After a final grace had been offered, while the boards were being cleared, Abbot Fingon invited his Templar guests to join him in his writing room, signing for Ninian to accompany them as he led them to a small whitewashed chamber on the east side of the cloister court.

Beside a cheery hearth, Fingon listened intently as the two Templars acquainted him with the background of their mission and described their examination of the Stone in meticulous detail. When Arnault produced the Breastplate, the abbot's gaze took on a thoughtfulness that reflected both profound respect and keen discernment.

"A curious and apt juxtaposition," he said. "These two gifts of heaven—the Stone and the Breastplate—have always existed for the same purpose: to bring the Light of the Divine within the reach of mortal men. With God's help, it may well be that we may use that common purpose to aid us in our understanding of His will."

When Arnault had related the prophecy concerning the Uncrowned King, the abbot gestured for silence and closed his eyes, repeating the words to himself as he committed them to memory. Having done so, he lapsed into a thoughtful reverie, fingering a wooden neck cross he wore on a leather cord.

"The realm has fallen into the hands of an apostate," he mused. "Someone close to the throne, it seems—and we must not assume that it is the king himself—has turned his back on the faith of Columba."

"Why do you say it could not be John Balliol?" Torquil asked.

"Because, given the diminished state of the Stone of Destiny, it is he who has most suffered, by having failed to receive the divine mandate that should have accompanied his enthronement."

"An excellent point," Arnault agreed. "But if not Balliol, then who?"

"Bear with me," Fingon replied. "The possibility we must first consider—based on your vision, Brother Torquil—is whether the extinction of the Canmore dynasty was the opening gambit in a campaign to reinstitute the darker aspects of the old pagan faiths. From the quelling of the Stone of Destiny, we may infer that this campaign has largely succeeded. Balliol himself may be only a tool. But if, on some level, Scotland is now being ruled in accordance with pagan traditions, the repercussions could be very serious, indeed."

"In what way?" Arnault asked.

Abbot Fingon's visage grew graver still. "A return to the old ways means a return to *all* the old ways," he said grimly. "In the days of the old religions, before the coming of Columba and his followers, the king was ritually wedded to the land. This was done in several ways, according to the region. In some of the Celtic lands, this marriage was consummated by union with a mare, which then was ritually slaughtered. But the shedding of blood remained a common thread—and sometimes, even by the time of the Romans, the blood offering was that of the king himself, or that of a suitable, ritually designated substitute."

Torquil was nodding as the abbot spoke, obviously aware of the tradition, and Arnault thought he recalled hearing references to similar practices in his native Brittany.

"The coming of Christianity mostly put a stop to this," Abbot Fingon went on. "In Scotland, when her kings embraced Christianity, Christ Himself became the sacrificial victim whose blood sustains the land and its people. The Stone of Destiny was given, through Columba, not just as a symbol of this union, but as the material vessel through which such sacramental virtue was carried over from one monarch to the next."

"In other words," Arnault said slowly, "in terms of kingship as well as the redemption of mankind, the divine sacrifice of Christ made all other sacrifices unnecessary."

Abbot Fingon nodded. "That is correct—as long as the bond between the earthly monarch and his divine surrogate was maintained through a properly constituted line of succession. At the death of one monarch, the power reverted to the Stone until the enthronement of his legitimate successor.

"Now, however, it appears that the link between the Stone and the monarchy has been broken, through at least two acts of regicide. So it may be that only another sacrifice, in imitation of Christ, will repair the damage and restore the Stone's life-giving power. This may simply mean a death in battle. I hesitate to make too close a connection here, between ancient practices and what most would find incompatible with our Christian faith, but we are speaking here of a very primal link between king and land."

"*Only blood may pay the ransom price,*" Torquil quoted thoughtfully. "That does seem to point to an oblation of atonement."

"The blood of the Uncrowned King?" Arnault ventured.

"So it would appear," Fingon replied.

"But—who is he, and how are we to find him?"

"Therein lies our first difficulty," Fingon said. "It would seem that John Balliol has not proven—for whatever reason—a suitable receptacle for the sacred kingship. By extension, I should point out that this makes his son likewise unacceptable."

"But Balliol was adjudged the most direct in descent from the Canmores," Arnault pointed out.

"The most senior—yes," Fingon replied. "But the law of primogeniture—the precept which says that a king must be succeeded by his eldest son—is a relatively recent innovation in Scotland. In earlier times, when the king was merely the 'chief of chiefs'—and the chiefs of many clans are still determined in this way—the king was elected from amongst a group of potential candidates of royal or chiefly descent, within a specified degree of kinship with the previous king or chief, known as the *derbfine*. The selection of John Balliol from among the other contenders reflects this tradition, in part."

Arnault nodded his understanding as Fingon went on. It had taken Luc and Torquil hours, that winter at Balantrodoch, to explain the concept to him.

"The individual thus elected was known as the *tanist*," Fingon said. "And in pre-Christian times, the *tanist* often secured his claim to the throne by killing off his political rivals as a sacrifice to the gods. Nowadays, in general, the *tanist* is simply the designated heir, who may or may not be the chief's eldest son.

"Taking all these precedents into account, and adding in the apparent importance of your Uncrowned King, it seems to me that if the sovereignty of Scotland is to be restored, this ancient king sacrifice of the *tanist*—the Uncrowned King—must be reenacted—but it must be done in a Christian way."

Arnault drew a deep breath as he realized what he thought Abbot Fingon was proposing.

"Are you saying that, instead of killing his rivals, this Uncrowned King we are looking for must be prepared to offer *himself* in sacrifice, in imitation of Christ?"

"In some sense, yes; that is my impression," Fingon agreed. "If the demands of the past and the needs of the present are to be reconciled, the old pre-Christian institutions must be redefined in spiritual terms."

"Suggesting that there may exist some spiritual *derbfine*," Torquil ventured, "from whose ranks a *tanist* will arise to assume the mantle of the Uncrowned King, in fulfillment of the prophecy."

"The notion of a spiritual *derbfine* is apt," Fingon agreed, "but it might be more accurate to say that this *tanist* will be *called forth*, in the manner of one being called to the priesthood. And of course, in a spiritual sense, a priest offers himself on the altar, along with Christ, every time he celebrates the Mass.

"But I fear your Uncrowned King may be called upon to make a more literal sacrifice as well as one of spirit—*only blood may pay the ransom price.* And only after that sacrifice has been offered and accepted will the Stone of Destiny be restored to full power for the benefit of *his* successors— who, again, must be found amid whatever *derbfine* emerges from which to reestablish the royal succession."

Momentarily struck speechless by the abbot's implications, Arnault could only gaze at him in disbelief. Not for several seconds did he summon sufficient composure to glance at Torquil, who appeared likewise overwhelmed.

"This will require careful contemplation," Arnault said slowly. "And even if what you say is true, there are practical considerations that must be addressed. Edward of England is ravaging Scotland even as we speak—and whether he may be a cause of what we believe to be happening, or is only reaping its benefits, the fact remains that if he succeeds in conquering Scotland, it may not be possible to salvage her sovereignty. We must find and identify this Uncrowned King before it's too late."

"I agree," Fingon said. "But if the Uncrowned King is to give himself to martyrdom, he must know what he is doing and why. He must be a willing sacrifice."

Arnault briefly closed his eyes, still staggered by the enormity of what apparently faced them.

"Father Abbot," he whispered, "I have no idea where to begin. I am a Templar, and this is not my land. But the Temple—the Inner Temple, that is—*does* have concerns regarding the Stone of Destiny, for it is meant to serve as cornerstone of the Fifth Temple, the New Jerusalem—surely, in some spiritual sense rather than literal. But the Stone itself—or the virtue it is meant to contain—is tied up with the Scottish succession. And for that reason, it is fitting that the Temple assist in resolving the earthly kingship of this realm—but, how?"

"For that," Ninian said, speaking at last, "we may be able to provide some guidance, for it is clear that we, like the Temple, have a decisive part to play in what is unfolding. Why else would *Cra-gheal* have instructed me to seek you out, if we were not intended to assist one another in resolving this?"

Abbot Fingon slowly nodded, digesting this declaration.

"I agree," he finally said. "And it seems to me that, under the circumstances, we may be justified in begging the boon of clarification from Columba himself. But it must be done in the proper spirit, and in the proper time." He glanced up at Arnault and Torquil. "Such things are best attempted at the time of the full moon, when all holy influences of nature can be marshaled in support of our prayers and supplications. The moon is now a week on the wane. Would you be willing to wait until the cycle turns again?"

The two Templars traded glances, but there could be no question of their answer.

"We will wait," Arnault agreed. For he could not see how they dared do otherwise.

Chapter Nineteen

THE THREE WEEKS THAT FOLLOWED SEEMED TO REINFORCE what Arnault had sensed as they rowed across from Mull: that Iona was somehow set apart from the outside world and the affairs of men. Abbot Fingon, observing how the Templars' borrowed black robes made them stand out from the rest of his flock, soon gave leave for the pair to adopt his own order's white robes, intending thereby to approximate the more familiar Templar habits they had left behind at Scone; but to Arnault it seemed that by putting on the habit of the Columbans, he was also absorbing some of the spirituality of their community, bringing himself into tune with the heartbeat of the land and being drawn more deeply into its rhythm. It made him no less a Templar; in fact, it made him more.

Every morning, just after the office of Prime, he walked down to the beach where Columba first had landed and stood there alone, watching the passing clouds reflected in the changing surface of the sea, as if they could show him the shape of things to come. The weather was halcyon, and yet in his heart of hearts, he knew it was only the calm before a storm. He sensed that once he and Torquil left the island, they would be plunging into the midst of a hurricane.

He spent some of his time meditating on the subject of the Fifth Temple, trying to deepen his understanding of its significance. Hitherto, the building of the Temple had always seemed to him an abstract accomplishment, something reserved for the future. Now he began to envision that Temple of the New Jerusalem as a tabernacle of many doors, suspended midway between heaven and earth. Like Jacob's Ladder, its purpose was to bridge an infinitude of space and time, so that pilgrim souls hungering for the Light might travel freely between the earthly realm and the divine.

The monks of Iona, like their house itself, seemed likewise to belong in a world set apart. Wearing their habit, Arnault took every opportunity to familiarize himself with their forms of worship, encouraging Torquil to do the same. While the Columban brothers conformed to a monastic rule that was not unlike the one with which the Templars were familiar, based on Cistercian and Benedictine usage, their meditations and spiritual disciplines and even the liturgies they held in common with the rest of the Church Universal all breathed an air of liberation. To Arnault, now breathing that same air, it somehow seemed that Ninian and Fingon and their fellow monks were gently unbinding things that were too tightly bound elsewhere in the world.

The day of the full moon was spent much as the days leading up to it, moving in the abbey's rhythm of daily prayer and praise and intercession, but also fasting in preparation for the night's work. After Mass, at which they all received Communion, while Ninian and Abbot Fingon withdrew to the seclusion of their cells and Torquil lingered a while in the serenity of the abbey church, Arnault paid a last visit to his favorite spot on Columba's beach. Down near the waterline, searching among the sea-polished stones, he chose a smooth pebble of the green and white marble that was unique to Iona. Closing his eyes, he fingered it lightly, acquainting himself by touch with its shape and grain.

"Kindly Columba, father and brother," he said softly, having learned from Brother Ninian that the Celtic saint did not turn away from the familiar pleas of family, "we need your favor on this night's work. You adopted this land as I have done. Now that land is in danger. I know that God's hand on earth works through men—and many years ago, I gave myself to be His instrument. I ask that tonight you grace us with your counsel, that I may learn how I and my brethren are to proceed. By the Son of the Mary of graces I ask this, by James and by John the beloved, by Michael *Cra-gheal*, of the bright-brilliant blades . . . Amen."

Just before dusk, the community gathered for Vespers, as was their usual wont. Afterward, instead of dismissing them to the evening meal, Abbot Fingon called Ninian and the two Templars forward and blessed them, in a ripple of Gaelic invocation of which Arnault caught only a few words. Then the abbot handed each of them a cup of glazed clay in which burned a votive candle, previously lit from the Presence lamp during the *Phos hilarion*. A fourth one he took for himself, before tucking a small flagon of holy water into the bosom of his habit and leading his three companions quietly from the church, heading toward Columba's mound. The rest of the community remained in the church to keep vigil on behalf of the four, softly chanting a litany of invocations to Christ and Mary and Columba and Bride and a host of other Celtic intercessors.

The evening was mild and clear, the face of the sea like glass, the first stars just beginning to appear. At the summit of the mound, on the site of Columba's cell, lay a smooth, flat boulder about two feet across, its center hollowed and smoothed, sheened with a pool of rainwater, pure and still. The sky to the west bore a lingering shimmer of daylight. To the east, the rugged hills of Mull were haloed with a silvery luminance that heralded the rising of the moon.

After bidding them to put aside their shoes, Abbot Fingon stationed himself on the east side of the stone, mutely signing for his companions to take their appointed places. Arnault moved to the west side of the stone, reverently donning the High Priest's Breastplate and also drawing from out of his white Columban habit the *keekstane* given him by Brother Ninian at Scone. Torquil and Ninian posted themselves to north and south.

Following Fingon's example, they placed their lamps before them on the level surface of the rock, bracketing the wash of rainwater between the four points of a cross. When this had been done, Abbot Fingon blessed himself and each of his companions with the sign of the cross, to the accompaniment of a quadri-partite invocation, spoken in the Latin of monastic usage, for Arnault's sake, but phrased with the imagery of its Celtic origins:

"In name of Michael of the White Steed,
Hide us under your shield
And defend us with your bright-brilliant blade.

"In name of Mary the generous,
Mother of the Shepherd of Flocks,
Enfold us in the mantle of the power of your Son.

"In name of Bride of many blessings, handmaid of the hearth,
Sing to us of your Nurseling,
That His name in our ears will open our hearts.

"In name of Columba the just and potent, shepherd of souls,
Guide us to your vision
And reveal what is hidden."

So saying, he unstopped the flagon of holy water, tipping a brief splash into the pool of rainwater. As ripples briefly disturbed the mirror surface, he said softly:

"Thou Michael *Cra-gheal*, Ranger of the Heavens, sanctify to us this water, fallen from heaven as the gentle rain."

A second splash of holy water followed the first, accompanied by a further blessing.

"Thou Mary tender-fair, Mother of the Lamb, sanctify to us this water, tears of the stars.

"Thou Bride, the foster mother, tranquil of the kine," he continued, letting a third measure of holy water fall, "sanctify to us this water, dew of the clouds.

"Thou Columba the benign, apostle of sea and shore," he concluded, emptying out the last of the flagon, "sanctify to us this water, mirror of heaven."

He set the empty flask aside, and all four of them waited in silence as the ripples in the pool subsided, leaving the rainwater pool once again as clear and as smooth as a pane of glass.

Slowly the white rim of the moon appeared above the eastern hills. Rising higher, it patterned the sea with silver dapples. As its lower rim cleared the skyline, Fingon turned to face it squarely, stretching forth his arms in a wide embrace.

> *"Hail unto thee, Mother of the stars,*
> *Fosterling of the Sun,*
> *Jewel of guidance in the night,*
> *Thou fair lamp of grace and beauty!"*

As he spoke, a soft wash of luminance spilled across the mound, touching their robes to silver. Its brilliance quickened the shallow pool of rainwater, transforming the surface into an iridescent mirror.

Beyond any doubt, Arnault sensed the sudden upwelling of power, rising from the pool to a cathedral arch above their heads. It was as if the small lights of their votive candles were become the pediments of four ascendant ribs supporting a soaring vault. The very air became luminous, faintly crackling with invisible energy. A wind stirred amid the surrounding rocks, bringing with it an elusive hint of fragrance and a sense of Presence immanently near.

With one accord, they turned their faces to the wind, Abbot Fingon holding out his hands in an attitude of supplication that recalled Ninian's gesture on the beach at Dunstaffnage.

"Kindly Columba, father and brother," he said in an almost conversational tone, "you know what troubles us. Will you not show yourself, that we may seek your counsel, as a wise teacher and shepherd of the heart?"

The fragrant wind lifted, brushing across the surface of the pool. The moon's bright-minted image dissolved in a haze of ripples. Instinctively Arnault leaned closer, the *keek-stane* closed in his right hand, waiting for the disturbance to subside. As the surface quieted, he caught his breath, for the likeness resolving before his eyes was no longer that of the moon, but of a man's face.

It was a striking countenance, sparse of flesh but graceful of mien, its innate asceticism gentled by a gleam of lively intelligence shining forth from the pale gaze. And it seemed no mere illusion, but a living face, as subtle and expressive as those of the men watching with him. Not for an instant could Arnault doubt that this image was, indeed, a vision meant to convey the real presence of the saint they had invited to be present among them. Though the chiseled lips did not move, he seemed to hear a voice that was not a voice, speaking to his soul.

My Stone has need of your care, Knight of Cra-gheal, it said.

"I know that, Father Columba," Arnault whispered aloud. "I have sought the Stone and sensed its sickness, but I seek guidance concerning an Uncrowned King, by whom it can be brought back to health."

A faint hint of a smile curved one corner of the saint's expressive mouth.

And for whose glory do you seek him, Knight of Cragheal? the saint asked.

"For the glory of the Threefold One, He Who is Chief of Chiefs," Arnault said boldly, employing the Celtic imagery he had absorbed in the past weeks, in the company of Ninian and the other Columbans. "And my Order's motto—the motto of *Cra-gheal*'s Order—likewise declares our service to God's glory. *Non nobis, Domine* . . .

"However worldly that Order's external purpose," he went on, "its inner duty is to erect the Fifth Temple, to the glory of God's holy name—for which the Stone of Destiny is to become the cornerstone, and Scotland its foundation. I am given to understand that the success of this mission stands or falls by Scotland's freedom, which is bound up with the waning power of the Stone—and neither can be restored save by the ransom of the Uncrowned King. I seek some sign by which to find him."

Caught up in the passion of his appeal, it was not until he had finished speaking that he became aware of a sensation of warmth radiating from the Breastplate. A rainbow aura emanated from the jewels, not crackling with energy as it had at Scone, but gently shimmering as it mingled with the silent moonlight. Amid the silence, Abbot Fingon softly spoke, not in pleading but in observation.

"The Magi were given the sign of the star to show them the way to Bethlehem," he said. "Were they not also looking for an Uncrowned King?"

The stern face in the mirrored rainwater smiled faintly.

My sons are wise—both my sons of Iona and those by adoption.

His luminous gaze returned to Arnault. *Know that he who is to be sacrificed in imitation of our Lord shares these traits in common with his Master: He will be a man of sorrows, obscure in his origins and rejected of other men.*

The saint's image was beginning to dissolve into the moonlight. Arnault leaned forward, the better to hear Columba's parting words.

Where the Stone is, there also will he be found. He shall accompany the Stone into darkness, and by him shall it be restored, to be that cornerstone upon which depend both an earthly kingdom and the New Jerusalem. Soon he shall make himself known—and you shall instruct him in his destiny.

Chapter Twenty

I HAD NOT THOUGHT IT POSSIBLE THAT EVEN A PUPPET KING could be so spineless," the younger John Comyn muttered to his father, the Lord of Badenoch. "Nor can I decide which canker gnaws worse in my belly: the arrogance of the English dogs, or Balliol's inability to stand and fight like a man."

The two were standing on the heights above the watch fires that marked the encampment of the Scottish feudal host, which lay sprawled before them among the forested hills and glens of the Grampian countryside. It was well past midnight. Behind them, ghostly dim under the light of a waning moon, lay a circle of standing stones known locally as Sunhoney—a name of benign association that did not at all reflect its ancient and dark affinities. It was for this, rather than for any strategic advantage, that the army had been led here at the elder Comyn's urging.

Following the rout at Dunbar, King John Balliol had abandoned his base at Haddington and withdrawn his forces

to the central Highlands. They had been on the move now
for weeks. Caught between vanity and fear, the king vacil-
lated daily between the two extremes, one moment blustering, the next moment quaking. So far, he had shown no gift
for strategy and even less for leadership, with no apparent
intention other than to keep as much distance as possible between his army and the English.

Now he was preparing to sue for peace, and to throw himself and his kingdom on the mercy of Edward of England.
King Edward, for his part, seemed content to lurk in mid-
Lothian, consolidating his hold over the east coast burghs in
a leisurely fashion.

"John Balliol is as worthless as an empty sheep's bladder
flapping in the wind," Comyn agreed, contempt edging his
voice. "If he will not play the part of a king, then he deserves
nothing better than to be stripped naked and flung onto a
dung heap. If he fails us, I will give the goddess his bones to
pick beside those of the Templars." His voice cracked suddenly, flaring into flint-edged anger.

"Treacherous, foreign-born knaves! They will pay, and
pay heavily for this latest outrage!"

John Comyn glanced sharply at his father, but the vehemence of the other's outburst warned that comment would
be ill-advised.

"The Master of England has taken Briochan's relics into
England," the Lord of Badenoch announced in a flat, gray
voice. "The ambitious Frère Brian de Jay is far more devi-
ous than we dreamed."

The younger Comyn gaped at this revelation. "He has
taken them to England—are you sure?"

"Would that I were not!" came the clipped reply. "The
goddess showed me in a vision—for which favor I paid
dearly! I suspected from the start that the disruption of
Briochan's resting place was no mere coincidence. I am
given to believe that his relics now lie hidden in a secret
place within the English Temple—which means that they

could not be further from our grasp if Jay had sunk them in the sea—or in a tarn by Balantrodoch, as was claimed when I first had inquiries made, regarding the disposition of the grave."

"What will you do now?" John asked.

His father's craggy face was haggard and drawn, his eyes red-rimmed with sleeplessness. Each night for the past three, he had sought communion with his dark patrons, withdrawing to the secret shelter of the ancient stones to invoke the power of the waning moon, each night offering increasingly costly sacrifice of blood and seed and soul. Only tonight had he received an answer.

"The obstacle is not insurmountable," Comyn said coldly. "We have, in our favor, the fact that the Templars very likely are not aware of our particular interests. Jay himself, however, is a most ambitious man—as evidenced by his fawning attendance on Edward at Berwick. While he may have some inkling that possession of Briochan's relics confers a potential for power, I would be willing to wager that he sees it largely as a means to further his own ambitions."

"By using pagan magic?" John asked, startled. "Surely a Christian would be profaned by dabbling in such things."

Comyn contained a disdainful smirk. "Some believe that at least a portion of the Order has been tainted by exposure to Saracen heresies—but I am less concerned with the state of Jay's soul than I am with recovering Briochan's relics. You have seen the use we make of Christian holy things; in like manner, he could profane the things we hold as sacred.

"To prevent that, I have been shown a way to force the return of Briochan's relics." Glancing behind them, Comyn drew his son closer, lowering his voice. "Jay's deputy, the Templar called John de Sautre, remains in Scotland. His brother, Robert, however, has gone south in Jay's following—and Jay has gone to Cyprus. The blood link between brothers is a powerful bond, as you know. If we can capture John de Sautre, we can work through him to get at Robert—

and *he,* in turn, can be compelled to steal back Briochan's relics and bring them to us."

The younger Comyn nodded, but his expression was doubtful. "I understand, in general, what you are proposing," he agreed, "but I would assume that this John de Sautre either rides with King Edward's advisors or has withdrawn to the main Templar preceptory at Balantrodoch—which, in addition to being strongly fortified, lies in an area now under English control."

His father raised a peremptory hand. "I do not propose to attack them in their lair, or even to penetrate the English lines. Our own position will be precarious enough in the coming weeks, if Balliol does, indeed, surrender. Edward will not fail to note our family's part in this rebellion.

"Nonetheless, the Templars present an increasingly vexing obstacle to our plans. I have learned by various means that the Temple itself apparently harbors factions in contention with one another. Some weeks ago, shortly after Berwick, two knight-brothers departed Balantrodoch for Scone, where they spent several days before departing in the company of a monk of the kindred of the cursed Columba.

"That they rode north from Scone, and in that company, leads me to believe that they may have been headed for Columba's Isle of Iona, in the west—possibly without the permission or foreknowledge of their superiors, for they left Scone in secret, having put aside Templar habit in favor of pilgrim attire. And not long after, the Master of Scotland rode out precipitously from Balantrodoch with an armed following, searching along the route they had traveled, making inquiries."

"Why should Templars go to Iona?" John said suspiciously. "And is it not a serious breach of their Rule, to put aside their Templar livery?"

"Breaches of their military discipline do not concern me!" Comyn said sharply. "And it is premature to worry that the visit of Templars to Iona could bespeak an alliance with those wielding the power of Columba. My more immediate concern is the very useful Master of Scotland, who is no longer safe in the fastness of his preceptory of Balantrodoch. Whatever the internal differences within the Templar Order, *he* holds the key to gaining access to Brian de Jay and the hiding place of Briochan's relics.

"I therefore intend to take advantage of de Sautre's foray into the west to send a contingent of our own in pursuit, to follow and ambush him and his men. Once we have taken them, we shall sacrifice those of lesser account to the goddess, and wreak such torment on de Sautre himself that he soon will be begging to do whatever we ask of him."

Sullen passion kindled in John Comyn's dark eyes.

"Let me lead them, Father!" he whispered. "I know what to do. I swear to you that I will make these Templars howl for the mercy of death!"

The elder Comyn shook his head. "Would that I could give you that satisfaction. But we both are needed here, to prop up our faltering puppet king and to try to hold together some semblance of an army. If Balliol is supplanted only to be replaced by Edward, our goal is no nearer than it was. My lieutenant Seward shall pursue the ambush, and Torgon shall go with him. He is the true servant of the goddess, and knows how to draw upon her power at need. Together they will obtain what we want, or die themselves in the attempt."

John de Sautre had nothing but jaundiced contempt for Scotland and its people. As far as he was concerned, the whole country was little more than a barbarous wilderness, a wasteland of gloomy forests, sullen lochs, and midge-in-fested bogs. Even the purple heather that covered the hill-tops in the summertime seemed garish and unnatural to his eye, like a perennial infestation of plague.

His dislike was particularly virulent as he watched his men break up their encampment on the marge of Loch Tay. The morning air was dank and cold, and a mist lay heavy on the water. Since leaving Balantrodoch, every step of the way had been hampered by bad roads and foul weather. After too many nights sleeping rough under drizzling skies, de Sautre's loathing for his surroundings had reached the point where he could no longer find words venomous enough to express it.

He wished, not for the first time, that he was back among the green and pleasant fields of his native Huntingdonshire, where those of common birth knew their place. The folk of this benighted land were unbecomingly independent. Only yesterday, the Templar party had come across a handful of crofters who sullenly refused to respond to any questions put to them in English, French, or Latin. Another time John de Sautre would have ordered them soundly beaten to teach them respect for their betters, but just now he had more pressing business to attend to.

Harcourt, de Sautre's second-in-command, approached him on foot, beating aside a swarm of midges as he came.

"The men are ready, sir," he said. "They're awaiting your orders."

De Sautre greeted this news with a sour grunt. "Tell them to mount up," he said. "Send d'Urberville ahead to scout the way. Tell him to keep silent on the move. If he catches any glimpse of our quarry, he's to report back immediately for further instructions."

He scarcely knew who was more deserving of his wrath: Arnault de Saint Clair, or the incompetent fools who had let Saint Clair and the equally infuriating Lennox slip through their fingers. Brian de Jay had left parting orders that the pair were to be kept under careful surveillance. De Sautre had entrusted the matter to three supposedly seasoned men, but Saint Clair and Lennox had proven too slippery for them. When Lamballe, Quincy, and Rutherford lost their quarry at Scone, de Sautre had been compelled to pick up the trail himself.

It had not been entirely easy to arrange his departure. King Edward had ordered all fighting men loyal to his cause to muster at Castletown in preparation for a march on Edinburgh. Though Templars were not obliged to answer to any secular authority, deferring only to the pope and their own superiors within the Order, Brian de Jay and his predecessor as Master of England had established ample precedent for Templar advisors to ride at Edward's side.

Accordingly, de Sautre had obtained leave to venture north, ahead of the English army, on the pretext of scouting out the terrain. Thus far, he had seen little along the way to suggest that Balliol's supporters had much fight left in them—a state of affairs that gave him flexible rein under which to carry out his own objectives.

He swung up on his charger as the knight named d'Urberville set off up the narrow trail and disappeared almost at once into the trees. They would give the outrider a few minutes' head start before following. Riding up alongside him, Harcourt drew rein and allowed himself an explosive sigh.

"Remind me again why we're waiting in this godforsaken place, being frozen and rained on and eaten alive by midges," he grumbled in an undertone.

"Because they've taken off on their own initiative, maybe even gone apostate, so we're obliged to bring them back!" de Sautre snapped. "If they've been to Iona, this is the most direct way back to Scone."

He had obtained his intelligence by bribing some of the servants attached to Scone Abbey. While professing ignorance of the whereabouts of their recent Templar visitors, who had spent most of a week in prayer and meditation with the monastic community, several of his informants recalled that they had ceased noticing the pair's presence at about the same time that a visiting Columban brother had also departed, shortly after news came of the Scottish defeat at Dunbar.

A casual walk through the abbey stables had discovered the presence of two leggy palfreys from the stables at Bal-

antrodoch, eating their heads off, and an obliging stable servant had volunteered the information that, yes, two Templars had left the animals in temporary exchange for a pair
of the abbey's sturdy rouncys, and were expected to trade
them back when they eventually returned to collect their
armor and other possessions left for safekeeping with the
abbot—who declined to speculate on the probable destination of the pair. But further inquiries along the road north
had revealed that a Columban brother and two bearded and
black-clad pilgrims with swords strapped under their saddles had passed that way at the appropriate time, and had
turned west after leaving the hospice at Dunkeld.

None of this squared with the orders shown de Sautre by
Saint Clair, authorizing him and Lennox to approach various
Scottish clerics regarding the instruction of King John's
conscience. De Sautre could concede the possible worth of
seeking counsel of the Abbot of Scone—but Columbans?
And why had Saint Clair and Lennox found it advisable to
do so in disguise?—unless it was to hide something.

"I still don't understand why they did it," Harcourt said.
"They're both veterans—well acquainted with the chain of
command."

"That really doesn't concern you," de Sautre said coldly,
for he shared Brian de Jay's suspicions that Saint Clair and
Lennox, obviously favored by the upper echelons of Templar authority in Paris, had brought their share of secrets
back from Outremer—secrets that an elite within the Order
were attempting to hoard for their own advancement. "To
act on their own initiative bespeaks contempt for the Rule of
the Order. At very least, they were obliged to report any re-
vision of their plans to a local superior—me. One way or another, I'll have them back at Balantrodoch to answer for
their actions."

Fortunately, the Rule gave de Sautre all the authority he
required to detain the two renegades under duress until they
could be compelled to make a full disclosure of their secret

activities. He would have welcomed an excuse to flog the truth out of them, after the labor, expense, and misery this journey had cost him, but that satisfaction would have to be reserved for Jay when he returned from Cyprus. Nonetheless, de Sautre intended to make life a misery for his errant confreres until a final reckoning could be made.

Arnault scarcely heeded the intermittent showers and even downpours that accompanied him and Torquil on their departure from Iona. The revelations of Saint Columba had given him so much to think about, that he had little attention to spare for the weather. When Torquil broke in on his reflections with the suggestion that they stop to rest the horses, he was faintly surprised to discover that the hood and shoulders of his black cloak were wet.

It seemed far longer than a week since he and Torquil had exchanged their farewells with Brother Ninian and Abbot Fingon on the beach at Iona, after changing back their Columban habits for the black robes they had worn for their journey there. Halting again for the hospitality of Dunstaffnage, and to collect their horses, they had been warned that Irish mercenaries were known to be still in the area, but they had not encountered any trouble on their homeward journey, other than the relatively minor discomfort of sleeping rough on damp ground.

The sky overhead was piled high with swift-moving clouds, hinting at more rain yet to come. Distractedly aware of the need to answer a call of nature, Arnault reined in and started to dismount.

"Watch the mud!" Torquil warned.

Arnault caught himself in mid-swing and glanced at the ground beneath his horse—fetlock-deep in mud—then grunted his thanks as he swung back up until he could move the animal a few steps forward to drier ground.

"I fear I'm more preoccupied than I realized," he said, jumping down. He handed his reins to Torquil before mov-

ing farther off the trail. "I've been trying to devise a plausi-
ble story for de Sautre when we get back."

"Well, he certainly can't be told the truth—at least not all
of it," Torquil said after a moment, as he, too, dismounted.
"All aside from what we actually *did* on Iona, I expect that
our mere independence to go there, and to put aside our
habits to do it, could be construed as rank insubordination."

"That wouldn't surprise me," Arnault said with a snort,
from behind a convenient bush. "He strikes me as a man just
looking for an excuse to flex his authority."

While they were acting under orders instigated by the
Master of *le Cercle* and issued by the Visitor of France, both
men knew that, according to strict interpretation of the Rule
of the Order, de Sautre could claim that they were still ar-
guably accountable to him, as their local superior.

"If it weren't for the fact that Luc should be advised of
what we've learned," Arnault went on, "I'd avoid Balantrodoch altogether, and head us straight for the nearest
east coast port where we could take ship for Paris. I confess,
I haven't a notion how we proceed, until we've had some
guidance from *le Cercle*." He emerged from the bushes and
took back his horse's reins. "I would be feeling far more
confident if we knew what's been developing in the rest of
the country during our absence."

Torquil only nodded agreement, both of them falling
silent as they set out walking for a while, to rest the horses.
Since leaving Dunstaffnage, they had yet to encounter anyone who could give them fresh news of any military or political developments since Dunbar. What they feared most
was the possibility that Edward might have pressed his campaign northward in an extension of his Berwick strategy,
giving his army leave to burn, slay, and "raise dragon"—displaying the dreaded dragon banner, under which no mercy
would be given, and none of the acknowledged conventions
of war would be observed. At best, the English king was

likely to be adding further victories to his credit, bringing Scotland ever more firmly under his sway.

"If John Balliol is still at liberty," Torquil finally said, "the Scots host will remain active in the field. He's still our king, even if he's a *bad* king. But what if he's been captured?"

"In that case," Arnault answered, "the outcome will depend on where the loyalty of his commanders lies: To the man, or to the realm?"

"The two should be one and the same," Torquil said.

"True enough—but are they, in John Balliol? I fear increasingly that they may not be."

After walking a while longer, they remounted. No longer traveling in Brother Ninian's company, they had abandoned the pretext of being religious pilgrims and now wore their swords strapped at their sides, though their borrowed black cloaks mostly hid the fact that they were armed, and covered the packs tied behind their saddles. They saw no one all the bleak morning.

The trail followed the line of the River Dochart, its surface like beaten pewter under the overcast sky. The water quickened as the afternoon wore on, the distant rush of a cataract gradually dominating all lesser sounds.

Pressing on through dense forest tracts of varied hardwoods and evergreens, increasingly in shade and damp, they urged their horses along a fragrant, muffling carpet of pine needles, nearing a clearing close beside the rushing waters, where Ninian had urged them to make camp on their outbound journey. All around, a vigorous growth of assorted hardwoods vied with majestic conifers and the bristle of pines, blue-green in the failing light, several of the trees with rookeries tangled high in their branches—virgin forest, never touched by axe or blade. Captivated by this tangible evidence of the splendor and beauty of God's creation, Ninian had not understood why both Arnault and Torquil maintained such watchful wariness as they pressed past it—until

Torquil pointed out, as the roar fell behind them, how such a sound could mask the approach of an enemy.

Again aware of this danger, as the trees thinned all around them and the clearing opened out, Arnault found himself straining to hear above the roar of rushing water and trying to pierce the deepening shadows of the forest as he and Torquil urged their horses to a quicker pace, glad that enough of the day remained to press well past this place before they must stop for the night. But even as Torquil's mount gave a wary nicker of inquiry, Arnault knew it was not their mere intrusion that suddenly sent dozens of rooks exploding upward into flight, their harsh caws of alarm all but drowned out by the rushing water.

Both men drew rein sharply, hands dropping to the hilts of swords as blue eyes and green probed amid the trees. A first flash of white, glimpsed peripherally on their left, immediately became one of a full dozen mounted men—six each of white-mantled knights and brown-liveried serjeants—moving slowly forward from the cover of the trees and shadows, lances braced at knees and helmets on heads.

Arnault checked, keeping his sword sheathed and warning Torquil with a glance to do the same, searching the faces, wondering whether they would be obliged to attempt fighting their way out against such odds, and against fellow Templars. Anywhere else in Christendom, he would have welcomed a chance meeting with brother-knights; but here, far from the nearest Templar outpost, he could only think that they had come for him and Torquil. His heart sank as one of the men kneed his warhorse to the front of the party. The Templar mounts dwarfed the Scone abbey rouncys.

"So, the prodigals surface at last," said John de Sautre, resting his sword across the pommel of his saddle. "I hope you have a good explanation for your actions in these past several weeks."

At a gesture from their preceptor, the knights of his entourage fanned out to surround the new arrivals. Their bearded faces were expressionless beneath their basinets, making Arnault wonder what de Sautre had told them about Torquil and himself.

"An explanation?" he echoed mildly. "Forgive me if I seem obtuse, Frère de Sautre, but you did see our orders. And surely Brian de Jay must have acquainted you with our mission before he himself left for Cyprus."

De Sautre's coarse lips curled in a sneer. "Mission? Is that what you are pleased to call it? No, I'm afraid that neither the Master nor your orders mentioned that the two of you were to be exempted from all the usual obligations of the Rule, including humility and obedience to your superiors. Oh, I'm sure you had some reason for going off on your own to visit some obscure community of heretics on the edge of civilization," he continued acidly, "but somehow I take leave to doubt that this mission of yours was sanctioned by any recognized authority within the Order."

Arnault could sense Torquil bristling, but he flashed his companion a warning look and said mildly, "Then you appear to be laboring under an unfortunate misapprehension. Our orders are discretionary, and come from the Visitor of France."

"Forgive me if I find that hard to believe," de Sautre said coldly. "Surely, knights under the direct command of the Visitor would be habited according to the Rule of our Order. To set aside our Lord's livery is to spurn His service. It seems you have as little respect for Him as you have for the Rule."

"We didn't always display our livery in the Holy Land, either," Torquil muttered. "But I wouldn't expect you to know that."

De Sautre turned to him with a glare, bright red patches flaring on his cheeks as Arnault put out a restraining arm.

"And what, exactly, is that meant to imply?" de Sautre demanded. "That you are operating under some hidden agenda of the Visitor, which absolves you of adherence to our Rule?"

"I regret that I am not at liberty to justify the Visitor's instructions," Arnault said, aware that de Sautre was not likely to back down, regardless of what he or Torquil said.

"Indeed?" De Sautre gave a bark of harsh laughter. "Then you can have no objection to accompanying us back to Balantrodoch, so I may satisfy myself as to the truth of your assertions. This is far outwith the usual chain of command, as you well know.

"As proof of your good faith and obedience, you will surrender your weapons. I trust I need not shame myself or the pair of you by requiring that you submit to being bound. I concede the possibility that your activities have, indeed, been authorized by the Visitor—much though I doubt it—but until inquiries can be made of Paris, or Frère Brian returns from Cyprus to clarify my own obligations as his deputy in Scotland, you will consider yourselves under arrest."

"With all due respect for your rank and office—" Arnault began.

"No!" de Sautre barked, gesturing with his sword. "I will have no more of your arrogance. You knights of Outremer are all alike—infected with the sins of pride and heresy. It's time you were curbed. If you are not brought to book for your actions, soon the whole Order will be called into disrepute."

Arnault could feel Torquil's eyes upon him in mute outrage, but he could see no option other than to surrender, and on de Sautre's terms. The men surrounding them were too many, and too well mounted to outrun—and in any event, he was reluctant to provoke bloodshed among these, his sworn brothers. With a sinking heart, he gave a nod to the Master of Scotland.

"If you send to Paris, the Visitor will confirm our special status," he said evenly. "But in the meantime, we will come with you."

Partially drawing his sword with his left hand, hilt first, he kneed his horse toward the nearest of de Sautre's men and prepared to surrender his weapon. Torquil sourly headed toward another man. The unexpected capitulation brought a pleased smirk to de Sautre's lips; but before his men could secure the surrender, a flurry of black-fletched arrows suddenly whisked from the gloom of the surrounding trees, unheard above the background roar of the nearby cataract, striking three men and wounding several horses.

As men and horses screamed and the Templars wheeled in alarm, knights and serjeants, looking around wildly for the source of the attack, at least a score of motley figures moved amid the cover of the forest beyond, nocking arrows to bows for a second assault—though they were not English longbows, and few of the arrows had the power to penetrate fatally, save where they struck unprotected flesh.

De Sautre's men were already scattering, even as he shouted orders, hunched low over saddles to afford smaller targets, casting aside their lances and drawing swords—for the quarters were too close for any conventional cavalry response. Some of them quickly dismounted, taking cover among the great boulders closer to the river, a few of them attempting to engage some of the closer bowmen hand-to-hand—though not always with happy result, for there were spearmen with the bowmen, and the spears had a longer reach than a broadsword—and an element of surprise as well, at least until the first Templar went down.

Meanwhile, it was the horses who were taking the brunt of the attack—and adding to the confusion—more and more of them loose, becoming a hazard of their own as their steel-shod hooves churned up the pine needles in ever greater alarm, frantic for an escape as the rain of arrows continued, eliciting the odd outcry or equine squeal. One big bay, stung by an arrow and still with a rider astride, nearly bowled over Arnault's smaller horse as it exploded into a bucking fit and ignominiously dumped its white-mantled rider at the feet of a dark little man who suddenly appeared from behind a tree—and was gone again, his dagger reddened with Templar blood, before anyone could even get a good look at him.

Steadying his mount, Arnault pulled back with Torquil and the rest in good order, all of them with swords now in hands, all of them now Templars against a common enemy. But as more arrows whizzed among them, Torquil was obliged to make a precipitous dismount as his valiant little rouncy went down with a piteous squeal, a feathered shaft deep in its chest and blood spraying from its nostrils.

As yet another flurry of arrows came raining down, Arnault ducked down and kneed his own mount closer so Torquil could shield behind it and catch on to his stirrup, to cling for dear life as Arnault whirled the little horse clumsily on its haunches to drag him out of the line of fire—but only at cost, for as Torquil scurried for cover behind a boulder, Arnault's mount met the fate of its stablemate, cut down by a hail of arrows that, individually, merely would have wounded, but in aggregate spelled its doom. Arnault rolled clear with a muffled *oof!* and scrambled to join Torquil, only just managing to keep his sword, as more arrows blacked the air, splintering and pinging among the rocks.

"I gather," said Torquil, "that we don't make a run for it just yet."

"I would if I could, believe me," Arnault muttered. "But we can't abandon our brethren to be slaughtered. Who *are* these men?"

"Not just common outlaws—that's for sure," Torquil said, both of them scrambling for safety as several loose horses came bolting past them to head upstream along the river. "And not a hunting party, either." He peered cautiously around the rock behind which they were sheltering, then leaned out farther for a closer look. "Good Lord, that one's got some kind of symbol painted on his fore—"

He ducked back with a muttered oath as an arrow whizzed past him, close enough to ruffle his hair. Arnault waited a beat, in hope that the shooter would turn to other targets, then risked a look in his turn.

The attackers were emerging again from among the trees, now arrayed in two ranks, with archers to the fore and spearmen gathering behind. All of them seemed to have foreheads painted with the symbol Torquil had seen on the first: a blue, roughly triangular shape with curved protrusions extending outward from the two upper angles, perhaps meant to be the horns of a bull or ram. Seeing it, Arnault was seized with an unaccountable sense of foreboding.

"*Jesu Christi!*" he murmured under his breath, ducking down.

Striding long-limbed behind the others came a powerful, bearded figure in a leather hauberk and helmet who appeared to be the leader of the band. His bare, muscular arms were covered with spirals and runic symbols traced out in blue, in addition to the symbol on his forehead, giving him the aspect of a pagan war chief of ancient times. Brandishing a spear high in his right hand, he flung back his head and gave a bull-throated bellow. The archers ceased firing and dropped back, allowing the spearmen to rush forward between their ranks.

Whooping and yelping, they charged down from amid the trees, bounding over rocks and other obstacles as they came. De Sautre's voice penetrated the din, ordering his men to stand fast. Gripping their swords more tightly—for without body armor of any kind, they were far more vulnerable than their fellow Templars—Arnault and Torquil braced themselves shoulder to shoulder as they watched the first wave of attackers engage with the Templars ranged at the forward edge of the clearing.

Oddly, the attack seemed largely a hit-and-run engagement. Yelling like demons, the Highlanders hurled themselves at the barricade of rocks and began jabbing viciously between the boulders with their long spears. Arnault and Torquil saw a serjeant fall in the first seconds of fighting—

though apparently only wounded—and two or three attackers also fell back groaning and clutching wounds. Glancing down the line, Arnault saw several spearmen lying either dead or wounded on the ground.

Even as this fact registered, a roared command from the Highland leader brought a rush of reinforcements. These were armed not with spears, but with swords and battle-axes, and with targes of hardened leather on their shield arms, studded with brass. From their numbers, Arnault guessed that the archers had abandoned their bows, and were now joining in the fray.

Another serjeant and a knight fell wounded, but the rest held fast, refusing to be pushed back. As the clash of steel against steel continued, never quite reaching Arnault and Torquil, they became conscious of a more insidious sound permeating the din of battle, throbbing like the rumble of distant thunder. There was a cadence to it, dull and heavy like the pulse beat of some monstrous leviathan.

Craning his neck to find where it was coming from, Torquil nudged Arnault in the ribs and directed his attention upriver, where a solitary figure in dirty white robes was watching from a stony point. What at first appeared to be a man's head trapped under the figure's right arm was, in fact, a painted drum—and the source of the throbbing sound, Arnault realized, as his eyes caught the movement of sinuous fingers flying above the painted drumhead.

And even as he listened—now picking out the rhythm more clearly, for knowing its source—the sound of the drumming began to pulse with a depth and volume not commensurate with the distance and far beyond the mere physical size of the drum, somehow rising above the roar of the river and the din of the fighting. The rough voices of the Highlanders joined in raggedly with a guttural chant that matched the cadence of the drumbeat, in no language Arnault knew but which made his blood run cold; for the chant somehow conjured up the memory of a farmhouse in

Orkney, where a freezing shadow had come lusting after the warmth of innocent human life.

Even as he made the connection, silently seizing Torquil's biceps in an urgent grip conveying danger and alarm, the drumming abruptly ceased. At once the attackers broke off combat, quickly fading back into the forest. Their Templar opponents checked, declining to pursue, seeming suddenly to sense a change in the air, looking around nervously for something they could not see.

The descending silence was as ominous as the calm at the eye of a storm. As they watched, hardly daring to breathe, thin tendrils of cold white mist began to rise up from the ground beside the river, near the feet of the now-motionless drummer—who, almost certainly, was some species of pagan shaman.

"Something's coming," Torquil murmured in a cracked whisper. His bearded face was pale under its healthy patina of weathering and freckles.

"I know," Arnault responded grimly, "and I think I'd better try to stop it. Guard my back. This is going to be quick and dirty—if it even works."

Shifting to both knees, he planted his sword in the ground in front of him like an upright cross as the drumming began again—softer, this time, and slower, and somehow even more sinister. He breathed a wordless plea for grace as he reached into the bosom of his borrowed black robe and brought out the packet containing the Breastplate. Unwrapping it with trembling fingers, he dared take no time to don it properly, or to prepare as he should; only cupped it reverently over his heart under his bare hands, swallowing hard as he called his inner faculties to order—for *something* definitely was coming.

"*Non nobis, Domine,*" he prayed aloud, softly. "*Eripe me de inimicis meis, Deus meus . . .*" Rescue me from mine enemies, O my God. Defend me from the workers of iniquity, and deliver me from these men of blood . . .

The drumbeat and chanting throbbed on, dragging at the senses. Out in the clearing, by ones and by twos, the other Templars were slowly lowering their swords, standing stupefied, eyes wide and staring. And all the while, the white ground mist rising before the pagan shaman was growing ever thicker and whiter, beginning to drift down the riverside toward the clearing in thick, ropy tendrils, driving a wall of cold before it. Grinning with malignant anticipation, the Highlander warriors began emerging from behind trees, softly chanting again, watching.

Tightening his concentration, Arnault repeated his prayer, unaware that the words that rolled from his tongue were now in Hebrew.

"Ha tzilayni mayoyvay elohai . . ." Rescue me from mine enemies . . .

But at these words, an answering warmth sprang up beneath his palms. The warmth grew warmer, joined by a glow, pushing against his palms like a living thing.

He opened his fingers outward and let it go—felt a surge of motion, like the flight wind of an invisible bird. The drumbeat faltered. The break in its rhythm disrupted the cadence of the chant. As the drummer and his followers struggled to reestablish the pattern, there appeared a sudden rift in the clouds overhead.

A long, slanting beam of sunlight spilled through the gap. Like a sword blade of transparent gold, it struck the ground in front of the advancing fog. The drumming faltered to a halt. The mist recoiled like a blind white worm, rolling backward and beginning to sink into the ground, subdued.

Continuing on, the beam of sunlight then spilled upriver toward the drummer, overtaking him in a zone of brightness. The shaman started up from his trance with a cry and staggered backward out of the light, shielding his eyes with the crook of his arm. An answering howl of dismay went up from the attackers, turning to shouts of alarm as the Templars shook free of the spell that had turned their limbs to lead, jerkily looking around them, swords rising in their hands.

The ray of sunlight disappeared, but the pagan shaman continued stumbling his way blindly toward the shelter of the trees, away from the river. Seeing him in retreat, most of his followers abruptly turned tail and ran, deaf to the exhortations of their rune-painted chief, who also began to make for the forest.

"After that man!" de Sautre shouted, punching his sword in the direction of the leader. "I want him alive!"

The Templars were quick to seize the offensive, making the most of their armored advantage as they drove after the fleeing Highlanders. Three more spearmen and a pair of swordsmen fell as the Templars overtook them. As several serjeants and a knight pressed on to harry the last of the fleeing Highlanders, de Sautre and three of his knights surged around the leader and a last pair of swordsmen, cutting down the two swordsmen without ceremony and then closing in on the leader in a concerted rush to surround and bring him down. A sharp scuffle ensued as they attempted to subdue him without using mortal force; and while their attention was momentarily diverted, Torquil turned anxiously to Arnault.

"Now would be a good time, I think, for us to be going," he said.

Arnault roused with an effort. Dazedly returning the Breastplate to its usual hiding place, he accepted the hand that Torquil held out to him and heaved himself upright, automatically retrieving his sword. Only then did he summon a wan grin for Torquil's benefit.

"That way, I think," he said, pointing the way upstream. "Let's go catch some horses and be on our way."

Chapter Twenty-one

I'D GIVE A LOT TO KNOW WHOSE THOSE MEN WERE," TORQUIL remarked later that night, as he and Arnault sat huddled over a tiny campfire in a secluded fir-wood. "They were certainly a wild and hairy lot—probably from far to the north—but nothing I've ever seen. And what about those symbols painted on their foreheads?"

"Some kind of clan totem?" Arnault guessed. "Or maybe a cult symbol? It looked like an animal head—a bull, I think. In magical terms, such a symbol might be used much as we might use the picture of a saint, as a common focus, except that it was—well, I won't say 'pre-Christian,' because what helped us repel the attack is also pre-Christian."

"Something from a different spiritual lineage, then," Torquil ventured. "Not Judeo-Christian, but—Celtic, perhaps?"

Arnault shook his head, gazing into the meager flame of their campfire. "If it was Celtic, it certainly wasn't Celtic in the sense that Brother Ninian and his Columban brethren would understand it. It wasn't even Druid, I don't think. Ninian told us that when Saint Patrick first brought Christianity to these islands, and used the shamrock to illustrate the Trinity, some of the Druids he encountered were already prepared for the coming of that way of looking at God. They regarded it as a fulfillment rather than a supplanting."

Torquil snorted softly. "Somehow, I don't think those men today saw it as a fulfillment."

"Nor do I," Arnault agreed. "Incidentally, did it seem odd to you that your relatively unsophisticated countrymen would attack an obviously better armed and armored band of mounted knights who were already spoiling for a fight? And forgive me if this seems proud, but I find it hard to believe that such a large band of Templars would not be recognized for what they are. Taking on such a force because you must is one thing. Deliberately attacking is quite another. The attack definitely didn't have the feel of them just stumbling upon us."

"No, I agree. More like a deliberate ambush."

The pair had ridden as far as they could before darkness finally forced them to halt for the night. They could only hope that they had left their fellow Templars far behind. Torquil picked up a stick and poked moodily at the fire between them, trying to forget how hungry he was. The saddlebags on the horses they had appropriated had produced little of culinary significance: a dry rusk of bread and a bit of moldy cheese in one, and nothing edible in the other. They had shared what there was of it, because they had nothing else and dared not call attention to their presence in the area, but they had concluded that de Sautre and his men must have been living off the land, probably demanding lodgings and food as they traveled.

"When de Sautre has a chance to think things over," Torquil said quietly, "I hope he appreciates that we stayed long enough to save his skin before giving him the slip." He paused to toss a few more sticks on the fire. "Of course, if he'd actually seen you do what you did, I don't suppose it would have done much to help our case."

"A point which poses yet another mystery," said Arnault. "Those ambushers weren't hunting *us*, they were hunting de Sautre and his men. We just happened to be there in time for what would have been the kill. The fact that they came prepared to use sorcery means that this wasn't just a skirmish between enemy forces. It wasn't even a grudge against the Order because Jay has been using Templars to fight against fellow Christians. Besides, I'm fairly certain our friends today weren't Christians. I think whoever was behind the attack has a different kind of grudge against the Templar Order. And I think I may know why."

"I'm listening," Torquil said.

Picking up his own fire-poking stick, Arnault rearranged the fire more to his liking.

"I haven't worked this all out yet, but I begin to see a connection between Jay and the de Sautres, and those missing pagan relics they *say* were disposed of in a lake that they can't or won't now identify, and a pagan sorcerer called Briochan—whose relics they probably were, and whose shade may well have been responsible for tearing apart Brother Colman's scriptorium. In fact, I seem to recall that Luc said there'd been some kind of amulet with a bull's face on it, among those missing grave artifacts."

Torquil whistled low under his breath. "Are you suggesting that Jay and his cronies *did* keep the relics, and those were Briochan's followers who attacked de Sautre and his men?"

"Something like that."

"But—why would Jay and his cronies want pagan relics?"

"Perhaps for the same reason that the Temple collects sacred relics: to gain access to the powers associated with them. We tell ourselves that we wield our relics in the service of God. I expect that those who revere Briochan's relics feel much the same way, using his relics in service of *their* gods. And it could well be that Jay and his associates were— or are—attempting to appropriate Briochan's powers for their own purposes.

"All of our brethren are aware of at least a few of the more conventional Christian artifacts in the keeping of the Temple—splinters of the True Cross, various saints' relics. Perhaps Jay or men like him have guessed that an elite few of us also guard more exclusive and more powerful treasures, whose very existence is unsuspected by the rest of the Order. Denied access to those, it could well be that some disgruntled faction within the Order has determined to gain access to alternative sources of extraordinary power—and might even be trying to use them to their own profit."

"That would certainly be in character for Jay," Torquil muttered.

"Unfortunately, I fear you may be right, reluctant though I am to speak thus of a brother Templar. And if the rightful inheritors of Briochan have come to suspect that Jay has stolen away their holy things, one can hardly be surprised if they might conclude that the Order itself is responsible. Hence, this afternoon's attack."

Torquil shook his head, frankly dismayed. "As if it weren't enough that the Stone is ailing, and the Scottish monarchy is being undermined by sorcerous interference, now you tell me that we have to worry about corruption among our own brothers!" He sighed heavily. "And de Sautre will deem *us* the renegades! What do you propose we do?"

"We still have our ongoing mission to accomplish," Arnault said, "and that is to prepare a foundation in Scotland for the building of the Fifth Temple. We must never lose sight of that. And whatever charges de Sautre may choose to lay against us at official levels, we've done nothing that *le Cercle* won't support. I expect that Gaspar and the Visitor can pull their usual strings behind the scenes to get us off—

perhaps with some formal reprimand and maybe even a token penance, but I have no worries on that account, so long as we aren't prevented from getting word to them—and Luc will see to that. Meanwhile, Luc can continue to act as liaison, so long as he isn't compromised by aiding and abetting us openly."

"That's fine for the long term," Torquil agreed, "but in the meantime, I should point out that we're still on the run, at least so far as de Sautre is concerned. It's a pity we didn't get a chance to ask him for news of the war—but I suppose we'll find out soon enough. Where next, then?"

"Scone, I think—and preferably before de Sautre gets there," Arnault replied.

"I think we'll be well ahead of him," Torquil said. "He has wounded. He won't be able to travel as fast as we can—and he's also short a few horses." He contained a snort of ironic satisfaction. "He can't have been happy to discover that we got away with two of the fittest ones."

"Aye, that will be one more grudge against us," Arnault said. "Meanwhile, Abbot Henry needs to be apprised of what we learned on Iona. After that, I'm none too sure. My instincts say we should get back to Paris as quickly as we can, and get our official status sorted out. That may be the only thing that will get de Sautre off our backs—and Jay, once he finds out about today."

For the next two days, subsisting on little but water, they took advantage of every hour of daylight to press eastward, avoiding settlements and only risking even a religious establishment when they paused at last to ask news and hospitality of the monks of Dunkeld. The news made their hurried meal lie like lead in their stomachs as they pressed on toward Scone.

During their absence, not unexpectedly, Edward had advanced northward from Roxburghe to lay siege to Edinburgh Castle, which had held out for little more than a week before surrendering. He had moved next on Stirling, which yielded without any resistance at all. The English king was now said to be somewhere south of Perth—which put Scone within easy striking distance.

The gates of Scone Abbey were closed when they arrived, for it was after dark, but the porter remembered them, and immediately let them in. By the time they had stabled their horses, making apologies to the brother hostler for the loss of the mounts he had loaned them from the abbey, word had been taken to Abbot Henry of their arrival and a lay brother was waiting to accompany them to the abbot's quarters. To their surprise, they found Luc de Brabant in the abbot's company.

"Good Lord!" Arnault exclaimed, breaking into a broad grin as he came to embrace the older man. "What on earth are you doing here?"

That Luc was likewise relieved to see *them* was evident, as he exchanged similar greetings with Torquil, but his sobering news soon dampened the reunion.

"You haven't heard, then," he said. "John Balliol has sued for peace. They're dickering over the terms, but it's only a matter of time."

"Where *is* Balliol?" Torquil asked.

"With what's left of the Scots army, somewhere north and east of here," said a Scottish voice from the direction of the fireside. "Word is that Longshanks has sent Bek of Durham to take the surrender. Once that happens, there's little to stop the English king from making himself sole master of everything between Berwick and the Moray Firth."

Both new arrivals turned to survey the speaker, who slowly unfolded from his chair. Apparently about the same age as Torquil, he was a brawny, broad-chested figure of a man, a full head taller even than Arnault—who was above average height—but with a thatch of curly auburn hair and bushy beard and startling blue eyes.

"Ah," Luc said. "William Wallace, you should make the acquaintance of Brothers Arnault de Saint Clair and Torquil

Lennox, Knights of the Temple—though one would hardly guess it, by their present state," he added, indicating their black robes with a sweep of a white-clad arm. "Will hails from Strathclyde—his father was a knight in the service of James the Stewart—but I met up with him down by Dunfermline. Under the circumstances, it seemed a good idea to bring him here with me."

The look of contrived innocence on Luc's face told Arnault that this was far from being the sum of the tale. Wallace himself undertook to supply further details.

"Och, I was being chased by a band of English hobelars," he said with a grin. "Their captain had been hounding me all the way from Kincardine. Brother Luc was gracious enough to let me climb a tree while he sent them off in the opposite direction."

"A lie which I have already reported to my confessor," Luc said, with a droll glance in Abbot Henry's direction. "What Will has omitted to tell you is that he was only in danger of being captured in the first place because he stopped to help me rescue some holy sisters whose cart had broken down a few miles from the town."

Wallace shrugged. *"Facis de necessitate virtutem,"* he quoted. "One makes of necessity a virtue."

This ironic use of one of Saint Jerome's more memorable observations brought a smile to Arnault's lips. Intrigued by this unexpected display of erudition, he began to share Luc's interest in Wallace.

"And may I ask what happened at Kincardine, that made this English captain so determined to capture you?"

Wallace shrugged and grinned again. "My spearmen accounted for nearly a third of his company. He seems to think I'm the one to blame for it."

"He's probably right," said Abbot Henry. "Even your uncle Robert would probably be forced to admit that you make a better soldier than a priest." Seeing the looks of inquiry from both Arnault and Torquil, he added, "One of

Will's uncles studied here for a time, before he was ordained, so I've no qualms about offering sanctuary to anyone who shares his name."

"I don't plan to be here for more than a few days," Wallace assured them.

"Where will you go when you leave?" Torquil asked.

"North, east—wherever the fighting is," Wallace replied, "until Edward of England learns that Scotland is more trouble to him than it's worth."

He retired shortly thereafter, pleading the accumulated effect of weeks on the run, with little sleep. When he had gone, Arnault and Torquil gave Luc and the abbot a concise report of all that had occurred since leaving Scone nearly two months before.

"The ambush incident is troubling," Abbot Henry noted heavily, "and I cannot say whether it relates to any of the rest of our troubles, but it's good to know that Saint Columba has not abandoned us. Still, this business of the Uncrowned King will bear further reckoning. Are we to wait for him to appear, I wonder, or are we meant to go in search of him?"

"I honestly don't know," Arnault said with a sigh, "and I'm too exhausted to make any immediate decisions until we've had a night's sleep. We daren't stay here long, because de Sautre will be only a day or two behind us, but I'd like to satisfy myself as to how the immediate crisis is resolving, before we move on."

"I can hide you for a few days," Abbot Henry said, "and even mislead de Sautre, if I must. What will you do then?"

"Return to Paris and seek retroactive permission for this bit of deception," Arnault said, plucking at a fold of his black robe, "and bring back letters of credence from the Visitor that will satisfy John de Sautre—and Brian de Jay—that we've acted within orders. In the externals, we have—but as Templars, we're of little use in any official capacity if our own brethren think we're apostate."

"*Are* you?" the abbot asked quietly. "Apostate?" he added.

Arnault exchanged glances with Luc and Torquil before carefully answering.

"Father Abbot," he said, "we have confided a great deal about our greater mission; and you know that the Stone and Scotland's sovereignty are at the heart of it. Let us say that I most fervently hope we may continue to operate within the structure of the Order. But I tell you frankly that, if forced to a choice, all three of us would choose that mission over our vows to any earthly Temple."

"Scotland is fortunate, indeed, to have such champions," Abbot Henry said quietly. "And for what it's worth, all three of you have my unqualified blessing."

"I value that more than I can say," Arnault said, with some relief. "Incidentally, concern for the Stone prompts me to ask what provisions you have made for its safety."

Abbot Henry looked at him owlishly. "Why, none, beyond the fact that the abbey is sanctuary. Dear God, do you think the English mean to take it?"

"If you were Edward of England," Torquil said, "would you not take it? It's clear he means to break this country, destroy its identity as a nation. Once he's secured Balliol's surrender, we think it likely that he'll appropriate any and every item he can that relates to Scotland's sovereignty—and the Stone will be right at the top of his list, along with the crown, the scepter—whatever he can find."

"Then, we must move the Stone, hide it!" the abbot replied.

"That much seems clear," Luc agreed, "and I should have thought of it myself. But I fear that is only half a solution. If Edward arrives to find it gone, he'll organize a search. He won't rest until he finds it. And he'll not scruple to use torture to get what he wants."

"Having been at Berwick," Torquil muttered, "I'll not argue *that*!"

"Then, if England's king wants a stone," Arnault said with a faint smile, "perhaps we'd better make sure he gets one."

Luc blinked. "What are you suggesting? That we make a copy?"

"Something like that."

"It would never work," Abbot Henry said. "The Stone is far too distinctive."

"To your eyes, perhaps. But how many Englishmen have actually had a good, close look at it? Edward himself has certainly never seen it, so how would he know a fake from the real thing?"

"Bishop Bek would know," said Abbot Henry. "He was at John Balliol's enthronement."

"That doesn't mean he actually looked at it closely," Arnault replied. "The Stone was encased in its chair and draped over in cloths until Balliol actually sat on it, and I *don't* think Bek was paying that much attention to furniture that day. I very much doubt that anyone who was present four years ago got more than a casual glimpse of the Stone itself—or that they would remember details, even if they did."

"He's right," Torquil agreed, sitting forward eagerly. "And if the deception succeeds, it at least will buy us some time—and it should prevent an excuse for local reprisals."

Abbot Henry slowly nodded. "We *must* not lose the Stone. Too much depends on it. Let's see: There's a stone quarry less than half a day's ride from here. I dare say the quarry master could supply us with a stone of approximately the right size and shape. But it must be done so that he doesn't suspect what it's really for."

"I agree absolutely," Arnault said. "I'd already thought of that. Tell me, Father Abbot: Would I be correct in assuming that the abbey might have a few buildings in need of repair?"

A ragged smile touched the abbot's lips. "What abbey does not?"

"I thought that might be the case. Perhaps it's time you commissioned some repairs. No doubt the stonemasons you send will be able to specify what sort of stones they're going to need." Arnault's gesture to indicate Torquil and himself elicited an answering nod from the abbot.

"That should be within their competence," he agreed.

"And in the short term," Luc said, "it might be a good idea to move the real Stone to a less prominent place—perhaps to the crypt."

The abbot's growing look of relief affirmed his increasing confidence in the plan. "An excellent suggestion. And if my people become accustomed to its absence from its usual resting place, they'll be far less likely to notice when the eventual substitution is made. But, when that happens, where shall we hide the real Stone?"

Arnault gave a weary sigh, massaging briefly between his eyes. "I haven't worked that out yet. Let me sleep on it. For the present, we'll plan to move the Stone down to the crypt tomorrow, and get on with procuring a substitute stone, and hope that the English king doesn't come banging on the abbey gates before we can make the substitution."

When they left the abbot, Luc showed them to beds in the guest house room he shared with Wallace, who was already hard asleep. Both Luc and Torquil soon slept as well, but tired as he was, Arnault found himself unable to drift off. His mind remained restless, alert, as if anticipating some event yet to be revealed.

After about an hour of gazing idly at the ceiling, watching the soft flicker of the room's night light, a soft rustling sound made him turn his head. Across the room, William Wallace had risen to a sitting position, bare legs dangling over the edge of his bed, head slightly bowed and arms lax at his sides. After exhaling in a great sigh, he slowly rose, clad only in his shirt, and turned toward the door, shuffling jerkily forward. His eyes, as he came toward Arnault, were half closed, apparently unseeing. Arnault quietly sat up as he approached, passing a hand before his face as he came abreast of the bed; but Wallace was oblivious, and kept moving slowly toward the door.

Instantly awake—and with no doubt that this was the reason for his sleeplessness—Arnault caught up his cloak and roused Luc and Torquil in passing as he tossed the cloak around his shoulders and started after Wallace.

"What is it?" Torquil said muzzily, groping for his sword, as Arnault motioned for him and Luc to follow him.

"Leave that. Just come with me. I couldn't sleep; and now Wallace is sleepwalking. I think there may be a reason. Come on."

Together the three Templars followed the big Scot outside and across the abbey yard. Wallace walked slowly but with seeming purpose, strangely stiff, apparently unmindful of the uneven cobbles under his bare feet. Seeing that he apparently was headed for the church, Arnault hurried ahead and opened the door. Wallace's eyes, as he passed beneath the watch lamp beside the church door, were vacant and unfocused. The Templars exchanged glances as they followed him inside.

Far down the nave, the sanctuary lamp seemed a tiny ruby eye keeping watch in the silent church, but wan candlelight also spilled from the archway leading into the north transept. As if the church had been lit by a hundred candles, Wallace made his way unerringly toward that wash of light.

"Is he going where I think he's going?" Luc whispered.

"Aye, visiting the Stone," Torquil whispered back.

Gesturing them to silence, Arnault hurried his pace, his companions close at his heels. The three of them reached the chapel doorway just in time to see Wallace moving behind the Stone, approaching it from the west. Before Arnault could decide whether he ought to intervene, Wallace folded to his knees and reached out blindly with both hands, laying them to either side of the depression on the Stone's upper surface.

His face was calmly expressionless in the glow of a lone vigil light on the altar, blank eyes shining like quicksilver. Arnault waited breathlessly. For a moment, nothing seemed to be happening, but then, to his astonishment, he saw that a pale, silver-blue glow was emanating from the Stone where Wallace's fingers rested.

Luc uttered an audible gasp and gripped Arnault's shoulder. Torquil made no sound, but his eyes were very wide. Together they watched as the glow spread itself up Wallace's hands and arms, continuing to expand until his whole body was enwrapped in a soft nimbus of pure light.

A fragrance like incense permeated the air, unearthly in its sweetness. To Arnault, the perfume had the quality of angelic sanctity. The blank look on Wallace's face yielded to an expression of rapture, blind eyes now lifting in wonder to something only he could see.

The light held him a moment longer in its shimmering embrace. Then it slowly began to fade away, like pure water spilling away through a cleft in a rock. With yearning hands, Wallace reached out as if to cling to the departing radiance. When it slipped through his fingers, he uttered a broken cry and crumpled to the floor.

As one the three knights rushed forward, Luc swiftly checking for a pulse.

"He's all right. He's only fainted," he reported. "Let's get him back to his bed."

Between them, they managed to carry Wallace back to the guest house without rousing alarm—no easy feat, for a man of his size. None of them ventured to speak until they had restored him to his bed.

"What was all that about?" Torquil whispered, as Luc tucked a blanket around the sleeping Wallace.

Arnault stood back and squared his shoulders with a sigh. "We'll wish to confer with Abbot Henry, and see what he thinks," he said softly, "but I am strongly minded to suggest that we have just witnessed the calling of William Wallace to the service of the Stone of Destiny—perhaps even to become the Uncrowned King."

"A lofty calling," Luc murmured, "but I pity him, nonetheless, if he is."

"He didn't seem to be aware of what was happening," Torquil whispered. "Will he remember any of this in the morning?"

Just then, Wallace groaned and stirred. Seeing that he was about to rouse, Arnault signed for Luc and Torquil to back away. The pair quickly retreated to their beds and lay down, positioned to allow surreptitious observation. Arnault was in the process of crouching down beside Wallace's bed when the big Scot's eyelids flickered and opened. Seeing a shape close beside him, he started up and groped for his sword.

"Peace!" Arnault said, staying his arm. "It's Frère Arnault. I heard you thrashing, and then I heard a moan."

Wallace's gaze focused. As Arnault's face registered, he relaxed back with a grunt and knuckled at his eyes.

"Sorry. I must have been dreaming. I suppose it's a measure of feeling safe here. Out in the field, that kind of thing could be the death of me."

"Having just come from a similar situation, I thought it might be something like that," Arnault said. "Are you all right?"

Wallace sighed and rubbed at his eyes again. He still seemed a bit confused. "What a strange dream . . ."

"How so?"

Wallace's expression softened, and Arnault caught a ghostly hint of the wonder he had glimpsed earlier.

"I was in a holy place," Wallace murmured. "The air was filled with heavenly voices, singing God's praises. There was a white-robed man—an abbot—offering Communion at the altar. He called me to partake of the feast, and I came . . ."

His voice trailed off and his eyes rolled upward in his head as he slipped back into sleep. When Arnault was satisfied that he would not soon rouse again, he withdrew to the corridor, Luc and Torquil hastily joining him.

"Could you hear what he said?" he asked.

"Aye," Torquil breathed. "Do you think he *is* the Uncrowned King?"

"For his sake in *this* life," Luc said, "I hope not—though methinks such service will have its own rewards, in the final reckoning. But I think the Stone has chosen. And if so, we must watch for the further signs, and be prepared to assist him in every way we can, to prepare him for the road ahead that he—and we—must walk."

Chapter Twenty-two

WHILE ARNAULT AND TORQUIL RETURNED TO THEIR BEDS, Arnault at last sinking into exhausted slumber, Luc went to inform Abbot Henry of Wallace's sleepwalking episode, and their interpretation regarding it. The next morning, during the hour between Prime and the daily chapter meeting, the abbot arranged to have the Stone moved into the crypt beneath the abbey church, with Wallace lending his brawn and Luc looking on. The abbot offered no explanation to the several lay brothers involved in shifting the Stone down the narrow stair but the entire community was aware that Edward's armies were north of the Firth, and that the abbey was apt to have English visitors at any time.

"Do you think the English will come here, Father Abbot?" one of the brothers asked, as they leaned a few paving slabs against the Stone to mask it.

"I hope not, my son," the abbot replied.

"They'll surely find the Stone, if they come down here," the brother said.

"But perhaps they will show it more respect, if they must bring it from the crypt," Abbot Henry replied. "And perhaps they will not think to take it, if it cannot readily be seen."

A little later, while all the brethren of the community were at chapter, a somewhat rested Arnault and Torquil quietly made their way down to the crypt, having put on the rugged homespuns and leather aprons of stonemasons, to take measurements of the Stone. To complete their disguise, they had even shaved off the beards that were so visible a sign of their membership in the Order, rubbing walnut stain on their cheeks and chins to drab down the pale skin thus exposed.

"There's something that puzzles me," Wallace said quietly, as he watched Arnault and Torquil take careful measurements of the Stone's proportions with a length of knotted cord. "Brother Torquil is a Scot, so it's right that he should respect the Stone of Destiny. But you and Brother Luc are French. And all three of you are Templars. Why should Knights of the Temple set such store by a Scottish symbol of sovereignty?"

"Because we know its history," Arnault said carefully, "and we know its potential. The Stone is more—much more—than a mere symbol. But even if it were only that, Edward would seek to possess it, to break that tie between Scotland's people and her past." His gaze narrowed as he chose his next words with care; for though Wallace appeared to have no conscious memory of the previous night's encounter with the Stone, he was clearly a part of what was now unfolding.

"Whatever more the Stone may possess, beyond its symbolism," he went on softly, "be sure that there are those in Edward's camp who suspect as much, and will doubtless urge him to seize it. For once it is in his hands, they will find the means to master its secrets."

Wallace's jaw clenched in sudden emotion.

"I would rather die than see the Sassenachs even gaze upon it!" he said with passion, apparently missing the additional meaning Arnault had ventured.

"To die for such a cause would be to waste your death," Torquil immediately responded, with a covert glance at his fellow Templars. "Scotland needs patriots such as yourself. If you would serve the Stone, you can help us find a fitting place to hide it."

Wallace simply blinked at him for a breathless instant, then crouched down to lay a hand on the Stone, nodding slowly, looking vaguely distracted.

"I can do that. It's a mickle great lump to be dragging around the countryside, but some of the hills between here and Dunkeld are as rugged as you'll find within a hundred miles of here. Actually, I can think of several places that might be suitable."

"I was hoping you might make such an offer," Arnault said. "You probably know the local countryside far better than any of the rest of us."

"I'll set out at once," Wallace said. "How much time do you reckon we've got?"

"There's no way to know," Luc said. "With luck, we shall have our substitute stone by tonight. But we must have a place to take the true Stone, before we make the substitution. And then we must work with all speed to take the true Stone to safety."

Within the hour, Arnault and Torquil set out from the abbey with a horse and cart from the abbey stables, now unrecognizable as Templars, in their stonemasons' attire, and armed with Abbot Henry's voucher for purchase of the stones they required. Wallace had left somewhat before them, mounted on one of the Templar mounts they had brought in the night before; and with Abbot Henry's blessing, Luc undertook to contrive a set of errands that would absent from the abbey those few others who had been aware of his fellow Templars' brief sojourn, along with his own horse and the second Templar steed—for the new day had brought with it the likelihood of a visit from John de Sautre and his men, even if the English stayed away.

They reached the quarry early in the afternoon. The supply of cut stone available was of variable quality. The piece most closely matching the proportions of the Stone itself was a block of honey-colored fieldstone.

"It's reasonably close for length and width," Torquil said dubiously, as he finished measuring it with his knotted cord, "but I wish it were taller. And it should be black."

"We can drab it down with mud," Arnault said. "It will just have to do. We haven't time to commission a better match—and anyway, that might give cause for suspicion. The main thing is that it will fit under the enthronement seat."

"Not unless you support it on blocks from below," Torquil said with a shake of his head, but he didn't press the argument any further.

They purchased enough extra stones to serve as camouflage on the way back, then returned to the abbey. By dint of the long daylight of midsummer, they arrived well before dark, with plenty of time to unload the stones in a tumbled pile in the abbey yard. Wallace had not returned, and de Sautre had yet to make his appearance.

But he did the next day, while Arnault and Torquil were laboring in the abbey stable to rerig a pack saddle suited to the abbey's largest draft horse—for when they moved the Stone, it must go by horse as far as the cottage where they had left the cart, since the sound of a cart leaving the abbey in the dead of night would arouse attention. Watching the abbey gate from the vantage point of the hay loft above where the pair worked, Luc, too, had been lying low since their arrival and, in the absence of his horse from the stables, was counting on the monks of Scone to conclude, if asked, that he had traveled on. His hiss of warning brought both of them scurrying up the ladder to join him in the loft, where the three of them lay on their bellies before a louvered window and watched their brother-knights ride into the abbey yard.

Most of the riders, including de Sautre, looked the worse for wear, and several were riding double—ironic restatement of early Templar seals, which showed two knights mounted on the same horse, in token of their vow of poverty. Bandages were visible on a few of the men, and two were leading horses with bodies tied across their backs.

But Abbot Henry was well prepared for their arrival, having sent a trusted servant north to watch the road, and claimed to have seen no renegade Templars. (Indeed, since Arnault and Torquil had borne little resemblance to Templars, either in their borrowed black robes, their stonemasons' attire, or the sturdy shirts and breeches that they presently wore, in anticipation of their coming mission with the Stone, the claim was not precisely a lie.) The abbot was pleasant and cooperative, even reminding de Sautre that the Templars of whom he inquired had left two horses when passing through some weeks before. And since it appeared that his men were sorely in need of remounts . . .

Though clearly vexed at his failure to turn up news of the renegades, de Sautre did accept the offer of their horses with a modicum of grace, and shortly rode on toward Perth with only two of his men now mounted double.

The afternoon stretched on, with no sign of Wallace. Meanwhile, rumors were rife of John Balliol's imminent surrender. Toward dusk, Luc came to the stable loft where the pair had been dozing, to pass on the sifting of news that had drifted in during the course of the day.

"How long do we dare to wait?" Luc asked. "You don't suppose anything's happened to him?"

"I devoutly hope not," Arnault replied.

"Maybe we ought to go ahead and make the switch tonight, whether he shows up or not," Torquil said. "We could temporarily hide the real Stone in the hay down below—or even set off in the direction of Dunkeld tonight, by a lesser route, and hope to make the contact later. Not knowing what the English are doing, I'm nervous about leaving it here any longer than we must."

Both he and Luc looked expectantly to Arnault, who thought a moment and then nodded.

"You're right. We'll pack up our gear and provisions and make the substitution tonight," he decided. "If Wallace hasn't arrived by the time we've done that, we'll hide the true Stone in here and wait another day. We'll give him until to-morrow night—and if he hasn't come back by then, we'll head in the direction of Dunkeld on our own. I'm sure that a word from Abbot Henry would gain us a few days' sanctuary there; and if Wallace does show, Abbot Henry can tell him where we've gone."

Torquil nodded. "I'm happy enough with that. I just don't want to stay here and do nothing."

Luc went off to acquaint Abbot Henry with their change of plans. It was agreed that they would meet at the church just past midnight, when the short summer night would be at its darkest. Luc returned to the ringing of the Vesper bell, with a basket of provisions over his arm, and the three of them knelt down in the hay of the stable loft and recited the office together with quiet passion, for they knew not when they might meet again.

Afterward they shared a light meal of bread and cheese and a little ale, each man alone with his thoughts. Arnault and Torquil armed themselves then, in the padded gambesons and leather hauberks of ordinary soldiers, and Luc kept watch while the other two dozed, for sleep would be increasingly precious once the Stone was moved from the crypt.

The shadows gradually lengthened and dusk finally began to fall. It was two hours past Compline, and not yet fully dark, when the abbey gate briefly opened to admit a big man on a borrowed Templar horse. Wallace immediately disappeared in the direction of the abbot's quarters; and as soon as a groom had dealt with the horse and gone away again, the three came down from the loft, Luc and Arnault quickly saddling two fresh horses from the abbey stable and Torquil harnessing the big draft horse with the pack saddle, muffling the hooves of all three horses with rags. Very soon, Wallace joined them.

"Thanks be to God!" Arnault exclaimed in a whisper, as the big Scot slipped into the stable. "You're not a moment too soon! We must move the Stone tonight."

"Aye, I've just been to see Abbot Henry," Wallace said. "I'm sorry if I've cut things a bit fine, but I think I've found what we need."

"You can acquaint us with particulars once we're away from here," Luc said, urging him and Arnault toward the door. "Start shifting the stones. Torquil and I will finish with the horses."

Arnault and Wallace slipped across the abbey yard to find Abbot Henry waiting for them in the shadow of the church porch, a shielded lantern in his hands as he met them by the pile of stones hiding the block of fieldstone chosen to stand in for the Stone of Destiny.

"I've sworn the gate porter to secrecy," he informed them in an undertone. "Barring some mischance, no one else should know of this."

It was the work of a few minutes to slip a stout leather carrying sling around the designated stone and, with the aid of two carrying poles, for Arnault and Wallace to heft its weight onto their shoulders and shift it indoors. The abbot lit the way for them as they picked their way carefully down the steps into the crypt.

There they exchanged the fieldstone block for the true Stone, Abbot Henry lingering briefly to blacken down the substitute while Arnault and Wallace used the same sling apparatus to carry the Stone itself back up the stairs. It was much larger by half than the substitute stone, and commensurately heavier, and even Wallace was trembling with the strain by the time they got it out to the yard.

Torquil was waiting with the big draft horse that would
have the honor of conveying the Stone. Only by dint of his
help and that of Abbot Henry—and much grunting and
wincing—were they able to shift the Stone onto the pack
saddle; for they must heft the Stone higher than their heads.
Abbot Henry came with them as far as the cottage where
Luc waited with the cart and the two saddle horses, one hand
resting on the Stone in its pack, obviously reluctant to part
with it. When they had shifted it onto the cart, Arnault and
Wallace tying sheepskins over it to cover it while Luc and
Torquil hooked up the pack horse between the cart's traces,
Abbot Henry gave the Stone a final pat and stepped back.

"God speed you, brothers," he murmured. "Even if this
scheme of ours should ultimately fail, you Templars will
have done more to secure Scotland's independence than
King John ever has."

"It is not alone for Scotland that we do this, Reverend Father," Arnault said quietly, as Wallace vaulted up onto the
driver's seat. "You have, in the Stone, a treasure more precious than you know. Luc"—he nodded to their fellow Templar as he and Torquil took the reins of the two riding
horses—"we'll send word as often as we can."

"Godspeed, all three of you," Luc said. "I wish I were
going along, but someone has to keep an eye on what Jay
and the de Sautres are up to."

Arnault only snorted as he and Torquil mounted up.

"Unfortunately, I'll warrant we've not heard the last from
them," he replied. "Father Abbot, we'll at least send word to
you when this is finished," he promised. "I hope it won't be
long."

"I shall be waiting," the abbot said, lifting his hand in
blessing. "Until then, may Saint Columba be your inspiration, and may God hold you in the hollow of His hand."

The summer sky was already paling in the east as they left
the abbey behind and joined the road toward Dunkeld. In the

next hour they began to pass a few fellow travelers, but the emptiness of the road was notable. It was as if the whole region were holding its breath, like a frightened hare immobilized beneath the circling shadow of a hawk.

"I'm beginning to know this stretch of road all too well," Torquil muttered above the creaking and rumbling of the cart's heavy wheels.

"Be grateful for small things," Wallace replied. "At least we have a road—for now."

No one commented on the clouds beginning to build in the east, for the prospect of rain was a daunting one, added to the already arduous task before them. Keeping a wary eye on the weather, they entered the fringes of Birnam Wood, speaking but little, and then in low voices. A mile farther on, at Wallace's direction, they left the Dunkeld road and struck out westward along a rutted woodcutter's track, following that until they entered a tiny clearing traversed by a thread of running water.

"We must leave the cart here," he told them, as he jumped down to unhitch the horse pulling the cart.

After bringing the big draft horse alongside, they shifted the Stone to its back and secured it, then overturned the cart to make it look abandoned. Wallace then headed down the little rill, which soon became a narrow burn, leading the horse with the Stone. The two Templars followed with the other two horses, carrying the poles and sling for the Stone.

They trudged along this muddy track for the best part of an hour, no one speaking, as other rivulets joined the one they followed and they eventually were obliged to shift to a narrow, stony track beside what was now a shallow but swift-running stream. The big pack horse could go only slowly, because of the weight of the Stone, and dropped its head gratefully as they halted where another, larger stream joined in from the right side.

"Now we turn upstream," he said, pointing. "There's a cave on up that glen, maybe another half mile. It's on the other side, but we can cross farther up. For the last few hundred yards, we'll have to carry the Stone."

Neither Arnault nor Torquil could summon any response save to press on.

They left the two saddle horses there, tied to a tree, and followed along with the poles and sling as Wallace continued on, still leading the horse with the Stone. From beyond the next bend in the stream, the sound of fast-flowing water recalled an incident both Templars preferred to forget, but they reached the fording place without incident and tethered the horse to a tree.

Uncovering the Stone, they fitted the sling and slipped the poles in place so that they could lift it out of the pack saddle. Then, shouldering their heavy burden, with Wallace on one end and the two Templars on the other, they eased their way down the bank and waded knee-deep, testing their footing with every step. The temperature was brisk under the overcast sky, but all three men were sweating by the time they reached the other side.

They set the Stone down on a patch of sand and paused to catch their breath. Pointing ahead, Wallace marked the place where the stream emerged from a ravine. The overhanging banks were sheer, but an old rock fall had left a narrow strip of exposed rock between the stream and the right-hand cliff wall. The Templars eyed the prospect with obvious misgivings, but Wallace flashed them a reassuring grin as they picked up their burden again.

The footing grew ever more precarious. Suspended from poles in their midst, the Stone was like some wayward pendulum, threatening at any moment to throw one or another of them off balance. With agonizing slowness, they edged ahead by inches, never shifting one foot until the other was firmly planted. Beside them, the stream was becoming a cataract, its swift-running waters ever ready to turn a misstep into injury or even death.

So engrossed was Arnault in minding his footing that he didn't realize they had reached the cave until Wallace signaled a halt. Only then did he raise his eyes to the dark, triangular rift in the cliff face, about eight feet above the streambed. Access looked just possible by way of a jagged ledge slanting up from the water's edge.

"It's easier than it looks," Wallace assured them between gasping breaths.

Arnault's shoulder muscles were burning by the time they gained the cave entrance. Torquil's face was scarlet with exertion, and even Wallace was looking strained. They eased the Stone's weight to the cave floor and stood there panting for several minutes, bent with hands braced on knees, too winded to speak.

Torquil was the first to recover. The failing daylight filtering in through the opening did not penetrate far beyond the entrance.

"How far back does this go?" he asked Wallace.

The big man grinned. "This is just the anteroom. There's a larger chamber beyond this one. It's round, like a Templar church—wee, but you'll like it. Give me a moment and I'll strike a light."

Crouching down on the floor of the cave, he produced from the leather pouch at his belt a tallow candle, a small bundle of dry moss, and flint and steel, from which he soon produced a flame. As a pale glow blossomed around them and Wallace held the candle high, a secondary gap could be seen at the rear of the cave, as wide as any doorway.

When Wallace had taken the candle into the adjoining cavern and set it firm on a few drips of wax, they carried in the Stone and set it in the center of the chamber. The feel of the place was good—perhaps fifteen feet in diameter and vaulted to nearly that height. After divesting the Stone of its carrying poles and sling, they hid these against the back wall, then came to briefly lay their hands upon it in farewell.

"You've chosen well," Arnault said to Wallace. " 'Tis a

fitting temple to shelter the Stone—at least for now." He
glanced at Torquil, knowing that the other Templar would
catch the layers of his meaning.

"Aye—until the King shall come into his own again," the
younger man replied. His answering glance made it clear to
Arnault that it was not Balliol he meant, but a king who
would never be crowned.

The man they believed would be that king merely sighed
and gave the Stone a final caress, having delivered it—at
least for a time—to a place where it might wait in safety.

It was not until several months later, in an office in the
bowels of the Paris treasury of the Temple, that Brothers Arnault de Saint Clair and Torquil Lennox learned of the resolution of that day's work. Thanks to the intervention of
Gaspar des Macquelines, and some inventive and largely
unverifiable reporting on the part of Arnault himself, their
actions in Scotland had been totally vindicated by the Visitor of France—who, a full week before their arrival in Paris,
had already received a pointed inquiry from the Preceptor of
Scotland. The reply later sent by Hugues de Paraud, Visitor
of France, coolly confirmed that the knights named in said
preceptor's complaint had acted with his full authority, and
implied that the earlier orders concerning these knights
(which said knights had shown to the preceptor) ought to
have been sufficient for no further questions to be asked.

Official news of the surrender of John Balliol, and Edward's
response to this latest Scottish rebellion, had also reached Paris
by the time Arnault and Torquil arrived: how Anthony Bek,
acting for the English king, had received Balliol's submission
at Brechin Castle and stripped him of the accoutrements of
kingship; had ripped the red and gold arms of Scotland from
his tunic, and broken the kingdom's great seal into four pieces,
and seized the crown and scepter, ring and sword—had taken
all of these away to the Tower of London, and Balliol and his
infant son as well, along with many chests of charters and

records looted from Edinburgh Castle, and even the castle's famous Black Rood of Saint Margaret—and the Stone of Destiny, formerly kept at Scone Abbey.

That latter rumor greatly subdued the homecoming of Arnault and Torquil to the Paris Temple. After a week's rest and discussion, having reported on their mission and returned the High Priest's Breastplate into the keeping of *le Cercle*, the pair were preparing to return to Scotland—still incognito—to confer with the Bishop of Glasgow, Robert Wishart, who was quietly fomenting talk of new rebellion in the west with James the Stewart.

But very shortly before their planned departure came a letter from Luc de Brabant, delivered to Gaspar des Macquelines by a Scottish knight named Flannan Fraser. Not being an intimate of *le Cercle*, Frère Flannan was not summoned to be advised of the letter's contents; but as soon as Torquil had fathomed the gist of the letter, he determined to toast his fellow Scot as a true and worthy son of Scotland, merely for bringing the news.

"Brother Luc says that English soldiers came during the first week of August, with authority from Edward of England to seize the so-called Stone of Destiny," Gaspar said, with a tiny, pleased smile. "What they took away with them—though God grant they may never realize this—was the stone you left for them. He says that Wallace was there to see the deed done, disguised as a rather tall lay brother, and that Wallace said to tell you that the cart the English soldiers confiscated to carry away the 'Stone of Destiny' was one you would know."

Both Arnault and Torquil exploded into delighted guffaws at that news; and at the looks of bewilderment from their companions, Torquil recovered himself enough to explain.

"He means that they took the cart we used to carry the true Stone to safety," he said, still trying to recover his composure. "And that, God willing, is as close as the Sassenachs will ever get to Scotland's most sacred symbol of its sovereignty!"

Part III

Part III

Chapter Twenty-three

LONDON IN SEPTEMBER OF 1297 WAS IN A FERMENT—LESS on account of the unseasonable heat than because of the staggering news recently arrived from the north. The map of Scotland spread before Frère Brian de Jay, Master of the English Temple, had been drawn to show the Temple's holdings there; but what riveted his attention was the account the Master of Scotland was giving him of the astonishing English defeat at Stirling Bridge.

Under the gaze of Stirling Castle, half the English army had crossed the bridge over the River Forth to be met by an inferior Scottish force under command of a baron's son called Andrew Murray and a renegade upstart named William Wallace. It should have been a clear English victory; yet the ragtag Scots had cut the English chivalry to pieces while their comrades could only look on helplessly from the other bank.

The incompetence of the English commanders, Warenne and Cressingham, made Jay grind his teeth. Their arrant stupidity, combined with the boldness of the Scots, had re-sulted in a defeat that had undone years of campaigning by King Edward, who was currently in Gascony fighting Philip IV. Cressingham, the king's treasurer in Scotland, had paid with his life; and his skin (so it was said) had been flayed and made into (accounts varied) a baldric for Wallace's sword, saddle girths for his horsemen, or small pieces that were sent throughout the country in triumph.

"As if this were not enough," John de Sautre concluded sourly, "these Scottish renegades continue to petition Rome for sanction of their rebellion."

At this, Jay sprang to his feet and slammed a fist on the table.

"God's curse on every last one of them!" he cried. "Every time we stamp out the flames of their revolt, some new spark ignites the kindling, and the fire blazes even more fiercely than before. Who is this Wallace? Where does he come from? He is a nothing—not even a knight!—and yet the Scots follow him as though he were their king!"

"They say Murray is the strategist of the pair," de Sautre pointed out.

"Murray is nothing!" Jay declared hotly. "It is Wallace who is the leader, and he claims his victories in Balliol's name! Balliol—a pantomime king disgraced by his abject surrender. Do you know where he lies now? Under house ar-rest, just outside London—allowed a huntsman and ten hounds, by God! Not even considered sufficient threat to re-main at the Tower, where all such spineless rebels should end their days! There he awaits the king's return, like a lap-dog pining for its master—and *still* he has such a cham-pion!"

He strode over to the window and glared out angrily over the nearby rooftops to where the Thames gleamed silver in the evening sun. The London Temple occupied a prestigious location that Jay, in a calmer frame of mind, found appro-priate to the Order's eminence. He much preferred to be here at the center of a mighty kingdom, rather than chasing around the dank landscape of Scotland, pursuing rebel High-landers and errant Templars, but Scotland still came under his provincial authority.

"There must be more to it," John de Sautre observed dis-tractedly. "Could Wallace be receiving assistance?"

Jay rounded on his subordinate with a glare. "Indeed! Per-haps from our disgraced brethren, Saint Clair and Lennox—the men *you* let slip through your fingers!"

John bowed his head to hide his expression. "We received confirmation from the Visitor that they had authority to work incognito, and on their own initiative. And since they es-caped us, there has been no further evidence of their pres-ence in Scotland. And it is only a guess that they are with Wallace's army."

"A guess?" Jay echoed caustically. "Guesses are all that is left to me, thanks to your incompetence."

"We did take a prisoner after that ambush," John re-minded him.

"Hardly through any cleverness of yours," Jay growled, "though I will concede that you extracted some intriguing information before he died. It would never have occurred to me that the Comyns would return to the old religions—and I find it fascinating to learn that the remains discovered in that grave near Balantrodoch appear to be those of the pagan wizard Briochan—as has been confirmed by my esoteric contacts here in London."

His displeasure dissipated, and he stroked his beard thoughtfully.

"Yes . . . and certain relics. Those offer us certain . . . pos-sibilities. Perhaps we may yet salvage something to our ad-vantage."

"Do you intend to turn these things against the Comyns?" de Sautre asked.

"Not exactly," Jay replied. "Other options suggest them-selves, if my researches should prove accurate."

Further elucidation was interrupted by a respectful knock on the door. Jay's curt acknowledgment brought Robert de Sautre scurrying into the room, his round face aglow with guilty satisfaction, like that of a schoolboy who has been stealing apples from a neighbor's garden. He cast a furtive glance into the corridor outside before quietly closing the door behind him.

"You have accomplished your errand?" Jay inquired with a lift of one eyebrow.

The younger de Sautre bobbed his head enthusiastically. "The gaoler could scarcely credit his good fortune, to be so richly recompensed for so trifling a task."

He presented his superior with a small leather pouch. Jay untied the strings and peered inside. "You are sure these come from Balliol?" he asked.

"I saw him take the clippings myself," Robert affirmed. "It was part of our bargain that I should be present. I did not wish to run any risk of deception or mishap."

John de Sautre grimaced, aware that his brother was inviting comparison with his own efforts. "What have you brought?" he demanded.

"Nail clippings and hair from that most royal prisoner, John Balliol of Scotland," Robert responded smugly.

The Master of the Temple stuffed the pouch into his scrip and passed a key to Robert. "Fetch the chest," he ordered, "and have horses readied."

"Where are we going?" John asked.

"To Westminster Abbey, to answer some of our questions and light the road ahead."

The elder de Sautre's brow furrowed in consternation. "Through sorcery?"

"Did not our Lord Himself practice the arts of prophecy?" Jay retorted. "Did not Saint John see visions of the days to come, foreshadowing the end of the world? What sin is it for us to do as they did? And what holds us back from doing so, other than a want of courage?"

"But—what has this to do with John Balliol? Stripped of his kingship, a prisoner of England, what threat is he to anyone?"

"That is what I propose to discover," Jay said. "I find myself increasingly curious about the Stone of Destiny—alleged to be the source of the mystical power which maintains the Scottish kingdom. On my advice, King Edward went to great trouble to secure it and have it brought south to London. And yet, despite losing so vital a national treasure, the Scots refuse to be put in their place. Worse, they find themselves a leader who has brought them a victory we could not have thought possible a few days ago!

"We then must ask ourselves," he concluded, "is Balliol's proximity to the Stone allowing him to draw upon its influence? Does he, even from here in England, exercise a kingly power which enables his champion to wage war against us in Scotland?"

"That hardly seems possible," John said, blinking at the map.

"What is possible is limited only by the breadth of a man's vision," Jay declared. "And I set no bounds upon myself in such matters. Be sure that the struggle in which we are engaged is no mere rivalry of crowns. It concerns the very soul of our Order."

"You're referring to the renegades, Saint Clair and Lennox?" John hazarded.

"Them, and all their impious associates," Jay agreed. "I am convinced that some faction within our Order is pursuing secret purposes of its own, which bode no good for England or the Temple."

His mouth twisted bitterly as he fingered the hilt of his sword.

"Many of those who served in the East have forsaken their true calling," he muttered. "They have returned from Outremer with their speech strangely accented, their minds twisted by exotic and heretical philosophies. But that is not the worst of it. Having surrendered to these seductions, they now are striving to subvert their Western brothers. Their objective is to impose their newly learned foreign ways over those of us who have remained faithful to our vows, praying for the victory of Christ's kingdom in those far-off lands while they idled in decadent luxury and dabbled in knowledge forbidden to any true Christian."

The de Sautres nodded their agreement without interrupting their superior.

"They have made a pact with the enemies of Christ," Jay continued in an impassioned tone, "abandoning His Holy Land in exchange for gold and the black secrets of the Assassins and the Magi. How else could Christian knights be driven off by infidels, unless they had betrayed God's holy trust for their own worldly gain? As part of this obscene bargain, they have agreed to remove themselves as far as possible from the scene of our former conquests, to give their new allies the ultimate assurance of victory. And what land in all of Christendom," he finished grimly, "is as remote from Jerusalem as the land of the Scots?—a country still infested with pagan superstition and dubious forms of worship."

"I still fail to see what Saint Clair and Lennox hope to achieve by aiding these Scottish rebels," John de Sautre said.

Jay's blue eyes were hard. "They see in the struggle for the Scottish throne an opportunity to gain ascendancy for themselves and found a new, unholy order—one dedicated not to the poverty and obedience of true Christian brothers, but to the vices that once were the mark of their godless enemies.

"Make no mistake: If they establish their authority here—as they clearly mean to do—it will be an end to us. We shall be copying petty accounts and guarding lonely watchtowers while they lord it over us with their fabled wealth and their sorcerous arts."

Robert de Sautre gazed at their superior with an admiration bordering on awe. "I would never have foreseen this, my lord. I doubt that any man but you could have conceived the enormity of their ambition or the blackness of their crimes."

"Are you with me then," Jay retorted, brushing the flattery aside, "or will you surrender meekly to these vipers which are bent on sucking on the heart of Christendom?"

"We are with you, my lord," John de Sautre affirmed grimly.

"Even to the death," Robert added with an inappropriate grin.

It was after nightfall when Brian de Jay and the two de Sautre brothers dismounted outside the main door of Westminster Abbey, Robert de Sautre cradling a narrow ivory casket under the shelter of his white mantle. The presence of soldiers at the main doors struck Jay as unusual—he could not recall such security at the abbey before the Stone's arrival in London—but he guessed that King Edward was merely being cautious regarding the safety of his prize.

Turning an indifferent eye to the splendor of the great church King Henry III had erected here, and followed closely by his two white-clad escorts, the Master of the Temple strode purposefully up to the serjeant of the watch and handed him a folded order, watched him come unconsciously to attention as he examined the seal. The document was a letter from the Archbishop of Canterbury, granting permission for the Templars to have a special Mass offered in the abbey for King Edward's victory and safe return from France. Jay always derived satisfaction from exercising his ecclesiastical influence; and in this instance, he took added pleasure from the deception involved. Tonight's foray was explained as an inspection of the physical layout of the part of the abbey church intended for use.

The three Templars were admitted and found the interior adequately lit for their purposes. Vespers and Compline were already over, and the monks would not return to the church until much later, for the office of Nocturn. Jay dismissed the guard who had admitted them, and had John de Sautre ensure that the door be secured behind them.

The martial impact of their footfalls echoed in the vaulted nave, where stone pillars loomed on either hand like so many frowning sentries, as Jay led his subordinates through the choir and the sanctuary to the old chapel of Edward the Confessor, the present king's avowed patron, current resting place of the Scottish Stone of Destiny. By King Edward's order, a fair bronze chair was being fashioned to house the Stone, but for the present it rested simple and unadorned in its place. Certainly of a proper size to have been Jacob's pillow, as the Scottish legends claimed, it looked surprisingly ordinary; but the Master of the Temple had learned enough of the mystic ways to know that such impressions were often deliberately deceptive.

Jay took the casket from Robert de Sautre and signed for him to remain at the entrance of the chapel, passing the casket to John as they moved into the presence of the Stone. As Jay went to bring a candle from one of the side altars, John de Sautre cast his gaze over the Stone of Destiny itself—a rather unremarkable-looking thing, he thought. As he did so, he was seized by the impression that there was someone standing at his shoulder.

A quick glance around revealed no one else present. He swallowed his uneasiness, knowing that to give voice to such an irrational notion would only invite the scorn of his superior.

Oblivious to his subordinate's discomfort, Jay came back to examine the Stone at close quarters. Other than a faint cruciform indentation, there were no additional markings suggestive of its sacred nature; and when he set his bare hand upon it and closed his eyes in meditation, it gave off no emanations of inner force.

Momentarily turning his back on the Stone, he took the

ivory casket from John de Sautre and set it on the floor beside the Stone, crouching down to unlock it. Inside were several items he had prepared in advance for this night's work, but what he removed first was a pair of wooden sticks, half the length of his forearm and inscribed with Pictish runes. After much time spent sifting records in the libraries at Balantrodoch and here in London, and numerous consultations with sources outside the Order, he had at last been able to determine some of the purposes for which these spell sticks of Briochan might be used. For one thing, they possessed an affinity for supernatural energies that could be utilized by a sympathetic spirit—and Jay was sympathetic to anything that promised to advance his own ambitions.

Clasping a stick in either hand, he returned to the Stone. Motioning John de Sautre to stay well back, he stretched out his arms over the Stone's upper surface and murmured an invocation in a voice too low for the other two men to hear. Repeating the invocation, he passed the sticks slowly back and forth, searching intently for some trace of mystical potency, however faint. He had been given to understand that the sticks would twitch downward if the object being so dowsed possessed any mystical potency. But though he repeated the exercise three times, he obtained no response to suggest that any residue remained of whatever energies had once been invested in the Stone.

Scowling, Jay set the sticks momentarily aside while he pulled from his scrip the pouch that contained John Balliol's hair and nail clippings. Carefully placing the pouch in the middle of the Stone, he reclaimed the sticks and began once again to sweep them above the surface of the Stone. His voice rose and fell in a guttural chant, summoning Briochan's guidance. But still the Stone remained stubbornly unresponsive.

With an exasperated hiss, Jay abandoned his efforts. Letting the rune-staves fall beside the pouch, he turned on his heel and began to pace the floor with angry strides. His subordinates kept out of his way, neither one daring to speak for fear of drawing his ire. After a moment, he came to an abrupt halt, his blue eyes feverishly bright.

"Nothing!" he whispered, flinging up a hand. "There is not so much as a trace of power that should have awakened when I exposed the Stone to the tokens of Balliol's presence! And yet we know that for centuries it has been the mystical key to Scotland's sovereignty. There must be something missing, something we have overlooked . . ."

It was Robert de Sautre who first took the chance of making a suggestion, drifting closer from his guard post by the chapel door.

"Might this not indicate," he said tentatively, "that either Balliol is no true king—or that this is not the genuine Stone?"

"Either that," John added in, "or *both* are false."

Jay cast his gaze over both men, considering, then slowly nodded.

"Such speculations are hardly likely to impress the king when he returns," he said coldly. "I fail to see how Balliol could be a false king, but if the king's men somehow managed to bring back a false Stone, we had better have some idea how to rectify the situation. We need more information," he continued, almost to himself. "And I do not think we can afford to be overly fastidious as to how we go about obtaining it."

Robert de Sautre blenched slightly. "What do you mean?"

Jay's tight smile bore altogether too much similarity to a grimace. In his heart he was not entirely easy about what he had in mind to attempt, but his ambition drove him on like a gale filling the sails of a rudderless ship, carrying it into uncharted waters that, for all their danger, might hold treasures worth any hazard.

For years, he had harbored increasingly definite suspicions regarding the existence of some esoteric cadre within the Order, who had access to mystical knowledge that conferred power. His attempts to seek them out had been singularly unsuccessful—perhaps because he was too cautious, knowing full well how interest in such subjects would be regarded as heretical, if it came to official notice. But gradually, he had found others outside the Order who were willing to accept him into their ranks, to teach him, and he was determined to be revenged on those who had rejected him. He was now certain that Saint Clair and the upstart Lennox were among their number.

Whatever it was that Saint Clair and his confederates were seeking, it seemed clearly bound up with the aims of the rebel Scots. It followed that whatever would do damage to one would also injure the other—and achieving such damage might well be possible by working through the Stone, which was said to embody mystical significance to the Scottish cause. Jay had long ago decided that no risk was too great to make himself master of its secrets, even if it meant dabbling in pagan sorceries.

Returning to the open casket, he reached along one side to finger out a flat-folded packet of parchment, the center overlap and turned-up ends sealed with wax. He opened this to remove what appeared to be a smaller, thicker piece of parchment inscribed with the triangular, horned shape of a bull's face. A musty, coppery smell came from it as Jay laid it on the Stone.

"You did well to send me that," Jay said, rummaging again in the casket. "Not only does it give us the symbol under which the Comyns' pagan sorcery operates, but the blood residual in the flayed skin will provide us with the admittedly unwilling blood offering of one of their co-religionists and the dark gods they serve. And this"—he removed a fragment of bone from the casket—"is from the forefinger of Briochan's left hand—he who served those gods a thousand years ago."

So saying, he set the bone atop the parchment token and handed flint and steel and a small charcoal brazier to John de

Sautre, directing him to set it alight while he again delved into the casket. The lighted brazier was set on the floor before the Stone, after which Jay laid a twist of parchment on the glowing coals and ordered John de Sautre to withdraw beside the chapel door with his brother, whence neither was to move or to speak. There was an edge to his voice that drove his two associates to obey him without question.

Curls of bitter incense rose to form a cloud of circling smoke as Jay gathered up the rune-staves and the finger bone of Briochan and resumed his original position. Like a priest standing over an altar, he once again elevated his arms, the rune-staves in his right hand, the bone fragment in his left, and began a Latin chant: the nearest embodiment of the ancient lore that he had been able to piece together from his contacts in London's mystical subculture.

Vestiges of ancient Celtic wisdom, Mithraic rituals introduced by the Romans, and other strands of magical tradition had been reinvigorated by an influx of cabalism and esoteric Sufi beliefs brought from the Holy Land by returning crusaders. Such information was carefully guarded, but Jay had discovered that a man with sufficient influence and wealth could unlock the hidden doors of the occult societies and gain access to much of their forbidden knowledge.

Now he armed himself with this knowledge as another man might don hauberk and shield to protect himself against a legion of enemies, and thus fortified, chanted his invocation with the fervor of a true initiate, oblivious to the uneasiness of his two fellow Templars.

"Per deam terrae sub pedibus et stellarum caelestium, per taurum magnum qui dexteram bellatoris firmat, iubeo te hanc sanguinem imbibere et secreta saxi sancti revelare."

Multiple repetitions brought no apparent response, and Jay began to doubt the efficacy of some element in the spell. Just when his patience had been stretched almost to the limit, however, he saw the parchment token on the Stone suddenly begin to quiver.

Smoke began to rise from it, acrid and sour, but he did not break off his chanting. Slowly a shadowy suggestion of shape began to form, drawing substance from the smoke, hunched over the Stone in a predatory attitude—a gaunt, bearded man in long tattered robes, disheveled hair hanging lankly over bony shoulders, a crown of withered leaves encircling his tonsured brow. John de Sautre suppressed a gasp, for he could have little doubt that the apparition was the same unseen presence he had sensed on first arriving in the chapel. Briochan had been here with them all along, either in anticipation of this moment or because his spirit was bound to the artifacts that had been taken from his grave, and had followed wherever they might be transported.

The specter turned its head, calling in a hollow voice like the cry of a lonely seabird sounding over the black waters of a benighted ocean.

"Goddess, O my goddess, queen of fire and wave, mistress of the depths of the birthing earth, I hear your call, but I cannot answer," it lamented.

The Templars shrank back from the outstretched hands as Briochan's shade drifted away from the Stone and made a halting circuit of the chapel, as if vainly seeking an exit, accompanied by the sullen clanking of chains he dragged at his ankles, hampering his every step. The eyes were wide open, yet he appeared not to see them until Brian de Jay accosted him by name.

"Briochan, servant of the once-great goddess," the Templar Master said sternly, "I charge you by your own lost deities and in the name of our Lord Jesus Christ to stand fast and harken to my words."

Briochan spun to face the Templar Master, his face contorted in a grimace of pain, as though Jay's words had the stinging force of a slave master's whip.

"Seek not to hold me, man of the cross," he blustered, *"or the goddess will surely feed your entrails to the starving hounds of darkness!"*

"Speak no idle threats, spirit!" Jay commanded firmly. "I possess the tokens of power that bind you to my will—both the heritage of your own spells and the last of your earthly remains. By the strictures of your own dark sorcery, you are compelled to obey me!"

Still clutching the relic of finger bone in one hand, Jay shifted the rune-staves to hold them like a cross between him and the spirit. Briochan's shade doubled forward, his ghostly essence writhing like a streamer of smoke tattered by a breeze, emitting a long, drawn-out moan. The sound was like the creaking of a ship's timbers under the pressure of the tide.

"*Say what you require of me, servant of the murdered god!*" he croaked, averting his tormented gaze from the Templar Master.

Jay indicated the Stone with a jut of his beard. "This is Scotland's Stone of Destiny, brought here to end the reign of her rebel kings. I order you to open its heart and show me the power that lies within. Tell me how its potency may be turned to my service."

He uncrossed the staves but continued to hold them ready. Briochan's shade eased itself upright, its tortured grimace yielding to an expression of hauteur. The entity spared a disdainful glance for the de Sautres, as though noticing them for the first time, before turning to face the Stone. The sullen clank of scraping metal accompanied him as his feet dragged their chains across the floor.

He overshadowed the charcoal brazier, taking greater substance from the smoke, and held his arms palm-downward above the surface of the Stone. As his eyes fluttered shut and his lips began a whispered invocation in the harsh Pictish tongue, a pale greenish glow emanating from his thin body slowly expanded to encompass the Stone in a pulsing aura of sickly flame.

A chill breeze stirred the air. The shade's chant of power subsided into an extended sigh, and for a moment the chapel was gripped by a breathless stillness, like a pendulum balanced at the far point of its swing.

Then Briochan's eyes snapped open, his head flinging back in a harsh explosion of cackling laughter. Jay went rigid with astonishment. As the laughter gradually subsided, lingering in the echoes amid the surrounding walls, the sense of derision was unmistakable.

"This is not the cursed Columba's gift to King Aidan!" the shade announced. *"This is an impotent lump of worthless rock, foisted upon you in the stead of the true Stone. Your king is a fool, as are all of you!"*

Brian de Jay's chin lifted in defiance, his brow darkening dangerously. Shifting the staves in his hands, he made a swift gesture that choked the wizard's laughter off short and sent fresh paroxysms pulsing through the shade's thin frame. But even that anguish could not entirely erase the scornful defiance from his features.

"I did not summon you here for your amusement," the Templar Master warned sharply. "If these words of yours are false, I swear that you shall never be free, but shall walk in torment through the land of the pagan dead for all eternity!"

Briochan's voice was dry and husky, but still carried the authority of his ancient calling. *"You have brought such mockery down upon your own heads, to be so lightly deceived,"* he retorted. *"You cannot put the blame on me, when you yourself have forced me to be the messenger of your shame."*

John de Sautre's throat was so dry, it was an effort to speak even a few words. "Does he speak the truth, my lord?"

"He does," Jay admitted reluctantly. "The spell is too strong for him to resist."

"Now will you free me, and allow me to answer the goddess?" Briochan demanded.

"No!" Jay retorted. "You will tell me who has the true Stone, and to what purpose they are turning it!"

Briochan raised his eyes to the chapel's ceiling, as though searching there for a vision. *"I cannot see so far, bound as I am by these cursed chains. The true Stone is meant for foundation, I know—for a temple of Columba's intention—but yet might it better serve the temple of the gods, should its power be thus diverted.*

"Wind and flame hold to no cause other than to destroy what stands against them," he continued, his tone now faint and faraway. *"The fates are in disarray, and the face of the king changes with the passing of day and night and day. The lightning hangs poised to strike to west or east, to affirm the line of kings or light the way of the goddess from out of the exiled depths."*

"What empty ravings are these?" John de Sautre whispered.

"Do not let him fob us off with these riddles!" Robert urged. "Task him, my lord, and squeeze the truth from his marrow!"

Briochan turned on the brothers, baring his teeth in a feral snarl. He stretched out his hands toward them, the fingers curling like the claws of a beast, and both men pressed their backs to the chapel's walls.

"Enough!" Jay cried, making a gesture of dismissal with the rune-staves.

A blast of cold, foul-smelling wind rushed through the room, and the specter vanished like a candle flame abruptly snuffed out by a draft from an open door. The ensuing silence seemed to enfold the three Templars like the stifling thickness of a death shroud.

Drawing a deep breath, Jay wiped a trickle of cold sweat from his brow and cleared his throat before replacing the magical items in their casket.

"Snuff out the brazier, and leave no trace of this night's work," he ordered John de Sautre. "And you—make certain no alarm has been raised by any sounds," he added to Robert.

As the latter hurried to obey, Jay crouched down opposite John de Sautre, laying a hand on the Stone.

"So the true Stone is still in Scotland," he mused. "But where?"

"The Comyns might have it," John de Sautre ventured, snuffing out charcoal with the pommel of his dagger. "That might explain why the ghost would not reveal its hiding place."

The Master of England shook his head, still thinking. "No, it is Wallace who is now wielding the power of kingship. Did he not raid Scone itself, driving out King Edward's justiciar, before his victory at Stirling?"

John de Sautre inclined his head in gruff affirmation. "True enough. The switch would have been made long before that; but if the Stone had been concealed thereabouts, Wallace might well have got his hands on it."

"Exactly," Jay agreed, as Robert de Sautre reappeared in the doorway and nodded his reassurance that all was well. "It strikes me that this upstart somehow may have found the means to draw upon its power, even without being crowned. And I begin to wonder whether our two errant brethren might, somehow, have aided him in this deceitful act of usurpation. We know they were about *something* at Scone, before riding on to Iona. If we are to retain King Edward's favor and patronage, we must somehow put an end to Wallace, and ensure that no Scots king thereafter is crowned upon the Stone."

"How are we to accomplish that?" John asked, as he packed the charcoal brazier back into the casket. "Wallace has already broken one army."

"If you wish to overcome a pack of ravenous hounds," Jay said thoughtfully, "toss them a bone and they will tear each other apart fighting over it. I think the Comyns have no more good will for Wallace than we—and we have a bone they are surely hungering for."

He slammed the casket shut on Briochan's relics and cast a darkling glare at the false Stone. "A fresh army is mustering to meet Wallace in the field, but it will take more than military might to defeat him. We must return to Scotland, brothers, and put an end to this matter once and for all."

Chapter
Twenty-four

IT TOOK MANY MONTHS OF CAREFUL PLANNING FOR THE
Master of England to advance his purposes. Not until July of
the following year did King Edward again march north to
wreak retribution in Scotland; but when he did, Brian de Jay
and John de Sautre were riding at his side, poised to further
both his ambitions and their own.

Meanwhile, those of their own Order whom they suspected of working to thwart their purposes—still regarded
as renegades by Jay and de Sautre, despite official vindica-
tion from as august a superior as the Visitor of France—
were camped with the Scottish forces fighting for the rights
of the still-captive King John Balliol, whose cause had been
asserted so forcefully the previous year at Stirling Bridge.

Still under secret orders from their superiors in Paris,
Brothers Arnault de Saint Clair and Torquil Lennox had returned to Scotland some eighteen months before, not as
Templars but in the guise of ordinary men-at-arms, quietly
offering their services to Bishop Wishart of Glasgow and

James the Stewart, the greatest magnate in the west of Scotland—and easing their way into the core of Scottish resistance focused in the southwest, which maintained that John Balliol's abdication and subsequent removal from kingship was invalid because obtained under duress. William Wallace, second son of a simple knightly family who were vassals of the Stewart, had been among those local patriots continuing to foment resistance to English occupation; and when he burst into prominence following his slaying of William Hazelrigg, the English Sheriff of Lanark, sparking the new rebellion that was to have its day of glory at Stirling Bridge, he kept silent about the true identity of two "scouts" who had attached themselves to his service and provided occasionally stunning bits of intelligence.

Nearly a year had passed since the battle of Stirling Bridge—a triumph that had cost the life of the brilliant and gallant Andrew Murray, mortally wounded in the battle. But the victory had led to Wallace's election as sole Guardian of Scotland, who thereafter styled himself "commander of the army of the Kingdom of Scotland, in the name of the famous prince the lord John, by God's grace illustrious King of Scotland, by consent of the community of that realm." Formal knighthood had shortly followed. Under the continuing leadership of Wallace—and taking advantage of the absence abroad of Edward of England—the Scots had reclaimed their native countryside, leaving only a handful of lowland castles in English hands.

But the Scots knew a further test was coming. A truce between England and France had enabled Edward to forsake his military campaigning in Flanders and return to England. In June, having summoned his northern levies for a new expeditionary force, he had begun his relentless advance up the eastern coast of Scotland, spreading fear and devastation as he came, intending to break the spirit of the Scots by forcefully demonstrating what price was to be paid for resistance.

From a Scottish perspective, one of the notes of optimism was that the English supply links were not yet reliable, and many of Edward's troops were reported to be near starving, some of them on the verge of revolt. Whether Scots tenacity could outlast English hunger and disgruntlement remained to be seen.

On this eve of the Feast of Saint Mary Magdalene, camped in the Wood of Callendar, near the town of Falkirk, it appeared they might. For the past several days, the English army had been stalled at Temple Liston, some fifteen miles to the east, by invitation of the Masters of the English and Scottish Temples; but reports just shared by Wallace with his commanders indicated that Edward intended to withdraw his hungry army all the way to Edinburgh on the morrow—for he had no inkling where his elusive foe was to be found. The plan of battle that Wallace had presented involved a quick march in the morning to fall on the English rear guard as they went, destroying their baggage train and killing as many as possible before falling back.

"What do you think?" Arnault murmured to Torquil, as they drifted back from the area before Wallace's tent where a few of the Scots leaders were still clarifying instructions with the Guardian. Clad in the light armor of hardened leather worn by scouts, dark-cloaked and anonymous, the pair blended easily with the following of commanders and more richly garbed Scots nobles now dispersing to their respective camps.

"As a Scot," said Torquil, "I think that it's a miracle they're continuing to listen to him. But they haven't got any better hope just now."

As they watched and listened to the men passing by, Torquil still marveled that Wallace had been able to take a nation that was beaten and demoralized and, by the sheer force of his character, set it back on course for victory and freedom, outstripping in valor and strategy so many who were his superiors in rank and experience. Yet the greater—

and more terrible—miracle was still to come; for as the weeks had passed and Scottish successes grew, there could be little doubt that Providence was elevating Wallace to a far higher estate—and that he was, indeed, the Uncrowned King foretold in prophecy.

Wallace's sacramental role had been sealed at the point when he had been appointed sole Guardian of the realm. John Balliol was a prisoner in London, and Wallace now fought in Balliol's name, as his champion and his surrogate. Some there were among Scotland's greater magnates who resented being led and governed by a man who was the second son of a mere knight. But to Arnault and Torquil, the relative humility of Wallace's birthright was but one of the signs they had been told to seek.

A man of sorrows was he, as well; for an act that had made him an outlaw under English law—his slaying of William Hazelrigg—had been precipitated by Hazelrigg's part in the brutal murder of Wallace's young wife. Wallace had slain Hazelrigg in a spirit of justice; but that act of retribution had not lessened the pain of his bereavement. That abiding sorrow was a further sign of his symbolic and sacrificial kingship. There remained one final trial, and it was the one the Templars most feared: a betrayal at the hands of his own followers.

Whatever their own fears, there was no denying the air of expectancy gripping the camp. The domestic smells of barley and turnips wafted up from the cooking pots as the men prepared their supper, but off to one side groups of men were practicing their swordsmanship. The force of their exchanges suggested pent-up frustration and an edge of resignation. Here and there the voice of a priest could be heard saying Mass for a group of soldiers; and indeed, the Mass that Arnault and Torquil had attended earlier had been joined by a greater number of soldiers than usual—a sure sign that many anticipated they would soon be face-to-face with the specter of death, and were seeking to armor their souls against his scythe.

The numerous spearmen, the common folk who comprised the main strength of the army, were hunkered down around the cook fires, exchanging desultory conversation as they sharpened the points of their long-hafted weapons. As the two Templars passed by, they could hear some discussing in hushed tones the best way to impale the horse of a charging English knight. Others were tinkering with badges and charms they hoped would bring them good luck, trusting as much in their old superstitions as in their prayers to Our Lady.

Down in a hollow to the west of the camp, the horses of the meager Scots cavalry could be heard whuffling and whinnying uneasily, as if at the approach of a lightning storm. To Arnault and Torquil came the sense of some less natural danger hovering near, closer than the English army that was encamped a full day away—and it was not the natural uneasiness any man might feel at the approach of battle.

As they circled back nearer Wallace's tent, they surveyed the faces of some of the Guardian's commanders. Sir John Stewart passed nearby—in charge of the archers of Selkirk Forest, who would have the daunting task of matching skills with Edward's famous host of longbowmen. John Stewart's brother, James the Stewart, was there as well, as were the Earls of Atholl and Menteith, Malise of Strathearn, and Malcolm of Lennox, who would have been Torquil's own lord, if he had not exchanged his feudal vows for those of the Temple.

John Comyn, Younger of Badenoch, was also prominent among them, wolfish and hard-eyed, representing his powerful family, who had contributed the main part of the Scots cavalry. Captured at Dunbar along with three earls and more than one hundred knights and esquires, he had been held a prisoner in England for many months, until King Edward sent him home in the hope that the Comyns would establish some peaceful stability in this troublesome country.

But like so many others, young Comyn had once again taken up arms in the cause of John Balliol. He professed loyalty to the Scottish cause, but there was that about his manner—an edge, a strange glitter in his eyes—that had spooked both Torquil and Arnault, by turns. While all signs pointed conclusively to Wallace as the Uncrowned King, they had yet to identify the shadowy "apostate" referred to in the prophecy.

Torquil was prepared to believe that the younger Comyn might well be that apostate; Arnault was proceeding on the assumption that they were looking for the leader of a secret cult, pointing out that young Comyn definitely had not been among the mysterious Highlanders who had attacked them on the way back from Iona—though whose those men might have been, they still had no idea.

Wallace finally withdrew to his tent with James the Stewart to confer over a hasty meal while the others dispersed to their own suppers, amid lengthening shadows. Though there were some discontented grumblings, most of Wallace's commanders seemed grimly satisfied to find themselves at last on the eve of a fight, even if it were not to be as glorious as many of them would have wished. Torquil turned to Arnault as they watched from the edge of the clearing.

"I think the men will not be happy about these orders," he said. "They're tired of these cat-and-mouse games. They want to stand and fight."

"And if they do," Arnault replied, "and if they must face Edward's heavy cavalry on ground of *his* choosing, they'll be ground into the mud."

"They held at Stirling Bridge," Torquil pointed out.

"Yes, but Edward was not present at Stirling Bridge, and the English have learned a few things since then. Also, Wallace had Murray at his side—perhaps one of the greatest strategists I have ever seen in action. It was a great tragedy for Scotland, that he later died of his wounds."

Torquil nodded, absently crossing himself in remembrance of the much missed Murray. "Aye, but Wallace has the gift of leadership. You've seen the loyalty he inspires. If, by some miracle, he does succeed in chasing Edward back across the border, the people might well offer him the crown. Would he take it, do you think?"

Arnault shook his head. "You know he is meant for other things. Besides, he is not highborn enough to win the support of the nobles which he would need, to reign as king. Moreover, his own sense of honor would not allow him to take such a step. No man is more worthy of the crown than he—yet he will fight to the death for the man who does wear it, or should wear it. And right now, that man is still John—" He broke off and frowned, his attention focused on something off behind Torquil.

"What is it?" Torquil asked.

"Turn gently," Arnault murmured, indicating the subject of his interest with a tilt of his head.

Slowly turning, Torquil followed the line of his mentor's gaze with apparently casual interest, to the unmistakable figure of John Comyn, standing with several of his retainers. Just walking away from them was a small, squat man in leathers and a saffron shirt, who was striding off in the direction of the western reach of the camp. Something about the look of the man made Torquil want to crane his neck to see if there was anything painted on his forehead, but he turned sidelong to Arnault instead, still watching the man— and Comyn—from the corner of his eye.

"Have I just seen what I think I've seen?" he murmured, his glance darting to Arnault's face.

"Later, I'll be interested to hear whether what you think you've seen tallies with *my* impressions," Arnault returned in an equally low tone, starting to head slowly in that direction—for Comyn had left his retainers and was now walking purposefully in the same direction the Highlander had gone.

At that moment, a man-at-arms from the Guardian's cadre of military advisors came shouldering between two lowland knights, raising a hand to catch their attention.

"Saint Clair—a moment!" he called, as Arnault and Torquil both turned. "By your leave, the Guardian requests a word."

With a fleeting glance at the departing Comyn, Arnault nodded to Torquil. "I'll rejoin you later," he said, with a meaningful nod. "See if there's word from that contact we were expecting."

"Aye."

As Arnault headed off toward the Guardian's tent with the messenger, Torquil returned his covert gaze in the direction of the younger Comyn, still making his way briskly toward the western reach of the camp—and directly opposite to the direction in which his own men were camped, on the army's east flank. Torquil's uneasiness had now become a distinct prickling at the back of his neck.

Taking care not to appear too furtive, he set off to follow, keeping pace at a discreet distance. Comyn proceeded through the camp like a man with a definite purpose in mind, looking neither left nor right, but Torquil was able to keep his quarry in sight without drawing attention to himself, weaving his own way quickly through the maze of tents and cook fires and milling men.

Comyn came at last to the horse lines picketed toward the western perimeter of the encampment, where the Highlander Torquil had seen before was holding two horses, talking amiably to one of the grooms. Comyn hailed both men in a friendly fashion, exchanging banter that Torquil could not hear as the two of them mounted up and rode slowly out and along the western perimeter of the camp—apparently in no hurry, but Torquil's sense of something being wrong was still as strong as ever.

A few words with a groom farther along the horse line secured Torquil a mount as well, and he headed immediately in the direction Comyn and his mysterious companion had just disappeared—and was able to catch just a glimpse of them as they passed into the screen of the forest edge and then briefly emerged to disappear again down the narrow defile of a stream leading directly away from the camp.

Now certain that Comyn was up to no good, Torquil followed, making use of skills hard won in the Holy Land to keep the pair always in sight yet never be seen himself. When, several miles beyond the camp, they appeared to be making for a ruined church, nestled down in a hollow beside a narrow stream, Torquil hung back amid the shadows of a veiling stand of trees to watch.

The pair drew rein in the ruined churchyard and dismounted, and Torquil likewise slid from his saddle. He slipped his sheathed sword from its hangers and slid it under his saddle flap before starting to work his way closer on foot, keeping to what cover was available, finally taking refuge behind a crumbling freestone wall—still at some distance from the stone shell of the building itself. But it was close enough to see that another horse was already standing hip-shot within the ruins of the church porch—and the brief glimpse Torquil got of a dark-clad figure who appeared briefly in the doorway to beckon young Comyn inside had something of the familiar to it; but he could not make out what it was.

Straining for some hint of what was going on, Torquil considered trying to make his way closer; but the Highlander remained with the horses, looking vaguely bored but apparently watching toward the north as he let the horses graze. Very soon, the dark dots of two additional riders could be seen approaching from that direction, causing the Highlander to poke his head briefly through the doorway into the ruins.

Hunching deeper into his hiding place, trusting that his leathers and dark cloak would continue to camouflage him, Torquil bit back a gasp—for the figure that emerged with young John Comyn, shaking back its dark hood to reveal a hard, bearded face that had seen more than its share of battles, was none other than the elder John Comyn, Lord of Badenoch, hitherto believed to be still in the north, defending his family's ancestral lands.

But even more appalling was the identity of the two men drawing rein in the churchyard. For their dark cloaks only partially covered bright white surcoats bearing the splayed red cross of the Order of the Temple; and as they, too, shook back their hoods, Torquil could have no doubt that he was gazing upon Brian de Jay and John de Sautre!

Chapter Twenty-five

THE IMPLICATIONS WERE STAGGERING. THAT THE YOUNGER Comyn should find it advisable to meet clandestinely with his father was bad enough; but to have arranged an assignation on the eve of battle with the Master of the English Temple and the Preceptor of Scotland—known to be riding with Edward of England as his advisors—was a betrayal of astounding magnitude.

And was it mere gold for which the Comyns were prepared to commit treason? For John de Sautre had a long, narrow casket tied behind his saddle, revealed as he swung down. And both Comyns eyed it hungrily as he unlashed it and tucked it under one arm, both of them watching both Templars warily as the four of them disappeared into the ruins again.

Torquil knew that he *must* find out more of their plans; but he dared not venture closer, for the Highlander was now tending all five horses, and idly scanning the approaches to the ruin, sure to catch any attempt by Torquil to spy upon what was going on inside.

There was one recourse open to Torquil that might work—used with some success in the past, though he had never dared to try it under such conditions. But desperate circumstances called for desperate measures; for if the Comyns and the Templars riding with Edward were preparing to work a betrayal, the cost to the Scottish patriots could be beyond reckoning.

Hunching down as small as he could make himself, Torquil eased his fingers into the pouch at his belt and, after probing briefly, brought out a roughly circular wooden disk, perhaps the size of a hen's egg. Called a *sian* or charm of protection, and cut as a cross section from a branch of rowan wood—long regarded as protective against the forces of evil—its two faces had been polished to a silken sheen and then inscribed by the monks of Iona during the appropriate cycles of new moon and tides, accompanied by appropriate prayers and blessings. One side bore the sign of the cross, burned into the wood, the other an inked inscription in the ancient Celtic tongue: *Mor do ingantaib dogni in ir genair o Muiri.*

Silently Torquil mouthed the words, his heart making of the line a prayer as his mind supplied the meaning: *The King that is born of Mary performs many wonders.*

Then, calling on knowledge he had gained during those weeks spent praying and learning with the kindred of Columba, on the blessed isle of Iona, he closed the *sian* in his right hand and pressed that fist to his forehead, silently reciting to himself the *Fàilte Mhoire*, the Hail Mary as he had learned it in the Gaelic. He could not remember the Gaelic for the rest of the charm of the *Frìth Mhoire,* or augury of Mary, but he knew the flow of intent, and trusted that the Mother of his Lord would hear him, even if the words were not exactly right.

"The augury mild Mary made for her Son, the Queen-maiden gazing downward through her palm . . ." He made a tube of the fingers of his left hand and blew through it thrice, in the name of the Three Persons of the Trinity, then held that tube to his left eye and turned his gaze toward the ruined church as he whispered what he could remember of the *Fàilte na frìthe.*

"The augury that Mary made for her Son, that Brigid breathed through her palm . . . The Son of the King of Life be my stay behind me, to give me eyes to see and hear all my quest . . ."

At first he could see nothing but a constrained glimpse of the man waiting with the horses in the gathering gloom of twilight. But then, as his breathing steadied and he reached deeper into his inner stillness, he saw-but-did-not-see four black-cloaked figures standing far to the east end of the church, before the ruined altar. Likewise, the whisper of voices became gradually audible through some faculty that was not physical hearing.

"Do not try to impress me with your courage, Templar," the Black Comyn was saying. "Save it for the field of battle. Let me see what you have brought us."

He took a stride forward, but Jay swiftly interposed, clapping a hand to the hilt of his sword by way of a warning.

"Not so quickly. Can you deliver to me what I seek in exchange?"

"Wallace?" Comyn retorted. "We can bring him to you. But you will have to slay him yourself."

A distant part of Torquil was aware of a queasy stirring in his stomach, but he kept himself focused and distanced from his outrage for fear of missing any vital piece of knowledge.

"Bring him *where*?" Jay retorted. "You will get no satisfaction from *me* until I know where Wallace is, and what his plans are."

Comyn's eyes narrowed. "And will you get satisfaction from your king, if you bring him not this victory? Do not try my patience, Templar. Before I will speak further concerning what *you* desire, I will examine what you have there. If that does not suit you, then draw your sword, and we shall settle our business with blood rather than words!"

The silence bristled between them, but then, abruptly, the Master of England curled his lip and lifted his hand away from his weapon.

"Very well, you may make your inspection," he said. "Brother John, over there will do."

He pointed to the pediment of a fallen pillar, its top sheared off to leave behind a rude table of stone. Impassive, John de Sautre came forward and set the casket on the rough surface. The other three men gathered round, and Jay presented the Black Comyn with a small key.

The Lord of Badenoch took a deep breath before unlocking the box. His gnarled fingers quivered slightly as he slowly lifted the lid. When he bent to view its contents, his whole face tightened. Frowning with concentration, he extended the index finger of his left hand over the open box and waved it slowly back and forth, as though testing the air by some arcane means.

The Templars exchanged glances, knowing that everything hinged upon Comyn's reaction. The younger Comyn watched the knights closely, alert for any hint of treachery. The silence drew itself out. Then the Black Comyn sighed aloud and raised his hands in an attitude of thanksgiving.

"These truly are the relics and spells of Briochan," he murmured reverently. "We shall welcome him home, and the goddess will shower us with her favor."

Jay reached out and banged the lid shut. Comyn rounded on him with an angry glare, but the Templar set his left hand on the lid in pointed possessiveness, right hand on the hilt of his sword.

"These relics go *nowhere*," Jay said, "until you first fulfill your part of the bargain."

The younger Comyn moved to his father's side, quivering with fury. "You are not in one of your Temples now," he declared. "This is our land, and you will speak with respect!"

"Nay, let us do as we have undertaken," Comyn said, raising a hand to calm his son. "You wish to bring Wallace to battle and slay him, Templar? It can be accomplished. Your king's army lies no more than a few hours' march from the Wood of Callendar, where the Guardian has made his camp. On the morrow Wallace will advance, hoping to catch the English host as they retreat and deal them a fatal blow."

Jay's right hand balled itself into a fist. "So near," he muttered. "Had we but known—"

"You know now, thanks to us," Comyn cut in sharply. "If you go forward to meet Wallace instead of withdrawing toward Edinburgh, he will have no choice but to stand and fight."

"And then what?" Jay demanded. "Will you stand with him?"

The Black Comyn's lip curled in a sneer of contempt. "William Wallace is a commoner and a usurper," he stated bitterly, "and I will not see my men fall in his cause."

The younger Comyn took his cue from his father. "At the point of battle, I will lead our cavalry from the field. The others' horsemen will follow. We will keep them safe from any folly of Wallace's, to fight another day. In time we can raise more foot soldiers to serve the cause of a king—but not a commoner."

"What of Wallace himself?" Jay asked. "Will he flee also, when he sees you abandon the field?"

"He is no craven, for all his common blood," young Comyn conceded. "He will stand his ground for as long as he can. And he will be yours for the taking—if you can catch him."

With preternatural swiftness, Jay seized the Black Comyn's wrist and pressed his palm down hard on the lid of the casket. Comyn's eyes flared with surprised outrage, but Jay held him firmly.

"Swear upon these relics you hold so sacred," the Master of England ordered, "that what you have said is true and that you will fulfill your promise on the morrow."

"By what right do you—" Comyn began.

"By right," Jay said coldly, "that what we have brought you are tangible relics of power. All you have given in exchange are words. Without your oath on this—we have no bargain!"

For the space of several heartbeats, the two men glared at one another, eyes locked in a battle of wills. The younger Comyn and John de Sautre likewise bristled, hands on sword hilts, uncertain whether to risk interfering, until finally the Black Comyn drew a hissing breath.

"I swear by all that I hold holy," he whispered through gritted teeth, "that what I have said is true and that I will not break my bond with you."

Satisfied, Jay released Comyn's wrist and took a step back, nodding for de Sautre to do the same. Neither made any attempt to interfere as the elder Comyn gathered up the ivory casket and cradled it possessively against his chest. His eyes widened, taking on a feverish inner luminance, as if Briochan's long buried power were already infusing his frame.

"Come," Jay said to de Sautre. "The king must have this news at once, before he begins to withdraw."

His subordinate mutely nodded his compliance, but as the two Templars turned to go, Comyn spoke again.

"We shall not meet again, Templar, for the hell of your own making awaits you."

An unearthly resonance to his voice chilled Torquil even more than the depth of the betrayal just agreed. Jay's response, however, was a disdainful sneer.

"If we do meet again," he said, "you will be kneeling before my king—or his headsman."

Turning on his heel, he swept out of the church, de Sautre in his wake. As they emerged from the ruined doorway,

Torquil suppressed a shuddering gasp and ducked his head, ending the augury. His pulse was racing as he huddled behind his bit of wall, trying to come to grips with all he had just seen and heard, vaguely listening to Jay and de Sautre mount up—and aware that the younger Comyn, at least, would soon be mounting up as well, to return along this route to the Scottish camp.

Indeed, young Comyn came out to watch with the Highlander as the Templars galloped off to the north. And while their attention was thus occupied, Torquil tucked the *sian* back into his pouch and began making his way quietly back to where he had left his horse, ducking low, mind awhirl with the implications of the betrayal.

That the Comyns should be conspiring with Brian de Jay to betray Wallace suggested that their ambitions far outstripped those of the Templar Master—and there now could be no doubt that the relics of the Pictish Briochan had *not* ended up at the bottom of a lake, as Jay and the de Sautres had claimed. Whether these were mere trinkets or whether they were objects of power such as the Inner Circle of the Temple guarded, Torquil did not know; but the thought of them in the hands of the Comyns sent a new chill up his spine.

But that must take second place to the wider-ranging treachery involving the betrayal of Wallace. Above all else, Arnault and the Guardian must be warned that Jay was riding to advise Edward of the Scottish position. As the only witness to Comyn's treachery, Torquil knew he had to make it back to Wallace's camp. The fate of the Scottish army must come first, and the deeds of the Comyns could be judged afterward.

When he had almost reached the safety of the trees, he glanced back at the ruined church and saw the elder Comyn coming out of the doorway, looking about wildly, agitatedly consulting with his son and the Highlander as he held out what appeared to be two sticks, holding them parallel to one another and ranging them in the direction of Torquil's hill, as if questing with them.

Torquil ducked behind a tree and gazed back fearfully—appalled—for before his very eyes, the Black Comyn's face seemed to be overshadowed by a greater darkness than the gloom of twilight, a fey gleam lighting the hollow sockets of his eyes that was visible even in the gathering darkness.

Recoiling, Torquil realized that some other entity had invaded the Black Comyn's body. Whether the secondary spirit was that of Briochan or the terrible goddess they both served, Torquil had no idea; but there was no doubt in his mind that he himself was in imminent danger of discovery.

Throwing caution to the winds, he broke for the deeper cover of the woods, heading for the clearing where he had left his horse, aware of young Comyn and the Highlander throwing themselves into their horses and spurring in his direction—and of something else stirring in response to whatever the elder Comyn was conjuring up, surely akin to what had come during that attack on the way back from Iona.

His horse shied back as he burst into the clearing. Ripping the reins loose, he flung them over the animal's neck and vaulted astride. Though the horse reared and plunged, he hauled its head around and launched it with a clap of his heels in the direction of Wallace's encampment. But though he quickly lost the sounds of mere human pursuit, a far worse pursuer had found his scent.

A shrill, ululating hunting call overtook him as he galloped headlong through the woods. He cast a fearful look over his shoulder and gasped to see a huge winged shadow-shape skimming low over the treetops in his wake, malevolent green eyes glaring down above a wide slavering mouth—without doubt, some horror set upon him by the Comyns, an unwanted demonstration of the power they could summon with the artifacts delivered to them by Brian de Jay.

Bending low in the saddle, he spurred his horse even

faster, low-hanging branches lashing him as he ran the gauntlet of the trees. The shadow swooped nearer, darkening the ground as it came. As the distance closed between them, it gave another ear-splitting howl and plunged.

Torquil sensed it coming and wrenched his horse aside. The animal stumbled and went down as a huge black wing swept over them like a reaper's scythe, an icy backdraft buffeting Torquil from the saddle. He hit the ground rolling and dived into a nest of brambles as the shadow-hunter turned in the air and prepared to attack again.

White-eyed with terror, his mount heaved itself to its feet, blood seeping from an ugly gash in its flank. With a shrill whinny, it wheeled and bolted in a flying shower of turf.

The shadow banked in midair. For a moment it hovered, as if uncertain which way to turn, perhaps distracted by the smell of blood. Quick to seize any diversion, Torquil scrambled free of the undergrowth and set off running in the opposite direction.

The rough ground kept conspiring to trip him up. As he struggled on, now gasping for breath, he heard the dread upbeat of wings and felt an icy wind buffet at the nape of his neck. He threw himself flat with an involuntary *whoof!* and gasped as icy talons swiped at his back. The pain of even a glancing blow was gut-wrenching; and in that instant he could entertain no doubt that not only his body but his very soul was in peril.

He elbowed himself up and started running again. Behind him he could hear the gurgle of bestial laughter as the shadow-entity closed in for the kill—and flashed on the utter certainty that he had glimpsed a like entity once before, compassing the death of Alexander III. Panting out a desperate plea to the Virgin for help, he cast about wildly for some natural defense against the powers of sorcery. But there was no running water anywhere, nor any stand of rowan wood—

Cursing himself for ten kinds of fool, he thrust his back against a tree and clawed in his pouch for the holy *sian* that had protected him not an hour before. As soon as his fingers closed around it, he felt a surge of renewed strength, as if all the company of Saint Columba were massing at his back, ready to defend him. Clenching the disk of rowan wood tightly in his right hand, he staggered to a halt and turned at bay, brandishing it, cross-outward, like a shield, quailing before the foul, freezing breath of the horror poised above him.

"Great Michael of the Battles, Ranger of the Heavens, be with me!" he gasped. "Jesu, Son of Mary, shield thou thy servant, soul and soul-shrine!"

In answer, the *sian* ignited in a blaze of pure white fire, kindling a fire in his heart that left no room for cold or fear. Its radiance expanded outward in a dazzling corona, as though he were holding the sun itself in his hand. Dimly, through the haze of light, he could sense the shadow gathering itself for its final onslaught, but he closed his eyes, concentrating on making himself a channel for the Light that was his shield in the face of the enemy.

The attack, when it came, was so ferocious that the force of it flung him backward off his feet. He struck the ground with a bruising jolt, and only just managed to retain his grip on the blazing talisman. The shadow pressed down on him from above, hungrily seeking a chink in his defenses. From flat on his back he gasped out another plea for help—to Saint Michael, to Mary, to Columba, to all the angels—even as he thrust the *sian* again between himself and his attacker.

Then, all at once, an eldritch screech ripped the air around him. In the same instant, the sun-disk exploded in his hand. Splinters of light burst upward in a fountain of white-hot needles, penetrating deep into the belly of the shadow. The creature screeched again and struck at him in a blind fury of flying talons.

Each blow seemed like a dagger slash. Torquil cried aloud in agony and tried to writhe away, right arm still upflung in warding, left arm shielding his eyes, a part of him nearly past caring whether the flying shards of light would take their toll of the shadow before it succeeded in ripping his soul from his body. Racked with pain and exhaustion, the last thing he remembered was the sight of the wooden talisman crumbling to ashes in his fingers before his senses abandoned him to the dark.

Chapter Twenty-six

AS THE LATE SUMMER NIGHT CLOSED IN WITHOUT BRINGING
Torquil back to camp, Arnault found himself increasingly
concerned. He had seen no sign of the younger Comyn either, but he could make no very specific inquiries without
possibly arousing unwelcome notice.

The atmosphere hanging over the camp was one of sim-
mering excitement as the Scottish army completed preparations for their march against Edward. Wallace himself had
been constantly on the move among the men, stopping to
share a joke or a bite of food with the common soldiers as
often as he paused to elaborate on his orders with their commanders. The Guardian exuded an air of confidence—
though there was no telling whether this was because he was
assured of success or because he knew that courage and fear
were equally infectious in these close confines. Either way,
Arnault could only admire the bond of trust that Wallace had
established with his men-at-arms, having shown them so
graphically at Stirling Bridge that a determined host of Scot-

tish spearmen could smash the assembled might of English chivalry.

Arnault wished he could be as sanguine about Torquil. As midnight approached, his forebodings took a sharp upturn when he finally glimpsed young John Comyn strolling past in the company of several of his peers. Falling in casually behind them, he worked his way close enough to overhear their conversation; but such snippets of talk as they let fall gave him no clues as to how young Comyn might have spent the past few hours.

Dropping back to a discreet distance, Arnault studied the younger man through narrowed eyes. John Comyn's demeanor appeared outwardly as bland as his talk, but even so, Arnault thought he could detect small signs of underlying tension in the way the man kept toying with the hilt of his dirk. Such uneasiness was perhaps only natural in view of the impending engagement, but Arnault found himself doubting that this could be the sole explanation—especially when Torquil had yet to put in an appearance. And there was still the unanswered question of the dark little man who apparently had summoned Comyn—who very much reminded Arnault of the men who had attacked the Templar band on the road back from Iona. If those had been Comyn men . . .

Drawing a deep breath, Arnault summoned his inner faculties to his aid. When he looked again with a keener eye, he at once became aware of a curious cast of shadow clinging about young Comyn's person, as if the younger man had been touched by something unclean that had left its mark on him. At Berwick, during the court of claims, he remembered glimpsing a similar suggestion of darkness surrounding young Comyn and his father—at the time, dismissed as probably nothing more than a deceptive trick of the eye. But that had been before John Balliol's inauguration, when Torquil had reported seeing the elder Comyn palm a consecrated Host at Mass—and long before the attack on the Templars . . .

Now the son's dark aura was clearly present, certainly no less unsavory than his father's had been—a discovery that filled Arnault with grave forebodings for Torquil's safety. And he could not conceive any good reason why Torquil should not have come back by now—if he were able . . .

He was reticent about confronting young Comyn directly, for it was possible the man would remember him from Berwick or Scone, as having been a Templar—a discovery that could well undermine his usefulness to Wallace. To get the answers he urgently needed, Arnault knew he would have to use another avenue of investigation.

Wrapping himself in his cloak, he made his way quietly to a secluded area on the outskirts of the camp. His destination was a hollow dell just beyond the reach of the watch fires. Here, behind a screen of young oak trees, he spread his cloak on the ground and sketched a circle of protection around it with his sword, which he then stuck into the ground before him as he sat down cross-legged. Delving into the neck of his gambeson then, he pulled out the cord on which the *keekstane* that Brother Ninian had given him hung.

After bowing low before the cross of his sword, he clasped the stone in his right hand and closed his eyes, drawing—though he did not know it—on the same strands of Celtic wisdom that Torquil had summoned with his *sian* of rowan wood, some hours before; for the *keekstane*, like the *sian*, possessed kindred resonances with Celtic spirituality. It had not occurred to Arnault that he might seek Torquil using the link between these two tools of spiritual discernment; but he found himself reaching out with the same kinds of imagery that both of them had learned on Iona, as he framed his petition to the forces of Light.

Thou Michael Militant, thou king of the angels, he prayed in the stillness of his soul, *shield thou thy servant Torquil with the shade of thy wing and the might of thy sword. By the power of the Chief of Chiefs, send me forth upon the road*

*taken by my brother-in-arms, that I may find him, safe and
still in thy service.*

So saying, he turned inward in spirit, seeking the silence
at the center of his being. Like the petals of a rose unfolding, that silence opened up to receive him. He stepped into
that silence and at once found himself slowly rising in spirit
above a sea of trees—the Wood of Callendar, he knew at
once, as he overlooked the familiar landscape.

Once oriented, he cast beneath him for some sign of
Torquil, and was drawn toward a shimmering thread of light
weaving its way westward across the forest floor—surely
the direction Torquil must have gone after the younger
Comyn. Just as some dark avatar of pagan times had left its
mark on young Comyn, so Torquil's talisman of light had
left its imprint on the ground over which he had passed. That
luminous residue of power would fade in due course, but for
now it represented a trail that Arnault could follow.

In spirit he set off along that shining route as it wound its
way through bog and briar and thickets toward the shell of
what appeared to be a ruined church. As he approached the
ruin itself, Arnault received his first intimation of something
amiss. The starlight that bathed the surrounding hillsides
stopped short of the burial ground that lay to the north of the
derelict church. As he moved closer in spirit to investigate,
his whole frame of vision was suddenly wrenched askew.

The scene around him spun and blurred. Even as he
fought to regain his equilibrium, he was hurled away from
the ruins like a stone from a catapult. A sensation of desperate flight seized hold of him, choking the breath from his
lungs as the landscape streaked past. Then an explosion of
darkness brought his momentum to a sudden shattering halt.

For a long moment, he lay stunned. When his senses
began to return, he had the confused impression of being in
two places at once. He was aware on the one hand of his
physical body, anchored to its circle of protection in the oak

grove. On the other, he found himself confronting a strange void.

His initial reaction was one of complete bafflement. Only gradually did it dawn upon him, with growing horror, that this pocket abyss of emptiness was all that was left of Torquil's protective talisman.

A choked outcry of denial burst from his lips. The emotional backlash jolted him rudely out of trance, sitting cold and stiff before the standard of his sword. For a moment, all he could do was stare with numb disbelief. Then, by slow degrees, feeling began to return to his extremities, bringing with it an aching surge of inner pain as his conscious mind began to grapple with the possibility that Torquil might well be dead.

His first impulse was to commandeer a horse and set off in search; but even as he thought it, he knew he dared not. In the dark, on the eve of battle, without some clearer indication to guide him, success was most unlikely. And much as it brought him personal sorrow, he knew that he had a higher duty to fulfill.

In going out to spy on the younger Comyn, Torquil had encountered something dark and deadly—perhaps something akin to what they had glimpsed on the road from Iona; something powerful enough to overcome the protective influence of the talisman blessed by the brethren of Saint Columba. If, as seemed quite possible, this dark and deadly something had been summoned at the instigation of Comyn himself, then it was equally possible that the Comyns were the source of the destructive apostasy that had brought about the downfall of the house of Canmore and the quelling of the Stone of Destiny. If they could do *that*, they might well have guessed the part Wallace was meant to play in reviving the Stone—and if so, it was only a matter of time before they would try to take his life as well, removing one further obstacle in the path of their ambitions.

It was likely that only the threat of English domination

had restrained them so far. But their power now seemed to be on the ascendant. Would the Comyns wait to see Edward defeated, and afterward turn on Wallace? Or would they first strike him down, and use their dark powers to try and drive the English from their land?

Either way, the life of the Guardian was in serious danger. If Wallace were to die in ignorance, an unwitting victim rather than a willing sacrifice, then Scotland's ruin would be assured. And if Scotland were to fall, there would be no Fifth Temple, no future haven for the Templar Order and the sacred treasures that they guarded for the good of all mankind. However much Arnault might grieve for the unknown fate of his brother-in-light, his first and highest duty was to remain here and protect the Guardian, upon whom so much depended.

Rising somewhat unsteadily, he retrieved his sword and cloak and started back to camp. During his absence, many of the men had settled down in their blankets to seize what rest they could before the dawn march. Arnault was conscious of a twinge of envy as he passed silently among them, making for Wallace's tent, for sleep was a luxury he himself could not afford, if the Guardian's safety was to be assured.

There were guards on duty about Wallace's tent, but they all knew him well by sight, and did not question him further when he announced his intention to remain close at hand in case the Guardian should require his services. After making a circuit of the area, Arnault settled down in the shelter of a nearby boulder and composed himself for the vigil yet to come. The guards were not to know that this quiet, modestly accoutred knight of foreign origin was maintaining wards that no enemy could breach without his knowledge. If his shoulders were bowed, it was because the burden he was carrying seemed as heavy as any cross.

The light behind Torquil's eyelids was very dim at first— or was it that his ability to perceive the light was somehow deficient? He seemed to have lain in pain and darkness for so long that he was almost afraid he was deluding himself with vain imaginings of an end to the night. He struggled to open his eyes—which were the only part of him that seemed at all capable of movement—but squinted at the pain the brightness caused.

The mere fact that he remembered his own name was a miracle in itself. Beyond that, he could remember little else, except an icy pain from which his soul shrank. He tried to focus on the point of light above him, reluctant to lose sight of it, in case it vanished. But instead of fading, the light expanded, broadening out until it formed a ring of golden fire, like a royal diadem.

Its radiance was filled with a warmth that Torquil had almost forgotten, in his eternity of endless cold and darkness. Though his body ached in every nerve, his soul reached out to it in yearning. Like some bottomless marsh, the darkness clung to him, trying to suck him back into its cold womb, but he began to struggle, determined not to let it bury him again.

The light itself came to his aid, casting down a beam of brightness like a life-rope to his soul. Eagerly he clutched at it—and felt himself floating upward into the midst of the ring of fire. Then the darkness receded, leaving him momentarily dazzled. When his vision cleared, he found himself gazing up into another human face, a trimly bearded face that smiled down at him as he tried to blink away the lingering haze from his eyes.

"Look you, he *is* alive!" a voice declared triumphantly; and only belatedly did Torquil realize that it was his rescuer who had spoken.

Frowning with effort, he studied the other more closely—a man somewhat younger than himself, with bright gray eyes and a mercurial cast to his features. His head was encircled by an aureole of brightness that Torquil might have mistaken for a nimbus or a crown, had he not seen that it was the light of the sun shining behind him through the surrounding trees. There was something elusively familiar about his countenance, but for the moment Torquil could not put a name to him.

Sinewy hands gripped his shoulders, easing him into a sitting position. He accepted that support without question while he bemusedly surveyed his surroundings, wondering how he came to be here. A localized twinge of discomfort made him look down to where his right hand lay open at his side. His palm was burned in the middle and covered with fine white ash.

"That mark on your hand seems to be your only injury, but you have the look of one who has survived a mortal battle," the other man observed, looking him over. "My companions declared you a corpse, and urged that we be on our way, but something told me there was life yet in this cold body."

For the first time, Torquil noticed that his rescuer was not alone. Near at hand were two other young knights, friends of his, by their familiar bearing. A dozen other men were waiting in the background with the party's horses. All wore mail and the colorful surcoats of Scottish nobles, and they carried the weapons of war.

His rescuer called for a waterskin. When it arrived, he helped Torquil to a drink.

"Robert, we still do not know who he is or on what side he is allied," warned one of the knights who was standing close by.

"Hush, man," said their leader dismissively, still supporting Torquil with his arm. "One act of charity is a slight matter, compared to the risks we've already taken—or those we shall take in future."

He spoke with casual authority. Torquil took another sip of water, then swallowed it at a hasty gulp as his jangled memory yielded up the name he had been searching for.

"You are Robert Bruce!" he exclaimed huskily. "The youngest of them. I saw you and your grandsire at Berwick."

Young Bruce gave a brief nod by way of acknowledgment.

"Then you will know that was only the beginning of the troubles that have plagued us since," he said with a grimace.

Torquil scarcely heard him. Other, more recent memories were starting to resurface. The Comyns and the Templars—the dark hunter pursuing him—the shield of light that must, after all, have saved his life . . . It all came back to him in a rush that made his head swim.

The betrayal of Wallace and the Scottish host!

He made an abrupt attempt to get up, only to fall back with an involuntary cry as a wave of pain racked his body from head to foot. Bruce let the waterskin fall and flung a bracing arm around him as he was overtaken by a fit of shuddering.

"Steady on, man!" he admonished. "Give yourself a bit of time to recover your strength. What misadventure brings you to this sorry state? If you were ambushed by brigands, they must have been merciful ones, to have left you without a drop of blood spilled."

"Not brigands," Torquil said hoarsely, with a shake of his head that set it to spinning. "Something far worse."

Before he could elaborate, one of Bruce's friends interposed.

"Robert, we must go. Leave this fellow the water—even some food, if you will—but let us be on our way, if we are not to fight."

A troubled expression crossed Bruce's face and he nodded his acceptance of what the other had said. Fearful of what might happen if he failed to spread the warning, Torquil clutched Bruce's arm and held him back.

"Give me a moment to speak with you alone," he implored.

The urgency in his tone gave Bruce pause. He took a closer look at Torquil's face, then waved his companions away. Once they were out of earshot, he eyed the other man expectantly, still crouched down beside him.

"All right, what have you got to say?" he said.

Torquil drew an aching breath. "First, tell me truly: Do you fight for Edward or for Wallace?"

Bruce's face hardened. "By what right do you question my loyalties?" he demanded, with a sharpness that told Torquil he had touched a raw nerve. "You have not even re-vealed your name, let alone your allegiance."

"My name is Torquil Lennox. Despite my raiment, I am a Knight of the Temple."

"Then you are for Edward," Bruce said, with a narrowing of his gray eyes.

Torquil shook his head, but even that slight motion brought on a brief attack of dizziness. He focused on Bruce to stop the spinning. He felt he could trust this man—though in truth, he had little other choice, if he was to reach Arnault in time to prevent a disaster.

"I am for Scotland, and therefore for Wallace," he stated with as much firmness as he could muster. "That makes me a renegade in the eyes of many of my brothers, but God's will is not always what wins the favor of men."

The anger faded from Bruce's expressive eyes.

"In such times as ours, it is a lucky man who can find a straight, unmuddied path to walk," he noted. "Truth be told, my father sent me to join Edward's army. If you were at Berwick, then I should not need to remind you that John Balliol was chosen as king ahead of my grandfather, who had the more just claim. Nothing he ever did has proved him worthy of the throne, so we will not help him hang on to it. With Balliol swept aside, a Bruce may yet wear the crown."

"Is it ambition, then, that sends you to Edward's side?" Torquil dared to ask.

"Take care that your tongue does not serve you ill!" Bruce warned. "Though I was sent to support Edward, and though I would cheerfully see John Balliol stay locked up forever, I will not take up arms against William Wallace. I will not make a man my enemy because he loves his country too much."

He sighed and glanced aside. "In defiance of both Edward and my father," he continued bleakly, "I am returning to Carrick. Some might see it as shirking my duty, but I see it as the only way of preserving my honor."

Torquil made another effort to rise, and this time the pain was more bearable. Bruce helped him to his feet and kept one hand on his shoulder to steady him.

"If you honor Wallace for his loyalty to Scotland, then I beg you to help me," Torquil said unsteadily, panting a little. "There is a plot afoot to betray him this very day, in which my brother Templars are playing a principal part—and also the Comyns," he added, knowing that would catch Bruce's attention, even if he cared little about Templar treachery. "I must get word to the Scots army before they join battle with Edward."

"A betrayal?" Bruce said. The keen look that came upon his face reflected curiosity held rigidly in check, for such an intimation powerfully underlined the urgency of Torquil's mission, regardless of what specific part was being played by his mortal enemies, the Comyns.

"The armies are close, that much I know," he said, glancing back at his men waiting by the horses. "Can you ride?"

Torquil took a deep breath. The freshness of the morning air was helping to clear his head. The greatest injury he had suffered was not of the body, and already the warmth of the sun and a measure of human kindness were combining to restore his strength.

"I am well enough," he said, "but my horse has fled, frightened off by my . . . attacker."

"You have yet to tell me who that was," Bruce said, "but

time is fleeting and precious. I doubt neither your courage nor the rightness of your mission."

He shouted an order to one of the serjeants in his following. The man joined them a moment later, leading a handsome chestnut stallion. Bruce took the reins and presented them to Torquil.

"No horse will bear you on your way more quickly than my own," he said. "His name is Talorcan, and he is the fastest steed in Annandale."

Torquil had to fight to find his tongue. "Your generosity does credit to the house of Bruce," he said. "How shall I return him to you?"

"Give no thought to that," Bruce told him. "Think only of Wallace. I have no wish to see him fall to a traitor's hand, even if he does uphold Balliol's kingship."

Torquil ran a hand along the stallion's sleek neck before climbing stiffly onto the saddle, given a leg up by Bruce.

"I haven't even thanked you properly for stopping to help me," he said as he gathered up the reins.

"You have not thanked me at all, Templar," Bruce replied, with one of his quicksilver smiles. "Just remember that one day I may need your help."

"If that day comes, then you shall have it, I promise you!" Torquil assured him.

"Then, take this as well," Bruce said, pulling his sheathed sword from its hangers and extending its hilt to Torquil. "A knight should have a sword, and I notice that you have lost yours."

"I cannot—" Torquil began. But Bruce pressed it into his hand.

"I will not be using it today," he said. "And I think you will, indeed, have need of it—and later, if you come to serve me."

Not speaking, Torquil slipped the sword into his own belt and gave Bruce a nod. As the earl gave his horse a farewell slap on the flank to send him on his way, Torquil could not help but wonder if there was more in this meeting than mere chance.

For the present, however, he knew he must set such speculations aside. Before him a battle was waiting to begin, and if he arrived too late, all Scotland might well pay the price for his failure.

Chapter
Twenty-seven

THE COMING DAWN BROUGHT NO SIGN OF TORQUIL. AS SOON as it was light enough, Arnault rode out beyond the Scottish encampment to question the forward sentries. Here he encountered a small Scottish skirmish force retreating in haste from their night foray toward the English lines. Last reported a full fifteen miles away, poised to pull back to Edinburgh, the English army appeared to have moved back half that distance during the night, and were now marching straight toward Falkirk.

Short of learning for certain that Torquil was dead, Arnault could think of no worse news. After questioning the skirmishers for further details, he kept one back and sent the others out again before galloping back to camp to relay the news to Wallace. He had already decided to refrain from mentioning Torquil's disappearance. Lacking information to the contrary, Wallace would simply assume that the younger knight was off on assignment elsewhere—an illusion best not dispelled, for the Guardian needed no further anxieties to burden his thoughts just now, when there was so much else at stake.

"You are sure this is the army itself, and not a scouting party?" Wallace asked, when he had heard the scout's report—a question prompted not by wishful thinking, Arnault knew, but by a steadfast determination not to make a hasty judgment based on ill-founded information.

The scout nodded. "The numbers alone confirm it's the main English host," he told the Guardian, "and moreover, they're arrayed for battle."

Wallace's fellow commanders gathered around him, their expressions grim as they confronted the new perils presented by the news.

"Odd, that they should change course so precipitously," the Earl of Atholl said. "Is it mere chance that brings Edward this way, or has some traitor exchanged news of our whereabouts for a sackful of English gold?"

"Blind mischance or treacherous design, it makes no difference now," Wallace said firmly, determined to cut short such speculation. "The die has been cast, and we must make the best we can of the situation."

James the Stewart shook his head, deeply troubled. "If we retreat now, they might well catch us from behind and make mincemeat of us."

"He's right, Wallace," the Earl of Menteith agreed. "There's nothing for it, but to draw up our battle line and let them do their worst."

"They'll do more than their worst if we meet them here," Wallace said, his calculating gaze already roving the surrounding landscape. "Apart from a few low hills, this is almost flat ground. There's little but scrub and a few trees to impede a cavalry charge. No, we'll face them, all right—but not on terms that suit Edward."

From one of his aides he took a map, which he unrolled and studied carefully.

"Here—and along here, just a short march back the way

we came," he said, letting several others hold it open so he could trace dispositions with one callused finger. "No, Edward won't care for that at all—and hopefully, he won't notice *that* until it's too late." His finger thumped on a marshy ground lying before the spot where he meant to make his stand.

"Pass the word to the troops that we'll march at once and make ready for battle when we get there." He looked up at the cavalry commanders, the earls and James the Stewart and the younger John Comyn among them. "Use the cavalry as a rear guard for now, and keep an eye out for the English until we reach our chosen ground. I'll send further orders when we arrive."

The Scottish host wheeled about in its tracks like a great beast being tugged by a leash—some six thousand foot, supported by a few hundred Ettrick Forest bowmen. The cavalry contingent tallied no more than six hundred horsemen. They made a brave sight with their spears and banners, and many of them gave a hearty cheer as they marched past in view of the Guardian.

But though their willingness to fight was undeniable, Arnault could not help noting, as he kept himself ready in Wallace's vicinity, that they were outnumbered by Edward's army almost two to one—and the English superiority in cavalry and bowmen was likely to prove the gravest threat.

Wallace was equally well aware of this. Nevertheless, he sat his horse with an air of unshakable confidence, returning the salutes of his men as he directed them toward their new positions. Even in the face of such odds, his indomitable courage and personal charisma enabled him to lift the spirits of those around him, imparting a strength of spirit that just might make it possible for the Scots to carry the day, making up in courage what they lacked in numbers.

Arnault made his own assessment of the strategic possibilities as the army formed up on Wallace's chosen ground. Veteran of many a battle, it occurred to him that the

Guardian might well have had this site in mind all along, in case some ill turn of fate should upset his plans for a surprise assault on the English rear.

The Scots were deployed on the southeast slope of Slamman Hill, with Callendar Wood at their backs to offer a ready sanctuary in case of the need for retreat. In front of them stretched a treacherous marsh formed by the junction of two streams—which would make it impossible for the English to make a direct assault without wading through the deep, muddy water.

Behind this marsh Wallace arrayed his footmen in four massive schiltrons: circular formations several ranks deep, each consisting of over a thousand men standing shoulder to shoulder. Rank upon rank of long spears protruded in all directions like the spines of a hedgehog, in a formation designed to leave no open flank or weak spot exposed to a cavalry assault—and the Guardian had personally supervised the training of these men, ensuring that they learned to bring down a mounted knight in the most efficient way possible, by spearing his horse. Encircling the schiltrons were palisades of wooden stakes that had been fixed into the ground and bound together with lengths of rope to give further protection. Any knight who could make his horse charge home against this double barrier of sharpened wood and cold steel would be impaled without making a dent on the defenders.

Groups of archers under command of the Stewart's brother, Sir John, were arrayed between the schiltrons, with the Scots cavalry kept to the rear as a reserve—a threat to any bowmen advancing from the English ranks, who could be easily routed by a well-timed charge. If the English knights were rash enough to hurl themselves ruinously against the spears of the schiltrons, Wallace hoped that the Scottish horse would be able to take advantage of their disorder to launch a counterattack and drive them from the field.

What he had sacrificed in terms of mobility, the Guardian had gained in the strength of his defense. He had made his army into a fortress and was daring Edward to assault it.

Arnault was one of several in Wallace's train as he rode before the schiltrons, making certain that all was in readiness. Near the edge of the woods, his inspection complete, the Guardian drew apart from his advisors and reined his horse beside Arnault's, where they had a wide view of the surrounding terrain.

"The land itself has always been our ally," Wallace said quietly. "If our earlier plans were undone by treachery, the loyalty of those present here may yet redeem it."

"I notice you name no names," Arnault said.

"Nor will I," Wallace replied. "In recent years, the allegiances of the Scottish lords have shifted like the movements of the tide. Whether they follow me gladly or grudgingly is of no consequence. What matters is that today they stand and fight for Scotland."

Arnault glanced back to where John Comyn was arraying his Comyn horsemen among the other cavalry, and wondered whether to voice his suspicions. He had no direct evidence that the Comyns were, in any way, connected with the English change of plans—or with Torquil's disappearance—and the prelude to a battle was a bad time to stir up dissension based on false accusations. Moreover, Comyn's men looked like they were preparing to do their duty by the Guardian.

"Sometimes a people's worst enemies are themselves," Arnault said, somewhat ambiguously. "But these, I think, will stand fast." He indicated the spiked ranks of the schiltrons.

"I have no doubt of their courage," the Guardian agreed. "I only hope I may prove worthy of it."

Arnault felt certain that no man could prove more worthy than Wallace; but before he could give voice to that sentiment, a hoarse outcry went up from many points along the

Scottish line. To the southeast, the sun was glinting off armor and spearpoints, and flags and banners were rising into view. The English vanguard had arrived: a mass of steel-clad knights, jostling forward in densely packed squadrons. Behind them marched the massed infantry, interspersed with columns of archers and crossbowmen, moving into battle formation as they advanced.

It was a daunting sight: one that caused many a man in the Scottish ranks to murmur a quiet prayer, Arnault among them. A chill of foreboding shivered up his spine—and more than ever, he felt the lack of Torquil's solid presence at his shoulder. But all he could do was commend his brother-knight to the mercy of God, together with all the Scottish host.

A breeze swept up the hill, carrying the sounds from the enemy ranks: the muffled rumble of horses' hooves, the jangle of harness, the sullen mutter of voices. Nothing daunted, Wallace spurred his horse forward, riding at a canter along the Scottish lines. Brandishing his sword, he stood high in the stirrups where all could see him, and addressed his men in a ringing voice.

"Men of Scotland, I have brought you to the ring!" he shouted. "Now let us see if you can dance!"

His challenge was answered with a cheer that could be clearly heard far to the south, where King Edward sat astride his great warhorse in the midst of his army. Despite a cracked rib, sustained during the night as he slept beside his horse at Linlithgow, the aging Lion of England had pressed forward at dawn.

Now, having heard Mass with the Bishop of Durham, who would command the right wing, Edward of England stared coldly up at the hillside with its great circles of bristling spears. Then he turned to the Master of the Templars, who had ridden up beside him.

"Your intelligence was correct, Templar. Wallace was trying to sneak up from behind and cuff my ear. He will pay for that impudence, now that we have him in our grasp."

Brian de Jay nodded in some satisfaction. "Aye, Sire. He has positioned his army badly, leaving himself no room to maneuver. He is depending upon that ill-clothed rabble with their pig stickers to keep him safe."

And if Comyn kept the remainder of his bargain, that ill-clothed rabble would be left defenseless, for the meager Scots cavalry—who included some of Scotland's most influential earls—would turn and flee without striking a blow. Jay had made no mention of that bargain, of course; and of the intelligence regarding the Scots position, he had given the king to understand that he and the Master of Scotland had come upon a skulking Scottish scout by happy chance, whereupon they had forced the prisoner to reveal the Scots position; the prisoner, alas, had died. It also remained to be seen whether Wallace could be taken.

The English host drew up before the somewhat innocuous stretch of marshy ground that lay between them and the Scottish schiltrons, squarely facing the enemy. The knights of the vanguard, under Roger Bigod and Henry de Lacy, Earls of Norfolk and Lincoln respectively, took up position on the left, while Bishop Bek's Durham chivalry formed the army's right wing. Between were ranged the spearmen in their thousands, mostly Welsh, supported by bowmen armed with longbows and crossbows. With numbers so greatly in their favor, spirits were running high among cavalry and footmen alike, equally eager to test their strength against the foe.

The knights on both flanks were already edging forward when the Earls of Norfolk and Lincoln rode up from the vanguard to inform the king that they would soon be closing with the enemy, both men's faces flushed with anticipation. Roger Bigod grinned broadly as he gestured toward the Scots.

"They've obliged us, Sire, by forming targets so large that they will be hard, indeed, to miss. A single shot should strike the gold, I think."

"Have you learned nothing from our clashes with the rebellious Welsh?" Edward answered coldly. "Even an untrained peasant can face up to your horsemen if he can hold a spear straight."

"Only if he has the nerve to stand his ground," de Lacy replied. "I swear to you, Sire, that we will rout them at the first charge and pay them back for our dead at Stirling Bridge."

"The Scots aren't going anywhere," Edward said, unmoved by his subordinate's fervor. "And our men have scarcely eaten in the past day. There's time to put food in their bellies before sending them to the fight."

"Sire, it's Scots blood they hunger for—not food!" Bigod declared. "They can no more be reined in now than a pack of hounds that have sighted the fox."

"It can only hearten the Scots to see us waver," de Lacy agreed.

Edward snorted—and winced at the pain of his cracked rib—but clearly, lack of sleep and food had not dulled the fighting edge of his men. On the contrary, it had lent an almost feverish intensity to their belligerence.

"Go, then," he said. "Clear the way for the bowmen, and then we'll make short work of those Scottish schiltrons."

The two knights wheeled about and galloped back to join their men. Their voices echoed back up the lines as they shouted orders and began the advance.

"And you, Templar," Edward said to Brian de Jay, "can I trust in your bragging, as much as I can in your scouting?"

"Sire, I have promised to take Wallace for you," Jay replied, "and so I shall. I shall bring him in a cage, if need be."

"There's no need to go as far as that," Edward said dryly. "His head is all I need."

Jay inclined his head in a perfunctory bow and rode off to rendezvous with his fellow Templars, who were gathered some distance away to the rear of the main body of cavalry. Between himself and John de Sautre, they had brought twenty knights and serjeants, including the younger de Sautre. Many were less than happy to be part of an invading army waging war on fellow Christians—and a few were even Scots—but they were bound to the Master of England by vows of obedience, so none raised voice against him.

"We'll stay well back with the reserve, for now," Jay said to John de Sautre. "It isn't our job to hurl ourselves against a wall of peasants' spears. We'll bide our time, and strike when we can do the most good."

"A prudent strategy," said Robert de Sautre, ever the sycophant. "Wait until they are at their weakest, then use our fighting prowess to deliver the killing stroke."

John de Sautre was squinting ahead at the bristling schiltrons at the foot of the hill, and the sheen of watery meadow that lay before them. "There will be killing enough, if our knights continue their direct advance," he warned, "but it will not be the Scots who will die."

"What do you mean?" Robert asked, his dark eyes widening owlishly in his round face. "Do you seriously think our knights incapable of overcoming the Scots, when only a ribbon of water stands between them?"

"'Tis more than a ribbon of water, I'll wager," John replied, pointing at the place where the two streams met. "If the horses become bogged down in *that*, our knights will be easy prey to the Scots."

"You are very likely correct, Brother John," Jay agreed. "All the more reason for us to hold back, and see if prudence or blood lust rules the day."

When the vanguard that was the English left wing came in clear sight of the marsh, the English earls were not so eager for the fray that they failed to discern the danger. Directing their column to veer sharply to the left, they skirted the edges of the boggy ground and continued toward the schiltrons. The English knights of the right wing, under Bishop Bek, also swerved wide to avoid the marsh, jostling and bumping each other in their eagerness to be the first to engage the enemy. Bek saw them falling into disorder and tried to have his bannerets call them back to re-form before charging, but his words of caution fell on deaf ears.

Ralph Basset, Lord of Drayton, rounded on the cleric and snapped, "Go back and say Mass, Bishop, and leave us to the business of fighting!"

The two wings then headed for the outer schiltrons. Stationed to the rear of the two central ones, Wallace watched the English cavalry advance with a mixture of apprehension and satisfaction.

"So much for the marsh," he muttered to Arnault.

"Aye, they'd have made fine targets for John Stewart's archers, if they'd been reckless enough to come wading through there," Arnault replied, with a tinge of regret.

"Still," Wallace said, "they've yet to learn they can't come at us in a solid line. By forcing the wings to go around, we've broken them up so that they'll be coming at us piecemeal. If they wear themselves out charging against the schiltrons, then we'll have a chance to push them backward into the water."

Arnault gazed down at the two huge columns of knights and could not help thinking that the plan was fine as long as his men could stand up to the initial attack—which was drawing nearer by the moment. The Scottish spearmen were bracing the butts of their weapons against the ground in readiness for the coming assault, and some of the archers were already making trial shots at the enemy, though to little effect.

Having passed through the space between the edge of the wood and the marsh, Roger Bigod and Henry de Lacy were leading the left wing to the attack. The line spread out and the knights pressed their speed to a gallop, battle cries now lifting above the thunder of pounding hooves. The thunder grew louder, shaking the ground underfoot as the distance closed.

The men of the schiltrons braced themselves for the impact, tightening their grip on the hafts of their weapons with hands grown clammy with the waiting. The knights in their heavy armor, their horses protected with steel plate and leather, bore down on the footmen with their lances at the ready.

The line of cavalry broke against the first schiltron like a wave dashing against a rock, to the sound of screams rather than the ocean roar. Some of the horses shied back before the bristling hedge of spearpoints, but others gashed their legs on the stakes or impaled themselves on the spear points of the Scottish front rank, who bent low to bypass the beasts' armor. The next rank of Scottish spearmen leaned forward over the shoulders of their companions, thrusting and jabbing at the riders. Some were run through and others were unhorsed, toppling to the ground to be either trampled or crushed by their companions.

On the other wing, the main body of Bishop Bek's knights likewise launched themselves headlong against the schiltrons, but they, too, broke against the wall of spears without budging the stubborn Scots. Bellowing orders through the din, the warrior bishop succeeded in diverting a cohort of knights less hotheaded than those in the vanguard, and directed these against the more vulnerable ranks of the Scottish archers who were strung out between the spear formations.

The men of Ettrick stood their ground and launched flights of arrows against the oncoming mass of knights, but they were too few in number, and their weapons lacked the lethal penetration of the English longbows. Bek's knights charged in, skewering unarmored bowmen with their lances and crushing them beneath the hooves of their steeds. The screams mounted as the archers began to give way.

"Why don't our cavalry attack?" Wallace demanded, tight-lipped, as he and Arnault craned for a better view. "Stewart's bowmen are being slaughtered! Without mounted support, they cannot stand!"

"I'll go," Arnault said.

Wheeling his horse, he made for the low knoll behind which the Scottish horse troops stood waiting. But when he topped the rise, he drew up aghast, for the majority of the Scottish knights had already turned their backs on the fighting and were rapidly dispersing from the battleground.

His arresting shout drew no response. Most of the horsemen were already beyond earshot. Among the banners far at the front, he could see that of the Comyns—*gules*, with three golden wheat sheaves—and suddenly, the likely reason for the younger Comyn's suspicious behavior the night before became all too clear: all part of a cunning betrayal, designed to leave Wallace at King Edward's mercy—and no wonder that Torquil, having apprehended it, had not been permitted to return to tell of it!

Now, betrayed as the prophecy had warned, the Guardian was fully committed to a battle probably beyond anyone's ability to salvage, and the loyal Scottish foot—the good, honest men of the community of the realm of Scotland— must stand alone against England's mounted might.

The sound of pounding hooves announced the arrival of Wallace himself, coming to investigate the delay. When the Guardian saw what was happening, the color drained from his face.

"What benighted, craven cowardice is this?" he demanded in a constricted voice.

Thinking desperately for some way to salvage something—anything—for the Scots, it occurred to Arnault that perhaps not all those with Comyn were active agents of the betrayal.

"It may yet be possible to rally them," he said. "I'll do what I can."

"Go!" Wallace agreed, with a backward glance at the English cavalry crushing his bowmen. "And may God give you His aid."

Without another word Arnault put spurs to his horse and set off at a gallop after the fleeing horsemen and the treacherous John Comyn. Returning to his men, Wallace dismounted and made a place for himself inside one of the center schiltrons and from there watched the terrible carnage being inflicted on his Scottish bowmen. Those not stretched dead already on the bloody ground were forced to flee for their lives. The Stewart's brother bravely tried to rally his men until he, too, was cut down by the English knights.

Only a handful of the Scots nobility had remained to fight on foot after the desertion of the Scottish horse, and were now sorely pressed as the English cavalry began shifting their attention back to the schiltrons. Macduff of Fife was ensconced amid the spearmen of his land inside their schiltron, and was exhorting their continued resistance as the English resumed their harrying. Wallace, too, shouted encouragement to his men, but each fresh assault reduced their ranks. With the Scots cavalry fled, and their archers driven from the field, the plight of the men holding the schiltrons grew gradually desperate.

The English knights swarmed closer, randomly attacking wherever there was the prospect of an opening. By now the fences of stakes surrounding the schiltrons had been trampled or smashed aside, and gaps began to appear in the Scottish defenses. More knights than spearmen had perished in the initial exchange, before eliminating the Scottish bowmen, but the blood of the English nobles was now on fire, and it had become a matter of honor to prove that a few bands of unwashed peasants could not stand against them. Yet time after time, the Scots held their ground and threw back their enemies in bloody confusion.

It was time for Edward to shift his tactics. Cursing his headstrong nobles for their costly bravado, he sent messengers ordering them to desist, lest their lust for blood and glory hand Wallace a victory by attrition. Even as his command was being reluctantly obeyed, he sent his archers marching over the streams and up the slope. What the reckless ferocity of his knights could not accomplish, the deadly accuracy of his bowmen surely could.

Sweating inside their armor and cursing the stubbornness of their foes, the knights withdrew to east and west, re-forming their scattered companies and giving their panting warhorses a respite from the battle. All along the lower slopes of Slamman Hill, the English archers began forming up in multiple ranks.

Brian de Jay, sensing that the decisive moment was approaching, led his band of Templars up onto the hill to join the rest of the English chivalry. Though eyed disdainfully by some of the English commanders, for holding back so conspicuously from the initial attacks, Jay declined to take affront, confident that he soon would be in a position to justify his actions.

Very shortly, a lone horseman came galloping toward the Templars, directing Jay's attention toward one of the central schiltrons. Amid those lesser men, even at this distance, the commanding figure of William Wallace radiated stubborn defiance in the face of hopeless odds.

"Now it truly begins," Jay said to the brothers de Sautre, when his informant had gone. "Our bowmen will soon flush this rebel out of his lair—and then he shall be ours for the taking."

Edward's Welsh archers took to the fore, seconded by a force of Genoese mercenaries armed with crossbows. They could not have asked for a more ideal target than the four great circles of closely packed soldiers, without skirmishers or horse to protect them. Orders were passed up and down the line, crossbows were loaded, arrows were plucked from quivers and longbows drawn by strong

Welsh arms. At a bellowed command, the bowmen un-leashed their attack.

The flight of arrows was dense enough to darken the sky and cause any but the stoutest heart to falter. Arching high in the air, they fell in a deadly hail upon the packed ranks of the Scots, slaying and maiming men in each of the schiltrons. Seeing gaps appear in the Scottish ranks, the English offi-cers renewed the command to fire, and another volley of missiles soared skyward, plunging among the Scottish spearmen with devastating effect. Wallace was in as much danger as his men, and those closest to him lifted their shields to protect him as the barbs rained down on all sides.

"They haven't the courage to close with us," Wallace shouted. "They can't throw sticks at us forever—and then we'll see them off!"

In spite of their desperate situation, the Guardian's show of confidence was not entirely feigned, for he well knew the arrogance of the English chivalry. It was that very trait that had proved their undoing at Stirling, and he clung to the hope that Edward would not be able to restrain their impetuousness, that they would charge prematurely, while the schiltrons were still intact. If he could inflict another bloody defeat on the proud English knights, the Welsh, who comprised the bulk of Edward's infantry, might yet desert him.

But with each fresh flight of arrows, more spearmen fell. The blood-soaked ground was thick with bodies, and the hopes of the Scots began to yield to grim fatalism. However much the English knights might chafe at the bit, eager to avenge their fallen comrades and kinsmen, Edward had made his wishes brutally clear. No member of the English feudal host was to venture forward again until the king's own royal trumpeter sounded the charge.

Brian de Jay was as impatient as any for the final assault to begin, and he watched with satisfaction as the Scottish ranks grew more and more depleted. After a time, it was difficult to tell how many still lived and how many were corpses with no more space to fall. Yet still the packed formations held their ground. As often as the English raised their bows to loose another flight of arrows, the Scots continued to stand firm, drawing strength from their common defiance as they braced themselves for death, determined to keep faith with those who had gone before them.

Warhorses snorted and stamped and knights impatiently brandished their lances until, at last, Edward gave the long awaited signal. In response to the trumpet call, the bowmen retired and the unleashed English chivalry resumed their attack from both wings. The surviving Scots tried to close ranks to meet the charge, but were impeded by their own dead, who littered the ground at their feet.

The wall of armored horsemen smashed into the depleted schiltrons at full gallop, with lances couched, and at last the weary and wounded Scottish infantry gave way before the furious momentum of their enemies. Ranks of spearmen were vengefully impaled and hurled to the turf, there to be ground into bloody pulp under iron-shod hooves. When one side of the schiltron collapsed, those left standing with their backs unprotected could only seek to flee before they were ridden down or killed where they stood.

In some cases panic took hold, causing men to fling their cumbersome weapons aside and run for their lives. Others maintained a semblance of order, retreating gradually uphill with their spears still extended to fend off their pursuers until they reached the treeline. All across the field, however, the schiltrons were breaking and the Scots army was being swept from the field. Brian de Jay saw Wallace's schiltron shatter and the Guardian himself fall back before the furious onslaught of the English knights.

"Now, brothers of the Temple!" he cried, turning toward his men. "As Christ is your savior, visit God's own vengeance upon these traitors!"

He adjusted his helmet and lowered his lance, then led the warrior monks forward to the attack. With their white surcoats and banners flying wild in the breeze, they charged across the field in a mighty wedge, for all the world like the point of a gigantic spear aimed squarely at the one man who was Scotland's hope for freedom.

Chapter
Twenty-eight

ARNAULT HAD NOT DRIVEN A HORSE SO HARD SINCE HIS days in Palestine, eluding Saracen patrols and enemy archers to deliver intelligence to the Grand Master at Acre. His present mission, if in service of a different Temple, was no less urgent: to halt the fleeing Scottish nobles and lead them back to the field before it was too late for Wallace and for Scotland.

By the time he caught up with the first of them, their initial hasty flight had been moderated to an orderly retreat. In the absence of English pursuit, they gave no appearance of fear or confusion—which reinforced Arnault's suspicion that it was no impulse of panic that had driven them off, but a prearranged plan to save themselves and leave the Guardian to his fate. How many had conspired to incite this act of cowardice, and how many had simply followed where others had led, he could not tell. Doubtless some, seeing the great mass of their companions fleeing the battle, had simply felt they had little choice other than to go along.

Those to the rear paid Arnault little mind as he rode along their flank, perhaps under the assumption that he was one of their own number who was simply tardier than the rest. A few taut faces registered flickers of recognition—and wary apprehension from a few, knowing him as a scout in the service of the abandoned Wallace—but wearing no man's livery, he aroused no particular attention as he galloped up the line looking for the most influential of them—and there were many, earls and barons among them. But he continued until he caught up with the front of the column, where Comyn and his men rode, then reined his horse sharply around to confront them.

"Hold, Comyn of Badenoch!" he cried. "And likewise, you others who call yourselves men of Scotland! What, in God's name, are you doing? Have your insides turned to water, that you scatter like children when the battle is scarce begun?"

The lead riders slowed, with a ripple effect that went back all along the line. Comyn, addressed by name, reluctantly brought his mount to a halt and gave Arnault an affronted glower without deigning to rise to the challenge, but his Comyn kinsman, the Earl of Buchan, brashly moved his horse a few steps closer to Arnault's.

"It may be scarce begun," Buchan retorted, "but this battle is already sorely lost."

"Aye, Wallace has led us wrong," the Earl of Atholl agreed, riding closer. "Why should we be the victims of his folly?"

Arnault raked them over with a steely glance, watching others of the leaders edge closer, moderating his words.

"It was not so long ago that you were grumbling against him for running from Edward," he reminded them. "And now that he makes a stand, you have turned tail and fled!"

"Wallace told us Edward was in retreat," John Comyn retorted hotly, "and that we had surprise on our side. Little truth there was in that vainglorious strategy! All the time,

Edward was marching straight for us, and the Guardian was leading us into the jaws of a trap."

Angry murmurs and shouts of agreement rose from the ranks of the horsemen. Comyn began to edge forward, seeking to bypass Arnault, but found his way blocked by his challenger's horse.

"The coward finds reasons for his cowardice," Arnault called out in a voice pitched so that all could hear, "and the farther he runs, the more excuses he finds. But that does not make them true, nor does it lessen his dishonor."

Others of rank were coming up from the rear to investigate—Menteith, Strathearn, even the Stewart—and these ranged themselves in loose, uneasy groupings around the two men. By the faces, Arnault sensed that many of them could feel their hearts agreeing with his words.

"Nobles of Scotland," he went on, "God has not given you authority over your fellow men for your own aggrandizement. It is your bounden duty to defend this land on behalf of all who lack the wealth or power to do so themselves—for the women who bear your children, for the men who tend your cattle and harvest your crops, who stand to fight beside you—and die beside you, if need be. If you turn your backs on such a trust, then what other purpose is there to your lives that is worthy of a knight's honor and bravery?"

A few of those who met his gaze flushed and looked away.

"Fine words," Comyn blustered, "from one who has shown no such bravery himself. Many of us here fought at Dunbar and at Stirling and at battles after, but what of this braggart who bears no ensign?"

He turned directly on Arnault, his voice filled with arrogant disdain. "What title or rank do *you* hold, that entitles you to address us in such a fashion? You are no Scot, by your accent—and yet you presume to harangue us about our duty to our nation. Can it be that you are serving the purpose of some other power, who would gladly see us destroyed to suit their own designs?"

Arnault had not intended to reveal himself, lest he endanger his greater mission—especially with Torquil lost, and with Brian de Jay riding in Edward's train. But the danger to Wallace—and to Scotland—was dire, and he knew that only drastic measures could help them now.

"It is true that I am no Scot by birth," he said boldly. "I am Breton. But know that I am also a Knight of the Temple of Jerusalem, Frère Arnault de Saint Clair, sent here to protect the rights of your lawful king and the freedom of your nation—and the life of Wallace."

An uneasy muttering rippled among them, and Comyn seemed clearly taken aback—much more so than Arnault would have expected. A knight sitting his horse near Atholl proved less rattled—or perhaps more thick-skinned—and called out scornfully, "When did the Templars ever care for anything other than their own wealth?"

"Aye," another mumbled. "And if you were sent to fight for Scotland, why does your Master fight for Edward?"

"Take yourself off to your prayers and your accounts," another said with feeling, to a sullen mutter of agreement. "We did not invite you to meddle in our business."

Refusing to be baited, Arnault addressed them with head held high.

"You need not heed *my* words," he said. "Your own conscience calls you back to the field of battle—and to your duty—as surely as any trumpet summoning men to war."

Comyn seemed to have overcome his initial discomfiture, and shouldered his horse hard against Arnault's, belligerent and arrogant.

"How dares a Templar call us to battle?" he demanded. "You have not answered why your brother-knights, led by their English Master, fight on Edward's side. Have they sent you here to lure us back, and thus ensure the slaughter of Scotland's chivalry? We are, none of us, so foolhardy as to throw our lives away, when we may yet win the day upon another field!"

Comyn's suggestion of treachery on the part of the Master of England made Arnault suddenly wonder whether it could have been Brian de Jay whom Comyn had gone to meet the night before—Jay, who, if Torquil had been apprehended spying on such a meeting, would have had no compunctions about killing a man he could later claim he had thought was an apostate from the Order. There was no time to speculate upon the details of any bargain struck by Jay and Comyn, but the very possibility of such an alliance made it doubly important that this betrayal should not succeed.

"I will not speak against a brother of my Order," Arnault said evenly, "and I cannot speak for his reasons in choosing to raise sword against fellow Christians. I *can* tell you that I answer to a higher superior than the Master of England— and that I am commanded to fight and die for a country that is not my own, but is favored of God. If I must ride back alone, I shall do so; but I will not leave Scotland's Guardian to stand without at least one more sword at his side."

"Two more swords at least," said a voice Arnault recognized, as James the Stewart kneed his horse forward from the ranks with half a dozen mounted men-at-arms at his back. "When these fled the field around me," he went on, gesturing toward Comyn and his men, "I assumed that our cause must be lost, and could see no reason to remain behind. I see now that I was wrong, and there is much yet to fight for, whatever the outcome of this battle may be. I do not speak for my men in this, but I and any who choose to follow are yours, for Wallace."

A muscle ticked in Comyn's tight-clenched jaw, and he jerked his horse around with a muttered oath, reining it hard so that it plunged and fought the bit as he glared at Stewart.

"And if you return now to find Edward victorious, and Wallace already dead, what then?" He gave a contemptuous snort. "Will you sue for terms, or give yourself up as a prisoner to be ransomed? *I'll* not entrust myself to Edward's mercy, while the road northward lies open!"

With that, he set spurs to his horse and galloped off, followed by his own men and most of the rest of the knights. Only a few peeled off to join Arnault and Stewart. When the others had gone, the pair were left with scarcely a score of men to lead back to the beleaguered army.

"We are few enough in number," James Stewart observed, following Arnault's assessing glance at their little band, "but having turned tail once, we'll not do so again, I promise you."

"God grant we may be enough," Arnault replied, "and pray we are not too late."

And clapping spurs to his steed, Arnault led them back the way they all had come, suddenly aware that, without consciously thinking it through, he had reached a fateful decision. For all that, hitherto, he had avoided shedding a drop of Christian blood, he could no longer avoid taking active part in the battle. The fate of the Temple was bound too closely to that of Scotland; and Scotland was bound too closely to Wallace for Arnault to hold back in any way. If fight he must, to keep the Guardian safe to fulfil his destiny, then he would have to trust in God to guide his sword.

With Arnault and Stewart at their head, the knights galloped back toward the sounds of battle, skirting the edge of the wood as they rounded the summit of Slamman Hill. The sight that awaited them brought them up sharply, for the field of battle had become a field of slaughter. The broken remnants of the great schiltrons were retreating as best they could, harried savagely by bands of English knights while the English foot advanced in their wake, cutting down stragglers and finishing off the wounded.

The dead were everywhere, amid bloody evidence of horrible wounds taken by arrows, lances, and swords. Drunk with blood lust, the English nobles careered to and fro amid the fleeing Scots, cutting down men who were struggling to join the remaining spear formations or scrambling desperately uphill toward the trees. Many of the surviving Scots were even driven downhill, to fall to the swords and arrows of the English footmen or drown in the muddy waters of the marsh.

"God, have mercy!" James Stewart murmured in a strangled tone, for somewhere amid this carnage was his brother, John, who had commanded the bowmen of Ettrick Forest—whether alive or dead, he did not know.

Mutters of consternation came from his men, as well. Honor had brought them back; but now, faced with the near suicidal prospect of actually reentering a battle so obviously gone wrong, they looked doubtfully at the man who had led them here.

But Arnault was standing in his stirrups, looking desperately for some sign of Wallace amid the pockets of furious fighting still in progress on the field before them—until suddenly a voice to his right warned, "Horseman, coming this way!"

Turning sharply, Arnault caught just a glimpse of a lone rider weaving toward them through the trees. A few of his men were already fingering the hilts of their swords, but something about the coppery glint of hair and beard, the set of the shoulders—

"Those are Bruce bardings on the horse," Stewart said with some surprise, "but the rider, I do not recognize."

"I do!" Arnault declared, relief flooding through him as that rider drew close enough to confirm, beyond all doubt, that Torquil Lennox was not lost after all.

He stood in his stirrups and raised an arm in hail, and Torquil bore down on them with surer focus, bringing his horse to a sliding, snorting halt.

"Thank God I've found you!" he exclaimed, his relief turning to horror as his gaze caught the carnage beyond. "Dear God, I am too late!" From his shock and dismay, he clearly had only just returned from wherever he had been, and knew nothing of the day's battle besides the dreadful slaughter he saw before him.

"And who is this?" Stewart demanded suspiciously.

"A brother in this venture," Arnault replied. "A Templar, like myself, and a countryman of yours. I had thought him lost."

"I nearly was," Torquil affirmed breathlessly. His handsome features seemed unnaturally pale, and he bore an air of fatigue that bespoke exertions far exceeding the rigors of a strenuous ride. "Last night, I discovered Scottish traitors selling information to the Master of the English Temple," he declared, omitting the names that Arnault knew already, and the means by which he had discovered this. "Jay means to personally hunt down Wallace and kill him."

As all Arnault's worst fears locked into place—and he knew there was more to the story than Torquil dared tell— he again swept his gaze across the bloody battlefield, searching frantically for Wallace.

"Where *is* he?" Stewart muttered beside him, as all of them strained to penetrate the confusion of battle, looking for that one tall, gallant form.

"Tell me I've not come too late!" Torquil implored.

"Look there!" one of the knights cried.

Following the line of his pointing finger, Arnault and Torquil turned to see not Wallace but the gleaming wedge of a Templar detachment carving a path across the bloody battlefield, coursing toward the woods like a pack of snow-white wolves on the scent.

"Now we must wager all, that *they* head for Wallace—as must we!" Arnault declared. "We cannot save this battle, my friends, but we must and shall save the Guardian! Ride with me, or abandon all thoughts of Scotland's future freedom!"

So saying, he drew his sword and sent his horse charging forward—not only to save Wallace, but to stop Brian de Jay from committing an act of infamy that would taint the name of the Templar Order for generations yet unknown. Torquil rode with him, and James Stewart and his knights formed a flying column behind them, determined to rescue Wallace and salvage both their honor and Scotland's hope from this day's betrayal.

They lost sight of the Templar column as their own course took them up a wooded ridge and into the trees. The rescue party broke ranks and galloped on, ducking and dodging branches as they rode up and over the spine of the hill. The trees were thinner on the down side of the slope, affording a glimpse of the Templar party breaking toward the open ground beyond.

There, ragged bands of Scots foot soldiers were retreating across the flat, beyond a boggy stretch of ground perhaps chosen by the men of their small rear guard in hopes that this would slow pursuit of their fellows. And in the midst of the band holding that rear guard, conspicuous by his height, was the indomitable form of Wallace.

Pounding down the hill, Arnault and his Scottish rescue party drove their tiring mounts on toward the Templar party, who were now starting to close in on Wallace and his small, desperate band of infantry. With the men of Jay's following so focused, the rescue party was among them before they realized.

Arnault came up on the flank of one of the younger knights and dealt him a heavy blow to the wrist with the flat of his blade. With a cry, the youngster dropped his lance and reeled back, glaring affrontedly past his nose guard; but by the time he had recovered himself enough to draw his sword, Arnault was already out of reach, moving on in search of a new target.

The attack became a melee as rider closed with rider—too close for lances now—and with the Scottish footmen now joining in with their rescuers, the Templar force found their prospects suddenly less certain. Torquil seized a serjeant's horse by the shank of the bit and gave it a twist, causing the animal to rear back and overbalance. Its rider fell heavily at the feet of a Scottish spearman, who immediately upended his weapon and rammed the point home through a chink in his armor.

The man's dying scream rang in Torquil's ears—a fellow Templar, killed because of him—but he wheeled his horse aside as a knight-brother bore down on him with a lance, a sweeping downstroke of Bruce's goodly sword deflecting and shattering the lance shaft, sending his opponent reeling in the saddle. Before the other could renew the assault with a fresh weapon, Torquil spotted the portly and unmistakable figure of Robert de Sautre and set off in pursuit, leaving James Stewart to take up the other challenge in his place.

Arnault, for his part, was fighting his way purposefully toward Wallace, who had planted himself on an island of firm ground with two of his spearmen. Together, they were just managing to hold off a mounted adversary.

Arnault spurred forward, intent on adding the weight of his own sword to the Guardian's defense, but before he could close with the other knight, his exhausted horse slipped in the mud and went down, half pinning one of his legs under the saddle.

Saved from crushing injury by the softness of the mud, and desperately holding on to his sword, Arnault struggled free of the stirrups and dragged himself to his feet as his mount clumsily heaved itself up and fled away limping. As he looked around to see how Wallace was faring, he found his way blocked by a white-clad form, unhorsed like himself, sword upraised to strike. He could attach no name to the face beneath the helm, but he knew the man from Balantrodoch, and the man knew him.

"Saint Clair!" he gasped, and swung at Arnault.

Arnault parried and gave ground, not wanting to slay a brother-knight, but he knew he must not let that cost him his own life. Sparks flew as he blocked a downstroke intended to sever his sword arm, and he whirled to counterattack, his blade slithering down the other Templar's to lock at the hilts.

"I am not your enemy!" he managed to spit out between clenched teeth, as he and his adversary strained against each other for a breathless moment. "Jay has betrayed the Order!"

"You are—apostate!" the other gasped.

"But I will *not* kill you!" said Arnault—and with a wrench, gave ground again and, when his opponent stumbled forward, dealt him a disabling slash to the back of the leg.

The other Templar let out an agonized cry and folded in his tracks, sword flying from his hand. Leaving the wounded man where he lay, Arnault rushed on again in search of Wallace.

Both the spearmen with Wallace had gone down, but Wallace was still on his feet, now fighting off two white-clad Templars, who were closing in on foot from opposite sides. As Arnault struggled toward them, hampered by the mud, he saw with sinking fear that Wallace's two adversaries were none other than John de Sautre and Jay himself.

"Hold!" he shouted. "It is not the work of the Temple to slay other Christian men!"

Jay turned at the sound of his voice, his features contorting in a snarl when he recognized his challenger.

"So, the renegade rears his head at last!" he sneered. "I swear by all that is holy, you are more Saracen than Christian, Saint Clair!" Aside to John de Sautre he said, "Send him to the hell that awaits him! I shall finish this rebellious Scot myself!"

John de Sautre turned on his heel and sprang to attack as Jay closed again with Wallace. Steel clashed against steel as his blade met Arnault's. The two men exchanged feints, circling warily as de Sautre sought an opening.

"Why do you follow him?" Arnault gasped, between clanging exchanges. "It is not too late for you to turn away from this bloody path. God forgives all things!"

De Sautre panted out a mirthless laugh. "Are you become my conscience? It is you who should look to the state of your soul—for you are about to go to judgment!"

With sudden ferocity, the Master of the Scottish Temple lunged and struck, the violence of his blow nearly disarming Arnault. In that instant, Arnault sensed that de Sautre knew only too well how far he had let Jay lead him into treachery and deceit—that it was the pain of that knowledge that now lent impetus to his attack, as he sought to batter down one of the few who knew him for what he was, their blades clashing and parting in a murderous exchange of blows.

Meanwhile, as Brian de Jay closed with William Wallace, feinting and probing to take his measure, he was finding himself surprised at how nimble the big man was, for all his size. In an instant that could only have been merest chance, the tip of Wallace's sword flicked under his guard and caught him low under the ribs.

Jay's armor held, but the blow itself was hard enough to drive the wind from his lungs. As Wallace's blade rose to press the attack, Jay attempted an impaling thrust, but it fell short and Wallace beat his blade aside.

Backing off, sobbing for breath, Jay raised his sword to block the next blow, but Wallace's sword came flashing down on his own with such force that the Master of England staggered in his tracks. He retreated again, and this time only narrowly succeeded in making the parry. As Wallace continued to hammer at his defenses, Jay knew with sinking desperation that he was about to be bested by this rough fighting man with no claim to nobility.

It was then, as he glanced in vain for some hint of assistance from some brother-knight, that a mighty blow from Wallace sent the weapon flying from his hand. The Master of England had only an instant in which to contemplate his death before Wallace brought his sword down in a final stroke that split the Templar's skull clean through.

The deed went unseen by Arnault, still engaged with John de Sautre and intent on letting the other man's insensate rage prove his own undoing. When de Sautre finally lunged just too far, leaving himself open to Arnault's out-thrust sword point, his own momentum drove him onto the blade. A choked outcry escaped his lips along with a gush of blood as Arnault pulled his sword free, and in shocked disbelief he looked down to see his life's blood obliterating the cross on his white surcoat.

"May God temper justice with mercy!" Arnault murmured, in as much of a prayer as he could muster for the dying man, as de Sautre sank to his knees, eyes already glazing.

But he was already turning to look for Wallace, who was pausing to give the coup to a foundered horse as he looked for *his* next foe. Behind him lay the crumpled corpse of Brian de Jay.

"You came just in time, my friend, and I thank you for it," Wallace declared, heading toward him. "Alas, I can find little other cause for joy this day."

"Nor I," Arnault replied, looking around for Torquil. "And we must be away from here."

They were somewhat to the side of the fighting, which continued to take its toll, but a possible way to end it came to Arnault as he spotted Torquil making his way toward him, roughly dragging a disarmed Robert de Sautre along with him. Apart from a red weal on his cheek, the younger de Sautre gave little indication of having put up much of a struggle.

With a glance at Wallace, Arnault raised his sword and his voice above the clash of weapons.

"Knights of the Temple, stand and desist!" he cried. "The Masters of England and Scotland are dead! In the name of the Visitor of France, I order you to break off!"

The clashing of weaponry faltered as, all around, the Templars began to disengage, warily flinging glances toward Arnault. In answer, Wallace called to the Scots to fall back. In the uneasy silence that took shape, all eyes turned to the bearded, dark-haired man in plain harness who was standing beside the Guardian of Scotland—and the other plain-harnessed man, a redhead, who was roughly dragging an obviously captive Templar toward them.

One of the Templars, wrenching off his helmet for a closer look at the pair, immediately backed off and thrust his sword into the marshy ground in obedience—a redheaded Scottish knight whom Arnault remembered well from a visit to Paris on behalf of Luc de Brabant—and before that, a long ride to Scone, to see a king crowned. Increasingly in Luc's service since then, Flannan Fraser would have had no part of Jay's treachery, but also would have been obliged by his vows of obedience to accompany the Preceptor of Scotland on this expedition with the King of England.

"Listen to him, brothers!" Flannan cried. "I know this man. He is Brother Arnault de Saint Clair—no renegade, but a true knight of Christ's most holy Temple! I myself know this!"

Blessing Flannan for the courage of his faith, Arnault went on, gasping as he caught his breath.

"Brothers, you have no business on this field of battle. We serve no king but Christ, and no man here is His enemy. Gather up your wounded and your dead and return to our house at Temple Liston. Brother Robert de Sautre will lead you—is that not so, Brother Robert?"

Still in Torquil's custody, the dazed younger de Sautre could not seem to take his eyes from the sprawled body of his dead brother, lying not far from that of Brian de Jay. He swallowed hard.

"Yes, Brother Arnault," he answered shakily. "It is as you say."

At Arnault's nod, Wallace's men moved aside to allow Flannan Fraser and such of his brethren as were still able-bodied to begin gathering up the wounded and the dead.

Torquil, not relinquishing his grip on Robert de Sautre's elbow, steered the portly knight closer to where Arnault was standing, drawing them both slightly away from Wallace.

"Before we leave the field ourselves," he said in a lowered voice, after glancing around to make sure no one else was within earshot, "there's something more you need to know about Jay and this one's brother. Last night, I saw them give the Comyns, father and son, a casket of pagan artifacts, as payment for betraying Wallace and the Scottish host."

"I had no part in that!" Robert de Sautre blurted.

Torquil shot him a forbearing glare. "It's true that he wasn't personally present at the meeting," he confirmed grudgingly, "but I think it highly likely that he was aware of his brother's . . . unhealthy interests."

Arnault bent his gaze on the cringing Robert. "Pagan artifacts, Brother de Sautre?"

"I never—"

"Tell me what you know of these artifacts," Arnault said quietly. There was steel and righteous anger in his voice, and Robert quailed visibly before him.

"I was told they were relics of an ancient sorcerer named Briochan," he confessed nervously. "Brother Brian and John secretly performed rituals with them—so John told me later. I did not witness it personally!" he babbled on. "Indeed, it was only recently that John acquainted me with any of these deplorable goings-on. I was appalled to hear of it, yet my vow of obedience to Brother Brian forced me to keep silent."

His sickly, craven attempt at a smile, as he wound down, did little to convince either of his listeners that he was entirely innocent. But nothing could be proved; and by Arnault's own reading of the other man's character, he guessed that the younger de Sautre was not one who would willingly choose a difficult path over an easy one. Without Jay to lead the way, he was hardly likely to involve himself in the hazardous business of ancient sorcery—not with the lure before him of vacant offices left in the Scottish and English Temples by the deaths of his brother and Brian de Jay.

"I take it," Arnault stated for de Sautre's benefit, "that you will see to it that these pagan rites will never again be practiced by any of our brothers."

Robert looked as if he might be physically ill as he raised a trembling right hand. "As God is my witness," he whispered. "There have been too many *misunderstandings* in the past, Brother Arnault. There need be no enmity between *us*. We are both of us concerned with nothing other than the good of our Order."

Arnault raked the other man with a hard, appraising look.

"I hope that what you say is true," he said softly. "The future will tell. And if your actions bear out your words, then perhaps no one will ever connect you with the misdeeds of your superiors."

The implied threat of exposure was not lost on Robert de Sautre.

"I assure you of my complete cooperation in anything which furthers the cause of our faith and the welfare of the Order," he promised, then glanced nervously toward his fellow Templars, who were preparing to depart. "Now, by your leave, I must go and attend to the wounded—and to the burial of my misguided brothers."

Torquil was not minded to let the younger de Sautre leave so easily, but released him at Arnault's gesture. With pious words of gratitude, Robert scurried off to join his companions. The Templars gathered their horses and the bodies of their dead and rode off, only Flannan Fraser pausing to salute the two brethren they were leaving behind.

"Thank God for Flannan Fraser's level head," Torquil said. "But as for de Sautre, I trust him no more than I did his brother and Jay."

"To expose him would only do the Temple more harm," Arnault replied. "And at least with Jay gone, it should no longer be necessary for us to conceal our identities. This schism in the Order is at an end.

"But I think we must ride now, before more English come. Having saved Wallace once, I do not relish the thought of having to do it again today."

The Scots knights were grouped together in subdued celebration of at least this small victory on a day of defeat, exchanging banter with the remaining spearmen they had rescued, none of whom seemed to bear any ill will toward those who had deserted them earlier. Wallace and the Stewart were deep in conversation, the Guardian with his hand on Stewart's shoulder—and from the grief in the latter's face, it was evident that he had been told of his brother's death at the hands of the English knights.

As Arnault made his way toward them, knowing he must urge them back to their horses, to be away from here, he knew that James the Stewart was not the only one who would have cause to mourn this day at Falkirk.

Chapter Twenty-nine

TO RISE AND BEHOLD THE DAWN WAS LIKE WATCHING CRE-
ation at work, which was why Arnault had risen somewhat
before it to make his morning devotions. The birth of a new
day was a recurring promise of new beginnings that was
sorely needed by the men encamped in the hills to the west
of Perth. Three days after Falkirk, the Scots were still licking their wounds as they contemplated a future now bearing
little prospect for hope.

Ragged remnants of the Scots army had collected here,
numbering scarcely more than a thousand men—enough, at
least, to carry out ongoing punishing raids, and ensure that
the English would not have the leisure to bask in the glow of
their victory—but that was small enough consolation. Wallace's other troops were either dead or scattered, the survivors hiding in cottages and thickets or crawling homeward
to try to sleep off memories of the carnage.

Word had filtered back that the Scottish nobles had halted
their precipitate flight and established themselves in the

north. Already John Comyn was playing the patriotic leader, drawing up plans for continued resistance and blaming Wallace for the defeat. According to their own account, Comyn and his friends had rescued the Scottish cavalry from a disastrous and ill-planned confrontation, and were now prepared to bear the burden of leadership that they believed had been thrust upon them.

No, the prospects were not bright at all; and though Wallace's premature and futile death had been averted, at least for the moment, it was by no means certain that the ultimate battle could be won. As Arnault knelt before his sword, facing the east, he could almost sense Jerusalem out there, beyond the visible horizon, tugging at his soul like a spiritual lodestone: the Temple of Solomon, the hill of Calvary, and all the other holy places now lost to Christendom. Many still spoke of a new crusade, greater than any that had gone before, but Arnault knew in his heart—and had known since his vision in Cyprus—that the Knights of the Temple were now men in exile, like the people of Israel, and must likewise find their Lord in new and unexpected places.

Surely this place was among the more unlikely. Nothing in this wild and verdant northern land resembled the baked plains and yellow crags of Palestine. Yet Arnault still believed that he and his brethren were being led here to establish themselves anew, for purposes that were still hidden in the mind of God. Where clarity of vision failed, it was necessary for faith to light the way. Though this country was not his own, Arnault tried to share the simpler faith of the defeated soldiers he saw around him, most still wrapped in slumber, their sleep haunted yet by dreams of fallen comrades and kinsmen, but also the dream of freedom for their land.

Concluding his prayers, Arnault crossed himself and got to his feet, shaking the stiffness of the chill morning out of his legs before sheathing his sword. Normally, he would have confessed his weariness of soul to Torquil; but he had

sent the younger knight off the previous day to bear word of
the Scottish defeat to Luc de Brabant—for *le Cercle* must
know of it as soon as possible, especially those details that
could never be recorded in any conventional report of the
battle.

Soon both of them must return to Paris for further instructions—and with Brian de Jay's vindictive pursuit now
at an end, they could even move openly as Templars again—
but for just now, he sensed that the struggle for Scotland's
independence had reached a crucial turning point, and that
he must be on hand a while longer to guide the Guardian
through the crisis. Exactly how, remained to be seen, but Arnault was content to trust the intuitions that had always
stood him in such good stead.

He cast his gaze toward the last place he had seen the
Guardian before turning to his devotions, then started slowly
in that direction. Even in the gray light of early morning, the
tall figure of Wallace was unmistakable, leaning on the tum-
bledown wall of a ruined field at the edge of the camp, twid-
dling a stalk of weed between his fingers. Something about
the way he was silhouetted against the dawn sky empha-
sized the man's immense dignity and, at the same time, lent
him an air of loneliness, like a single strong oak rising out
of a deserted landscape.

Arnault slowed as he drew nearer, for Wallace was staring
out across the empty field with yearning eyes, as though he
beheld the whole of the land he loved in this one stretch of
ground—a moment that did not invite intrusion. But before
he could decide whether or not to return at a more opportune
moment, the other man turned and greeted him with a weary
smile. Though the Guardian could have snatched only a few
scant hours of sleep in nearly a week, he had spent too long
as a hunted outlaw to be easily caught unawares.

"You are abroad early, Arnault—or Brother Arnault, I
suppose I may call you now," Wallace said, casting aside his
bit of weed.

"Arnault alone will do as well now as it did a week ago," the Templar said easily. "I'm sure you have enough to concern you, without troubling over a trivial matter of titles. As for the hour, I find it's a good one for prayer."

"Prayer," Wallace repeated. "Of late, I've found little enough time for that—too little, if the truth be told. A miracle would serve us well, at this point."

"Sometimes it is God's will that we make our own miracles," Arnault said. "And if the world, in all its brokenness, confounds our efforts, God Himself redeems our failure through the consolation of His grace."

"Aye, you've known your own share of defeats, you Templars," Wallace acknowledged bleakly. "Otherwise, you would still be in the Holy Land—not here, where the enemy have the same faces and the same faith as ourselves."

"Men are men, wherever they are," Arnault said, "but when they fight over matters of faith, the conflict is at least an honest one."

Wallace pulled a jagged pebble from the drystone wall and flung it out over the field, watching it arc through the air and disappear amid a welter of bracken. His expression was meditative and solemn, as though he sought a sign in the falling of the stone that might guide him in this hour of decision.

"When your Templar brethren chased me through the forest, I fought by instinct for survival," he recalled, "and you and those you brought with you were a welcome sight. Now, though, I begin to wonder if I should thank you for saving my life. It might perhaps have been better if I had died on the field of battle, sharing the honor of those who fought to the death, and gaining for myself a peace I have been denied in life."

"Sometimes the price of peace is too high," Arnault reminded him, "as King John Balliol has discovered. The kind of peace you speak of is also dearly bought, for the price is despair."

Wallace gave the Templar a dark look. "I know only too well that it is a sin to take one's own life. But it is no disgrace to wish for death in battle."

"And if you had died, who would there be to lead the people of Scotland?"

"Let them lead themselves," Wallace said sharply. "That is what they must do now anyway, for I am resigning the Guardianship. I no longer know what there is to guard, or for whom I should be guarding it."

This unexpected admission caught Arnault unprepared. Small wonder that Wallace had seemed so troubled.

"To give up so high an office after so short a time—one that you have carried out with both wisdom and dedication—surely you cannot mean to do this?" he said.

"I have, on occasion, been accused of speaking too plainly," Wallace allowed, "but never of making my meaning obscure. I was not born to high office, nor did I deliberately seek it out. Not so long ago, I was an outlaw hiding among the caves and trees like a wild beast, depending upon the common folk for my safety. Three days ago, I trusted my fate to the nobles who are the rulers of the land, only to find that they care nothing for what happens to me. Very well, let them have this country to themselves, if that is what they want. It is what they were raised for, after all."

"A pack of squabbling lords is not what Scotland needs," Arnault pointed out. "It needs a king."

"I have given every fiber of my being for that king," Wallace declared vehemently. "I can do no more."

"I am not speaking of Balliol," Arnault said. "Scotland's king is not the one who surrenders to his enemy and accepts a comfortable captivity, as Balliol has done. The king is one who remains with his kingdom, even to the death."

"We have no such king."

"On the contrary, it seems clear to me that we do, if he will but admit it to himself."

Wallace frowned and looked away. "I have never sought the crown, nor would the nobility grant me it, if I did."

"There is more to kingship than a crown of gold and a fine throne," Arnault said. "While the Stone of Destiny remains, Scotland has a king, even if he is not recognized as such—not even by himself. You served the Stone, and in return have been marked for a singular destiny. Surely you must know this in your heart."

"I know no such thing," Wallace said. "It is all well and good for you and your religious brethren to sermonize about destiny and kingship, but I must deal in the solid realities of my life. I have lost my home, my wife and family, and now I have lost more than a battle; I have lost the promise of victory that was all I could use to persuade my highborn allies to follow me and bring their soldiers to support the cause of Scotland's freedom."

Arnault did not interrupt, for he knew that he must allow Wallace this moment to give full vent to his grief and frustration, if any sort of healing was to come, in the end.

"The title of Guardian is a hollow sham," Wallace continued. "It serves the illusion that this realm yet retains a vestige of its sovereignty, separate from that of England, but let some other man take it up, and make of it what he wants. I'll go to the farthest north and follow a life of obscurity, until even the name of William Wallace is forgotten. Either that, or I shall travel to France and fight in the service of a king who will be grateful to have a champion. At the very least, I may find my last battlefield."

He turned away from the dawn to face the still benighted sky of the west, throwing his troubled features into shadow.

"You speak lightly of your own death," Arnault said quietly, "yet you would not have it serve the cause you profess to love. The King of Heaven laid down his life for all mankind without being recognized as a king, even by those closest to him."

Wallace rounded on him with a flash of anger. "Your

speech borders on blasphemy, Templar," he warned. "I have told you once that I seek no crown, and I tell you so again!"

"The divine purpose thrusts upon us many things we would shun if we followed only earthly desires for comfort and peace," Arnault noted. "Do you think it was mere chance that brought you to us, when we sought to save the Stone of Columba from King Edward? It was at that moment, when you were recognized by the power of the Stone, that your destiny was set forth."

Wallace went very still, warring emotions flicking across his honest, open face.

"How could you possibly know that? *I* do not know! And what is the Stone to you? Who are you, to tell me this?"

"I am a Knight of the Temple," Arnault said, "and *my* destiny is to serve my Order, and the glory of God's name, to my last breath.

"The Temple, too, has its destiny—more than just its mission in the Holy Land. And that greater destiny, if you will, is now threatened by grave danger, as is all of Christendom. Meeting that danger has led a few of us here, to Scotland, where our attempts to clarify and deal with this danger have been frustrated repeatedly—sometimes even by those within our own ranks, who have fallen into the ways of corruption.

"You saw some of them at Falkirk—and sent one of them to be judged for his crimes by the All High God. So did I. But they are not the only ones we have to fear, or the ones we must fear the most. Others who serve the Darkness more directly have asserted themselves on this same disputed ground, restoring banished pagan sorcery and seeking to bring back the ancient gods, with their bloody ways, from the outer dark into which they were cast centuries ago."

He paused a beat. "But I have told you more than you wanted to hear, or even can grasp."

Wallace's gaze had dropped from his in confusion, but there could be no doubt that Arnault still had his attention.

"The balance here in Scotland is precarious, as you must know," he went on. "The struggle for the throne will determine far more than whether this family or that will gain a period of ascendancy; it will decide whether this Christian nation may survive at all—and with it, the fulfillment of that greater purpose for which the Order of the Temple was founded."

After a pause, Wallace at last spoke in a hushed voice.

"Speak to me of the Stone, Frère Arnault," he whispered. "The rest"—he fluttered a hand in rejection—"I know not how to answer. But the Stone—there *is* some kinship I felt with it, some . . . calling. But I don't know what it means."

"Nor do I—or at least, only a part of it," Arnault said. "But when one's own insight or reason fails to bring sufficient enlightenment, one must seek the wise counsel of those with clearer vision. My own quest took me to Iona, and the kindred of Columba. It was there I learned more of the forces at work here, and where my duty lay in the midst of this war."

"If you know that, then you know more than I," Wallace said.

Arnault inclined his head. "I can tell you this: The Stone, which we both have helped to preserve, was given by Saint Columba himself, as a visible sign of the bond between the king and the land. That bond was known of old, but seen in the light of the faith of Christ, its truth is even clearer. The strength of the king gives strength to the land, and vice versa; and what harms one harms the other. The power which arises from this link—the land's sovereignty, if you will—was preserved, focused, contained by the Stone of Destiny; and it lent both authority and power to the king. But the extinction of the line of Canmore severed that link between king and land, and now the Stone itself has been robbed of its potency."

"But—if the king draws his power from the Stone," Wallace said slowly, "and the Stone draws its potency from the king, what is to be done when there *is* no king, and the Stone has been rendered inert?"

Grateful that he had managed to divert the Guardian's attention to the cure rather than the cause of the problem, Arnault carefully went on.

"Before a true king can be established, the Stone must be restored to its former state. We have learned that this can only be done by one who stands in the place of the king without ascending the throne: an Uncrowned King, if you will, who has all the attributes of a king without laying claim to the crown."

Wallace frowned, looking vaguely uneasy. "With all you have learned, all you have seen, are you suggesting that I am the one you seek?"

"I am," Arnault said quietly. "And if I were to tell you that I had this of Saint Columba himself, in a vision at Iona, that would only frighten you. But ask yourself this: Has any man achieved more for Scotland than you have, or suffered more for her sake in loss and betrayal?"

Wallace met the Templar's gaze squarely, swallowing only with difficulty. His face had the look of a man who was preparing for the worst in spite of himself.

"You're right," he whispered. "I *am* frightened." He paused to take a deep breath. "So, what is it you would have me do?"

"At the risk—again—of being taken for a blasphemer, I would have you follow in the footsteps of the King of Kings, Who gave up His life for His friends," Arnault replied, in as much warning as he dared give directly. "I would have you take up your appointed destiny—and do not surrender to the false sweetness of despair, no matter how fiercely fortune may beat against you. The man who will not surrender cannot be defeated, nor can his honor be taken from him. Hold fast to this, whether it be through death or victory, and you will achieve the salvation of your land—but only if you hold true to that purpose and refuse to abandon it, whatever may come in the future."

Wallace walked several paces away, rubbing at his beard, then strode back, shaking his head. "You keep returning to my destiny," he said. "For yourself, you have fortified your faith with old wisdom, with counsel and revelations I do not have. I *want* to believe that I can still make some difference, but—"

"If you agree," Arnault said quietly, "I believe that a share of what I have seen can be yours, as well."

The offer brought Wallace up short. He gazed long at Arnault, apparently sensing that the Templar was offering more than fine words—perhaps more than he really wanted to know—but after a moment he gave a clipped nod.

"I agree."

Behind them, the camp was just beginning to stir. Probably, no one would disturb them for a while, especially if they appeared to be deep in private converse. Taking a leaning seat against the wall beside them, Arnault swept a hand in invitation for Wallace to join him, then pulled from its habitual resting place beneath his tunic the perforated scrying stone that Brother Ninian had given him. As he removed it from its leather thong, he briefly explained its nature to Wallace, who stared at it skeptically.

"A *keekstane*?" the Guardian declared. "I had thought such superstitions fit only for old women and simpleminded children. Is it to such talismans as these that we should entrust our lives?"

"We entrust ourselves to God," Arnault said, "but sometimes He guides us in unexpected ways. Sometimes He would even have us be as children—for in that way, we best demonstrate our trust in His Providence."

So saying, he slipped a dagger from its sheath and quietly offered it hilt-first to Wallace. Made of steel reforged from a blade broken in battle in the Holy Land, he had carried it with him since the retreat from Acre, as a memento of the reason they were fighting. But some instinct had always prevented him from putting it to ordinary use, and only now did he realize why.

"Make a small wound in your palm," he instructed. "Once a little blood has welled, I shall give you the *keekstane* to hold.

"What, in some kind of pagan blood sacrifice?" Wallace said doubtfully, as he hesitated.

"Not at all," Arnault replied. It was, however, true that the dagger, no less than the *keekstane*, must be blooded, to serve the ultimate purpose to which Wallace was called. "The *keekstane* possesses spiritual virtues that enable it to serve as a window between the Seen and Unseen, and the blood serves as a link between yourself and these virtues. Think of it being akin to the way a saint's physical relic serves as a connection with its owner's spiritual essence—an instrumental means for penetrating the veil that normally screens the future from our mortal eyes."

Wallace searched deep into Arnault's eyes. He looked very apprehensive, but also very determined. "Very well," he finally said. "I've trusted you before, in far greater matters. I'll not hold back now."

Closing the dagger firmly in his right fist, he set its point to his left palm and, with a quick stroke, opened a small cut about a finger-width long. A coin-sized pool of blood slowly formed in the palm of his hand, and when Arnault had slipped the dagger back into its sheath, he placed the *keekstane* flat over the wound, pressing it close with his fingertips.

"Close your eyes now," he ordered, "and picture the Stone as you last saw it. Fix its image in your mind . . . and ask in your heart for a vision of your destiny . . ."

As Wallace obeyed, Arnault closed his own eyes and breathed a hasty prayer.

Kindly Columba, send him clear vision . . .

Then, reaching out for his own mystical connection with the *keekstane*, he cast his thoughts back to the revelations he had previously been granted of that other Stone, asking for a sharing of that vision with Wallace. He could feel a tingle beneath his fingertips, the *keekstane* growing warmer; and then, through more than the eyes of memory, he was looking upon the Stone of Destiny.

And Wallace was with him, standing in awed wonder on the opposite side of the Stone. He appeared surprised and yet strangely accepting, as if feeling, for perhaps the first time since losing home and family, that he had come to the place where he belonged.

As they both gazed down at the Stone, there blossomed at its heart a faint yet steady light, filled with both peril and promise. To Arnault, it seemed for a fleeting moment that he glimpsed the face of Saint Columba in that light; but then the light shrank to a mere point.

Unease flared briefly then, as if in response to their presence there. The darkness beyond the Stone thickened, and a stench of seaweed and dank earth teased their nostrils as ghost-whispers of a pagan chant echoed up through the gloom. A chill shivered up Arnault's spine as he sensed a malignant entity hovering unseen on the edge of their awareness, and even Wallace flinched a little.

The light, however, did not waver, and Arnault could see that Wallace was holding firm to that sight, taking courage from it in spite of the sense of imminent menace that threatened to intrude. Fueled by their faith, the light expanded and the dark retreated before it, the vile smell and the aura of personified evil also receding.

The unholy chant faded, giving place to sounds of distant combat. The battle din mounted amid the thunder of hooves and the clash of arms. The screams of dying men mingled with an exultant clamor of victory as Arnault and Wallace found themselves enfolded in radiance like a golden ray of sunlight.

Banners waved on every side—the flags and ensigns of Scotland—and the clamor became discernible as the acclamation of a king. A throne took shape amid the glow, and seated upon it was a crowned figure whose face they could not make out.

Then the cheers subsided, and the golden light faded, and the chamber sank once more into a darkness that was only faintly illuminated by the point of light at the Stone's heart. It was smaller than a candle's flame, yet it held the sole hope of fulfillment of the vision of the new king.

Beside Arnault, Wallace's hand had closed around the *keekstane*, and he was slowly shaking his head, eyes still tightly closed.

"I cannot see," he whispered. "I must see further. I must See!"

Gently Arnault set his fingers back on Wallace's, willing calm, searching his mind for a way to extend the vision— and remembered a way, learned on Iona.

"I can help you see further," he murmured. "Keep your eyes closed. First, give me the *keekstane*." He watched the other's trembling eyelids as he plucked the stone from Wallace's bloodied hand.

"Now close your fist . . . and relax it slightly, so that your fingers form a tube in your left hand . . . good. Now blow three times through that tube while you invoke the Trinity— but say it in the Gaelic."

Wallace's brow furrowed and his lips parted as if to question; but then he drew a deep breath and let it out, lifted his fist to his lips and blew three times.

"*In ainm an Athar . . . agus an Mhic . . . agus an Spioraid Naoimh . . .*"

"Now . . . turn your face to the east," Arnault said softly, "and lift the tube to your left eye, and look through it at the sun . . . and let yourself See . . ."

Trembling, Wallace obeyed, squinting at the light—and as Arnault again closed his eyes, he was back in that other place before the Stone. Wallace was still there as well, but kneeling now before the Stone to set his bloody hand upon it.

At that touch, new light spilled forth from the billow of gauzy curtains within a narrow doorway. Its invitation was for Wallace only, its cool breeze fresh and sweet with the scent of lilies, and Arnault watched with wonder as Wallace turned toward that doorway and slowly rose, clearly reluctant yet acquiescing, and began to walk toward it. A part of him longed to warn Wallace; but another part knew it was for this purpose that he had brought Scotland's Guardian to this place between the worlds—for only here might he learn what was asked of him, and either accept or reject what had been ordained for him.

Wallace disappeared through the doorway into light, and utter silence enfolded Arnault, overlaying the growing bustle of domestic sound in the campsite not far away. His own sense of isolation became so intense that he was half minded to attempt going after Wallace, to confront whatever had taken him, even if, in doing so, he violated his own sworn duty. But before he could make any such decision, the light at the heart of the Stone of Destiny flared up like a bonfire igniting, and the dark chamber dissolved before it like mud being washed from a windowpane by a torrent of cleansing rain.

Abruptly Arnault found himself back on the edge of the field, with Wallace still beside him. The morning sun shone fully upon them, and the light showed up the pallor of Wallace's face. Arnault hardly knew whether to ask him what he had seen.

Wallace licked his lips and flexed his hand, the blood in it now mostly dried, and took a deep breath to steady himself back into the world of the Seen.

"God's will can ask much of us, truly," he said at last, with a slow, distant nod. "I will do what I see now that I must, but I do not know if I can bear it as I ought."

But Arnault, too, had glimpsed at least some inkling of what he, too, must bear, and met Wallace's haunted eyes with a compassion that was as deep as it was blind.

"Whatever awaits you," he vowed, "I swear that you shall not bear it alone, while I live."

Wallace only looked down at his bloody hand, flexing it again before bending briefly to wipe it clean on a patch of dewy grass.

"I do not think you know what you are promising, my friend," he whispered as he straightened. "I do not think you know at all."

Part IV

Part IV

Chapter Thirty

THE SIX YEARS FOLLOWING FALKIRK WERE HARSH ONES FOR Scotland. Wallace himself spent much of that time attempting to drum up support on the Continent, but to little avail, and eventually returned. Though Scottish patriots under a succession of Guardians and combinations of Guardians after Wallace made periodic attempts to reassert the kingdom's independence, Edward of England continued his relentless campaign to impose English sovereignty on the land, so that by mid-June of 1304, nearly every Scottish leader of note had reluctantly done homage to the English king.

Apart from a few scattered pockets of resistance, only Wallace himself, Sir John de Soules, the most recent Guardian, now sheltering in France, and the garrison at Stirling Castle, under command of the young Sir William Oliphant, had refused to capitulate. And Wallace was in hiding in the north, Stirling Castle under siege by Edward himself, unlikely to hold out more than another month or two.

Arnault and Torquil had arrived back in Scotland at about
the same time Edward began the Stirling Castle siege, once
again moving freely as Templars, again carrying orders, as
they had at Berwick eight years before, that would absent
the Master of the English Temple from the king's side. For
though the current Master, one William de la More, was
deemed to be pious and upright as well as competent, un-
tainted by his predecessor, and was only following long established general policy of the Order—that the Master of
England should advise the English king in matters of military strategy, as Brian de Jay had done—*le Cercle* had
deemed it advisable to reduce this potential source of English advantage by having said Brother William summoned to
report to the Grand Master in Cyprus, as they had done for
Jay eight years before.

Brother William had received his orders gracefully, unaware of the affinities of the knight-brothers who delivered
them save that the men were sent under authority of the Visitor; and Edward had issued writs of safe conduct for
Brother William to clear the port of Dover and sent him with
a letter to the Grand Master, praising his services to the
crown and asking that he be sent back as soon as possible.
But it would be at least midwinter before Brother William
returned from Cyprus—and by then, Arnault and Torquil
would have been able to cautiously begin setting in place the
next phase of *le Cercle*'s master plan, without fear of unwitting interference from their English superior.

The slow evolution and crafting of that plan had been accomplished only with difficulty during the six years since
Falkirk. Though the pair had made periodic trips back to
Scotland during that time, gauging the pulse of developments unfolding there, they and *le Cercle* had also known
that William Wallace's time as the Uncrowned King had yet
to run its course; and Wallace himself passed many months
in France, pleading the Scottish cause with king and pope.

As for the Comyns, the deaths at Falkirk of Brian de Jay

and John de Sautre had precluded finding out anything further about the casket Torquil had seen them give to the Comyns; and since, in subsequent years, the Comyns had seemed to derive no untoward gains that might be attributed to the assistance of sorcery, further speculation in that regard had been put into abeyance against the receipt of further information.

Meanwhile, the fortunes of the Order as a whole were also demanding careful examination and consideration, for France was becoming almost daily a less than hospitable home. By 1303, resolving a long-standing struggle for power between king and papacy, the king's agent, Guillaume de Nogaret, had succeeded in deposing the hapless Pope Boniface VIII, alleging misconduct of a most heretical and blasphemous nature. Subsequently imprisoned, Boniface soon had died under bizarre circumstances, having beaten his own head against the stone wall of his room. Some said that other hands might have guided his head to the wall. Since the Order answered directly to the Roman pontiff, who was its spiritual protector, it was necessary to view any attack on the papacy as a potential danger to the Order as well. The French king still reposed sufficient trust in the Temple to allow some French treasury functions to be based at the Paris Temple; but in times like these, no king could truly be trusted.

Even in matters that did not directly concern the Order, Philip IV was proving less than trustworthy. Though formerly a supporter of John Balliol's restoration—since turmoil in Scotland would inconvenience Edward in pursuing his continental wars—that support had ended two years before, when Philip entered a treaty with Edward at Coutrai in 1302. It now appeared that yet another urgency was being added to the Order's race against time: to see whether the Temple could establish its new spiritual home, anchored in the mystical erection of the Fifth Temple, before the Order's enemies in France ousted it from its physical home, now based largely at the Paris Temple.

All of these considerations were well known to Brothers Arnault de Saint Clair and Torquil Lennox as, amid the dusk and drizzle of the eleventh day of June, they picked their way across the boggy, salt-tanged Carse of Stirling, whose marshy flatlands were subject to tidal flooding along the meandering course of the River Forth. Besieged Stirling Castle lay less than two miles across that carse, encircled by the armed hosts of Edward's army, daily battered by his mighty siege engines, the Parson, the Berefrey, and his newest plaything, the War Wolf.

But their destination was Cambuskenneth Abbey, not the English lines; and the English king would have taken grave exception to any secret meeting with the man who had summoned them there.

The pair had first made the acquaintance of William Lamberton, the dynamic and capable Bishop of St. Andrews, when he was still chancellor to Wishart of Glasgow, during those taut, exhilarating days when Wallace was first bursting into prominence. Even then, young Lamberton had been well wedded to the patriot cause, and soon had shown himself to possess a keen intellect, a remarkable ability to flex according to circumstances, and a fervent longing for a return to the precepts of Celtic monarchy that had guided the Canmore kings. In the aftermath of Stirling Bridge, when Wallace's influence was at its highest, it had been no difficult matter to persuade the new Guardian that Lamberton would make a worthy successor to Bishop William Fraser, one of Scotland's longest serving advocates, who recently had died in France.

In the intervening years, Bishop Lamberton had proved an untiring champion of Scotland's liberties, running the dangerous gauntlet of English warships to risk repeated trips to Paris and Rome to plead Scotland's cause, serving in various combinations of Guardianship among such men as John

Comyn, Ingram de Umfraville, the younger Robert Bruce, and Sir John de Soules, yet always walking that fine line from which even Edward of England had not presumed to topple him; for Lamberton had an unerring instinct for knowing exactly how far he dared push the English king while still retaining his own integrity and his position of influence in the affairs of Scotland.

In addition, Arnault and Torquil had discovered, he entertained more than just a political affinity for Scotland's Celtic past, and was even conversant with many tenets of the Columban spirituality practiced on Iona; and while they had not confided the whole of their mission to him, Lamberton seemed to sense that the pair were more than they seemed, and apparently was willing to accept that, at the appropriate time, they would reveal what further he needed to know. He knew how they and Wallace had spirited away the true Stone of Destiny, though not—by his own request—where it lay; and he had become a staunch ally among Scotland's clergy hierarchy.

Meanwhile, he continued to pursue the practicalities of their common goal in his own ways, with tact, sensitivity, and an unswerving focus on eventually restoring Scotland's independence. Like almost everyone else, the Bishop of St. Andrews had made an outward peace with Edward, rather than face exile or imprisonment, but Arnault knew full well that his love of country and his hunger for its freedom had not been quenched.

"It's dangerous for him even to have come here," Arnault said to Torquil, as they drew rein in the last of the screening trees before they must set off across a final stretch of meadowland between them and the abbey gate. "He could have met us any of a number of other places, farther away from Edward and his army."

Torquil lifted his gaze to the dark silhouette of the castle perched on its crag, then returned his attention to the abbey, where a few torches were beginning to show beside the gate.

"Well, it looks safe enough," he said. "Have you come up with any idea what he might want?"

"None," Arnault replied. "So I suppose we're just going to have to ride over and find out."

Hooded heads lowered against the drizzle, the two continued on across the last few hundred yards separating them from the abbey. The gate porter swung the gates wide at their approach. Within, a cowled brother was waiting to take their horses into the abbey stables, out of sight, and two more were standing on the porch of the abbey church—black-robed Augustinian friars. They bowed in acknowledgment as the two knights swept toward them in their distinctive white mantles. One of the monks stepped deferentially aside while the other opened one half of the double door. Arnault and Torquil greeted them silently in passing as they entered the church's gray, candlelit interior.

A black-cloaked and hooded figure was kneeling in prayer before the high altar. As the two Templars approached, spurs ringing on the stone flagging, the man rose and crossed himself before turning to push back the hood from a tonsured head only now beginning to gray at the temples: William Lamberton, now six years a bishop, but still only forty-one, nearly a decade younger than Arnault.

He was clothed in the plain black of a Benedictine beneath his traveling cloak, a sure sign that this assignation was, indeed, as secret as Arnault had been led to believe. Though the bishop showed a winning honesty in his brown eyes, and an authority to his bearing that any man would admire, both Templars had learned that Lamberton had an uncanny knack for altering his manner to seem the most unassuming and commonplace of men. No doubt in Edward's presence he was a very model of humility, giving no indication of the threat he genuinely presented to the king's plans for dominance.

"Thank you for coming, brothers," he said in a low voice

that was pitched not to stir echoes from the surrounding stonework. "You were not hindered in obtaining leave?"

Arnault smiled faintly. "You perhaps are not aware that the Master of England has again been sent from King Edward at a time when his presence nearby might have been inconvenient. As a consequence, we are able to travel freely about our business."

"Would that I could say the same," Lamberton said with a thin smile. "My friend the king still has me watched, and it was not easy to slip away. I am like a religious novice who must prove his worth before being allowed to act without supervision."

"From what I hear, it is a dangerous business to tempt Edward's wrath these days," Torquil said.

"With advancing years some men grow in wisdom," the bishop observed. "Others, however, grow in bitterness—and the fruit of that bitterness is all too often an unreasoning cruelty, all the more unbridled if it is wedded to power."

"Yet Edward now has nearly all that he wishes," Arnault said. "Surely there remains no need to vent any sort of rage."

Lamberton allowed himself a shrug and a bitter smile. "Given the mass surrenders and submissions of this past year, there are few candidates left for his revenge. Accordingly, those few who remain must suffer doubly for it—and young Oliphant, sadly, is one of the latter. Trapped inside Stirling Castle with only a few score of men, he has become the focus of all of the king's long-simmering frustration."

"So we are given to understand," Torquil said. "We have heard that Oliphant wished to send to John de Soules in France, to learn whether the Guardian would allow him to surrender. They say that he does not deem himself of sufficient authority to authorize surrender, since it was the Guardian who gave him Stirling, to hold for the crown and community of Scotland."

Lamberton lifted a ringed hand in impatient denial. "It was not allowed. Edward's patience is at an end. He no longer has interest in negotiating any terms for surrender, however favorable they might be to him. Since rumor has it that this is the last battle of the war, he has decided to use young Oliphant's honorable resistance as an excuse to try out all his new siege engines. Perhaps you have seen some of the results of these past weeks' work. The defenders cannot last much longer, I fear—and God help them all, when surrender eventually comes, as it must."

"War is ever a brutal business," Arnault said. "But surely Edward does not mean to take retribution beyond the brutality of the siege itself. Surely the rules of chivalry still apply."

"Perhaps you have not been to the English camp, as I have been," Lamberton said with a curl of his lip. "But you both were at Berwick. The king's outbursts of savagery have spread fear among his own people, and this siege looks likely to end in a massacre unless he can be restrained by some of the cooler and more chivalrous heads who surround him."

"If you have asked us here to avert such an outcome, I fear you will be disappointed," Torquil said. "Tolerance is the best we can hope for from Edward, and no appeal for leniency from us will carry any weight."

The bishop turned his face toward the Rood cross, his face still and taut in the dimness. "May God forgive me if I say it is not the fate of the castle and its garrison that mainly concerns me, though I pray it will not come to the worst. It is what happens after that, for Scotland—whether this is, indeed, our final and irrevocable defeat, or whether something can yet be salvaged, even if it is no more than the tenuous flame of a single candle to relight the fire of freedom."

"There is one spark which still burns, however faintly," Arnault said.

Lamberton turned to look at him, well aware that Arnault referred to the Stone of Destiny, and how the Stone pertained to their present discourse. That King Edward had come to doubt the authenticity of the stone being held at Westminster was almost certainly a contributing cause for his vindictive malice against all remaining Scottish rebels in recent years.

Mere weeks after the battle of Falkirk, he had sent a band of knights to Scone again, with orders to strip it bare of any and all remaining treasures. They had found no trace of the true Stone, of course. But after Lamberton's return from his consecration in Rome the following year—which had been spent trying to recruit support for Scotland's cause—Arnault and Torquil had enlisted the new bishop in the service of the Stone, though they had withheld that vital connection of its mystical link with Wallace.

Now, clearly, Lamberton took Arnault's meaning regarding the symbolism of the Stone, but his head shook almost imperceptibly.

"What we need is not a symbol of kingship, but a man we can crown upon it."

His words came as some surprise, for Lamberton had long been a staunch ally of Wallace, and a firm supporter of John Balliol as king.

"John Balliol was crowned upon that Stone," Arnault said slowly. "Are you saying that you have abandoned his cause?"

"With some disquiet—yes, I have," the bishop admitted, looking away with a sigh. "With Balliol as our absent king, we have come to this: humiliation and surrender. And Balliol now has lain in exile in France for five years and more, too spineless to take back his throne, and has said he will never return. If we can find no more suitable ruler, then perhaps we should simply accept Edward as our liege lord and be done with it."

"Surely, that is not what you propose to do?" Torquil blurted out, appalled.

The bishop stayed him with a gesture. "Fear not, Brother Torquil, I am not yet come to that," he said. "Oh, I will bow the knee to Edward for now, as I have done before, since that is a necessary strategy to gain time. But we can hardly strike back, can we, if all our leaders are dead, imprisoned, or in exile in France?"

"What of Wallace?" Arnault asked. "Have you spoken to him of this?"

Lamberton let out a heavy sigh. "I owe my episcopal see to Wallace—and there is no man more noble in all of Scotland, and none who loves this country more. Yet, we have come to such a pass that his best qualities now work against him—and Scotland."

"How so?" Torquil asked.

Lamberton clearly was ill at ease in discussing this topic, and toyed with his crucifix as he spoke.

"He will not abandon Balliol, no matter what. To him, the point of honor is a simple one: Balliol has been rightfully crowned king, and so he will remain, even unto death. Wallace cannot abandon that principle, nor can he feign obeisance to Edward—not even to buy the time we need to muster our strength once more."

"He would find no mercy from Edward, even if he did," Arnault pointed out. "Edward has made an official decree that there is to be no peace offered to Wallace unless he delivers himself utterly and unconditionally—into his *will*, not his mercy or his grace."

"He would be safer placing his head inside the mouth of a starved lion," Torquil muttered.

"Precisely," Lamberton agreed. "There is no safety for Wallace here, and yet he will not leave the country again, whatever the danger. John de Soules and others of our leaders—the Stewart, Umfraville—are not to be granted safe conducts to return from France until Wallace is given up—and worst of all, Edward has personally charged various of the earls and barons with Wallace's capture."

"Surely they will not agree to such an undertaking," Torquil said disgustedly.

Lamberton shrugged. "They must, to secure their lands from threat of seizure—and who can blame them? Moreover, some of them say it is Wallace himself who has brought Edward's wrath down upon us, and that if he is delivered, Edward will leave Scotland in peace."

"If they truly believe that, then they deceive themselves," Arnault declared.

"Men with their own worldly interests at heart are ever their own dupes," Lamberton said. "However, the sum of all this is that we must have a leader and we must have a king. Above all they must be one and the same man, not a struggling Guardian and an absent, powerless figurehead."

The bishop's distress made clear how much it grieved him to speak thus of parting company with a man whom he so admired and to whom he owed so much. Arnault saw there was nothing to be gained from arguing the point, and he knew that Lamberton, as always, had Scotland's best interests at heart.

"What course is it, then, that you intend to pursue?" he asked.

"We must have a fresh candidate for the throne," Lamberton replied, "one who can do all that Balliol was incapable of doing and who, unlike Wallace, can claim the kingship by right. There is only one such man. Comyn yet has designs upon the throne, but he is tainted with an evil I can scarce contemplate without feeling my flesh grow cold. He was the ruin of every effort at joint guardianship, and he will be the ruin of Scotland, if he is given the chance."

"You speak of Bruce, then," Torquil said.

It was offered quietly, but something in his tone caught the bishop's attention.

"That is more than an intelligent guess on your part," he said.

Torquil's hand had drifted to the hilt of the sword Bruce had given him, and he looked to Arnault, who nodded for him to continue.

"He *is* the senior Bruce heir, since his father's death two months ago," Torquil said.

"And?"

Torquil exhaled slowly, not taking his eyes from the bishop's. "When I encountered Bruce some years ago, on the very day of the battle of Falkirk, I had an intimation that he was destined to be king. Even though it might have been only a trick of the light as I beheld him, the more I pondered it, the more it seemed a true sign."

"I pray God that it was," Lamberton murmured.

"Even so," Torquil went on, "it makes me uneasy that Bruce submitted two years ago, and has served Edward ever since."

"It won him a bride and the promise of future allies in Ireland," Lamberton said. "And in that, he has done no more than the rest of us, for all that he did it sooner. Perhaps he merely saw, before we did, the futility of continuing to fight for Balliol's lost cause."

"You think, then, that he has been biding his time, waiting for the right occasion to make his move?" Arnault suggested.

"That is how I read his mind," said the bishop. "It was only a matter of time before his father died and the way was cleared in that regard. In these past months, I have come to believe that if victory and freedom are ever to be ours, then we need a fresh vision of the future. It is my hope that Bruce may be able to provide that—and today I propose to put the question to the test."

He answered the Templar's questioning looks with an ironic smile. "I have invited him here today to meet with me secretly, so that I can determine whether or not we have a solid foundation of hope for the future."

"You intend to speak to him of the kingship, while he is yet in Edward's service?" Arnault asked, caution in his tone.

"I myself am in Edward's service," Lamberton pointed out, with a droll arch of one eyebrow. "I would have to look hard indeed to find more than a handful of men who are not. What I seek is a remedy for that situation."

"Why have you asked us here?" Torquil asked.

"As you were quick to see, the situation is a delicate and difficult one," Lamberton admitted. "I judged it best to have neutral but sympathetic witnesses on hand, to seal whatever arrangement I can reach with Bruce. There is also the matter of the Stone of Destiny. While I place every trust in the word of Abbot Henry, I have it only by his report that the stone Edward stole is, indeed, a mere substitute. You, on the other hand, can confirm by your own witness that the true Stone is safely concealed, merely awaiting a king to be crowned upon it and claim its ancient authority."

The two Templars exchanged measuring glances. With Balliol abandoned, Bruce was, indeed, the only viable candidate—and a good one, if he could be persuaded to put Scotland's good before the mere advancement of his powerful family. But though Bruce had been discussed and cautiously approved by *le Cercle*, based on Torquil's insights, they had not expected Lamberton to endorse him quite so soon. They had come here half expecting to discuss a plan to ensure the safety of the Stone, should Edward truly become King of the Scots at last; but instead, the bishop was displaying a sense of imagination and purpose that might yet rekindle the nation's fortunes.

"It is a bold step you are taking," Arnault said at last. "And perhaps the time is past for too much caution. I will confess to certain . . . experiences which foretell a future king who might answer your prayers. His face, however, I have not seen, and I hesitate to give him a name. If you have judged Bruce rightly, then it may be that you have seen the way forward. We will certainly do what we can to facilitate your plan, if this seems to be what is intended."

Before Lamberton could respond, the door creaked open and one of the monks waved a signal to the bishop.

"Bruce has arrived," Lamberton said. "I need a few minutes to speak alone with him before I call upon your support. I ask you to conceal yourselves in the side chapel, where you will be hidden from view but still able to overhear us."

The pair nodded their brisk agreement and moved into an alcove to the right of the sanctuary. A few moments later the main door opened again to admit Robert Bruce.

Now a mature man of more than thirty years, a little younger than Torquil, the Earl of Carrick was plainly dressed and without escort, sword and dirk at his waist—and probably mailed beneath his robe—but outwardly unthreatening. As he strode down the aisle, his demeanor carried no hint of deference, either for the man he had come to see or for the holy place where they met. For all his boldness, however, his expression was one of curiosity as much as irritation.

"I hope you appreciate the risk I am taking, in agreeing to a clandestine meeting, my lord bishop, when King Edward is only a few miles distant and in a disagreeable mood," he said.

"Risk has become as much a part of our existence as drawing breath these days," Lamberton responded. "Without it we can do nothing at all, unless we would live like creatures of the sea, forever mute and moving with the tide."

"Your tongue is as able as ever, but I am not here to admire your eloquence," Bruce said.

"Then, why are you here?" Lamberton countered.

"Surely that is for you to explain, since it was you who issued the cryptic invitation."

"You would not have responded unless you had some inkling of my purpose, Robert Bruce. While it may not be exactly the same as your own, the two coincide to a degree that cannot be ignored."

"What purpose of mine do you speak of?" Bruce asked defensively.

"To become king," Lamberton answered flatly.

Bruce's expression froze, and he eyed the bishop in stony silence.

"You are as unwilling to deny my assertion as you are to confirm it," Lamberton said. "But what lies in the heart cannot remain forever hidden, or it will wither away to nothing but the lost and bitter dream of an old man who passes his final years cursing his own want of courage."

This bald statement caused Bruce to bristle. "I have no want of courage, I assure you of that!"

"Then, will you remain Edward's servant forever?" Lamberton asked.

"For as long as you, maybe!" came Bruce's hot retort.

Lamberton raised his hands in a placatory gesture. "Peace, my lord, I have not asked you here to quarrel with you. With your father's recent death, you are now a candidate for the throne in your own right. All hope of Balliol even being willing to act as a king is now lost, so it is time to look elsewhere. Would you agree with that?"

"Most heartily," Bruce replied. "But would you have me declare my desire for the throne when, just across the river, our liege lord Edward is preparing to roast men alive for far less presumption?"

"You have kept your intent hidden for long enough," Lamberton said evenly. "Do not let an excess of caution be your undoing."

"There is no shame in acting with caution and wisdom," Bruce said. "If I had followed Wallace's stiff-necked course, I would have lost my lands, my titles, and my family to become a fugitive running from cave to cave, fleeing Edward's men and my own people. One does not become king from a position of weakness, but of strength."

Lamberton lifted an eyebrow. "Is that what you think? Did not Balliol start from a position of strength? He was king, by the will of Edward of England and the assent of the community of this realm, and still he lost it all. Is it not better to start with nothing, and to win the crown, than to begin with the crown and lose all, including honor itself?"

Bruce's brow darkened. "John Balliol's crown has been empty for some time. Nor do we even possess that symbol of that kingship. Edward took it, along with all of the other symbols of our sovereignty. It is no longer even possible for a man to be properly crowned King of Scots."

"In that you are mistaken," the bishop said mildly.

Passion flared in Bruce's gray eyes, confirming that Lamberton had not misjudged the man. Ambition there certainly was, but also something more.

"The Stone of Destiny never left Scotland," Lamberton stated flatly. "What Edward has placed on display in Westminster Abbey is a worthless copy."

Bruce's gaze narrowed. "You know this to be true? You have seen it yourself?"

"In all honesty, I cannot say that I have," Lamberton confessed, "but I have witnesses here who will confirm what I have told you. Brothers, would you please join us?"

Arnault and Torquil emerged from the side chapel, white mantles almost aglow in the dim light. Bruce stiffened as he cast a suspicious eye over their Templar robes, but then he looked again at Torquil's face.

"You are familiar to me," he said uncertainly.

"On the morning of Falkirk, you gave me your horse—and a sword," Torquil confirmed, briefly holding his hand away from the hilt of the weapon. "You found me lying unconscious and, like the Good Samaritan, you came to my assistance."

"So I did," Bruce acknowledged with a nod. "And you did tell me then that you were a Templar." He paused a beat. "Has the sword served you well?"

"It has—and would serve *you* now, if you mean to fight for Scotland and her crown."

Bruce's gaze flicked to Arnault, then back to Torquil. "How is your Order involved in this?"

"Officially—not at all," Arnault replied. "But like the bishop, we seek a free and strong Scotland. He believes you are now the only man who can accomplish that."

"And the Stone?"

"Brother Torquil and I were among those who removed it to a safe hiding place. So was Wallace."

"You mean he has known of it for all these years?" Bruce exclaimed. "Now I begin to understand part of the reason for his persistence."

"The important thing," Lamberton said, "is that through his efforts and those of these knights, we can crown a king with the full authority which only the Stone of Destiny can bestow."

"Do you mean now, while Edward holds Scotland in the compass of his fist?" Bruce asked sharply.

"No, not now," Arnault answered. "Even if our current state were not so perilous, it still would not be the right time. If the next king is to be more than the puppet shell that Balliol was, he must have not only the support of the people of Scotland—and be willing to fight for them. He must be enthroned upon a Stone that is fully reempowered. For we believe that a fault with the Stone is at least partially to blame for the failure of Balliol's kingship."

Bruce merely stared at him in astonishment for a long moment, glancing at the bishop to see whether this extraordinary suggestion had raised an episcopal eyebrow. But Lamberton was gazing back at him without a flicker of misgiving.

"Reempowered," Bruce repeated softly. "What does that mean? I know that the Stone of Destiny is reputed to have mystical properties, but I confess that until now I had given little thought to such tales—especially as I believed the Stone was in London."

"The spiritual heritage of any land is based in truth," Arnault said quietly. "And your Celtic heritage contains more truth than, perhaps, you realize. Your Stone of Destiny is far more than a mere symbol of your land's sovereignty."

He deferred to Torquil to elaborate, in light of the bond already established between the two.

Choosing his words carefully, Torquil told Bruce how Brother Mungo had first hinted that the Stone might be ailing, and how their further investigations had led them to Iona, and something of what they had learned there of the link of the Stone with the land and the king. Without divulging the purposes or even the existence of the Templar Order's Inner Circle, he told Bruce of their suspicions that sorcery had been used in the extinction of the Canmore line, and that the Comyns were practitioners of such sorceries, underlining that assertion with an account of what he had seen the present Comyn's late father do at John Balliol's inauguration. Nor did he shrink from mentioning his own near death while fleeing from the Comyns, and his supposition that they had summoned whatever dark force had pursued him.

"You did avoid specifics that day, regarding your attacker," Bruce allowed, when Torquil had finished. "I thought it strange, even then, that there was no wound upon you . . . save for that mark in the palm of your hand."

"What had saved me, the previous night, was a protective charm given me by the monks of Iona," Torquil said boldly. "And they are prepared, when the time is right, to assist with the reempowering of the Stone. Meanwhile, you must prepare yourself to be worthy of the Stone's endorsement of your cause."

Bruce rubbed at his beard, obviously still uncertain.

"This matter of the Comyns—you did hint of their treachery, that day of Falkirk," he said. "I knew they had some strange ways, but never did I suspect they might hazard their souls in this fashion, and so against Scotland's interests. Perhaps that explains the threat I always felt, when I tried to share the Guardianship with John Comyn. But—can they truly have brought about the extinction of the Canmores?"

"The evidence we have is circumstantial," Arnault allowed, "but it is very suggestive. I would prefer not to elaborate. Simply be warned that Comyn is a very dangerous and ambitious adversary, and will resist you with every power available to him."

"That much, I already know—whether or not he is in league with these dark forces of yours!" Bruce said with a snort.

"Do not dismiss this warning," Lamberton said. "Perhaps you now understand why I was prepared to risk this meeting, so close to Edward's wrath. Make no mistake, he is still a deadly danger—but I fear that fellow Scots, not the English, may prove the greater danger."

"As dead from one as from the other," Bruce muttered.

"No, *not* as dead from the one as from the other!" Lamberton said sharply. "You are speaking of things you do not understand. But a safe way lies amid the dangers, if you will be guided."

Bruce started to speak, then thought better of it and closed his mouth again, exhaled slowly before venturing to answer at last.

"I will speak, then, of things I *do* understand. If you would not have me declare myself king now, and you are not yet ready to crown me, why did you call me here?"

"Because it is now, when things are darkest, that hope is most sorely needed," Lamberton answered. "It is now that we must secretly begin laying the groundwork for the future, or resign ourselves to unending subservience. It is a curious way of things that the best time to form an intent must often needs be the worst time in every other respect. When all is dark, it is then that the beginnings of light are most clearly seen."

Bruce met the bishop's gaze unflinchingly. "Speak plainly then, and tell me what it is that you ask of me."

"That you declare now your intent to win the crown," Lamberton answered, "whatever the cost may turn out to be. You spoke of the hardships Wallace has brought upon himself by his constant defiance of Edward—and for now, you have succeeded by judicious actions in avoiding that fate. But in the end, you will have to make sacrifices as well. Unless you are prepared to live an outlaw's life, to spend years hunted and in fear of betrayal, just as Wallace has done, why should any man think you worthy of the crown?"

"It is mine by right!" Bruce declared, one fist clenching in his passion. "Nor will Scotland find me wanting, when the time comes!"

"In that case, I may ask our friends to proceed regarding the reempowerment of the Stone, knowing that their efforts will not be for nothing," Lamberton said mildly. "For my part, I will do all I can to prepare the way politically, without betraying myself to Edward; and if you need assistance from me to maintain your own position, you may call upon me."

Bruce looked away. "I am under pressure to do homage to Edward for my English lands, now that my father has died," he said.

"Then do what you must, as we all must do," Lamberton replied. "But meanwhile, agree that you and I shall be allies, and shall consult one another before attempting any major enterprise, and shall warn one another of any danger."

"I agree," Bruce promised. "And when you look for a king to crown, you may call upon me and I will answer." He turned to Arnault and asked, a little less certainly, "Will it truly be possible to reempower the Stone?"

"With God's help, I believe so," Arnault said. "Then a true king can be crowned, and the darkness lifted from the land."

"You speak, I think, of more than Edward's oppression," Lamberton said quietly.

"I do," Arnault replied, but he did not elaborate. For not

only must Wallace play his part through to the end, by ancient rite that neither Lamberton nor Bruce would easily understand—nor need they—but the dark powers stirred by the Comyns would have to be dealt with.

"Your words hardly inspire confidence," Bruce noted grimly.

"Perhaps not confidence," Arnault allowed, "but there are grounds for hope. I fear that dark times lie still ahead for all of us—and perhaps sacrifices as yet unimagined."

Chapter Thirty-one

WITHIN THE NEXT FORTNIGHT, WORD THAT BRUCE HAD ENtered Edward's homage was well overshadowed by the capitulation of the Stirling garrison, finally worn down by weeks of daily bombardment by the English siege engines. Not content with mere victory, England's king refused to allow the garrison to surrender with the military honors they had earned by the courage of their defense. Instead, he threatened them with hanging and disemboweling unless they performed abject abasement before him—a demand only minimally mitigated at the plea of some of Edward's own supporters, whose sympathies had been engaged by the gallantry of the young Scottish commander. Following their capitulation, Sir William Oliphant and his companions were summarily sent off to prison, a gesture meant to demonstrate Edward's implacable intentions toward anyone who continued to oppose him.

By the end of August, after nearly a year's absence, Edward returned to England, convinced that the Scots had finally been brought to heel. All of Scotland now lay within his grasp. The Scottish magnates had all submitted save those still in France, and all royal castles were under English control. Only William Wallace remained at large—for how long, no one could say—and those of the Scots nobility charged with his capture knew only too well what would be the consequences if they failed the English king in his demands.

The autumn came and then the winter, passing as winters do in Scotland, with little activity and much waiting. The new year saw Robert Bruce cast increasingly in an unwelcome role as the English king's principal advisor on Scottish affairs. Between February and May, he was called upon to take part in two parliamentary sessions aimed at establishing an ordinance of government for the land—not the realm—of Scotland, a distinction not lost upon the Scots required to assist with this exercise in assimilation. While Bruce was at Westminster, Edward lavished many marks of favor upon him, granting him the lands formerly belonging to Sir Ingram de Umfraville, while publicly commending him for his good counsel. Clearly, the King of England was taking pains to conciliate the one man capable of asserting a claim to the Scottish crown, unaware that Bruce had already pledged his future endeavors to the cause of Scottish freedom.

By midsummer of 1305, most of the skeins were in place for what now must unfold. Abbot Fingon and Brother Ninian had come in the spring from Iona "to spend time in retreat" with the monks of Scone Abbey. Very shortly, Arnault and Torquil took them for a brief visit to the Stone, and observed while the pair erected mystical protection to obscure its whereabouts from any who might seek it by means other than physical, as its time approached for renewal.

Le Cercle likewise had sent reinforcements in the form of Father Bertrand and Brother Christoph de Clairvaux, ostensibly come to Balantrodoch to conduct an audit of the preceptory's accounts—a matter requiring several months' residence. They had also brought the High Priest's Breastplate and Gaspar's assurances that, if time allowed when the actual need came, he would join them for the required working; for perhaps uniquely among those of the Inner Circle, he had a true inkling what would be the cost to Arnault, who had been his finest pupil, when the time came actually to channel power back into the Stone.

"He says that the Breastplate will enable you to harmonize the three strands of sacred tradition brought together in the Stone—Hebrew, Christian, and Celtic," Father Bertrand told Arnault, "for the Stone bridges all these spiritual paths."

It was late July when Arnault and Torquil arranged for what would be their final meeting with Wallace. All spring and early summer, Wallace had continued to roam the Scottish mountains and glens, harrying the English whenever and wherever he could, but each passing day brought all of them a step closer to the fateful moment of resolution, which had been seven years in the making.

The actual day of their meeting was the Feast of Saint Mary Magdalene, July 22, the seventh anniversary of Falkirk. After guesting overnight with the Bishop of Dunkeld, Arnault and Torquil rode out just at dawn to keep a secret rendezvous with Wallace at a site of the latter's choosing, deep in the woods nearby. Though the clearing appeared to be deserted, a tall figure in weather-beaten clothes emerged at Arnault's low whistle, almost indistinguishable from the surrounding trees. Both Templars dismounted, but Torquil stayed with the horses as Arnault went forward to offer the rebel leader his hand.

"I remember another dawn meeting," Wallace said quietly.

His handclasp and then a quick embrace were as powerful as ever, but to Arnault's searching gaze, as they withdrew deeper into the wood, the former Guardian looked worn and gaunt. His eyes had the hollow, haunted look of a mariner who has been too long at sea and hungers only for some sight of the land long promised. So John the Baptist might have looked, in the final days of his ministry by the River Jordan. Like the Baptist, Wallace had seen the man who was to follow in his footsteps, and knew that he himself would not live to witness the coming of the kingdom.

They sat on a log in another sunlit clearing while Arnault handed over a number of dispatches from Wallace's secret supporters. All were without seal or signature, but Wallace needed no such signs to recognize the writing hand of Robert Bruce among the rest. The rebel leader read the letters closely before putting them away in his belt pouch. Only then did he move on to question Arnault about more personal news.

"You'll be pleased to hear that Luc de Brabant currently has charge of Balantrodoch," Arnault reported with a smile. "The Master is in London on business with the Master of the English Temple—and Robert de Sautre has been sent on a pilgrimage to Rome, so at least for the nonce, *he* is not a worry. The rest at Balantrodoch are all good men."

Wallace permitted himself a flicker of a grin. "A happy disposition, that will serve a multitude of good purposes. Have you seen or spoken with Abbot Henry?"

"I have. I told you that two of our Columban friends had come from Iona to assist us. In addition to their prayers, they have been lending their skills in the abbey scriptorium. I fear that when Edward's soldiers made their second visit, they took away many of the abbey's records and manuscripts instead of a stone."

Wallace smiled, pleased. "I notice that Edward still hasn't publicly admitted he was duped."

"Nor will he ever, I suspect," Arnault said. "Unfortunately, the private knowledge alone has proved galling enough to goad him to a war of many excesses."

"True enough," Wallace agreed, and sighed wearily. "I feel as if this land of mine has been at war for centuries. I cannot honestly remember the last time I slept easy in a bed, or shared a pint of ale in a tavern in the company of friends."

The weariness in his voice was plain to hear. He sighed again and looked away. "We both know my time will soon be running out," he murmured. "I only regret that I haven't been able to give Scotland a miracle worthy of all the widows and martyrs this war has made."

"That miracle is still to come," Arnault reminded him. "You yourself have foreseen it."

Wallace turned his head to confront the Templar squarely. "Yes, I have . . . and may God have mercy on me, when that hour comes nigh."

There was dread in his eyes, which Arnault was chilled to see, for in all his journeys and battles, he had never met a braver man. But he had learned of a way he might lighten at least a portion of Wallace's burden, even though it would heighten his own.

"William," he said quietly, laying a hand on the other's taut shoulder, "there is something you can do for me that will help both of us, when that hour comes." He pulled the *keekstane* from under his tunic and unlooped it from its leather thong, laid it in Wallace's hand. "Do you remember how we blooded this, on another such morning?"

Wallace briefly closed his eyes as his hand closed around the stone.

"Aye," he whispered.

"I told you then that blood can create a bond—and it can."

Before Wallace realized what he was about, Arnault unsheathed his dagger and, without further ceremony, nicked his left palm. Wallace gaped as he saw what Arnault had done, closed fist going to his lips as he stared at the blood welling in Arnault's hand.

"I know not what this means," he whispered. "I cannot let you take my burden."

"And I cannot take it from you," Arnault said. "But I can

share it. Whatever torment the future holds, you will not be left to bear it alone—not while I have life and breath."

Wallace looked away, still fingering the *keekstane*.

"You have taught me just enough to understand what I think you propose to do. It is not that I doubt your ability to do as you say. Acceptance would come easier if I did not count you a friend."

"Then you must think again," Arnault said. "It is only *because* we are friends that I can make this offer. All it requires on your part, beyond what you have already offered, is the bond of your blood with mine."

As he held out the hilt of the dagger, Wallace slowly closed his fist around it, the other hand gently laying the *keekstane* in Arnault's blood. In an instant his own hand was bleeding, and he handed back the dagger.

"This will be a bond between us?" he murmured, as Arnault sheathed the blade.

The Templar held out his hand, with the *keekstane* lying in his blood, never wavering from Wallace's searching gaze.

"I will be with you in spirit, I will know when you are taken, and I will know when you have need of me . . . *on that day*."

"Jesu help us both," Wallace murmured, closing his eyes as he set his bleeding hand atop Arnault's, with the *keekstane* between them, trembling as the Templar's hand closed around his and then drew him closer. A strong arm circled his shoulders and drew his forehead against a white-clad shoulder, and a peacefulness enfolded him as the other wove ties between them that would only be broken in death.

He wept as Arnault held him: for the pain he knew was coming, for this beloved land he was giving his life to secure, for the sunrises and sunsets he would never see, for the anguish this white-clad man must bear with him. And after a while he had no more tears, and raised his head in faint self-consciousness, and flexed fingers stiff with blood, his own and Arnault's mingled. The Templar merely smiled minutely and wrapped the bloody *keekstane* in a piece of clean cloth he had pulled from his scrip, then tucked both back into its recesses.

"If there was ever any doubt that you are the one," he said quietly, "all doubt ended just now. The prize *will* be worth the cost, my friend. Believe that, no matter what else may befall."

Wallace sighed, then slowly nodded. "Thank you. I will carry that thought with me. It will help lighten my journey."

"Where do you propose to go from here?" Arnault asked.

"South and west, toward Glasgow. A friend has offered me the shelter of his house. For the time being, anyway."

After a slight pause, he drew a deep breath and continued. "I don't doubt I've a spy or two in my company, just waiting for the chance to set the hounds on me. There are lords enough in the south, eager to win Edward's favor. If one of them doesn't get me, another will. Someone loyal to me will send word to you, when the time comes."

Heavyhearted, Arnault nodded. "They shall find me at Balantrodoch. There may be many battles ahead, but I promise you that one day, Scotland *shall* have a true king."

Wallace almost smiled. "King Robert Bruce. It has a good ring. What a pity I didn't see it sooner. I've spent too much time in the past seven years fighting for the wrong man."

"You were Scotland's champion, not Balliol's," Arnault reminded him.

"And shall be Bruce's, from this moment onward," Wallace replied. "Though distant, the blood of the Canmores does flow in his veins. He is—has always been—the right-ful heir to the Scottish throne. And heir to the power of the Stone of Destiny. I am ready to do what I must, to ensure that its power is restored."

His expression turned wistful. "I just wish I could be there to see it," he said softly. "I wish faith need not be blind. But if we saw things clearly, I suppose it wouldn't be faith."

July yielded to August, and the waiting intensified. Arnault, waiting at Balantrodoch, dreamed of Wallace's capture the night it happened, two days after Lammas, and on the strength of that dream sent a trusted messenger off to Paris the next morning to fetch Gaspar—Flannan Fraser, himself now a member of *le Cercle*, albeit a very junior one. Brother Christoph and Father Bertrand he sent to Scone, to alert the others. Confirmation of the long dreaded news came three days later, by way of the messenger Wallace had promised.

"Near Dumbarton," an exhausted Glaswegian tanner reported, between gulps of wine in Luc's office at Balantrodoch, as Luc, Arnault, and Torquil listened soberly. "Men in the service of Sir John Menteith burst into a house where he was staying—one of our own must have betrayed him. The king's constable has him now. They will take him to London by easy stages, to show him off along the way."

"Dear God, it begins," Luc whispered, when the man had gone, as Arnault stared numbly at the door that had just closed and Torquil stared at both of them, stunned.

The three Templars left that very day for Scone, to join the others keeping vigil in preparation for even worse to come.

News of the capture reached John Comyn of Badenoch at about the same time the guardians of the Stone were gathering at Scone, and brought a smile to the lips of the man who, since the death of his father, now headed the powerful Comyn family. After a day's indifferent hunting from one of his castles near Elgin, Red John Comyn had been dining amid his retainers with an elder kinsman, Alexander Comyn, brother to the Earl of Buchan and, therefore, a cousin of the Comyn himself. More scholar than soldier, in recent years Alexander had taken over most of the running of the Comyn estates.

"Your work?" he asked, gnawing on a meaty beef bone, when the messenger had bowed himself out of their presence and the buzz of speculation filled the hall around them.

Comyn only drained his cup, smiling as he filled it again. "Let us merely say that I am well served. Tell me, cousin, how stand the accounts in my Galloway estates?"

With a shrug, Alexander tossed his gnawed bone to one of the wolfhounds lying in the rushes at their feet and allowed the subject to be changed.

Later that night, having drunk more heavily than was his usual wont, Comyn retired alone to a private chamber where he often slept when his darker affinities required solitary contemplation. The news regarding Wallace was *most* satisfying. Not only would his capture satisfy the English king's demands on Comyn and the other Scots lords charged with delivering him, but his execution—for that was a foregone conclusion, once he was delivered into Edward's hands— would be fitting punishment for presuming to lord it over his betters.

There had been a time when Comyn had even feared that Wallace might be the mysterious Uncrowned King of whom he and his father had been warned, so many years ago; but after that one brief year of glory, Wallace's influence had declined steadily—and the manner of his impending death should ensure that he suffered *most* satisfyingly for his impudence. As Comyn lay back on the narrow bed and closed his eyes, light-headed from wine, he put Wallace from his mind and thought upon how he might next use the sorceries at his disposal to enhance his position.

The night was close, oppressive, and after a while he stripped off his clothing and lay down again. Focus was not coming easily tonight. In the five years since his father's death, under the tutelage of the shaman priest Torgon, he had come into a measure of the powers previously wielded by his father, but he did not yet have the mastery he craved—and feared to spend too much time at Burghead, for *she* was there, as well as Torgon, and extracted payment for each new power granted.

But something in the very air kept tugging his thoughts back to the Pictish fortress—a heaviness like thunder, a metallic flavor to the warm wind blowing in off the sea. Something of its taste reminded him of his first draft at that dark well, and of another visit, the first time he went there after his father's death . . .

There had been no bull sacrifice that day. Instructed by Torgon—though the pagan priest did not accompany him down those dark stairs—Comyn had dragged another sacrifice into that darkness, toward the flickering torchlight that dimly lit the pool. The dark-haired boy had been too drugged to struggle much, wrists bound tight behind his back, wilting dull-eyed and compliant against the curbing at his feet as Comyn intoned the ancient chants, Torgon's bronze sickle held aloft in invocation.

When the waters began to froth and boil, Comyn had used that sickle. There had been blood—a great deal of it—but little sound save a strangled gurgle, right at the beginning, and then the brief thrashing as he held the dark head under the water until the weakening death throes all but eased. And when he then tipped the twitching body into the water, *she* had come, rearing out of the depths to take the offering.

Even to that moment, with murder on his hands, he had not been sure that the memory he had of that other time, with his father, had been anything but a dream. As a sickly green radiance bubbled upward, engulfing the sacrifice, he had sunk back, weak-kneed and open-mouthed, as the spectral form manifested before him, his body shuddering in mingled revulsion and the stirrings of something akin to carnal lust. The lambent eyes had fixed him with a force that compelled his utter attention and obedience as a voice seemed to fill the shadowed cavern.

"Your every thought is known to me, little mortal . . . and every secret desire. Your flesh hungers for my embrace, but

your soul lusts even more for the promise of my power. Both you shall have, as your father before you, but only as you bend your will to mine."

John Comyn had bowed low, too overwhelmed to speak, trembling before the beguiling potency of all that was offered.

"You shall yield to me utterly, to be my scourge that shall drive out the servants of the murdered god. Do this, and I shall give you the power you crave—even the earthly crown of this land . . ."

The crown—

With heart pounding, the blood singing in his ears, he had dared to lift his face to her again, his hunger for power igniting a reckless courage.

"I *will* have it!" he whispered. "The bargain is agreed!"

"No bargain is agreed without the offering of your blood—not this paltry virgin sacrifice!"

In a burst of green-tinged bubbles, the limp body of the boy had bobbed abruptly to the surface of the pool, to tumble briefly with dead eyes open and wide-staring in a glaze of horror, until her gesture sent it back into the depths.

And Comyn, enflamed, had given her his blood, gashing his hand and plunging it into the pool—and had twisted and cried out as something in the water held him fast and drew him backward over the curbing, free arm flailing, his face only just clear of the water.

"Now we have a bargain!" came that dread voice, both terrifying and irresistibly seductive, as the apparition filled his vision.

And he had yielded utterly before the force of that utterance, no longer caring for any mortal danger as evil invaded and possessed him, a choked moan of mingled anguish and passion gurgling from deep in his throat as he was ravished, body and soul. Pain and pleasure had collided in an explosive climax—and exploded now, plunging him into something between dream and vision, again at the edge of that dark pool, but now in spirit, not mere memory.

And *she* was there, terrible in her fury, serpent hair writhing around her bony shoulders, taloned fingers flexing in menace as she reared out of the pool.

"Why have you been so long from me?" she demanded, her voice like a lash. *"You will come to me in my dwelling place! The Uncrowned King goes to be slain, and a flicker has stirred in that which was safely dead. His death can restore it to life!"*

He cringed before her, only slowly dragging himself from the dregs of passion to sober focus. "The Uncrowned—Wallace?" he blurted. "And *what* can be restored?"

"His willing sacrifice can give life to that accursed hallow that was the altar stone of Briochan's adversary, he who brought the new religion to this land."

Briochan's adversary . . . an altar stone . . .

Suddenly it came to Comyn, through his stunned bewilderment, that she was speaking of Columba, and the Stone of Destiny.

"But—the Stone is in England," he managed to protest. "Its power is no use to England's king."

A shrill howl of frustration rent the air like ripping gauze.

"No! It lies yet within this land of Alba—protected by the servants of the murdered god, who has the power to bring the dead back to life. And life for the Stone means death to all our ancient ways."

"But the Uncrowned King—Wallace—is on his way to London," Comyn faltered. "If the Stone is still in Scotland—"

"The Stone will draw life from the land, once it be quickened by the sacrifice," she said sharply, *"and that is echoed in the Between, where distance has no meaning! The Stone's renewal is the danger, if it drinks of the well of grace which is the Uncrowned King."*

"Then, I shall find the Stone and those who guard it!" he declared, refocusing his courage and intent. "Give me the power to do this, and I shall destroy both!"

"Come to me, then," came her whispered response. *"My priests shall teach you. And I shall give you such power as may wreak my contempt upon the Stone, and destroy it and the white-robed ones who guard it—the servants of the lost temple. By this shall I win you the crown that you seek . . ."*

The thrill of that promise was enough to stir new passion in Comyn's blood, but he gave himself instead to exhausted sleep, not stirring for what remained of the night. When at last he roused, his body was sore in every limb, and his groin ached as if he had been kicked. With a groan he struggled to his elbows, squinting against the sunlight streaming into the room—and gasped as memory came flooding back.

Last night—news of Wallace being taken! And then, in his dreams, a summons from his dread patron, warning that the Stone of Destiny lay not in England, as he had long supposed, but somewhere here in Scotland, waiting to be reempowered by the death of Wallace. But the promise of the crown was his, if he was bold enough to take it!

Heaving himself to his feet, he drew on clothes and staggered down to the hall, where his cousin was already at work on the accounts.

"Fetch horses," he ordered brusquely. "We must ride at once to the shrine of the goddess at Burghead. Our enemies will be gathering, and it is from Burghead that we shall strike at them."

Chapter Thirty-two

AT SCONE ABBEY, UNAWARE THAT THE FORCES OF DARKness had taken interest in the Stone of Destiny, its protectors immersed themselves over the next fortnight in holy preparation for what was to come, fortifying themselves with prayer and meditation, clinging to each new snippet of news that came in from a succession of observers set along the route by which Wallace's captors were taking him toward London.

They were four Knights Templar, a Templar priest, and two Columban brothers. The latter two, having been there since the spring, could move openly amid the community; the Templars took discreet residence in the cottage where some of them had lodged for John Balliol's inauguration, never venturing outside during daylight hours, for the presence of so many Templars would have been remarked.

Designating the smaller of the cottage's two rooms as their chapel, they kept vigil by twos, night and day, sending forth their prayers to strengthen and fortify Wallace and channeling energy into the distant wards that hid the Stone. In addition, the Columban brothers joined them for many hours each day, sharing aspects of Celtic wisdom likely to be of use regarding the Stone; and when the Columbans must return to the abbey, Arnault and Torquil reinforced their teaching, seeking to integrate the Celtic and Templar wisdom.

They did not yet venture near the Stone itself, for they dared not risk drawing unwelcome attention to its location by premature activity in its vicinity. But nightly, assisted by at least one other member of *le Cercle* and one of the Columban brothers, Arnault composed himself with prayer and trance and went out upon the *Via Spiritus*, with the *keek-stane* in his hand, to pay homage to the essence of the Stone, as reflected in the spiritual realms, and then briefly to touch the Uncrowned King. Lest he arouse some human hope of physical reprieve, he did not reveal his presence to Wallace, but always he left a benison of peace and courage, so that he knew his friend slept dreamlessly as time and Edward's men moved him ever closer toward his destiny.

By the night that Flannan returned from Paris with Gaspar, the pair having all but ruined several relays of horses in their haste to reach the Stone in time, Arnault had learned that Wallace and his captors were within two days' journey of London. Once he was in Edward's hands, his trial and execution would not be long in coming.

"It will not be an easy death," Arnault said quietly, to the group of them gathered in the cottage to welcome Gaspar— the Templars only: Arnault and Torquil, Luc and Father Bertrand, and Brothers Christoph, Flannan, and Gaspar himself, for Abbot Henry and the two Columban brothers were keeping vigil in the abbey church. Flannan was posted by the door, lest eavesdroppers come upon them unbeknownst.

Gaspar closed his eyes and sighed, wearily massaging the bridge of his nose, a cup of wine unheeded in his other hand.

"When he returned to Scotland, and determined to stay,

his capture was inevitable. He knew this. Having so chosen, we must ensure that his death is made to serve a greater purpose." He sighed heavily. "I like it not, though, that he must suffer a traitor's death. Have any of you ever *seen* a man hanged and drawn and headed?"

"*I* have," Flannan said bleakly, turning his head slightly toward them.

"That, perhaps, is hardest to bear," Torquil said. "He is no traitor. Wallace never swore allegiance to Edward Longshanks, and no man was truer to his king than he—little though Balliol deserved such loyalty."

"The legality of his allegiance will have little role to play at the English court just now," Luc said. "Coveting your Scottish lands, Edward has spun himself a web of hatred for the Scots—and at its heart is Wallace, to whom he has attached a host of long-nurtured grudges and resentments. Your brave Scot has become too much a symbol of the liberty Edward is determined to eradicate once and for all. By destroying the symbol, the king believes he will also destroy the ideal it represents. In truth, killing Wallace will serve a purpose Edward does not dream."

Torquil glared moodily at the floor. "I accept that his death must be made to serve as sacrifice. But a traitor's death is a hard one. Must it be this way?"

"We like it no more than you do," Arnault said gently, "and I speak from a certain personal interest. But we have been shown the way to restore the power of the Stone, for the benefit of this land and for that Fifth Temple we are commanded to build. It is not for us to question that this is so. Nor are we required to be the instruments whereby the sacrifice is made. It is enough that Wallace himself has willingly accepted his role. And our charge is to ensure that his sacrifice achieves the purpose for which it is intended."

Wordlessly Torquil nodded, dropping his eyes from Arnault's, hitching angrily at his sword belt. Flannan, the only other Scot in the room, had been taking it all in, but now he shook his head.

"Brother Arnault, may I speak freely?" he asked.

"Of course."

"I am still disturbed by this notion of—well, human sacrifice. I am youngest here, in *le Cercle*, but—"

As he broke off, looking distinctly uncomfortable, Arnault signed for Luc to take his place as door warden, and gestured for Flannan to come and sit beside him.

"Flannan, you have only voiced what all of us have felt, at some time. We do not assist or condone the judicial murder that will be done to our friend William Wallace, a few days hence. It is his assent that transforms that murder into an oblation. Consider it a lesser rendition of an old, old play, beginning even before our Lord was offered in the ultimate sacrifice."

"Treacherous ground, my friend," Father Bertrand warned.

"Aye, blasphemy, and worse, in other company," Arnault agreed. "But sometimes there are no clear demarcations between old and new. That is for testaments and even religions. Our human ability to discern the direction of our spiritual evolution is more a continuum, as is the magic we of *le Cercle* learn to wield in service of that evolution."

He could see Gaspar nodding slightly, at the edge of vision, and he continued.

"According to what I have learned from our Columban brethren, whose knowledge spans the shift from older to newer expressions of faith in these Celtic lands, the particular magic touching on the Stone derives from sources beyond human memory. As abhorrent as we may find the notion of human sacrifice, we should recall that, in its purest sense, it was never practiced lightly. Blood has ever been the most potent of links between the human and the Divine—which makes the ritual shedding of blood awe-ful. Why else did our Lord redeem us with His blood, and command that the wine be changed into His blood in the Eucharist?

"Wallace's death will mirror that ultimate sacrifice—as above, so below—and will release energies capable of renewing the potency of the Stone of Destiny. But unless those energies are properly harvested and contained—not in a physical sense, but on a spiritual level—they will dissipate like mist. Fortunately, the Stone is a fitting vessel to receive those energies."

"Thus fitting it to be the cornerstone of the New Jerusalem, the Fifth Temple?" Flannan ventured, looking greatly reassured.

"That is our hope," Arnault said. "That was why I asked Gaspar to send the High Priest's Breastplate. In addition to affording protection during the procedure—especially if there should be sorcerous opposition—we hope the outcome may give us some further confirmation that the Temple's true destiny does, indeed, lie in this troubled land."

Flannan slowly nodded, then glanced at Gaspar, who sighed and set aside his cup.

"That is another urgency upon our work, Arnault, for I fear that France may not harbor us much longer. If this land be not the place ordained for our next work, I begin to sense the cold edges of despair for our very survival. You should be aware of what has been developing in Paris."

"Things have deteriorated further?" Arnault asked.

"I fear they have. A malignant star seems to have risen over Christendom. The situation within the Order grows worse with each passing day. The brotherhood has become rife with factions, each considering itself to be the one true heir to the traditions of our predecessors—and each is prepared to accuse the other of heresy and worse crimes. When your Robert de Sautre was there, en route to Rome, he stirred up considerable disquiet."

Arnault grimaced, thinking of Brian de Jay and John de Sautre: both ambitious, both deluded, both dead. Bertrand

and Christoph, both usually resident at the Paris Temple, nodded their agreement.

"Who would have thought to see us so divided among ourselves?" Christoph observed. "And yet, these divisions merely reflect the chaos that is overtaking the world at large. Malice abounds everywhere; trust is a thing of the past. And nowhere is this malady of spirit more in evidence than within the French court."

"All too true," Gaspar continued, picking up the thread. "Philippe le Bel is devoured with suspicions. His counselors know this—and instead of reassuring him, they are playing to his fears to secure their own advancement. The worst amongst them is the lawyer Guillaume de Nogaret. By means best known to himself, he now has the king's ear, and daily he fills it with poisonous calumnies."

"Nogaret is a toad," Arnault said disgustedly. "It was he, I recall, who championed the king's request to join our Order."

"Toad he may be," Gaspar agreed, "but he is a powerful toad. Philippe is totally in his thrall—and has become even more capricious since the death of his queen."

"The queen is dead?" Luc interjected. "Jeanne de Navarre is dead?"

"Aye, some four months ago."

"But, she was only—what—thirty or so?"

"Thirty-four," Gaspar supplied. "The court physicians attribute her death to natural causes, but Philippe has persuaded himself otherwise. He has accused Bishop Guichard of Troyes, a member of the queen's entourage, of poisoning her—even though there is no evidence to support such a charge."

"But—why would he say such a thing?" Arnault asked.

Gaspar shrugged. "Who can fathom the mind of the man? Rumors persist that agents of the crown had a hand in the deaths of both Boniface and Benedict. I am loath to believe that a consecrated monarch could so forget his divine office as to sanction such crimes, but I cannot help wondering whether his recent delusions might be the result of a guilty conscience turning upon itself."

"Or of a toad's venom," Arnault muttered.

"That is, indeed, a possibility," Father Bertrand allowed. "Nogaret's influence at court is considerable, and Philippe's vision is so distorted that he cannot see anything but what Nogaret and his other ministers show him. Thanks to their lies, the king is becoming persuaded that the Templar Order is rife with heresy and sorcery."

As Arnault and the other Scots-based Templars exchanged glances, Gaspar went on.

"I fear it may be only a matter of time before the king is incited to move against us," he said. "The fleet has been advised—those captains who can be trusted—and they are primed to stand ready to evacuate the Order from France, as from Acre. But we cannot risk putting the treasures on board without some guarantee that a safe haven stands ready to receive them."

"It will be ready," Arnault promised. "The cornerstone of the Temple is ready to be set in place, and Wallace's sacrifice will secure the foundation."

Gaspar nodded heavily, again rubbing at his forehead as he shook his head.

"I only wish I could believe that this will be the only sacrifice required," he said heavily. "But I greatly fear that others will follow—not because God Himself wills it so, but because there are evil powers loose in the world which are always hungry for blood. There are always idolators who are ready to offer holocausts to the evil that resides in their own hearts and minds—for gold, for gain, for power, for riches, for the right to pride themselves on virtue. They delude themselves into thinking they are purifying the world; in fact they are merely blackening their own souls, stoking the fires of hell for their own reception."

"Then we must be certain that our own efforts work to reverse this," Luc said quietly. "Wallace will arrive in London very shortly, and we must be ready. If we miss this opportunity, we will not have another. Wallace will have suffered and died in vain, and the Order will be doomed."

"He's right," Arnault said, shifting his gaze to the rest of them. "We must go tomorrow to where the Stone lies hidden; we dare not cut things too fine. I suggest we travel in two groups, lest we draw too much attention to our presence in the area. I believe our Columban brethren have made the necessary arrangements with Abbot Henry, for supplies and horses," he added, with a glance at Father Bertrand.

The priest nodded. "Everything is in readiness. Abbot Henry would go with us, if he could."

"His prayers will go with us," Arnault said. "We could not ask for more."

That same night, in the fastness of the fortress of Burghead, one who courted far darker forces knelt by a dark pool, again having made the sacrifice to summon his dark patron. This time, the shaman-priest Torgon had accompanied him, and stood behind him with the casket containing the relics of Briochan. As the waters churned and boiled, and *she* approached, John Comyn glanced over his shoulder at the pagan priest; but Torgon was standing motionless with his eyes closed, a pungent wind lifting strands of his long, stringy gray hair, the open casket held forth in offering.

"Art thou prepared to receive my priest Briochan?" came the soft, seductive whisper of her voice amid the shadows.

"I am," Comyn said steadily.

Blood afire with the promise of new power, he rose and turned toward Torgon, boldly reaching into the ivory casket to take out two of the rune-staves, earlier identified as the appropriate ones for the work to come, remembering how his father had seized the staves before Falkirk, and the power he had called. As he lifted his eyes to those of the pagan priest, he felt himself drawn into their power, caught and held, a willing captive for what had been prepared, this ten-day past.

"Briochan, my beloved, be present before your god-dessss," said the voice behind him.

In answer to that command, tendrils of smoke began to rise from the casket, gradually weaving a head crowned with laurel leaves, tonsured like Torgon . . . but it was *not* Torgon. As the face solidified, overlaying Torgon's, Comyn was aware of a shift—that it was that other who now held him steady for what had been agreed. And as that other bade him take that next step, from which there was no turning back, Comyn brought the two distal ends of the rune-staves together, like setting flame to tinder.

Green fire flared in a blinding light, power crackling down Comyn's arms to envelop him in a mantle of otherness that overlaid his own consciousness. In that instant, he felt his perceptions stir, shift; and then Torgon was taking his arm, leading him blindly up the stairs to the surface, to the topmost tower of Burghead, bidding him turn his face toward the south.

"Be his voice, Briochan," Torgon murmured, touching his hand in bidding him to raise the staves. "Seek out and find our enemies. Show him where they lie!"

Aware of that other, with him and in him, Comyn cast his senses outward, along the sight lines of the rune-staves in his hand. Partnered with Briochan, he discovered that sensory impressions were strangely enhanced. Sight, hearing, taste, touch, and smell had all been sharpened to an uncanny degree of acuity.

The touch of his clothes against his skin, the taste of salt sweat on his lips, the sound of men quietly talking in the yard below—all these things came to him with a sharpness he had never experienced before. In mounting excitement, he spread his sensibilities wider, like a net, reaching out beyond the confines of the fortress to the south.

As his field of perception broadened, his nostrils flared wide at the scent of something that both drew and repelled him. Its sweetness was that of church incense, causing the dark aspect within him to snarl and spit in revulsion. But it was also the trace he was seeking: the signature of a hostile sanctity that would lead him to where the Stone of Columba lay hidden.

He closed his eyes and mind to all other sensations in order to focus on that one impression. The scent drew him southward. Like a wolf on the hunt, he followed it over wood and water, mountain and glen. Skirting the hateful beacon that was the cathedral at Dunkeld, he reached the thread of a river and followed until he came abruptly before a cavern mouth that reeked of the fragrance of holiness.

Stomach-turning in its potency, the fragrance told him that he had found what he was seeking, though it lay behind a veil that must be torn. Knowing he had found it, his darkling aspect rejoiced at the prospect of attacking and destroying the altar stone of his patron's saintly adversary.

With the site indelibly imprinted in his mind, Comyn pulled back within himself, feeling that other entity fall away.

"I know where the Stone is hidden," he said to Torgon, "but it is well protected. I sensed no physical protectors, but they will come—and they will be the weak point. When they gather in the presence of the Stone, their thoughts will be on what they hope to accomplish—and that will also be their time of greatest weakness. It is then that we shall strike in earnest. We must make ready."

The next day dawned fair. Immediately after the conventual Mass of the abbey, Torquil set out for the cave where the Stone lay hidden, with Brothers Christoph and Flannan, Father Bertrand, and the two Columbans. Meeting afterward in Abbot Henry's chamber, Arnault and Luc listened as Gaspar told them of his dreams in the early hours of the morning.

"It could be that all our talk of this work last night set my mind to fearing," he said, as he rubbed at his forehead.

Luc shook his head. "No, there's trouble in the air—and I think your headache confirms that you were catching glimpses of it. When our Columban brethren joined us in the spring, they said they'd been sensing something brewing all through the winter. We were aware of it at Balantrodoch, too. We just can't seem to work out where it's coming from."

"Could there be English patrols in the area?" Gaspar asked.

"Possible, but not likely," Arnault said. "Besides, it isn't conventional soldiery I fear. I've told you before about my suspicions regarding the Comyns."

"I thought the old Comyn had died," Gaspar said.

"He did," Luc said, "but his son is cut from the same cloth. Torquil saw both of them there, that night that Jay and de Sautre gave the casket to them—and he told you about what came after him, after they'd spotted him. Thank God for His grace—and for that talisman Torquil was carrying!"

"Do you think this Red Comyn has inherited his father's full powers?" Gaspar asked.

Arnault shrugged. "Inherited or assumed, I couldn't say—but we cannot afford to rule out that possibility. From the evidence thus far, I fear the worst. We've learned that the late Comyn put a great deal of money and work into restoring an old Pictish fortress up on the north coast, deep in the heart of Badenoch country—and when we've tried to probe in that direction, there's a psychic haze, almost a fog, that none of us have been able to penetrate. Given the delicacy of our waiting game, we haven't dared to go up there in person."

"You think it's sorcery obscuring the fort?"

"Probably. But whether or not this Comyn is dabbling in such things, his focus is on political gain. As much as he hates the English, he doesn't want to see anyone but himself become the next king of Scotland—even if it's only as a vassal of Edward. If he has any inkling what we're up to—whether or not he's in league with his father's old allies—he'll certainly try to interfere, to whatever extent he's able."

The second party left Scone late in the afternoon—Arnault, Gaspar, and Luc—armed with Abbot Henry's blessing. Other travelers on the road to Dunkeld were few, and those the party did encounter hurried on about their business, sparing curious glances for three Templars obviously on some portentous errand; but they had decided that they needed the symbolic comfort afforded by the habits of their Order more than the anonymity that would have accompanied disguise.

The settling dusk was heavy and still, warm even for August. When they stopped to rest the horses, shortly before the place they intended to leave the main road, the only thing moving anywhere was a large black bird catching the air currents high above them, wheeling in leisurely spiral patterns that seemed to spell ill omen.

"I don't think I like the look of that bird," Gaspar remarked to Luc, as he adjusted his horses's girth.

"I don't either," Luc replied, "but it's out of bow-shot range, even if we'd thought to bring a bow."

Arnault overheard them, and cast an anxious glance skyward as he mounted again.

"Never mind," he told them. "We'll soon be among the trees of Birnam Wood."

The leafy precincts of the forest seemed welcoming at first. But as the three pressed on, the patches of shadow amid the trees began to take on a sinister quality. For a while, Arnault wondered if it was just a trick of his imagination—until he noticed that Luc and Gaspar were also casting uneasy glances over shoulders.

"Something isn't right here," Gaspar muttered under his

breath. "Whatever it is, it has no liking for anyone who travels under the sign of the Cross."

Darkness was approaching as they threaded their way along the series of streambeds that led toward the Stone's hiding place, Arnault in the lead. They forded the stream at a shallow point and struck out westward along the north bank. The river was running low, leaving margins of sand and rocks on either hand. It looked different from what Arnault remembered, and he was relieved when they came within sight of the ravine leading to the cavern where, for the past seven years, the Stone of Destiny had lain hidden.

The others had already established a picket for the horses at the mouth of the ravine. Leaving the horses for Torquil and the others to deal with, Arnault took Gaspar and Luc up to the cave to visit the Stone.

Christoph was sitting just inside the entrance of the outer chamber, his sword thrust into the ground before him, and rose to sketch a sign in the air before the opening, before stepping back to admit them. Light spilled from the narrow doorway that led to the inner chamber, and Arnault gestured for Gaspar and Luc to precede him.

Inside, the chamber of the Stone had been transformed into a worthy shrine to contain it. Candles were set at the four quarters, with the real Presence of the Sacrament established in the east by a pyx and a votive light burning in a cup of red glass. A faint hint of incense hung on the air—a breath of frankincense mixed with something clean and slightly citric.

The Stone itself lay in the center of the space, now set upon a small rug of the sort Arnault had seen used for prayer in the Holy Land. Fingon and Ninian were kneeling behind it, each with a hand upon it, and looked up as the three newcomers entered, but Gaspar waved them back to what they had been doing.

As the Columban brethren returned to their labors, murmuring between them in the Gaelic tongue, Gaspar studied the Stone from afar, finally turning to Arnault.

"I hadn't thought to ask before, but—assuming this sacrifice has the desired effect, do you know now who Wallace's successor is to be?"

"Aye, Robert Bruce."

Gaspar lifted his eyebrow in surprise. "The same whose grandfather challenged Balliol for the crown?"

"The very same," Arnault replied. "Little did we guess then that their mutual animosity prefigured a battle between the forces of darkness and light. But Bruce is definitely our man."

"And Wallace—you're *sure* he is the Uncrowned King?"

"Alas for him—I am," Arnault replied.

Leaving the two Columban brothers to continue their deliberations, the three emerged from the cavern. Before the entrance, the others had traced a sweeping line in the sand delineating a crescent-shaped area of protection, studded with the swords of all the other knights. Led by Father Bertrand, they were erecting a warding wall of prayer along the boundary so formed. The Columbans joined them after a while, weaving moonlight into the protection as the late sun set and the moon rose, all but full.

As they settled, then, around a small fire to partake of an evening meal of travel rations, Arnault withdrew to a sheltered spot far to the right of the protective crescent, where he could sit with his back against a tree. After sticking his own sword into the ground like a protective talisman, he drew up his hood, under the ensign of the cross of his Order, and took out the *keekstane* from his belt pouch, as he had each night since learning of Wallace's capture.

Holding the opening of the stone before his gaze, he let a series of slow, deep breaths serve to center his thoughts as his spirit slipped across the threshold of awareness into

trance, and breathed a prayer learned amid the kindred of
Saint Columba.

"The Son of the King of Life be my strong shield behind
me, to give me eyes to see all my quest . . ."

A moment's shift in perspective sufficed to anchor his
physical aspect to the ground beneath him. Using the hole in
the stone as a window to another dimension, fixing his focus
on a bright point of moonlight glinting from the cross-hilt of
his sword, he sent his spirit from his physical body and set
off in search of Wallace.

That other's soul-signature, imprinted in blood on the
stone in his hand, drew him toward its source like steel
drawn to a magnet. The intervening distances melted away
as Arnault sped southward across moor and mountain and
meadow in his soul-flight, no longer seeing with merely
mortal eyes. Towns and villages whisked past him, blurs in
the deepening twilight, until finally the silver serpentine of
the Thames led him to the turrets of the Tower of London.

Walls and ramparts of mere stone posed no barrier to one
seeking access in spirit-form. The presence he sought grew
ever stronger as Arnault plunged downward through the
many levels of the citadel until he reached a cramped cell,
deep in the bowels of the Tower complex. Shackled by
heavy chains to an iron staple set in the wall, the rebel Scots
leader lay on a heap of moldy straw in one corner of the
chamber. He was filthy and battered, his face scarcely rec-
ognizable beneath a mask of grime and bruises, but to Arnault, his very presence blazed forth like a beacon shining in
the midst of darkness.

There was an English gaoler attending to Wallace's
chains. The man stooped to make sure the locks were secure
at wrists and ankles, then stood back and gave the prisoner
a spiteful kick in the side.

"*That's* for all the schoolboys you burned alive!" he said
vehemently.

Wallace contained a grimace as he turned his face toward his tormentor. "Is that what's charged against me?"

"Aye, and more than that," came the sneering retort. "You'd best make your peace with the devil tonight, because tomorrow you go to Westminster Hall, to answer for your crimes."

He spat on Wallace and shuffled out, clanging the door fast behind him. Left alone, Wallace settled back on the straw and closed his eyes in resignation—but not before Arnault had glimpsed the grim turmoil in his soul.

Moving closer in spirit, he willed the other to sense his presence as a touch of hand to hand, as he had done at that last meeting, not a month before. At once Wallace's eyes flew open, the initial surge of his doubt and despair like the blast of a hurricane; but Arnault held steady and kept his focus set on pressing through it until that instant when Wallace realized that it was he.

Grateful recognition brought a flood of renewed hope and relief as the bond between them tightened, like a handclasp between friends who know they are soon to be parted. Eschewing words, Arnault projected his promise and assurance that Wallace would not be alone in that final hour—that he and others were prepared to play their parts in renewing the power of the Stone. As he did so, an image came to him of a great Temple spanning heaven and earth, whose cornerstone was the Stone of Destiny.

Therein was enthroned the holy Lamb of God, Whose resplendence filled the Temple with a supernal Light that spilled from its manifold windows in a dazzling tide. Enfolded by that tide, his soul cradled in its healing balm, Wallace surrendered gratefully to the joy of that vision and was content to set aside his fears, at last giving body and mind to the exhausted release of blessed sleep.

Less contented, Arnault withdrew to his own body, drained and wearied from his long spiritual journey, articulating a final prayer for Wallace.

Thou King of the blood of truth, forget not Thy servant in Thy dwelling place, do not omit him from Thy treasure-house . . .

When he shortly roused from trance, he felt light-headed and almost sick. Shivering despite the balmy summer night, he wrapped his mantle more tightly around him before putting away the *keekstane* and going to rejoin his companions, all too aware that food would only replenish his body, could do nothing for the fact that he was sick at heart.

"At least the wait will not be long, for us or for him," he said quietly, as Torquil offered him a chunk of bread and Luc unstoppered a wineskin. "Tomorrow they bring him to trial. The verdict is of little doubt—or the sentence."

Chapter Thirty-three

THEY POSTED WATCHES FOR THE NIGHT: TWO KNIGHTS AL-
ways on guard before the outer entrance of the cave while
the others rolled up in their blankets in the outer chamber, to
take what rest they could. Arnault withdrew to sleep in the
Presence of the Sacrament, before the Stone, laying the
packet of the High Priest's Breastplate upon the Stone to
serve as a further protection and shield. Father Bertrand and
the two Columbans kept a rotating vigil, maintaining a bulwark of prayer around the Stone.

Even within the protection of Sacrament and Stone, Arnault found it difficult to sleep. Food had dispelled the worst
of the chill residual from his scrying exercise, but when at
last he finally dozed off, his slumber was haunted by shadows and whispers. He drifted uneasily in and out of a series
of formless dreams until he was abruptly roused by a shrill
whinny from one of the horses tethered out beyond the cavern.

He came instantly awake, instinctively reaching for his

sword as he sat up. Ninian had been praying, the other two clerics were rousing. Gaspar had been lying down across the doorway from the outer chamber, but was already on his feet, sword in hand. With an emphatic staying gesture toward Arnault and the three clerics, he disappeared into the outer chamber.

Bertrand and Fingon came to kneel on either side of the Stone, their hands upon it; Brother Ninian kept his place before the Sacrament, laying his hands upon the pyx as his head bowed in more fervent invocation. Unsheathing his sword, Arnault came as far as the doorway to the outer chamber and rammed the weapon into the sand. Beyond, Gaspar had taken up a defensive stance in the opening to the outside, flanked by Luc and Flannan. Torquil and Christoph were not to be seen.

"Where are the others?" Gaspar said to Luc.

"Gone to check the horses."

"Could it just be a wild animal of some kind?" Flannan asked.

Luc shook his head. "I don't think so. There's something very wrong about the feel of—"

Before he could complete his sentence, the air beyond them lit up with a sizzling crackle of energy.

On their way down to the horses, Torquil and Christoph pulled up short at the warning tingle of pure evil very near, swords instinctively lifting in warding. For a split instant, Torquil thought he glimpsed the ghostly flicker of a misshapen human form skulking against the trees far ahead. Around them, other flash points flared in the darkness, strung out like fireflies along the ward-line of their personal protection. A stink like burning seaweed briefly wafted past them, acrid enough to halt them, choking, in their tracks.

The horses went wild. The picket line snapped and they scattered like sheep, plunging off into the surrounding trees. A few stampeded past Torquil and Christoph, and a host of shadows broke from the surrounding trees in swooping pursuit. Farther off, a horse screamed.

It was no time for heroics. As one, Torquil and Christoph bolted for the safety of the cave mouth. As they fled, something caught viciously at Christoph's arm, but he twisted away with a cry, opening a shallow gash along the wrist, and pelted after Torquil until they gained the safety of the guardian boundary. There they added their swords to the three already holding the protective line, joining hands then in a human bulwark to reinforce the line just behind its boundary.

Their pursuers were hard behind them—and vaguely visible now, but only in side vision: six or seven of them, vaguely humanoid, but twisted and deformed, with grasping talons that raked the air in mortal threat, and eyes glowing an eerie green at the level of a tall man's head. Hydra hair streamed from their misshapen heads like trailers of decaying moss, and their gnarled, angular bodies were rough and gray as weathered rocks, the gaping mouths lined with a double row of razor-sharp fangs.

In a concerted rush, they flung themselves at the defense barrier, the force of their impact reverberating in showers of silvery sparks, but the barrier held. As a second onslaught again jarred the barrier, Father Bertrand came from within with an armful of unlit torches. He thrust one into the watchfire, crying, *"Per ignem Dominum Nostrum Jesum Christum Filium Deum, te consecro!"*

As the fire flared, he passed the torch to Gaspar, who brandished it before the barrier.

"By the power of the Most High, I abjure you to depart, or perish in these flames which the Almighty has sanctified!"

The wraiths fell back, hissing, and Bertrand continued lighting torches, passing them to the others, who struck them in the ground between the swords to fortify the line.

The wraiths recoiled before them, then broke and fled,

disappearing into the shadows of the wood with piercing yowls of rage and frustration. Behind the barrier, hearts still pounding, the Templar party drew cautious breaths of relief, trying to peer beyond the wall of fire. Blood was dripping from Christoph's injury, and he let Bertrand ease him to a sitting position as Gaspar summoned the Columbans. They came at once, *tsk*ing over the wound.

"What manner of fiends were these?" Christoph gasped, as Abbot Fingon bathed the hurt with holy water, murmuring in Gaelic. The wound smoked as the water made contact, eliciting an indrawn hiss of obvious discomfort; but it melted away under the cleansing stream, and Christoph flexed the arm gratefully.

Torquil watched, waiting until Fingon had signed a cross over the site of the former injury, then gave the other Templar a wan attempt at a smile.

"From blessedly limited prior contact with such things, I would have to guess that this confirms that the Red Comyn has, indeed, learned to use the relics of Briochan, Saint Columba's ancient adversary."

"Do you think he's physically present in the vicinity?" Gaspar asked.

Torquil shook his head. "I have no idea how close he has to be—and I don't think I particularly want to go out there to find out. I think we and the Stone are best served if we make our stand here. The cave itself will offer some protection to the Stone—and this is the only way in."

He swept an arm before their bulwark guarding the cave mouth, and Gaspar nodded.

"If he's fathomed our intention regarding the Stone, I expect he'll attack again."

"I would think it almost certain that he found the Stone because of the very protections we've erected around it," Torquil replied. "And if the Comyns were responsible for eradicating the Canmore kings, they'd not want the Stone to be reempowered, since that was the foundation of Canmore power. That means this is only the beginning."

They set new torches beside the ones still burning between the swords, ready to be relit at the first sign of renewed attack. Arnault came out briefly to inspect the line of their defense, but he knew he must husband his strength for the defense of the Stone itself—and for that more awe-ful work of the morrow, when he must serve as channel to reempower the Stone. Peering out beyond the boundary line, he could catch occasional furtive hints of movement darting through the inky blackness under the trees. Every now and then, something would brush against the edges of their mystical rampart, touching off a brief crackle of hostile sparks.

He retreated to the Stone's sanctuary at the first signs of the second attack, just after midnight. The barrier withstood the assault, but the fabric of its defenses was left weakened by the strain. Restoring the mystical barrier to full strength was costly in terms of vital energy.

"If we can hold until dawn," Gaspar said grimly, "the power of the attacks should diminish. Fortunately, it is an axiom of the Unseen, that the powers of darkness gain strength during the hours of darkness. Happily, the greater Light is constant. But after the dawn, I fear the attacks will change character, to focus on preventing the actual reempowering."

Two more attacks came before the dawn, each repulsed, but all the Stone's defenders were aware of the drain on their vitality. When the dawn finally came, they joined in prayers of thanks for their deliverance while Father Bertrand celebrated Mass upon the Stone and all of them partook of the fortifying grace of Holy Communion. Afterward, Arnault briefly emerged from the cave to join Torquil, who was standing behind his sword and gazing down into the ravine below.

"Any sign of the horses?" he asked.

Torquil pointed grimly. "Aye. Look there."

Just at the edge of the streambed, about twenty yards from the perimeter, Arnault spotted the skeletal remains of a large animal, its bones picked clean.

"I fear that may not be the only one," Torquil continued, "but I can't say I'm eager to go looking for them."

Gaspar overheard him, and came to join them. "Never mind the horses for now. I don't want you or anyone else venturing beyond our defenses. Daybreak has bought us a respite, but we are still under siege."

Flannan had drifted closer during the conversation—least experienced among them in esoteric matters—and jutted his chin toward the area beyond the defensive line. "What will happen if we *can't* hold the defense during the reempowerment?"

"We *must* hold it—not only for the sake of our own souls, but because Scotland's future and the fate of the Temple's Fifth Foundation depend on it," Arnault said bleakly. "And the danger will only increase as the time of Wallace's execution approaches."

Luc took charge of the outer defenses, again arranging watches so that some could rest while two at a time took the active watch behind the sword wall. Gaspar, Arnault, and the two Columban brothers, meanwhile, withdrew to the sanctuary of the inner cavern where the Stone of Destiny lay hidden. Here, they set about preparing the chamber for the work that lay ahead.

Arnault unsheathed the dagger that was blooded with his and Wallace's blood and laid it on the Stone. The *keekstane* already lay in the shallow depression atop the Stone, symbolically occupying Wallace's place as the Uncrowned King. Gaspar was removing the wrappings from the High Priest's Breastplate.

The Columban brothers, meanwhile, had set fat candles alight in the sand at east, south, and west, and were quietly circling the chamber amid murmured prayers in the Gaelic tongue, Abbot Fingon with burning incense in a bowl of glazed clay, Brother Ninian with a like bowl of holy water, sprinkling the walls and floor. Seeing that the pair had their part of the preparations well in hand, Arnault turned to Gaspar, who was unpicking the threads closing a pair of small pockets stitched to the back of the Breastplate.

"I've never used the *Urim* and *Thummin*," he said quietly. "I've never even seen them."

"The Lights and Perfections," Gaspar said with a faint smile. "Hold out your hands."

From out of the pocket on the right he took the *Urim*, a flat, oval piece of flawless quartz, clear as rainwater, of similar size to the gems stitched to the front of the Breastplate. This he laid in Arnault's right hand. The *Thummin*, placed in his left, was of matching size, but of polished onyx. Both were engraved with mystical inscriptions, like the other stones on the Breastplate.

"Do we know the meaning of the symbols?" Arnault asked, feeling their cool substance and the faint tingle of their promise as he closed his hands around them.

"In general," Gaspar replied. "The stones themselves are only the vessels for the mystical attributes, of course—much as the Stone of Destiny is the receptacle for the grace that sustains the sovereignty of this land. Combined with the uniquely Celtic nature of the virtues focused in the *keekstane*, they should enable you to See what is needful, when the time comes."

Arnault nodded, touching both stones to his lips in turn, before carefully setting them on a strip of folded linen that Gaspar laid across the Stone of Destiny. Both of them then rose, Gaspar retreating to the west, where Arnault's sword still stood sentinel in the doorway, Arnault himself moving to the north of the Stone, to face south toward London and Wallace. Abbot Fingon was already waiting in the east, Ninian in the south.

"Shall we begin?" Abbot Fingon quietly asked Arnault.

Drawing breath and exhaling deeply, Arnault nodded.

"Then, let the Keeper of the Gate begin by invoking *Cra-gheal*, under whose protection we prepare to do battle," Fingon said quietly, nodding toward Gaspar.

Lifting his upturned palms to waist level, Gaspar closed his eyes and spoke.

"Great Michael, *Cra-gheal*, the red-white, defender of the gates of heaven, clothe us this day in the armor of sanctity. Michael the victorious, of the bright-brilliant blade, may you stand between us and harm."

"Mary of graces," Fingon said next, "of fairest, purest beauty, call down for us the grace of the Lamb, the Word made Flesh, that He may unite to Himself His servant William, receiving his soul as a worthy oblation, renewing the covenant with this holy realm."

"Blessed Bride, handmaid of virtue," Ninian took up the chant, "entreat for us the grace of the Consoler, the Comforter, bright fount of wisdom, that our hearts may be cleansed and we found worthy to serve the Three."

It fell to Arnault to complete their fourfold invocation. Lifting his heart and voice into the Sacred Presence, he commended them all to the intercessions of Saint Columba, who had brought them all together in their common cause.

"Kindly Columba, ever blessed, patron of this land's enlightenment, assist us as we seek fulfillment of the prophecy, that this land may be baptized anew into the Light. Amen."

Having now made such outward preparations as were possible, he picked up the *keekstane* and came around to sit in the south, with his back against the Stone of Destiny, settling inward in spirit as he closed his hand around that talisman, which was his link with Wallace. A few slow breaths slipped him smoothly into trance, and thought and image blurred as his soul took flight, borne on the wings of vision. When his senses righted themselves, he found himself once again with Wallace, but he held apart from any fuller contact, only observing as he sought to orient himself.

The Uncrowned King had been brought into the broad, vaulted expanse of a great hall, wrists bound behind him like a common criminal, his head now crowned with a circlet of laurel leaves, in mocking acknowledgment of the power he had wielded in the land now claimed by another king. A sea of hostile, leering faces parted before the prisoner as he was chivied up a long central aisle and made to climb a flight of makeshift steps to the top of a wooden scaffold.

On a broad dais opposite the scaffold was enthroned the steely-eyed king who had brought Wallace to this reckoning: the aging Edward of England, flanked by his Lord High Justiciar and the Prince of Wales, his golden crown a pointed contrast to the prisoner's coronal of laurel leaves—still powerful and very dangerous, at last poised to vent his years of anger and frustration on the man who, for so long, had thwarted his Scottish ambitions. The icy eyes scarcely flickered as he nodded for a clerk herald to read out the charges.

Conserving his strength for later, Arnault did not dwell on the details of the judicial proceedings that followed—perfunctory, in any case, the trial little more than an ugly mockery. No witnesses were called; no plea was entered; no defense was allowed. Wallace could only stand silent as a voluminous list of crimes was read out against him, beginning with the murder of Sir William Hazelrigg, the English Sheriff of Lanark, and ending with charges of treason against the king himself.

This last charge was the only one that Wallace even attempted to repudiate.

"Edward of England, you are no king of mine, nor ever were," he declared in ringing tones. "I never swore you fealty, and never did you homage. Kill me if you must, but be sure that of this charge, at least, I am wholly innocent!"

The statement earned the prisoner a heavy blow to the face from one of his gaolers. Pandemonium broke out as the court spectators roared and jeered, but died away as Edward raised a hand and the bailiffs of the court beat their staffs on the floor, demanding silence.

As the hubbub subsided, the king's justiciar rose from his chair to deliver the foregone verdict: that William Wallace of Elerslie, styled knight, was guilty of all charges, including treason, and would answer with his life.

Arnault's senses reeled with Wallace's as the stark finality of that verdict sank in, for the bailiff then pronounced graphic details of that peculiarly English form of execution specifically devised for traitors—that the prisoner should be hanged by the neck and cut down while still living, his manhood struck from him, his bowels drawn from his body and burned before him, his head then to be struck from his body and displayed on Tower Bridge, as a warning to other would-be traitors against the king's grace. In final and emphatic reinforcement of the Scottish lesson, the body of the condemned was to be quartered and the parts sent north for display by the open sewers of cities in the land where Wallace had fought to free his country.

". . . and may God have mercy on your soul," the bailiff concluded, though with little conviction.

The traitor was then remanded to the place of execution at Smithfield Elms, where sentence of the court was to be carried out forthwith, before the setting of the sun.

Sick at heart, Arnault attended in spirit as Wallace was taken from the hall, bound hand and foot to a hurdle, and dragged through the streets of London. The circuitous journey took almost four hours, during which Arnault dipped in and out of trance to ensure that all was well with the Stone. The crowds lining the streets along the way swarmed close on either side, yelling obscenities and pelting the prisoner with garbage—for Wallace was deemed an enemy of England, and deserving of this fate.

The condemned man bore the abuse in stoic silence, his face a mask, eyes fixed on distances above the heads of the crowd, drawing solace from his faith and from a vague awareness that Arnault somehow was with him, as they neared the place of execution.

They had come within a quarter mile of the place when Arnault roused for his final preparations, the *keekstane* still closed in his right hand. He had been leaning with his head against the Stone—using it, in fact, like Jacob's pillow of old; and as he let his eyes open slightly, deliberately willing them not to focus, lest he lose his connection with Wallace, he was aware of Gaspar kneeling to his right, the two Columban brothers to his left.

"They're nearly there," he whispered.

As if from a distance, he was aware of Gaspar reaching above his head to take the *Urim* and *Thummin* from the altar, laying the stones over his eyes as he closed them again. Not lifting his head, he raised his right hand to press the *keekstane* to his brow, feeling the gentle pressure as the two Columban monks bound all three stones in place with fine linen bandages, reminiscent of the tomb bindings of the pharaohs of ancient Egypt. So configured, the stones formed the upward-pointing triangle of the element of fire—fitting focus for channeling celestial fire, when the time came.

With physical sight thus closed away, Arnault sought and found the balance point among the stones' affinities; and as Gaspar fastened the Breastplate around his neck, he felt himself sinking to an even deeper level of rapport, all of the stones now enhancing one another. But even so deep, a part of him yet remained in contact with his surroundings, as he felt hands set under his elbow to urge him upright.

"Sit up now," he heard Gaspar softly say.

He slowly sat, letting them guide him to turn and rise up on his knees, moving around to the north side of the Stone. Again facing the far southern reaches where Wallace lay, he settled back on his heels and laid both hands flat on the Stone—and flinched before the renewed flood of Wallace's perceptions, beneath a burning sun at Smithfield.

Little of visual input now, with his eyes bound blind, but

that was as well, for his connection with Wallace had height-ened all other senses. The shouts of the crowd soon yielded to the roaring of his blood in his ears as the rough bite of a rope began to choke out that other life—and the hangman's noose was only the beginning of a traitor's death.

But neither of them must falter now. It was time now to push the contact through, to be truly *with* Wallace to support him in these final minutes. Pain convulsed at Arnault's throat and chest as instinct bade the other fight to breathe, bound limbs going into spasms, and Arnault drove his will through the blood-haze of near-suffocation to make Wallace aware that he was not alone. Through growing panic and dimming awareness, as Wallace began that wavering slide into unconsciousness, Arnault made the connection—and began to share the other's pain.

Wallace was too near oblivion to respond save by a surge of anguished gratitude, his body too focused on mere survival; but even that acknowledgment strengthened Arnault's own focus, though it also heightened his discomfort. Seconds of chest-searing pain and asphyxiation seemed to stretch into minutes, hours—then ceased with a jolt as Wallace was cut down.

Arnault found himself gasping for breath, even as his head cleared along with Wallace's, but he knew the respite would be brief, and was only prelude to far worse. As he braced himself, all too aware that the butchers soon would begin their work, he did his best to pour strength and courage into the man with whom he suffered, seeking to still the queasy start of visceral dread as, far to the south, the executioners showed Wallace their instruments.

The pain, when it came, was sudden and piercing, and far worse than ever Arnault could have imagined. A hoarse cry burst from his lips as he doubled over the ragged fire sud-denly searing at his groin, and his head hit the edge of the Stone with enough force that a part of him worried he might have damaged the stones bound on his brow—though at least the bandages gave some protection against the blow. Though all instinct bade him clutch at his agony, he somehow managed—just—to keep his hands on the Stone; but gasping for breath, he nearly choked on the anguish of a second cut. The roar of Wallace's pain—and his!—vied with the roar of the crowd at Smithfield, and he greatly feared he could not hold the link.

But then there were hands on his shoulders—Gaspar's, and Fingon's and Ninian's—shoring up his strength. Briefly his breathing grew easier, as they helped him dissipate the sharpest edge of the anguish; but then, without warning, new pain seared at his belly like a stream of molten metal burning out his entrails.

The agony of disembowelment was blinding in its intensity, dragging tortured senses toward physical shock and oblivion. Though Arnault fought against it, his body curled in on itself, his hands slipping toward the edge of the Stone, nails shattering as he clawed at the pain. But as Gaspar's strong hands on his pinned him to his purpose, keeping his hands flat in contact with the Stone as his pain hammered with each agonized heartbeat, Arnault slowly became aware of a Light, very far away, beginning to penetrate the shadow of impending death like the sun breaking radiantly through a storm.

It spilled down on Wallace from unfathomable heights, like the promise of welcome rain beginning to fall toward parched earth, and his failing spirit yearned instinctively toward it, more than ready to abandon the frail shell of flesh that now housed only pain and torture. In that instant, though it still was far away, Arnault felt a sudden stir of awakening power, like the rising of a storm.

It is finished! he sent to Wallace. *The land has been served, the power awakened. Go, good and faithful servant, to claim the place awaiting you in the Light . . .*

So saying, he drew apart from the dying man, catching the merest flash of the welcome axe descending to sever soul from body in a single bloody stroke. Like a floodgate bursting wide, the instant of Wallace's release set free a mighty rush of mystical energies.

The power crested and broke, sweeping northward over mountains and valleys like a tidal wave. Arnault fled before it in spirit as the torrent came thundering after him, for no mere mortal could channel its force, save by the virtue of the Stone itself, mediated through the High Priest's Breastplate.

He felt soul reunite with body in a solid *thunk*, there where he knelt before the Stone, and unerringly his bloodied fingers crawled to the dagger lying atop the Stone, closing around its hilt to lift it heavenward.

"Adonai, Chief of generous Chiefs!" he cried aloud. "Behold, Jacob's pillow: footstool of angels and seat of kings! The Uncrowned King comes to You in willing sacrifice, in faithful imitation of the holy Lamb. Now may the covenant be renewed, whereby this realm of Alba became a dominion of Light. Of Your grace, fill again this Stone, to be once more the consecration seat of Scottish kings, and cornerstone of the Temple of Your New Jerusalem!"

Standing on guard outside, with Luc, Christoph, and Flannan, Torquil became suddenly aware of a profound and spontaneous quickening of his inner senses. The clouds veiling the darkening sky were suddenly rent asunder by a blast of silvery radiance as bright and unbridled as a lightning flash, cascading from the sky in a molten stream. The Stone of Destiny was the lodestone that drew it, and Torquil's heart surged in grateful joy as he realized Wallace's sacrifice was complete.

But even as he wavered between grief and exultation, there came a rumble deep in the bowels of the earth underfoot. A crack split the ground a few yards beyond the boundary line, emitting a sudden effusion of noisome black smoke. Warning cries went up from Luc and Christoph as more cracks appeared beyond their containment barrier, vomiting up twin streams of shadow.

The darkness spread like wildfire up and down the line created by the wards. A blast of wind stirred the trees as a monstrous form began to take shape in the midst of a noxious-looking cloud. Instinctively Torquil sketched the sign of the cross before him as he glimpsed that nightmare spirit that had pursued him the night before Falkirk.

Shadows burst from it, hurling themselves at the bulwark of the magical boundary before the four knights. Torquil felt the impact deep in his soul as buffet after buffet reverberated on the shielding energy. Earth flew as the shadows scrabbled at the earth, endeavoring to burrow under the Templars' zone of protection, seeking to destroy the Stone of Destiny before it could be reempowered.

The attack intensified as darkness reared up to curtain the sky, as the demon-minions pressed all along the barrier. Even within the barrier, the air grew stiflingly cold, dense as water in the lungs. Torquil's ears began to pound, and he could feel his chest laboring under the effort of catching his breath.

The pressure mounted. Torquil felt a sudden, sharp pain in the back of his nose, followed by the copper-taste of blood in his throat and the trickle of blood on his lip. The pounding in his ears became a pulsating ache. Even as he covered his ears with his hands, half turning from the barrier, he saw Father Bertrand moving into the opening from the outer cave, raising his hands in invocation.

"Father of mercies, send down the help of Your angels, lest we perish in the midst of our enemies!" he cried.

The formula filled the attackers with snarling rage, but it also shattered Torquil's paralysis. Gulping breath, he darted to his sword in the defensive bulwark and thumped to his knees before it, laying his hands upon its cross-quillons as he flung back his head to shout out the motto of their Order:

"*Non nobis, Domine!*"

Without hesitation, the others did the same, even Bertrand laying his hands on Gaspar's sword, for Gaspar was engaged in guarding Arnault and the Stone. As each new voice added its strength to the exhortation, blue fire sizzled along each blade and into the ground, fortifying the bulwark, barring the way to the evil trying to pass by.

Within the chapel of the Stone, the walls of the cavern were heaving and contracting like the womb of a beast laboring to give birth. Reaching for the link to the power still swirling high above them—and still with eyes bound by *Urim* and *Thummin* and *keekstane*—Arnault had the impression that something evil was trying to tunnel its way in from outside, something spreading veins of shadow over the floor and walls, squirming toward the Stone like tentacular worms.

The source of that dark power lay far to the north, perched at the very edge of the land. In a flash of visionary insight, he knew its name, could see it in his mind's eye: a place called Burghead, an ancient citadel, a place of dark sacrifice, hulking on a bleak headland that overlooked the sea.

That knowledge gave new power. Knowing the source of the attack, Arnault now set about countering it—and the key lay already upon his breast, focused in the twelve mystical stones ranged across the very Breastplate of God's armor of Light. Drawing Fingon and Ninian to either side of him, he called upon names of divinity that had served when the Breastplate was fashioned by and for the High Priests of Israel, guardians and servitors of the first four Temples, solemnly intoning each name, letting its syllables vibrate in the sanctity of Sacrament and Stone, then drawing together and fusing the strands of Christian and Celtic tradition:

"*Elohim . . . Ee-he-vau-he . . . Adonai . . . Shaddai el Chai . . . Christus Dominus . . . an Ni Math . . .*"

The jewels of the Breastplate lit with unearthly radiance. Even behind the bindings of his eyes, Arnault could See their variegated fire filling the cavern. But through the oracular lenses of *Urim* and *Thummin*, he also became aware of four other puissant Presences manifesting in the midst of the cavern, winged like eagles and armored in light, each with a shining star bound upon its noble brow.

Even in the confines of the cavern, their flowing hair was spangled with stars. The resplendence of their mere presence caused the shadows to recoil. Through a blur of dazzling colors, Arnault saw the newcomers sweep throughout the cave, scouring the walls with holy fire. Then came a final rending shriek from above, and all at once the air was free again, the angels gone.

Stunned, Arnault stared after them, not resisting as Fingon and Ninian stripped the bandages from his eyes and rescued the three stones, laying the *keekstane* in the depression in the center of the Stone and then positioning the *Urim* and *Thummin* to either side, in the same triangular configuration in which they had been bound to Arnault's brow. But Arnault's gaze had turned heavenward, where the ceiling of the cavern seemed to melt away to reveal the shining storm of power now funneling down from above.

Reaching toward it with his right hand, Arnault lowered his left hand to set the point of the dagger into the hole in the *keekstane*, which rested atop the Stone of Destiny, both dagger and stone signed both with his own blood and that of the Uncrowned King. Then, like a woman drawing down thread from a spindle, he willed himself to be a living conduit, bridging the span between heaven and earth, opening himself to channel to the Stone, through blade and window, all the grace so hard won by the Uncrowned King.

The jewels of the Breastplate flared brighter as the power began to spiral downward, they and the *Urim* and *Thummin* and the *keekstane* buffering the force of the flow to levels endurable by mere human flesh, the passage filling Arnault with such joy and peace as made all their sacrifices seem as nothing. Before his wondering gaze, the Stone of Destiny became once more a vessel of aery transparency. The power flowing smoothly through the hole in the *keekstane* was like clear, crystal water, building until the Stone was like a glass box filling up with scintillating radiance.

When the power was brimming, the flow subsided at last to a trickle. By the time the glow died in the jewels on the Breastplate, the Stone of Destiny was full of light, a living thing once again.

Outside, the dark entities broke off their attack with a long, drawn-out shriek of denial, scattering like dry leaves before a gale. The last Torquil saw of them was a wild thrashing among the trees that died away into the distance like the echo of a storm. Breathing hard, he drew himself up, his sword still vibrating in his hands, wondering if he dared sheathe it. Slowly the others stirred, unbending cramped hands from their own blades, as pale and winded as Torquil. Father Bertrand stared wordlessly at his hands, wondering at what he had done. Christoph looked numb, Flannan disbelieving.

"I think it's over," Luc said, first to break the silence.

"Aye, it is," Torquil agreed, "but what about the Stone?"

The answer came from behind them.

"All is well. The Stone of Destiny lives."

All of them turned. Brother Ninian was standing in the mouth of the cavern entrance, Abbot Fingon leaning on his arm. Both monks wore expressions of mingled weariness and gratitude.

"What about Arnault?" Torquil asked anxiously.

"Temporarily overcome by his spiritual exertions," Abbot Fingon replied. "Brother Gaspar is tending him. A few hours' rest should restore him from his ordeal."

They took the precaution of maintaining their defense perimeter, but nightfall brought no sign of threat from any quarter. After a few hours, satisfied that all was well for the moment, Torquil ventured into the inner cavern, anxious for word of Arnault. He found the older knight reclining against the Stone, his Templar mantle pillowing his head and a cup of mulled wine in his fist.

"I confess I'm still feeling a bit shaky," he admitted, in response to Torquil's inquiry, "but a night's sleep will mend the rest of that."

"It must have been—unspeakable—the pain, I mean," Torquil said with a shiver.

Arnault briefly closed his eyes. "It wasn't only the pain that was unspeakable. The unspeakable is not always a bad thing. But as for that—let us simply say that, if ever I have say in the way I am to die, I pray that it may not be by hanging and drawing. On the other hand," he managed a faint smile, "the privilege of channeling the power of the Stone makes even the other seem a mere distraction. I only wish that Wallace could have shared that part of it—though perhaps he did, for the service he has rendered to the land, this day, will surely merit him a seat in Paradise."

Hesitantly Torquil laid his hand on the Stone, closing his eyes as his close-honed perceptions caught a hint of its renewed potency.

"We should move it as soon as possible," he said to Arnault, caressing the Stone as he looked up again.

"I agree. Have we horses, still, to do it?"

Torquil grimaced. "We have at least one less than when we started—and God knows how far any survivors ran. If you don't mind, however, I think I'll wait until morning, to go looking for them."

Arnault nodded his head and smiled again. "My thought, precisely. Tomorrow is plenty of time. Meanwhile, the Stone itself will serve as some protection to us—and in any case, I expect that we've exhausted Comyn's resources, for the time being."

"So one would hope," Gaspar said, joining them. "You're sure Dunkeld Cathedral will be a safe resting place?"

"As safe as any, at least until Bruce is in a position to lay claim to its powers," Arnault replied. "Abbot Henry has already made the arrangements. Bishop Crambeth is a friend and supporter of Bruce, as well as a patriot and a devotee of

Saint Columba. Dunkeld is also reasonably convenient to Scone. That will be important, when the time comes."

"How soon might that be?" Gaspar asked.

Arnault frowned slightly. "That depends on how much time it takes Bruce to prepare the ground. Before being crowned on the Stone, he must first prove his worthiness by claiming back at least some of the castles and fortresses now under Edward's command. For such a campaign to succeed, he must gather allies and forces, and be ready to strike when the opportunity arises."

"And if Comyn attempts to seize the Stone in the meantime?" Torquil asked.

"The Stone exists in both a physical sense and in its essence, which bridges the world of the Seen and Unseen—which is why it is intended as the cornerstone of the Fifth Temple," Arnault said. "Now that it is reempowered, its own virtues will keep it hidden from the kinds of sorcerous searching Comyn might employ—so he would have to try to find it in a physical sense. Scotland is a big place. And I somehow suspect that, in the next months, Edward of England will be demanding a great deal of his vassals in Scotland, as he begins consolidating the kingdom he thinks he has won. That will affect Bruce, as well; but he has us working for him. Comyn will have to shift for himself."

Gaspar glowered, folding his arms across his chest. "It would save a great deal of worry if we could do something about Comyn *now*, while his powers are in disarray."

Arnault shook his head. "Not yet, I think. However heinous Comyn's crimes may be, on a spiritual level, we dare not bring any of that into the open. He is still head of one of the most powerful families in Scotland, whose support any King of Scots will need, and we are still the Temple. We cannot be seen to take sides.

"I now know precisely where the seat of his power lies— the most dangerous part of his power—and eventually, we *will* need to deal with that. But now that we have the means to properly enthrone a true King of Scots, Robert Bruce must become the focus of our efforts. And it is Bruce who must determine how best to deal with the very real political power that Comyn wields."

Chapter Thirty-four

IN THE DAYS THAT FOLLOWED, THE STONE OF DESTINY WAS secretly and safely moved to a new hiding place in a crypt chapel beneath Dunkeld Cathedral. Bishop Matthew Crambeth, a staunch patriot and a contemporary of Abbot Henry, willingly took charge of the Stone on behalf of the kingdom, and allowed Brother Ninian to become a temporary part of his household, to maintain a fitting watch on the treasure he guarded.

While Arnault was busy arranging for the safe disposition of the Stone, Torquil rode south to Annandale to carry word of these events to Robert Bruce. Luc and Flannan returned to Balantrodoch, Abbot Fingon returned to Iona, and Gaspar and the others of *le Cercle* took the Breastplate back to Paris, where threats to the entire Templar Order were achieving ever sharper focus.

By early September, Arnault had rejoined Torquil with Bruce in Annandale. The next six months were marked by feverish if clandestine activity as Bruce and a growing co-

terie of intimates set about laying the groundwork for a new
rebellion against Edward of England. Returned to Bruce's
side, Arnault and Torquil functioned as unofficial aides-de-
camp and military advisors, again working in civilian attire,
carrying confidential dispatches back and forth between
Bruce and key members of the Scottish nobility.

Then in February of the following year, with plans still in
a state of flux, Bruce surprised his Templar allies by declaring an intention to meet face-to-face with the Lord of Badenoch, in an attempt to win John Comyn over to their
common aspiration against England.

"I mean to treat with him in Dumfries," Bruce told Arnault, before sending him and Torquil to make arrangements. "Neither of us, without the other's support, can take
and hold the crown. He and I must find out where we stand.
Go and do what must be done."

He had chosen Dumfries because it lay only a short distance to the east of the adjoining territories of Carrick and
Galloway, held respectively by the Bruces and the Comyns.
As such, the town was a natural meeting place for the heads
of the two rival families.

Even so, Arnault remained uneasy as he prowled the
grounds of the Franciscan church, which occupied a prominent position in the town's southern quarter. It was the tenth
of February 1306. He had serious reservations about the
wisdom of a direct confrontation with Comyn, for he had yet
to convince Bruce of the extent of the danger involved—or
to reveal the full circumstances of that danger.

His doubts were shared by Bruce's principal co-conspira-
tor, Bishop William Lamberton, who was currently in residence at Berwick, presiding over the English council
delegated by Edward to rule Scotland—and doing all he
could to allay King Edward's suspicions. But Bruce had
overruled Lamberton's objections as well as Arnault's.

"I am not unmindful of your warnings," he had told Arnault earlier that day. "Even if Comyn has secretly embraced

the pagan past, he still commands one of the largest followings in Scotland. I dare not attempt to fight him and Longshanks at the same time. If there is even a chance we can persuade him to abandon his apostasy and join us, then we will have won a double victory."

"You have no inkling what you are inviting," Arnault had said darkly. "There are some things from which I cannot protect you."

"You look as nervous as I feel," Torquil observed to Arnault, as they met under a sturdy maple tree, breath pluming in the cold, both of them restlessly scanning the area.

Today, to better blend with their surroundings, they had taken up the brown habits of Franciscan friars, hoods drawn up to obscure their beards and close-cropped hair, though they wore mail and swords beneath their robes.

"I wish he were not doing this," Arnault said.

"You'll get no disagreement from me," Torquil countered. "But politically, he must make the attempt."

"Politically, he must do many things. It isn't the politics that worry me today."

Torquil snorted. "You think it impossible then, that they might find a common ground?"

"I do," Arnault replied. "And if they did, *that* would make me nervous—because I do not think I could stand to have Bruce work with him, under any circumstances."

He glanced over to where Bruce was conferring with a cluster of trusted companions, speaking earnestly with Sir Christopher Seton, perhaps his closest friend. An Englishman by birth, son of a Yorkshire knight, Seton was married to Bruce's sister Christian, and fiercely loyal to his brother-in-law—as were his brothers, John and Humphrey, also in Bruce's immediate entourage. Bruce's own two brothers, Thomas and Neil, had carried the invitation to Comyn's castle at nearby Dalswinton, whence he now awaited their return, with or without Comyn. He had proposed to Comyn that they each bring along no more than a half a dozen of their closest adherents. In Bruce's case, these were all members of his immediate or extended family save a knight called Roger de Kirkpatrick and the Templars, the latter of whom he did not mean to count in his quota of guards and escorts.

The February day was bright and chilly. The still-bare trees cast spidery shadows across the short, frosty turf, and snow still lay mounded off the footpaths that ran beside the church and among its monastic buildings. Torquil turned at the sound of footsteps on gravel and bobbed his head politely in greeting to one of the friars who was passing by on his way into the town. Most of the brothers were keeping discreetly out of the way, aware only that high-ranking visitors were to use their premises for a confidential meeting. Their abbot alone knew the identity of those visitors.

A clatter of hooves on the cobbles outside the church gate drew the Templars' attention: Thomas Bruce, just pulling up to dismount. Flushed with excitement, the young knight ran to join his older brother, his report tumbling from his lips in an excited undertone. Robert Bruce responded with a nod and clapped Thomas approvingly on the shoulder.

Parting company with his kinsmen, he approached the two Templars and beckoned them aside, by the entrance to the cloister walk. He had left his sword on his saddle, and was armed with only a long Highland dirk set with a cairngorm in the pommel—which at least was better for fighting in close quarters, if he had to defend himself from Comyn treachery.

"Thomas tells me that the Comyn will be arriving with Neil very shortly," he informed them. "Comyn's uncle Robert will be with him, along with four of his cousins, in keeping with the terms of my invitation. You'd best take up your positions."

"I still advise against this," Arnault said. "Comyn's adherence to the old religion includes the practice of sorcery. Should he attempt to invoke the powers at his command, even the sanctity of this consecrated ground may afford you scant protection."

"I have only your word for it that these tales of witchcraft and evil spirits are true," Bruce said, with a hint of impatience.

"And I can only give you my word that I have told you nothing but the truth," Arnault said. "Do not wish for proof. *That* is something you do not wish to deal with."

"Be that as it may," Bruce replied, "the Comyns and their friends are too significant a force in Scotland for me to call myself king without first enlisting their support—if that is possible. If it is not, best to have it out now, and know where we stand."

"Then at very least, be on your guard," Torquil urged. "The hopes of Scotland rest upon you."

"Would you have me avoid confronting the Comyns out of fear?" Bruce countered, with a faint, wry smile. "Or would you prefer that I move against them without even giving them the chance to join me? No, in spite of our past differences, John Comyn may yet care enough about this land to see the empty destructiveness of prolonging our rivalry."

"Then, God grant that your tenacity may one day stand you in good stead," Arnault said.

"And hope," Torquil added, "that Comyn won't risk doing anything that might attract Edward's attention. We could hardly be much closer to the English border."

"The king's justices are in session right here at Dumfries Castle," Bruce pointed out ironically. "I find that having the enemy in close proximity concentrates a man's mind most sharply on his duty."

"Whatever happens, both our prayers and our swords are with you," Arnault assured him.

"I value your support," Bruce said, "but I hope neither aspect of your vocation will be required this day."

He rejoined his kinsmen and began chivying them toward the porch of the abbey church, casting a wary eye beyond the church gate in the direction his brother had come. With eyes narrowed, Torquil watched him go.

"However ill-advised this meeting may be," he said to Arnault, "I become more and more convinced that Wishart and Lamberton were correct to enlist our support for this man. Now that he has grasped the nettle, he is clearly determined to see things through to the end."

"Whatever that end may be," Arnault replied. "But we'd best take up our positions."

Retreating into the cloister yard, the two Templars hid themselves in vantage points chosen earlier, from which they could observe what went on both in forecourt and church. Arnault took up a post very near the sacristy door, which gave access to the nave. Even though they were out of earshot, the demeanor of Bruce's companions suggested that they, too, were harboring misgivings; but Bruce's own confidence seemed to allay their fears. As he exchanged bantering remarks with them on the steps of the abbey church, his followers' bearing brightened appreciably.

It was not long thereafter that Neil Bruce appeared at the gate, heading up a party of horsemen. At Neil's side rode Red John Comyn of Badenoch, easily distinguished from his companions by the somber richness of his clothing and the Comyn bardings on his fine horse. Accompanying him were an older man with graying russet hair—the predicted uncle—and four others who, from their looks, were surely cousins of some degree. All but Comyn himself wore fighting harness, swords at their sides, but Comyn, like Bruce, was armed with only a dirk.

Directed by their Bruce escort, the Comyns dismounted and strode across the forecourt with studied disdain, keeping shoulder to shoulder like the ranks of a schiltron. In contrast to his supporters, who never ceased scanning for possible ambush, Comyn carried himself with the confidence of a man entering his own great hall. He had never lacked for arrogance, but now that pride of bearing had about it a cold imperiousness.

His manner displayed no hint of conciliation as he and Bruce exchanged formal greetings. His men hung back glowering, their hands hovering close to the hilts of their swords. If Bruce's temper was aroused by his counterpart's demeanor, however, he gave no outward sign of it as he invited Comyn to enter the church with him.

"This is neutral ground, which should be acceptable to us both," he observed. "Its very sanctity ought to serve as a guarantee of peaceful behavior and Christian restraint."

"We have come here in peace, and in the interests of our nation," Comyn stated loudly enough for everyone to hear. "I hope that you can say the same, Robert Bruce."

Bruce forbore from responding to the implied insult and led the way into the church's dim interior. Arnault had slipped in through the sacristy door, and ghosted to a hiding place inside the great pulpit, peering through a chink between two boards to watch as the two Scottish leaders came down the nave, speaking as they walked. Torquil remained outside, to keep an eye on their restless followers.

The two were not yet close enough for Arnault to hear what they were saying, but he was relieved to see that Scotland's king-in-waiting was taking his advice to bring Comyn to the protection of the sanctuary for their meeting. They stopped beneath the Rood screen, where Bruce paused to cross himself as he glanced toward the altar and its Presence lamp. Comyn only clenched his jaws, silently regarding his rival with open insolence.

Arnault strained to hear, for the two were that bit too far away to make out everything they said, but Comyn's monosyllabic responses soon elicited greater volume on Bruce's part. In bits and snatches Bruce's words became audible, and Arnault could hear the appeal in the other man's tone.

"It has been our downfall, Comyn," Bruce was saying. "Too often in the past, we Scots have turned upon each other, leaving ourselves easy prey to those who see us as a subject for conquest. We must unite now, if the flame of our freedom is not to fade away entirely—while we can yet remember what it was to be a free nation."

Comyn's lip curled. "You speak of freedom, but it is a freedom under King Robert," he sneered. "You would make yourself king while John Balliol not only lives, but has an heir to follow him."

Arnault saw Bruce's jaw tighten, and knew he was checking his temper only with an effort.

"You are no fool, Comyn. You know as well as I that Balliol is no king. He lies in France, under the pope's house arrest, and has sworn he shall never return to Scotland. Support me in this labor, and you shall have all of my lands of Annandale and Carrick to add to your own. You will be the foremost lord of the kingdom."

"I am that already," Comyn retorted. "It was I who made the peace with Edward, which saved the kingdom. It was I who persuaded him to restore all lands and properties to those who had fought against him. It was I who insisted that we Scots retain our own laws and customs and freedoms. There are many who know they owe all of those things to my prudence, and they will repay the debt they owe me."

"What good is prudence, if the kingdom be lost?" Bruce said. "King Edward is aging and unwell, and his days are numbered. We have weathered him like a violent tempest, but when the storm clears, we must be prepared."

"I am amply prepared, both for Edward and for you," Comyn retorted. "I have resources at my disposal that would make you tremble."

"Do you?" Anger darkened Bruce's brow. "If you speak of the unholy rites and practices revived by your father, I know of these things, and they do not frighten me. It is you who should be fearful that your blasphemies be exposed."

Comyn's jaw tightened, and a momentary flicker of surprise showed in his eyes, but he quickly recovered his composure.

"I make no apology for cleaving to the ways of my ancestors," he replied. "They made our people strong in the past, and can bring them unlimited victories in the years ahead."

"If that is what you truly believe, you are merely deluding yourself," Bruce said. "If you are trafficking in such matters, you have put your very soul at risk, but it is not too late to disavow them. God can forgive all things. For the sake of your own salvation, forswear the dark deeds I have heard spoken of, and consign these practices to the darkness whence they came. Then we can put this behind us and still be allies."

"*Allies?*" Comyn echoed derisively, his voice rising in pitch. "There can be only one king in this realm, and why should it be you? I have as good a claim as you—better, for I have the power to defend it, which you lack. Who, more than I, has the right to sit upon the Stone of Destiny?

"Oh yes, I know the Stone is still in Scotland," he continued, offering a feral smile in response to Bruce's startled expression. "Restored, moreover, to the full extent of its mystical powers. Once it upheld the Canmore kings, but my patron saw it drained of power. Now it is powerful again, but the Canmores are no more. It is for a new royal line to take up the crown—and Scotland's sovereignty—and to remake the land. My father opened the path before me, and I will follow it to its end. I intend that the Comyns shall be the new royal line, not Bruce!"

As Arnault watched and listened, his deeper instincts had begun to sense a subtle change in the atmosphere of the church. All at once, Comyn raised his left hand and clenched it into a fist.

Bruce gave a gasp and staggered, knees threatening to buckle under him. Eyes wide with outraged astonishment, he struggled to keep himself upright, but his movements were ponderous, as if his limbs were weighed down with leaden chains—to Comyn's gloating satisfaction. His right hand had arrested in mid-reach toward his dirk, the fingers flexing, straining to gain it, but with no success.

"This is only a taste of my true resources," Comyn murmured, his voice mocking. "Did you think that the trappings of your infant religion could save you?"

Comyn's voice had changed, and Arnault sensed that it was no longer the Lord of Badenoch who was speaking. Instead, he had become merely the mouthpiece of whatever malevolent entity to which he had submitted himself, host to a monstrous spirit that was now making its presence manifest.

So close to the source of the ensorcellment, Bruce could not seem to summon sufficient strength of will to break free of that magically induced torpor. By fractions of inches, he managed to curl his fingers around the hilt of his dirk, but he could not seem to free it from its sheath. Comyn, by contrast, calmly drew his own weapon and lifted its point toward Bruce in lazy menace, his left fist still clenching at the power that held Bruce helpless.

"Your spirit is strong," said the sibilant voice that issued from Comyn's lips, "but it will avail you nothing!"

Bruce tried to speak, but managed only a strangled croak. The fingers of his free hand dragged at his throat, as if trying to tear away an invisible noose.

Flinging caution to the winds, Arnault rose up from his hiding place in the pulpit and thrust the first two fingers of his right hand toward Comyn like a blade, invoking the protection of the archangel Michael to repel the powers of darkness.

"Michael of the battles, shield your servant!"

His voice made Comyn whirl to confront him, vague recognition flaring in his haunted eyes, and the face contorted in a grimace of hatred as eldritch power spat and sparked on the blade he turned toward Arnault.

In that brief instant of distraction, the spell that held Bruce wavered, and he wrenched his dirk free of its sheath to plunge it to the hilt in Comyn's breast. An unholy shriek burst from Comyn's throat, surely shrill enough to etch glass, but Bruce grabbed at a handful of tunic and held the weapon hard in place with all his strength. Comyn's spine arched at an acute, unnatural angle, blood bubbling from his gaping mouth. Then, all at once, his legs gave way and he collapsed to the floor, leaving the dagger behind in Bruce's fist.

Blood was rapidly soaking the front of Comyn's tunic. His limbs twitched spasmodically, but other than that, he was not moving. Staggering back a pace, Bruce kicked Comyn's dirk out of reach and pressed his free hand to his brow, shuddering, evidently unharmed but still partially dazed by the sorcerous assault to which he had been subjected, apparently unaware how Arnault's intervention had given him the edge necessary to save himself.

"God, what have I done?" Arnault heard him whisper.

Staring at his own bloody weapon, just beginning to comprehend the sacrilege he had just committed—to slay Comyn before God's altar—Bruce turned and staggered back up the nave. As he burst from the church door, the bloody dirk still in his fist, out of the shocked babble of confusion rose a harsh cry of *"Murderer!"*

The accusation came from Comyn's uncle Robert. Silhouetted in the doorway, he charged at Bruce with sword in hand and murderous intent. Still fighting to shake off the lingering effects of ensorcellment, Bruce parried clumsily and twisted enough for Robert Comyn's blade to glance off the links of his mail shirt. With a strangled cry, Christopher Seton darted in to Bruce's defense, cutting down Comyn's uncle with a lethal sword stroke to the head.

"What has happened?" one of Bruce's brothers cried, as Comyn and Bruce supporters surged closer.

"I think me that I have killed the Red Comyn," Bruce rasped, dazedly displaying his bloody weapon.

"You *think*?" said Roger de Kirkpatrick. "Then, I make sure!" he cried, breaking for the altar steps where John Comyn lay sprawled.

The import of their exchange evoked a roar of outrage from the rest of the Comyns, who tried to stampede after Kirkpatrick. But Arnault was faster, darting between them to wrench Kirkpatrick around by an arm and wordlessly bellow as he swept his sword before the Comyns and they stumbled back from the arc of the blade.

"Hold!" he cried, in the voice he had used to command many a green recruit in the Holy Land. "Can you not see that devilish spirits have been at work here? Will you add to their mischief by slaying each other in this holy place?" he demanded, thrusting Kirkpatrick from him, in the direction of Bruce.

The Comyns shrank back uncertainly, torn between the desire for revenge and the need to carry news of Bruce's deed back to their stronghold at Dalswinton, their initial bravado diminished less by Arnault's words than by the realization that they were clearly outnumbered. At a muttered word from the senior of the survivors, the Comyn party began edging cautiously toward the door. Torquil interposed to prevent the Bruces from following them.

From a nearby window, Neil Bruce and one of Seton's brothers watched the Comyns gather up the body of Comyn's uncle and retreat toward the gate, where their horses were waiting. As they began to mount up, the rest of Bruce's supporters clustered around him. Bruce was pale, but gave his friends a reassuring nod, with a special word of gratitude for Christopher Seton, whose swift response had saved him from Robert Comyn's vengeance.

Arnault dared to relax just a little, cautiously sheathing his sword, but the affair was not yet over. The din had alerted the abbot, who came jogging breathlessly into the church by a side door, attended by two of his friars. At the bloody scene before the altar, all three clerics stopped short, faces aghast as they crossed themselves.

"You swore there would be no violence committed in this holy place!" the abbot said accusingly to Bruce.

"That was never my intention," Bruce managed to whisper. "Comyn—had other plans."

"There have been dark forces at work here, Father Abbot," Arnault said in Bruce's support, declining to specify what particular dark forces had been involved. "Comyn was the first to draw steel. Bruce had no choice but to slay or be slain."

"That may be, but the vilest sacrilege has been committed!" the abbot retorted, as his friars knelt beside Comyn's body to whisper prayers for the departed soul. The one crouching closest to the head looked up in surprise.

"This man yet lives!"

Startled, the abbot bent close to feel the pulse at Comyn's throat as Arnault moved warily closer.

"So he does," the abbot confirmed, "but not for long, I warrant. Carry him into the sacristy. We can at least give him what solace the sacraments may afford him, in what little time remains to him."

"Father Abbot," Arnault said sharply. "There are dangers here you do not understand."

"I understand my duty as a servant of Christ," the abbot replied, giving Arnault a hard look as his two friars lifted Comyn's body by the arms and legs. "I cannot undo the sin committed here, but at least I can ensure that it is followed by one act of charity."

Arnault looked doubtfully at the stain of Comyn's blood on the altar steps, smearing across the floor as the friars half dragged him toward the sacristy doorway. Realizing there was no way he could prevent the abbot from doing what he felt was right, he glanced back up the nave, where Bruce had withdrawn to remonstrate with Roger de Kirkpatrick in the open doorway. Beyond them, he could see Torquil at guard behind the Bruce, and out in the yard, Comyn's men mounting up under the bristling guard of Bruce's remaining kinsmen.

He started up the nave to join them. He reached them as Kirkpatrick was turning to rejoin the others in the yard—seeing off the Comyns, who had the body of the slain Robert Comyn draped across the front of one of their saddles. Bruce favored Arnault with a nervous nod as he came back inside and glanced toward the altar, and the smear of blood on the altar steps.

"You were right to warn me not to treat with Comyn," he said to the Templar. "In place of unity, I have found bloodshed, and I fear there must be more of it before this business is finished."

"I fear you have the right of it," Arnault agreed, "not merely because the Comyns will not let this go unchallenged. Now do you believe what I told you of the other?"

"I cannot deal with that now," Bruce said hastily.

"There will be some successor to take up those powers—"

"Later!" Bruce said, beckoning to Thomas and Neil, who came running. "Now that my hand has been forced, I must secure my position as best I can.

"Gather our men," he instructed his brothers, as he walked with them back toward the doorway, "and see that they secure the castle and the great hall of Dumfries. Then send word to our supporters that the time has come to rise up and drive the English from our cities and castles. Let the fiery cross be carried all across Scotland, to signal that our time of servitude is at an end. I could have wished for more time to prepare, but after what has taken place here, I have no choice but to move against Edward now, and let the dice all fall where they may."

"And the Comyn territories in Galloway?" Thomas said.

"Those must be taken as quickly as possible, before they have time to ready a defense," Bruce replied.

As Neil and Thomas mounted up and hurried off to carry out their instructions, Bruce next addressed Humphrey Seton.

"Send word by secret messenger to Bishop Lamberton at Berwick, informing him of what has taken place. Tell him to stay in Edward's confidence for as long as he can, but to be prepared to join me, when I summon him. I will go to Bishop Wishart in Glasgow, and beg for absolution. Please God, we may all meet soon thereafter for my coronation at Scone."

Bruce was recovering quickly, taking matters in hand, already organizing his uprising, already with the bearing of a true king.

"What you have told me of the Stone of Destiny had best be true," Bruce said to his Templar ally. "I will need every source of aid I can muster in these coming weeks."

"We will see that you are crowned upon the Stone as soon as it can be arranged," Arnault responded. "Thereafter, no one can challenge your kingship."

"I can guarantee you that some will," Bruce replied, "and Longshanks will be at their head."

Before he could comment further, a terrified shriek came from inside the church. As he and Arnault ducked back inside, the sacristy door flew open and the abbot and one of his friars came bursting out, eyes wide and terrified, faces deathly pale and distorted with dread. Arnault bolted toward them, but was nearly bowled over as the panic-stricken men shouldered past him—and fetched up short as a blast of arctic air gusted after them.

"Torquil, to me!" Arnault shouted urgently.

Torquil was already racing down the nave, sword in hand; but as he reached Arnault's side, a pulsing blackness filled the sacristy doorway, dissolving then to reveal John Comyn clinging to the door frame, apparently heedless of the blood drenching his robe. The Lord of Badenoch looked to have aged a century in the mere minutes since his presumed death. Though he was hardly older than Torquil or Bruce, his hair had gone completely gray. The sunken eyes were red-rimmed, lit with a brooding gleam of lambent green, and the skin of his face seemed to have no flesh behind it, as if the entity possessing him was sucking away the last vestiges of his vitality, to give itself a few more precious minutes of animation.

The abbot shrank back behind Arnault. His friar had continued running up the nave.

"I was placing the chrism on his brow, when suddenly he rose up in ghastly life!" the abbot babbled. "Black flames sprang from his body and engulfed the room with choking, stinging vapor. I fear that Brother Mark is dead. We had no choice but to flee for—"

He broke off with a cry as the ensorcelled figure lumbered forward, making for the front of the altar. Bruce and his remaining men had surged into the church behind the two Templars, but pulled up short at the sight. The abbot scuttled to supposed safety behind a statue of the Virgin, in an alcove near the door, where the other friar was already cowering in terror. In passing, Arnault noted that the faces and hands of both men were dappled with scorch marks.

Shouting for Bruce to stay back, Christopher Seton boldly advanced toward Comyn, sword in hand. His two brothers rushed forward to support him, but all three of them stopped dead as an ear-splitting howl burst from the corpse's lips, shredding the air with its harshness and intensity.

An icy blast of wind roared up the nave, tumbling the Setons backward. Bruce and the Templars were also buffeted off balance, and had to struggle to stay on their feet as Comyn bestrode the stain of his blood and lifted both arms above his head in a gesture of summoning.

A grating voice burst from his throat in harsh command, and a nimbus of black flame burst forth around his desiccated frame. As if in answer, to fill the void of that blackness, a whining wind invaded the church, bringing with it a maelstrom of invisible energies. Precious candlesticks toppled from the altar with a clang of metal against stone, and a weighty Gospel book was hurled aloft in a flurry of loosened pages, as if to show disdain for such items of piety.

Arnault could have no doubt that Comyn—or his patron—was the source of the tempest; and only extraordinary measures would suffice to stop him. Bracing himself against the storm, squinting against the biting gale, Arnault handed off his sword to Torquil and closed his fist around the hilt of the dagger he had used to empower the Stone, forged in the land of Christ's birth from a blade broken in holy crusade, made trebly sacred by the blood of Wallace. Shifting to grasp it by the blade, he cocked back his arm and summoned all his remaining strength in a muttered prayer for divine aid—then threw the weapon with all his might.

Time seemed to slow as the dagger tumbled point and pommel and point and pommel, releasing a rainbow-burst of radiance as it embedded itself point-first in Comyn's heart. Comyn's body staggered back with a ululating wail, and lambent eyes gaped incredulously at the cruciform hilt protruding from the shattered chest. With a final strident howl, the possessing entity fled the body of its host, leaving the corpse itself to crumple before the altar, like a deflated airbladder. The storm departed with it, leaving behind an incongruous silence that was broken only by the harsh breathing of those who had barely survived this fresh horror.

Arnault was the first to approach Comyn's body, bending cautiously to set his hand on his dagger, confirming that this time Red John Comyn of Badenoch was truly dead. As he pulled the dagger free, he turned to glance back up the nave, where Torquil was holding Bruce and his men from approaching any closer.

"We should pray for Comyn's soul," he announced, as he straightened up from cleaning the dagger on a corner of

Comyn's cloak, "that he will find whatever rest there may be for one such as he."

Diffidently the abbot advanced to his side, Bruce and the other friar approaching more warily. The abbot clutched his crucifix tightly in his still-trembling hands as he chanted a brief prayer in a hushed tone. Bruce gazed down at his old rival with an expression still betokening disbelief, and slowly shook his head.

"For all that I disliked the man," he muttered to Arnault, "I still can scarcely credit that he came to this."

"The powers of corruption take their toll of victims," Arnault said. "These have held sway for many centuries."

Bruce's eyes flashed with righteous determination. "They shall do so no longer in a land that has *me* for its king," he vowed.

Arnault faced him squarely. "Then allow me to act as your agent. The evil you have witnessed today is rooted at a place called Burghead, far to the north. If you will grant me the authority to act in your name, I know what must be done."

"I grant it willingly, and my prayers go with you," Bruce replied. "I will not rest easy until I know that such an abomination no longer darkens our land."

Arnault gave him a curt nod, then turned to Torquil.

"Go with him," he said. "I will deal with the other. For a time, at least, with Comyn dead, those at Burghead will be without a leader. There can be no better time to strike."

Chapter Thirty-five

ARNAULT RODE TOWARD BURGHEAD FIRST VIA THE TEMplar commandery at Balantrodoch, where he apprised Luc and Flannan of what had happened and, with their assistance, selected a detail of thirty knights and serjeants who had not been tainted by the past regime of Brian de Jay or the de Sautre brothers. Included among their number was the current Master of Scotland, Walter de Clifton, who hardly raised an eyebrow when Arnault requested the use of men for a holy war in the north. Luc had primed the Master very well.

"I know little of these matters, but I have complete trust in Brother Luc," Clifton had said. "I am eager to learn, and have no love for what you have described. Choose what men you wish, only allow me to join you."

Luc accompanied them as far as Scone, where Abbot Henry had already received warning of the deed done at Dumfries and had dispatched a trusted messenger on to Iona, to notify Abbot Fingon of an imminent coronation.

After a good night's sleep, a last hot meal, and a fortifying Mass, Arnault and Flannan rode on with the Scottish Master and their band on the long ride toward Burghead, leaving Luc to help oversee preparations at Scone.

They passed first through Dunkeld, the knights in their white mantles, serjeants in brown, the black and white battle banner of *Beaucéant* before them. Scotland lay still in the grip of winter, and the elements themselves seemed set to turn them back as they pressed north and west along Strath Tay and Glen Garry. The icy northern gales met them head-on, pelting them with rain and hail and dampening spirits as they soaked through raiment.

Each night, when the horses had been cared for and they took their sparse meal of travel fare and sought to thaw and dry around their meager campfires, Arnault would give his men careful preparation for what they might face when they reached their destination. Later, bolstered by their communal prayers, they confessed one another of their petty failings, as had always been the way of the Temple, for only coming to battle clean and grace-full might they hope to weather the worst that might come.

But these were not men of the stripe who had been led astray by Brian de Jay. Warfare and the disciplines of monastic life, under the solid rule of Luc and their new Master, had tempered their souls like well-forged swords, giving them the will to endure hardships that would have defeated men of lesser strength. And Arnault fired their hearts with a sense of purpose that sustained them in defiance of the elements, and would not suffer them to be turned aside from their God-appointed task.

Elsewhere in Scotland, especially across the south, as the fiery cross of battle was being carried from town to town, summoning loyal Scots to rally under Robert the Bruce, another Templar was playing his own part in the battle to defend their cause: accompanying the Bruce to seek absolution from Bishop Wishart of Glasgow, for the sacrilegious murder committed at Dumfries.

"My Lord Bishop, I have killed the Red Comyn—slain him before God's holy altar!" the Bruce confessed, falling to his knees before Robert Wishart. "I never meant to do it—I truly had called him there only to seek a resolution of our differences, for the good of all Scotland. But he drew on me! He—seemed to call dark forces to unman me, to render me helpless before him. But then his focus was distracted—and I slew him."

"But that was not the fatal blow, my lord," Torquil interjected. "Comyn yet lived when we came into the church. The abbot had him taken to the sacristy to give him last rites, but he somehow revived, and again tried to attack the Bruce. Another finished him, to save the Bruce's life."

"Another?" Wishart said, shrewdly cocking his head.

"None of either Bruce or Comyn loyalties, I promise you," Torquil replied, his tone making it clear that the bishop should not inquire further on specifics.

"Then, it appears that Robert has not, in fact, committed sacrilegious murder," Wishart replied. "Certain it is, however, that the Comyns will not see it thus."

"Indeed, they will not, my lord," Bruce murmured, hardly able to believe this turn of fortune.

"Very well. For that you did, indeed, cause grievous bodily harm to a sworn enemy, and in God's church," Wishart went on, "I give you the penance to spend this night in prayerful contemplation of the consequences of your action, prostrate before the Blessed Sacrament. Make a good act of contrition for your sins, and a firm resolution to sin no more." He lifted his hand to sketch the sign of blessing over Robert's hastily bowed head.

"May our Lord Jesus Christ absolve you, and with His authority I absolve you, from all the sins of your past life, the Father, the Son, and the Holy Spirit. Amen.

"Now," he said, rising to his feet with a dusting motion of his hands, as if to put this all behind them. "We have much work to do. I have longed for this day. I have in my keeping certain royal vestments and regalia, secretly kept against this glad time when a King of Scots might again reign over us. These must be taken to Scone. Brother Torquil, in particular I thank you for the services rendered this realm by the Temple, and will ask your further assistance in preparing missives to summon certain others whose support will be required, to properly crown our king. Do your orders permit it?"

"They do, my lord," Torquil replied. "My brief is to remain with the Bruce until he is crowned, and to do all within my power to help that come about. I was a Scot before I was a Templar, but happily the two loyalties are joined in this, our present enterprise."

"And I was a Scot before I was a bishop," Wishart replied with a grim smile. "I think we understand one another. Come into my study, my sons, where we will make preliminary lists of what must be done. Then, while Robert makes his penance this night, you and I, Brother Torquil, will set about producing the letters of summons that can be entrusted to no others. Scotland's freedom is dawning at last!"

In the north, however, little evidence could yet be seen of any dawning. Though many of the southern castles and towns were already yielding to Bruce and his followers, news was slower to penetrate the bleak Highlands, where winter still held sway. Arnault and his Templar troop used every hour of daylight to hasten their journey, not halting until the horses could no longer see their footing. Clattering past small villages as night descended, the eerie gray of twilight lent them a spectral appearance that sent frightened country folk scurrying indoors.

Stories quickly spread of a phantom host flying by night across the land, who might carry off any man foolish enough to stumble into their path. Some said it was Saint Andrew leading a company of warrior saints to spread the call to arms throughout Scotland. Others suggested they were led by the ghost of William Wallace, seeking out his betrayers to wreak God's vengeance upon them for their treachery. Had they known the truth, they would have been no less fearful, for this was indeed a company waging a holy war—though not against any mortal foe—bent on a mission fitted only to those who rode with Saint Michael himself for their captain.

The Templars rode up the valley of the River Spey into Moray and the Comyn heartland of Badenoch, where word of John Comyn's death had gone before them. The loss of the Comyn chief appeared to have left the people of this region confused and demoralized, and certainly no one ventured to challenge a column of Knights Templar riding in full battle array. On Arnault's instructions, they avoided the towns and castles, keeping to the sparse country tracks that led them through the rugged hills toward their destination, some of them so narrow that the riders must go single file. Making a wide detour around Elgin, they came at last in sight of the fort of Burghead, rising up against the stark background of the cold North Sea and a cold winter sky.

Arnault called a halt, and the whole company drew rein to survey the outermost rampart, which lay now a few hundred yards off. They could see no signs of activity, but Arnault had no doubt that they were being watched by hidden sentries. He gave the order to ready arms.

His men adjusted their helmets and loosened swords in scabbards, some of them unlimbering crossbows. Shields that had been slung from saddlebows were shouldered for defense, and lances were lifted, their pennants fluttering in the icy wind. At Arnault's right hand, a serjeant rode closer with *Beaucéant* streaming above him, famed throughout Christendom as an emblem of holy war. As Flannan moved in at his left, Walter de Clifton leading the column to deploy in battle order, Arnault's heart stirred at the prospect of going into action, his brothers arrayed on either side of him, ready to give their lives for their faith and for each other.

The company started forward at a trot, keeping to their line in an imposing show of discipline. Heads bobbed up behind the Burghead battlements, and cries of alarm rang out, echoing thinly through the wintry air.

The Templars continued to advance without drawing any missile fire from above. Arnault signaled the company to halt within bowshot range of the gates; then he and Flannan rode forward to inspect the fortifications at closer range. They kept their shields at the ready, but none inside ventured to fire upon them.

"Very old," Flannan said. "In its day, this would have been a formidable defense. But you can see where the ramparts have been patched and repaired. It should be no great challenge to scale the wall head."

"With luck, it won't come to that," Arnault said.

They had the wherewithal to assault the fort with ropes and grappling hooks. Nevertheless, Arnault hoped to resolve the business without bloodshed. The handful of faces that could be seen peering down at them over the walls were more nervous than defiant. He was willing to wager that most of them had never before faced so heavily armored a company; and they were right to be dubious about their chances of defending a stronghold as timeworn and dilapidated as this one.

A new figure appeared above—one with evident authority, from the manner in which the others deferred to him. Arnault kneed his horse a few steps forward, taking the risk that this might draw fire.

"I am Frère Arnault de Saint Clair, Knight of the Temple," he announced. "Who commands here?"

"I am Alexander Comyn, brother to the Earl of Buchan and kinsman to the Lord of Badenoch," the other man replied. "Since learning of the Red Comyn's death, I have assumed responsibility for this fort, and hold it in the name of his son, who is not of age."

"Have you also assumed responsibility for the barbarous practices that have taken place here?" Arnault demanded. "If so, you must set your soul at a cheap price."

This observation provoked grumblings of uneasiness from the men around the Comyn commander, and earned Arnault a smoldering glare.

"It is those who basely murdered my kinsman on holy ground who have courted damnation!" came the angry reply.

"I will be plain with you, Alexander Comyn," Arnault said. "It was ancient sorcery and unholy practices embraced by his father that were the Red Comyn's undoing. If you know this place, and are aware of the evil that dwells here, you must surely see the truth in what I say."

He could see that his words had struck home. At the same time, however, Alexander Comyn was clearly determined to retain his dignity in front of his men. It would require delicate handling to persuade this Comyn to do what he must know to be right, without unwittingly provoking him into resistance.

"Yield us this unholy place, I pray you," Arnault urged. "It is not worth the price of your immortal souls."

"This is some trickery!" Alexander replied. "Are you the vanguard of Bruce's army, come to wipe us out? Has he not the courage to ride at your head?" he challenged.

"I swear by Christ's blood that we come here to do no man any harm," Arnault assured him. "We have come only to cleanse this site of the taint that has lain upon it for too long, and to free all who dwell hereabout from its deadly curse."

"And what then?" Alexander Comyn pressed him. "Will you require our submission?"

"When we have carried out God's work here, we shall leave and not return," Arnault promised. "We have come to fight the servants of darkness, not you or your people. You have my solemn word on that."

The two men regarded each other with hard calculation while their respective followers looked on in hushed expectancy. Obliquely Alexander Comyn surveyed the dozen men who stood in the ramparts beside him, more waiting in the yard below—but were they enough? His Highlanders were a proud breed, and looked ready to do whatever their leader asked of them, even if it should mean a fight to the death—but the battle-hardened knights before him, with their deadly lances and crossbows and great warhorses, bearded faces resolute beneath their steel helms, were not foes any man would willingly challenge.

"I must trust what you have said," Alexander Comyn said at last. "Enough have died for my kinsmen's false dream—and it becomes more and more of a nightmare, the longer we suffer it to continue." He turned to his men and ordered, "Open the gate!"

There was a moment's hesitation before the Comyn soldiers overcame their instinctive reluctance to give way before a potential enemy. A glowering look from their leader, however, prompted them to carry out his order without further delay. The great bolts were hauled back and the gates slowly drew apart, leaving the way clear for the Templars to enter.

The knights formed themselves into a well-ordered column and Arnault led them forward into the compound. All of them kept a wary eye for any sign of attack, but no hostility was offered. Descending from the rampart, Alexander Comyn curtly issued orders for his men to fetch their horses and equipment in preparation for immediate departure. Now that the decision had been made, Arnault noted, the men of Badenoch appeared only too willing to comply.

At Arnault's command, six of his knights remained on horseback to oversee the Comyn withdrawal, ranging themselves in strategic positions where they could observe the whole interior of the fort, especially the Comyn men now gathering up their belongings. Eight more knights climbed up onto the rampart with crossbows. Leaving Walter de Clifton to supervise the withdrawal of the Comyns, Arnault and the rest dismounted to press on through a second gateway leading to the mound of the citadel.

Dominating the courtyard beyond was a pair of weathered monoliths, rearing up twice as high as a man. The one on the left depicted a huge bull, its head lowered for the charge, its powerful muscles sharply delineated by lines etched deep in the rock. On the other was the crude yet potent image of a woman rising out of the sea, a human skull hanging between her pendulous breasts. Each of these figures was surrounded by a swarm of abstract patterns: circles, spirals, and lightning bolts, brightly painted.

"Pagan gods?" Flannan murmured under his breath to Arnault.

Arnault only nodded, but many of their fellow Templars grimaced at the sight, muttering prayers and warding themselves with the sign of the cross. Others, more military in their thinking, cast calculating looks toward the citadel, which surmounted an earth mound at the far end of the promontory. Arnault found his gaze drawn toward a dark slot in the ground to one side of the path leading up the keep. To his inner senses, the opening seemed to exude an invisible miasma of dank decay, but before he could make a move to investigate, he was hailed by Walter de Clifton, who gestured back toward Alexander Comyn.

Comyn's men had finished hastily gathering up their belongings. Lingering out in the outer courtyard, they looked more than ready to abandon this ancient, haunted fortress. But the late Comyn's kinsman wore a determined expression as he approached the Templar commander.

"I have revised my thinking, Templar," he told Arnault in a low voice. "You may smash every accursed stone in this place, and do so with my blessing. But this is still a Comyn holding. If you are still here on the morrow, then we will meet again with swords drawn."

"If we are still here when the sun rises, then we shall already be dead," Arnault said baldly. "In that event, you and your people had best flee as far from here as possible."

Alexander went a little pale, clearly sensing that this was no dramatic exaggeration, but a sincere warning. As he hesitated, a sudden movement on the path above them drew all eyes as a cracked voice split the air like the sudden caw of a gore-crow.

"Begone from here, unbelievers, if you value your wretched and unworthy lives!"

The speaker was a gaunt, white-robed figure with a sweeping gray beard, powerful hands grasping a gnarled black staff. Crowned with a circlet of spiny gorse, he was tonsured ear to ear in the Celtic manner, the back hair hanging in two greasy plaits on his shoulders. On his brow was traced in blue the smudged shape of a bull's head. A golden torc loosely circled his thin neck, and wide bracelets of hammered iron were clasped to his sinewy forearms. Beside him stood a much younger man, similarly but less elaborately attired, his wide sleeves obscuring some bulky object he clasped to his breast, over which his head was reverently bowed.

Curtly beckoning his acolyte to attend him, the old man descended the slope in a series of goatlike bounds to halt fearlessly a few yards before Arnault and Flannan, his black eyes blazing as he thrust out his staff to bar the way forward.

"Come no closer, Templars!" he warned. "And you, fool! What have you done?" he demanded of Alexander Comyn. "Would you allow these intruders to defile this shrine of your ancestors? Slay them, as is your duty!"

"My duty is not to you, Torgon!" Alexander retorted. "I owe you naught but my contempt. You can be damned, for all I care—and so can any who stand in your defense!"

He turned his back in pointed disdain. Outraged, the

shaman drew back his staff as if to strike, but Arnault lifted his sword in warning to come no closer. With angry vehemence, Torgon rammed the heel of his staff into the ground at his feet and barked a curt command at his assistant, who hurried forward to present him with the ivory casket he had been hiding under his robes.

Alarmed, Arnault thrust Alexander behind him and prepared to ward them both, for he sensed with a sudden and unshakable certainty that the chest contained the relics of Briochan, which Torquil had told him of seeing handed to the Comyns by Brian de Jay, eight years before. Torgon spat contemptuously, and darted back between the two standing stones.

Brandishing the casket aloft, he offered it to the cloudy heavens above, as a torrent of invocation poured from his lips. Thunder rumbled in apparent response, but Arnault dared not let himself be moved.

"Your cause is lost," he told the old man. "Your patrons are dead, and those you serve will soon be swept away forever. It is not too late for you to turn away from this madness and ask God's forgiveness for your sins."

"What care I for your murdered god?" Torgon snarled. "It is your childish faith which shall fade away and be forgotten, in ages yet to come. My patron is Briochan—he who serves those who live as long as the earth itself. Come, Briochan!"

In answer came a boiling up of baleful energies from the ground between the monoliths, quickly enveloping Torgon like a suit of new clothes, overlaying his visage with a spectral image Arnault had seen before, in the vaulted treasury at Balantrodoch—Briochan, indeed, summoned in defense of the deities he had championed in ages past! At the same time, as Torgon's voice rose on an eldritch screech, a bitter wind swept in from the sea, bringing with it the stench of rotting seaweed. A deep boom reverberated from the subterranean stairway, shaking the citadel to its foundations.

Undaunted, Arnault reached into the neck of his surcoat and pulled out the *keekstane* he had brought from Iona, again worn on its leather thong. With his other hand he raised his sword. Sighting down its length at Torgon-Briochan, he closed the sacred stone in his raised fist and made bold to petition Saint Columba, invoking his authority to drive back once again those forces he had beaten into submission centuries before.

"Kindly Columba, beneficent, benign: In name of the Three of Life, in name of the Sacred Three, in name of the Secret Ones, and of all the Powers together—shield me from thine ancient enemy. O Michael of the white steed, lend me the sword of thy protection!"

At the same time, he opened his left hand to display the *keekstane* in his palm, directing its window toward Torgon.

A flash of white light burst forth from the heart of the scrying stone, leaping across to Arnault's other hand and coursing down the length of his blade on the path he directed. With a searing *crack*, the bright beam struck the casket of pagan relics, dashing it from Torgon's clutching hands.

The manifestation of Briochan vanished like a snuffed candle flame. Torgon's eyes flared with redoubled rage, and he pointed an indignant finger at Arnault.

"Now you have earned my wrath!" he howled. "I shall send you such pain as you have never imagined!"

Fists clenched, he crossed both scrawny forearms before his breast in a clang of iron armlets; but before he could formulate any further intent, he was caught in the throat by a crossbow bolt. The force of its impact knocked him sprawling at the feet of the two great monoliths, a final paroxysm racking his frame as blood gushed from his lips and he at last was still.

Turning, Arnault saw Alexander Comyn handing the crossbow back to Walter de Clifton, who began calmly winding the weapon to take another bolt. With cold deliberation, Comyn drew his dirk before striding over to examine the shaman's prostrate form. From where he stood, however, Arnault could see there was no need to strike again.

Confirming this, Comyn turned to the shocked acolyte, who cringed at his glance.

"Take yourself away from here," he said coldly. "Return to whatever village or farm it was that spawned you, and find yourself such obscure occupation that you never come to my attention again."

With quaking hands, the young man hastily stripped off his pagan accoutrements and dropped them in a heap by his master's body. With a last fearful look at Comyn and then at Arnault, he scuttled off past Clifton toward the open gateway, like a frightened field mouse fleeing to its nest. Alexander Comyn snorted in derision.

"It appears that I have inherited both the responsibility and the curse of Burghead," he explained, his face a tight mask of self-control. "If there is to be blood on anyone's hands, it should be on mine. I do not wish to see a fresh cause of feud, when there are too many scores already to be settled."

Arnault inclined his head in acknowledgment of the other man's wisdom. "I hope that when we next meet, it will be under friendlier circumstances."

"I would not depend upon it," Comyn replied. "Friendship is in short supply in these troubled times."

Turning on his heel, he strode off in the direction of the gateway, where his men were waiting with the horses. Seizing the reins of his own steed, he mounted up and rode off, sparing no backward glance. His men fell into line behind him, and soon were disappearing into the distance. With the departure of the Comyn soldiers, the Templars stood down from battle alert, looking to Arnault for further instructions.

"Search the place," Arnault told them, "and gather up anything that seems unclean to you. Burn what will burn, and sprinkle the rest with holy water. We must cleanse this place of its evil."

He himself directed the destruction of the monoliths. Looping ropes around the great stones, mounted knights heaved them over so that they crashed to the ground like fallen giants. Both shattered; and hammers and picks were then used to smash them into pieces.

Meanwhile, Torgon's staff was broken and cast onto a bonfire, along with various items of shamanic regalia and the body of Torgon himself. To this cleansing blaze was added the chest of relics. As the flames consumed them, Arnault cast a measure of salt on the flames and pronounced a formal edict of interdict, banishing the spirit of Briochan to whatever afterlife awaited him. He prayed silently that with Briochan's departure, there would be no further revival of his cult.

Once these tasks were completed, he turned to that dark stairway leading down into the earth, where final rites must also be performed. He took with him Flannan Fraser.

"Just keep reciting whatever prayers you think appropriate," he told the other knight, as he handed him a torch. All around the mouth of the stairwell, a dozen knights were already kneeling in a circle, swords thrust into the ground before them like crosses, hands on the cross-hilts. One of them was Walter de Clifton, the Master of Scotland.

"We are prepared to support you as you have taught us," the Master said. "But what should we do, if you should not come out?"

"If that should come to pass," Arnault said, "fill in this opening with earth and stone, consecrate our grave with your prayers, and return to Scone, to inform Brother Luc. Then be guided by his instructions."

Clifton inclined his head. "Go with God, my brothers."

"We shall," Arnault said with a smile. And turning his gaze to the rest kneeling around him and Flannan, he said, *"Non nobis, Fratres."*

"Non nobis, Domine," they responded, in reiteration of the Templar motto that had sustained the Order through nearly two centuries of service to the Light. *"Non nobis, sed Nomini Tuo da gloriam!"* Not to us, Lord, not to us but to Thy Name give the glory.

Again grasping the scrying stone in his free hand, Arnault held his sword at arm's length before him like a crucifix as he led the way down the steps into the gloom that waited below, Flannan behind him, accompanied by the whispered aves and paternosters of those remaining above ground.

"God before me, God behind me, God above me, God below me . . . I on the path of God, God upon my track," Arnault murmured, stringing together phrases from the prayers that Brother Ninian and Abbot Fingon had taught him, using them to focus his intent.

"The compassing of God and His right hand be upon my form and upon my frame . . . the compassing of the High King and the grace of the Trinity. May the compassing of the Three shield me in my need . . . from hate, from harm, from act, from ill . . . Christ Himself is shepherd over me, enfolding me on every side. He will not forsake me, hand or foot, nor let evil come anigh me . . ."

A moldering stench rose to met them as they descended, an unsettling mix of salt water, rotting vegetation, and damp earth. Flannan's torch behind Arnault cast his shadow long on the steps before them.

"The air seems thick, like pushing through water," Flannan noted, though he did not sound afraid.

"Fear itself is trying to stifle us," Arnault said. "If we do not let it master us, then it can do us no harm. Say your prayers and trust in God."

At the bottom of the steps they paused before a threshold, beyond which they could hear a low, rasping breath, like steel grating against sandstone. A noisome exhalation gusted past them, extinguishing the torch and plunging them into pitch blackness.

"Valiant Michael of the white steed, I make my circuit under thy shield!" Arnault said into the darkness. "For love of God and for pains of Mary's Son, spread thy wings over us and shield us, thou Warrior of the King of all and Ranger of the Heavens." Drawing breath, he went on more boldly.

"The mantle of Christ be placed upon me, to shade me from my crown to my sole. The mantle of the God of life be keeping me, to be my champion and my leader."

A roseate radiance blossomed from the cross-hilt of his sword, brightening to a flame as pure and colorless as adamant. In the same instant, Flannan's torch flared into life once more. The reeking gloom retreated precipitously before these twin beacons of the Light. Shoulder to shoulder, the Templars edged their way across the threshold, into the cavernous chamber beyond.

The torchlight revealed a broad expanse of shining blackness rimmed by stone, a sullen pool so densely black that neither the torchlight nor the radiance surrounding Arnault's sword could penetrate its depths. Tendrils of greenish vapor rose off the surface in sickly coils. Peering more closely, Arnault could discern sluggish stirrings of movement within the womb of the dark.

Taking a firmer grip on the sacred scrying stone, looping its thong from around his neck, Arnault began reciting fragments of prayers he had rehearsed with Luc before setting out on this crucial mission, again calling on the wisdom of Saint Columba.

"The strength of the Triune be our shield of cleansing . . . be the Cross of Christ to shield us upward . . . be the Cross of Christ to shield us downward . . . be the Cross of Christ to shield us roundward . . ."

At the pronouncement of the first few lines, the vapors rising from the pool recoiled. A shiver passed across the surface, penetrating deep into the inky blackness below. As Arnault continued his words of exorcism, the waters began to churn into a scummy froth, exuding venomous green bubbles as something monstrous took shape in the depths, driving rapidly toward the surface.

Arnault braced himself, tightening his grip on sword and *keekstane* as a huge, distorted female form erupted from the roiling water like a leviathan, casting a foul spume over the two knights as she reared above them. Both men recoiled from a blast of fetid breath, Flannan lifting his torch in a warding-off gesture, but Arnault never faltered as he brought his chant to a close with a ringing *Amen.*

The apparition snarled but kept her distance. Dwarfing them in size, she glowered down at the two Templars, lips drawn back in a feral leer that exposed rows of yellow, rotted teeth. Her face was wizened and wrinkled like that of a crone, but her breasts were huge and full beneath the shroud of foul, lank hair trailing down to the water like tendrils of rotting vine.

"So, little soldiers, have you come to feed my blood hunger?" she demanded in a heavy rasping voice. *"Give yourselves to my embrace, and I will suck you dry and feast upon the marrow of your bones!"*

Arnault only held his sword steady, murmuring under his breath, "Columba, be thou a bright flame before me." Behind him, he could sense Flannan's taut dread, but the other man did not retreat. The entity before them slavered and snarled, but Arnault sensed indecision. Stronger than her age-old hunger was a note of growing fear.

"You have no power over us," he stated firmly. "Your worshippers are either dead or scattered like withered leaves, and your name is fading from the face of the earth."

The creature greeted this pronouncement with a cackle of angry laughter.

"Spineless worms!" she shrieked. *"Maggots! I will rip your flesh to tatters and bite into your hearts like ripe, succulent fruit!"*

"You shall do no such thing, for Columba's task is accomplished at last," Arnault responded, his voice unwavering. "In name of the King of life, in name of the Christ of love, in name of the Spirit Holy, the Triune of my strength, be banished!" he cried.

At his declaration, a crystalline beam of white fire blazed forth again from the window pierced in the *keekstane*. Brighter than either the torch or the glow emanating from Arnault's sword, it filled the room with a supernal light that banished every shadow. It burned away the stench of decay, leaving behind a fragrance like incense smoke. The demoness shrank back with a shrill wail, recoiling into the dark sanctuary of her birthing pool.

"Go now into that abyss whence you came!" Arnault ordered. "By Michael chief of hosts, by Uriel of the golden locks, by Gabriel seer of the Virgin of grace, and by Raphael prince of power—may God's angels and the sword of Saint Michael sever you from this world!"

With a swift casting gesture, he flung the *keekstane* into the pool. White flames spread instantly across the surface, rushing up the creature's trailing hair to engulf her in a blazing nimbus of purifying fire. Her scream shook the walls of the underground chamber before she sank beneath the burning water, as if dragged down by a powerful undercurrent.

The room itself convulsed. The flames shot higher, licking the roof overhead. Spurred into movement, Arnault seized Flannan by the arm.

"Go! Get out of here quickly!" he urged.

They bounded up the stairs, taking two at a stride, as the blistering heat of the inferno roared up the stairwell after them. As they burst into daylight, throwing themselves to either side, their fellow Templars grabbed them and pulled them well clear of the circle of swords still ringing the stairwell opening.

Fire and smoke erupted upward, but could not seem to pass beyond the outline of an invisible dome above, delineated on the ground by the circle of swords. As a final catastrophic boom rocked the headland, the earth convulsed, the stairwell collapsing in on itself. The final echoes dwindled into stillness as the smoke slowly dissipated.

The Templars flocked around Arnault and Flannan. Clapping the other knight on the shoulder, for he had done well under fire, Arnault cut short an anxious flood of inquiries with a reassuring wave.

"We're all right," he gasped. "The danger is past. Let us give thanks to God. Brother Walter, summon the brethren."

He drew a deep breath and cast a grateful look around him as they came, the newcomers adding their swords to the others as all of them knelt outside that holy circle, hands clasped on the cross-hilts symbolizing their faith, and bowed their heads to recite a solemn Te Deum. The sun was sinking behind the hills to the west. Here and there, a bonfire still spat and crackled as the last of the pagan paraphernalia was reduced to ash. Night was descending upon Burghead, but it would be a night free of the evil that had haunted this country for so long. When they had finished their prayer, Arnault sheathed his sword and signaled his men to fetch their horses.

"Let us be gone from here before darkness falls," he ordered. "Whatever struggles may yet be to come, this battle at least is won. *Non nobis, Domine!*"

"*Non nobis, Domine, sed Nomini Tuo da gloriam!*" the rest responded, in fervent affirmation.

Chapter Thirty-six

FOLLOWING THE CLEANSING OF BURGHEAD, ARNAULT TOOK his men back to Balantrodoch, where he would acquaint Luc with far more detail of the success of their mission than could have been gleaned from any of the others, even Flannan. But first Luc had news of a different but no lesser import, which he imparted to all the men in a hastily convened chapter meeting.

"The rebellion is now well and truly afoot," he informed them. "I have had word several times from Brother Torquil, who rides with Bruce as a military advisor. In addition to taking Dumfries and Dalswinton, Bruce has made himself master of the castles at Tibbers, Ayr, and Dunaverty. His supporter, Robert Boyd of Cunningham, has taken Rothesay Castle, and has laid siege to Inverkip. The only castellan in the west who has refused to yield is Sir John Menteith of Dumbarton. Otherwise, Bruce now has effective control of the Firth of Clyde."

"Is there still an English fleet anchored at Skinburness?" Walter de Clifton asked.

"There is," Luc replied. "But with control of the firth—even without Dumbarton—Bruce can still count on allies and supplies being able to reach him from Ireland and the Outer Isles."

"That's as may be," one of the senior knights rumbled, "but I like it not, that the Order seems to be being drawn into a dispute among fellow Christians. The mission to Burghead served God's holy cause—none who were there can deny it. But no more right is it for us to fight for this Robert the Bruce than it was for some of us to have fought for Edward of England, under Brian de Jay."

"That is true," Arnault said carefully. "And no one asks us to fight for Bruce. What is required is that we help maintain the peace, as has always been the purpose of the Temple, wherever we are sent—and that, if need be, we lend our swords to prevent Edward's forces from interfering in the wishes of the Scottish people; to see their own king crowned, and to regain their freedom."

In the absence of instructions otherwise from their superiors in France, the chapter agreed that such intent was reasonable; and following evening prayer, Luc released all of them to retire to beds for the first time in several weeks. In a subsequent meeting, in private with only Arnault, he was able to reveal information he dared not share with the others of their Order.

"I need not tell you, I think that questions are still being asked in some quarters concerning the manner of John Comyn's death," Luc said, "but the senior members of the Scottish clergy have been told enough of the truth to justify Bruce's actions. Thanks, in part, to Torquil's quick thinking, Wishart of Glasgow has given Bruce formal absolution for the slaying—and Bruce, in exchange, has sworn a formal oath to uphold the freedom of the Scottish Church. Wishart preached a rousing sermon from the pulpit, exhorting the Scottish people to fight for Bruce as for a crusade. As a result, oaths of fealty are pouring in from every quarter."

"Then, Bruce now has support from the Scottish clergy, the Scottish nobles, and the Scottish people," Arnault replied. "Not all, of course—but at least the way is paved for him to receive the formal seal of kingship: the power that will attend his enthronement on the Stone of Destiny. And *that* will help him unite all the factions, to stand against Edward of England."

Plans were already set in motion for Bruce to undergo a more conventional coronation and enthronement at Scone Abbey—as conventional as such could be, in a state of war with England, and with so much of the traditional regalia still languishing in London. This public ceremony was to take place in less than a fortnight, on the Feast of the Annunciation, this year falling on the twenty-fifth of March.

After some further consideration, Luc and Arnault agreed that Bruce's mystical enthronement should take place secretly at Dunkeld the night following—to which end, Brother Ninian had sent word that Abbot Fingon would be on his way to Scone from the Columban house on Iona, and that Abbot Henry would be contributing to the secret ceremony. Satisfied that these worthies could supply any knowledge that might otherwise be lacking, Arnault was guardedly optimistic as he and Luc set out from Balantrodoch on the road north to Scone.

They arrived at the abbey with two days to spare, to find Torquil there ahead of them and already briefed by Abbot Fingon and his fellow Columbans. Brother Fionn had accompanied the abbot, bringing the Columban number to three. That night, Arnault apprised them of the events at Burghead, and Torquil filled him in on the past month and more with the Bruce.

Bruce himself arrived the day after, in more stately procession, bringing in his train a large number of Scottish magnates and high-ranking clerics. The atmosphere hanging over the abbey was tense with expectation. Though most of those present knew nothing about the secret preparations

being made by Arnault and his companions, all seemed
united in the unspoken conviction that Scotland's future was
about to be decided for centuries yet to come.

The morning of the twenty-fifth dawned fair. As preparation for the public ceremony of enthronement and crowning—itself always a secular affair—a solemn High Mass
was held in the abbey church. Listening to the readings, focusing himself for what would come as the day unfolded,
Arnault found it faintly ominous that this year's Feast of the
Annunciation should fall on the Friday before Palm Sunday.
Perhaps it was a suitable occasion for the formal acclamation of a king, but he could not help reflecting that a king
thus hailed might well face great sufferings before coming
into his kingdom. He sensed Torquil's uneasiness as well, as
the two of them moved forward to receive Communion from
Bishop Lamberton. Bruce, accompanied by his wife and
brothers—incipient queen and princes, as soon as the crown
was placed upon his head—seemed as calm as could be expected.

A brief recess followed the Mass, so that appropriate re-
arrangements could be made inside the church, for in the absence of the Stone, the enthronement ceremony was to take
place there, rather than outside on the Moot Hill. Bringing
out the regalia he had brought with him from Glasgow,
Bishop Wishart produced episcopal robes appropriate for a
king, a circlet of gold, hastily contrived, and most impor-
tantly, a royal banner of the arms of Scotland, which had belonged to Alexander III. In place of the absent Stone of
Destiny was set a regal chair, on a dais at the upper end of
the nave, surmounted by rich draperies of brocade and cloth-
of-gold.

Upon completion of these preparations, the only person
not yet arrived for the ceremony was the Countess of
Buchan. A staunch supporter of the Scottish cause, Countess
Isabel had claimed the ceremonial role of her brother, the
Earl of Fife, whose hereditary privilege it was to set the

crown on the new monarch's head—an infant when John Balliol was crowned, and now a captive hostage of Edward. But when, after an hour's further delay, she still had not arrived, it was decided not to wait any longer.

"Further delay would not be wise," Bishop Lamberton noted with misgiving. "Many of us have come at grave risk to life and office. There will be repercussions enough, when Edward learns what is being done here. The ceremony must go forward without her."

Lamberton himself presided over the ceremony, assisted by Bishop Wishart of Glasgow and Bishop David Murray of Moray. As host, Abbot Henry of Scone was likewise prominent in the order of ceremony, together with his colleague, the Abbot of Inchaffray.

Among the noblemen present were four great earls: John of Atholl, Malcolm of Lennox, Alan of Menteith, and Donald of Mar. Bruce's four brothers were also in attendance, as were his wife, Elizabeth, his nephew Thomas Randolph, and his close friend Christopher Seton, who so recently had saved his life at Dumfries.

Following the inaugural addresses, Bruce was seated on the royal chair and duly invested with the regalia that Bishop Wishart had provided: the robes, his own sword, the banner of his Canmore ancestors, a white wand in lieu of a scepter, and a golden circlet of kingship. For those who had been present at the enthronement of John Balliol, fourteen years before, comparisons were inevitable—though superficial, other than those drawn by Bruce's Templar champions. Though all the external trappings of tradition had been correct on that occasion, including the presence of the Stone of Destiny, Arnault, Torquil, and Luc well recalled how strongly they had felt that something vital was wanting. Now, despite so many outward changes and substitutions, at least all was right with the man himself—and tomorrow night, God willing, Bruce's kingship would be validated upon that most precious symbol of Scotland's sovereignty: the Stone of Destiny.

But for now, the crown must suffice. Following the enthronement and crowning, Bruce received the acclamation of all present, and took oaths of fealty from those who had not already sworn him allegiance. Anxieties over the absence of Isabel, Countess of Buchan, were relieved when she arrived later in the day, having ridden one of her husband's horses at great speed. In respect for tradition, it was decided that the enthronement and crowning would be repeated on Palm Sunday, so that her family's hereditary role might be carried out. That night, while the monks of Scone Abbey hosted a banquet for the new king and their other eminent guests, those who had reason to look beyond the fleeting celebrations of the day slipped off to make sure all was in readiness for the momentous events to come.

Early the next morning, Abbot Fingon and Brothers Ninian and Fionn made ready to set out for Dunkeld in advance of the main company. To them had been entrusted the relics of two Scottish saints: the arm bone of Saint Kentigern of Strathclyde and the crozier head of Saint Fillan of Strathearn, brought to Scone by their hereditary keepers, the Dean of Glasgow and the Abbot of Inchaffray respectively. With the willing consent of these two churchmen, the three Columbans were taking the relics to Dunkeld with the intention of invoking the saints' blessing, in addition to those of Saint Columba, on behalf of the new king and his embattled kingdom. Arnault met the party at the gate to see them off.

"The plan is for the rest of us to steal away after Vespers," he told Abbot Fingon. "Relays of fresh horses have been arranged along the way. With luck, we should be with you between Compline and midnight."

"Then, God speed us both," the abbot said, inclining his silver head.

As much as possible, those expecting to make the night journey devoted the daylight hours to rest and meditation on Saturday, in preparation for the work that lay ahead, though the new king's attention was required for assorted meetings with various supporters throughout the day. All members of the company, not excepting Bruce himself, abstained from food from the middle of the afternoon; and after Vespers, when the king announced his intention to retire early, most of his train took the opportunity to do the same. Within an hour, the abbey precincts were quiet, so that a cloaked and hooded party of six were able to set out secretly on the road north. Torquil led the way, with Abbot Henry and Bishop Lamberton flanking Bruce. Arnault and Luc provided their rear guard.

Dunkeld lay fifteen miles to the north. The little band covered the distance in haste, stopping twice along the way to change horses. The stars were burning bright in a frosty, deep black sky as the six approached the gates of the cathedral ward. A sleepy porter let them in, little mindful of the identity of the newcomers, and after leaving their horses in the care of two servants of Bishop Crambeth, Bishop Lamberton and Abbot Henry led their charge to the rear door of Crambeth's house.

A trusted servant was waiting to admit them, and to whisk the king upstairs to bathe and exchange his riding clothes for garments more suitable to the ceremonial occasion. While he was making himself ready, Torquil standing by to take him to his destiny, the others retreated to the lamp-lit crypt beneath the cathedral, where all was in readiness for the mystical event to come.

There, before the altar of a chapel in the crypt, was set the Stone of Destiny, temporarily draped with a snow-white cloth. Before it, to the west, lay a trestle table covered with a fair linen and draped across one end with a precious cope from the cathedral treasury. At the other end was set a silver basin and ewer and a linen towel. In the center was a wand of peeled ash wood and a coronal of twined laurel leaves and rosemary.

Three wooden lamp stands were ranged to the north of the Stone. The two at either end held the holy relics of Saint Kentigern and Saint Fillan, brought earlier that day from Scone. Upon the center stand, in honor of Saint Columba's historic association with the Stone of Destiny, Bishop Crambeth himself had placed Dunkeld's most famous treasure, the Monymusk Reliquary—and would be joining in their work tonight, in reward for having been the Stone's guardian this past year. Sometimes carried into battle before Scottish armies, like a Celtic Ark of the Covenant, this tiny house-shaped casket, embellished in the Celtic style and hardly larger than a man's hand, contained holy relics of Saint Columba himself.

But first the chamber must be prepared for the work to come. As the others ranged themselves around the Stone— all save Torquil and the Bruce himself, who had not yet arrived—Arnault drew his sword and, acting for the Church Militant, made a solemn circuit of the room, beginning in the west, tracing a sacred circle with his blade, his Templar robes ashimmer in the lamplight. Luc bore a lighted candle behind him, Brother Ninian following to sprinkle the boundaries of the circle with holy water. They did not close the circle in the west, for that must first serve as the mystical gateway through which the king would enter the sacred precinct thus created.

The casting of the circle being accomplished, Arnault took up his post outside the western gate, sword grounded beside him, to await the arrival of the king. The three Scottish clerics stood in the east, between the altar and the Stone, Abbot Henry flanked by Bishops Lamberton and Crambeth. Luc moved to the south, where Arnault and Torquil would join him. The three Columban brothers ranged themselves between the Stone and the trestle table, Abbot Fingon nearest the end with the basin and ewer, all of them expectantly facing the west.

The king was not long in coming. Shortly before midnight, following the sound of a door closing somewhere above them, two sets of footsteps on the stairs into the crypt heralded the arrival of Torquil, the Bruce's naked sword borne before him, and then the Bruce himself, now wearing the snow-white alb of a priest—or a sacrifice. His empty scabbard hung at his side. As they came slowly down the length of the crypt, Abbot Fingon laid the towel over his arm and took up the basin and ewer, moving quietly into position just inside the gate. Arnault came to attention, raising his sword in salute, as Torquil took up station opposite him and Bruce stopped between them, facing the abbot.

Briefed while he prepared with Torquil, the king extended his hands over the silver basin as the abbot poured water over them in symbolic purification, drying his hands on the towel after the manner of priests serving Mass and then laying it back across Fingon's arm. The two exchanged bows, after which Torquil conducted him through the gate and on to stand between the table and the still-draped Stone, turning then to place the king's sword on the table before retreating to a post beside Luc.

Arnault closed the western gate with the symbolic stroke of his sword's point across the stone floor, then laid the blade along that line in reminder of the protective circle it represented. As he took his place with his brother Templars in the south, Abbot Henry pulled the covering from the Stone behind Bruce. To Abbot Fingon, as keeper of the accumulated lore and wisdom of Iona, fell the lore-speaking role of *seannachie*, traditional conductor of ritual inauguration in Celtic tradition, speaking from between his two Columban brethren.

"Robert Bruce, successor to the High Kings of Alba," he said. "You stand within a sacred circle, cast by a sword hallowed by service to the Light, among those prepared to bear

witness as you are enthroned upon the Stone of Destiny, inaugural seat of your predecessors. Before you stand three
who are sworn to the service of holy Columba; behind you
stand three Scottish clerics, whose prayers shall sustain you
as king. At your left hand stand three knights of God, earthly
instruments of Michael of the white steed, God's own captain general. And at your right lie the relics of three sweet
saints of these blessed isles. Permit me now to bring you
into their presence."

Gesturing toward the three lamp stands he stepped to
Bruce's side and took his elbow, turning him to face the
north, then moved forward a step, betaking himself into the
symbolic presence of the three saints.

"Blessed Saint Kentigern," he declared with a reverential
bow, "we, your successors, invite you to be present amongst
us, as we mark the enthronement of King Robert Bruce, in
keeping with tradition handed down from the days of your
ministry. Grant us, we ask, the grace of your prayers and
protection, that the virtues vested in the Stone of Destiny
may be visited upon him, and this realm of Scotland be freed
from the yoke of foreign dominion."

He next addressed himself to Saint Fillan. "Blessed Saint
Fillan, shepherd of souls," he prayed, "we invite you likewise to be present in our midst. Support us in our labors, by
your prayers and intercessions, that King Robert Bruce may
receive the blessing and sanction of the Father of Mercies,
to deliver the people of Scotland out of the hands of their enemies."

His third and last address was directed to his own patron,
to whom so much was owed by so many in this chamber.

"Columba, beneficent and benign, our father in faith," he
prayed, "the time foretold by you in prophecy is now at
hand. The Uncrowned King has laid down his earthly life,
thereby renewing the virtues of the Stone of Destiny. Bear
witness now to the enthronement of his successor, Robert
Bruce, and pray with us that he may receive all grace and

power from the Threefold One to secure the freedom of
Scotland, and in so doing lay a firm and lasting foundation
for the Temple of Light."

In the pregnant hush that followed these words, the
faintest breath of a wondrous perfume touched at Arnault's
nostrils. Sweet and aromatic, the scent went to his head and
heart like a draft of wine, lightening his spirit with intimations of joy. The others seemed to smell it, too. In the same
moment, it seemed to Arnault that the lamplight pervading
the chamber was growing clearer and brighter.

The immanence was centered on the three reliquaries on
the north side of the dais. It brought with it a sense of living
Presence—or rather, Arnault corrected himself—three separate Presences, each radiating a shimmering fragrance of
sanctity. Brightest among them was the one in the middle,
powerful enough to cast a mantle of light over the Stone of
Destiny. In that moment, Arnault felt all his fears abate, his
heart too filled with wonder to hold anything else in that moment, until finally a purely human voice broke the spell—
Lamberton, quietly reciting a bidding prayer to signify the
commencement of Bruce's investiture.

A chorus of hushed amens concluded the bishop's prayer.
Thereafter, Abbot Fingon addressed the company in his role
as *seannachie*.

"Hear now these words regarding the sacred kings of
Scotland," he began, "and learn what it truly means to be a
king."

The disquisition that followed mirrored much of what Arnault had learned during his sojourn on Iona. Abbot Fingon
spoke briefly of the history of the Celtic peoples of these
isles, going on to recite the names of Alba's kings from the
time of Columba onward. This formal lesson in history was
accompanied by a discourse on the traditions and responsibilities long associated with Scottish kingship.

"In giving to King Aidan the Stone of Destiny to be his
coronation seat," Abbot Fingon recalled, "Saint Columba

was instituting a practice by which the Scottish people might know and recognize their true monarch. For the king must be to them as a good shepherd to his sheep: their guide in times of confusion, their protector in times of trouble. So let it be with you, Robert Bruce, in whose veins the blood of the Canmore royal line flows true."

This exhortation served as prelude to a formal panegyric in which the abbot recited the lineage of Bruce's own family, at the same time noting and praising the heroic deeds of generations past. As Arnault listened, he reflected silently that none of the exploits of Bruce's forefathers could equal, let alone surpass, the challenges that lay ahead of Bruce himself. Such success as he had already achieved was darkly overshadowed by much greater dangers yet to come. But Arnault dared to hope that, once invested with the Stone's mystical powers, Bruce would find the fortitude within himself to reforge his kingdom in the image of greatness, past and future.

"Witnesses present on behalf of the Scottish people," Abbot Fingon concluded at the end of his recitation, "I present unto you Robert Bruce of Annandale, undoubted King of this realm of Scotland, inheritor thereof by the laws of God and man, who has pledged himself willing to accept the kingship. Let him now be invested with the tokens of royalty, that he may become in name and in fact what he is already by right of birth and sacrifice."

At these words, Arnault stepped forward to join the abbot in conducting Bruce before the Stone. Bruce briefly closed his eyes as Fingon then began calling forward the individual members of the company to carry out the investiture.

First to approach was Abbot Henry of Scone, with the precious cope signifying the mantle of kingship. This he laid upon Bruce's shoulders, clasping the gem-studded morse upon his breast—very like the High Priest's Breastplate, it suddenly occurred to Arnault.

"Receive this kingly mantle as an emblem of authority," Abbot Henry said. "May it please Almighty God to grant you all meritorious virtues, that you may wield that authority in accordance with His will."

Torquil then took up Bruce's sword, now serving as a sword of state, and lifted it to kiss the cross-hilt of the guard before presenting it to its owner, hilt uppermost.

"Receive this sword, likeness of the symbol of our faith, as an emblem of courage and fortitude. May it serve you well in the defense of your land and your people."

Before taking the sword, Bruce bowed his head and likewise kissed the cross-guard. Then, closing his right hand around its hilt, he turned to salute each of the four airts, beginning with the east, where the altar lay. Finishing in the north, he paid lingering reverence to the three saints whose veiled presences enlightened the otherwise empty northern side of the chamber. When he had completed his salutations, he sheathed the blade in the empty scabbard at his side.

Bishop Crambeth next came forward to invest Bruce with the white wand. "Receive this rod as a token of governance," he said. "May you rule your subjects with wisdom, and administer the laws of this land with mercy and discernment."

When Bruce had received the wand, Abbot Fingon and Arnault formally assisted him to be seated on the Stone. The king's fingers tightened on the wand and he briefly closed his eyes, but all of them were well aware that the culmination was yet to come. It remained for Brother Ninian to step forward with the coronal wreath, to set this upon Bruce's head in place of a crown.

"Receive this coronal as a token of kingship," he said quietly, "bearing in mind the memory of those who came before you, not least William Wallace, whom we also honor here as Scotland's Uncrowned King.

"The laurel leaves are symbolic of your victory, and victory yet to come," he continued, "but they also recall the crown with which William Wallace was invested on the day of his death; the rosemary betokens that remembrance. Therefore, wear this crown in a spirit of humility, never forgetting his sacrifice in imitation of that King who is above all Kings, and before Whom every knee should bend. May you be as ready, at need, to lay down your life for the sake of those you shall rule."

Bruce's taut face betrayed the depth of his inner emotion, his fingers clasped so tightly around the white wand across his knees that Arnault feared it might snap.

"I so pledge my readiness," he said softly. "And as God is my witness, henceforth I and all those who come after me who bear the name of Bruce shall take rosemary as the badge of their family honor, in faithful remembrance of William Wallace and of all the many others who have died to uphold the cause of Scottish freedom!"

The invocation of Wallace's name served to remind all present that Bruce had one last duty to perform: to bind himself to the Stone of Destiny and receive its mystical empowerment. Arnault once again came forward, starting to draw the dagger that had shed Wallace's blood. But before he could do so, Torquil stepped between him and Bruce, his arm across Arnault's chest, his glance darting between the two men.

"Not that blade," he murmured. "It is this night's blood which now shall bind the king to the Stone. That blade served well, but it also shed Comyn's blood. It would not be fitting that it be used for this holy rite. The point has worried me since that day at Dumfries."

Chilled, Arnault let the dagger slip back into its sheath, appalled that he had not thought of it. But as Bruce looked at them uncertainly, Torquil slowly eased his own sword partway from its scabbard and sank to one knee, offering the hilt to Bruce.

"The day of Falkirk, you gave me this sword," he said. "I hope and pray that I have done you honor by it. You said I would need it, if I came to serve you. I would have it serve you now, if that is your will."

Bruce's gray eyes met his, searching, uncertain. Then he closed his hand around the hilt.

"Will you assist me?" he asked.

"Most willingly," Torquil said.

Nodding his acceptance, Bruce gave the white wand to Arnault, then drew the blade the rest of the way from its scabbard and laid the sword across Torquil's hands. Torquil braced the weapon as Bruce closed his left palm around the tip of the blade, never taking his eyes from the Templar's— and sharply pulled his hand away, flinching slightly.

The hand he opened to display to the four quarters was bleeding, and he closed his eyes as he lowered it beside him, so that his bloody palm came to rest upon the Stone of Destiny. By that simple action, he made himself at one with Wallace and the Stone. And in that moment of unity, the power vested in the Stone yielded itself to him.

No outward physical sign attended the act, save that Bruce drew and exhaled a long breath, but all within the circle were aware, to varying degrees, of a surge of energies rising up to encompass Scotland's new king. Like tongues of sacramental fire, the power flowed and flickered around him. Bruce's still face was momentarily suffused with blind rapture as his spirit drank of the tide of enlightenment. Nor did the tide subside until this new human vessel had drunk its fill of the Stone's indwelling power.

For that timeless moment, utter silence reigned. Then the supernatural brightness of the room yielded peacefully to the familiar dimness of earthly lamplight as Columba and his fellow saints retired to the other side of that veil that marked the boundary between the Seen and the Unseen. A faint residual fragrance hovered for a moment in the wake of their departure, and Arnault sensed his fellow Templars gently exhaling as the tension faded. As he bestirred himself enough to lay the white wand back in the Bruce's slack hand, Torquil quietly sheathing his sword, Abbot Fingon broke the silence, once again speaking as *seannachie* for this earthly Chief of Chiefs.

"All hail Robert Bruce, King of Scots!" he said fervently. "Thanks be to God, together with all His angels and saints, for the work that has been accomplished this night in our midst!"

This acclamation was heartily echoed by all present. At the sound of their voices, Bruce lifted his head with the mildly startled air of a man awakening from a dream.

"And thanks be to you, my true and honorable friends," he said haltingly, "for I think that, without the aid and guidance of your vision, the flame now passed to me would have perished long ago, and with it Scotland's hopes for liberty.

"But this moment, which marks the ending of one journey, likewise marks the beginning of another," he continued, gaining confidence. "Before us lies a road fraught with perils. It runs through the valley of the shadow of death, but I swear to you that no fear of either death or darkness shall hold me back from leading you to the other side. The Light which abides with us now is an eternal light of freedom which cannot be quenched. Let us pledge our loyalty to one another, knowing that so long as our faith holds true, the minions of darkness shall never prevail against us!"

Epilogue

BRUCE'S WORDS CONTINUED TO ECHO AND REECHO IN THE back of Arnault's mind as they made their way back to Scone in the small hours of the morning. He wondered if the moment of empowerment had gifted Bruce with a vision of future events, as Wallace before him had been vouchsafed a glimpse of things yet to come. Such foreknowledge, as Arnault knew from his own experience, was often as much a burden as a blessing. Small wonder, then, if the new king should choose to keep silent concerning what he himself had foreseen.

They returned to Scone as swiftly and secretly as they had gone. Mere hours later, the rising sun ushered in the solemn observances of Palm Sunday, couched in the celebration of a pontifical High Mass to set a public seal on Bruce's crowning. The morning offices were followed by a reenactment of Friday's ceremony of enthronement and crowning, but for Arnault, these events had the quality of a dream. Though he was present in body throughout the investiture and the swearing of fealties, his mind and spirit were preoccupied with contemplations of the previous night.

His own next duty—in which intent Luc concurred—was that he and Torquil should return to France as soon as possible, to report the successful outcome of Bruce's enthronement. It would mean but little to the Order in general, for claiming a crown and daring to hold it against the wrath of the English king would be two different things. But the other members of *le Cercle* would eagerly welcome the news that the sovereignty of Scotland was once again vested in a rightfully appointed king. Arnault and his allies might have won a few battle victories, but the outcome of the war itself was yet to be decided.

Later that evening, amid the leave-takings of various dignitaries setting off for their own lands, Arnault received an invitation to meet with Robert Bruce in the abbey's cloister garden for a few private words alone. The evening stars were just beginning to appear when he entered the garden. Bruce was pacing up and down in the shelter of an arbor, its interlacing branches still thin and bare, with only buds showing at the tips of each twig. He welcomed Arnault's arrival with a smile, gesturing then that they should walk a while.

"I called you here first to thank you once again for all your help," the king said. "But I also wish to ask about a question weighing on my mind."

"Then, ask," Arnault said. "I shall do my best to answer it."

"My Scottish bishops have endorsed my kingship," Bruce said, "because they know they can trust me to uphold the independence of the Scottish Church and its clergy. The monks of Iona similarly have given me their support, knowing that I will honor their Celtic ways. But you and your companions remain something of a mystery to me. I have been wondering why members of the Order of the Temple should go to such lengths to see me enthroned according to the traditions of Columba."

Arnault was taken slightly aback by the question, for the reasons were many and complicated, and not all could be shared with the Bruce.

"You are right to deduce that we have our reasons," he said thoughtfully. "If I hesitate over my answer, it is because the reasons are by no means simple to explain."

"After what took place last night," Bruce said with a wry glimmer of humor, "you might be surprised what I would be willing to accept."

Arnault studied the new king for a long moment. Looking deep into the other man's eyes, he perceived clear evidence of the changes that the Stone's empowerment had wrought: a deepening of mind and insight, a clearer vision of what it truly meant to be a king. It occurred to him that Bruce's inquiries were prompted by the same influences that had been guiding their common purpose all along. Taking some of the initiative sometimes allowed by his oaths to *le Cercle*, he decided that it was meant that the other man be vouchsafed some partial knowledge of the greater truth.

"The Stone of Destiny is not the only artifact of power known to our Order," he said. "Some of us within the Temple have made it our life's work to recover and preserve such treasures for the good of all mankind. Our hope in the past was to establish a grand reliquarium for these objects in Jerusalem. With the fall of the Holy City, however, we now believe that Providence has singled out another place for that purpose."

Bruce's brow furrowed. "Scotland?" he hazarded incredulously.

Arnault confirmed it with a nod. "To serve as home for our greatest treasures, Scotland itself must be a free nation. We could not sit idly by and let her fall victim to the acquisitive greed of England's king."

"But there were Templars aiding Edward at the battle of

Berwick, at Falkirk," Bruce protested. "More than once since then, Edward has commended the Master of the English Temple for his services."

"That Master had an agenda of his own," Arnault replied, declining to be more specific, "and the Order is not the unified brotherhood it once was. That makes it all the more important that those of us who are appointed guardians of these secret treasures find a safe and inviolate haven for them."

A long silence fell between them as Bruce assimilated this revelation.

"If you hope for Scotland's freedom," he said at last, "you must know that the fight is only just beginning. If it is to be truly won, the cost will not be light."

"Where there are great issues at stake, often the price of resolution is proportionately dear," Arnault said. "But in this case," he added, "I think you have already been shown a reason to hope for victory."

"Whether God should see fit to deliver Scotland out of the hands of her enemies remains to be seen," Bruce said. "But I owe my crown, in part, to you and Brother Torquil, and I consider myself in your debt. If, in the future, I am in a position to render you assistance, I give you my oath that I will do so."

"I could ask no more of you than this," Arnault said with a smile. "And your offer is all the more precious because I did not have to ask. It is a pledge that my superiors will be anxious to hear."

"How soon do you plan to take them the message?" Bruce asked.

"Brother Torquil and I should set out first thing in the morning," Arnault replied. "There is much to be done—but much also to hope for."

"Then we shall both live in hope," Bruce declared, extending his hand, "until the coming of a brighter day."

Partial Bibliography

Addison, Charles G. *The History of the Knights Templar*. Kempton, IL: Adventures Unlimited Press, 1997. (Reprint of 1842 London edition.)

Adamnan. *Life of Columba*. Translated by Alan Orr Anderson and Marjorie Ogilvie Anderson. London/Edinburgh: Thomas Nelson and Sons, Ltd., 1961.

Baigent, Michael, and Richard Leigh. *The Temple and the Lodge*. London: Jonathan Cape, 1989.

Barber, Malcolm. *The Trial of the Templars*. Cambridge, England: Cambridge University Press, 1978.

————. *The New Knighthood*. Cambridge, England: Cambridge University Press, 1994.

Barron, E. M. *The Scottish War of Independence: A Critical Study*. Inverness: Robert Carruthers, 1934.

Barrow, Geoffrey W. S. *Robert the Bruce & The Community of the Realm of Scotland*. Edinburgh: Edinburgh University Press, 1975, 1994.

Bower, Robert. *Scotichronicon.* (Fifteenth century chronicle) General editing by D. E. R. Watt. Aberdeen: Aberdeen University Press, 1989.

Burman, Edward. *The Templars: Knights of God.* Wellingborough: Aquarian Press, 1986.

Carmichael, Alexander. *Carmina Gadelica.* Edinburgh: Floris Books, 1994.

Gerber, Pat. *The Search for the Stone of Destiny.* Edinburgh: Canongate Press, 1992.

Knight, Christopher, and Robert Lomas. *The Second Messiah: Templars, the Turin Shroud, and the Great Secret of Freemasonry.* London: Century Books, 1997.

Kurtz, Katherine, ed. *Tales of the Knights Templar.* New York: Warner, 1995.

Partner, Peter. *The Murdered Magicians.* Also published as *The Knights Templar and Their Myth.* Oxford, England: Oxford University Press, 1981.

Paterson, Raymond Campbell. *For the Lion: A History of the Scottish Wars of Independence 1296–1357.* Edinburgh: John Donald Publishers, Ltd., 1996.

Prebble, John. *The Lion in the North.* London: George Rainbird, Ltd., 1971.

Prestwick, Michael. *Edward I.* London: Methven, 1988.

Robinson, John J. *Born in Blood.* New York: M. Evans, 1989.

———. *Dungeon, Fire, and Sword.* New York: M. Evans, 1991.

Runciman, Sir Steven. *History of the Crusades, Vol. III, The Kingdom of Acre and the Later Crusades.* Cambridge, England: Cambridge University Press, 1954.

Simon, Edith. *The Piebald Standard: A Biography of the Knights Templar.* Boston: Little, Brown, 1959.

Upton-Ward, J. M. *The Rule of the Templars.* New York: Boydell Press, 1992. Translated from the French of Henri de Curzon's 1886 edition of the French Rule, derived from the three extant medieval manuscripts.

About the Authors

KATHERINE KURTZ is the author of the internationally bestselling Deryni books and other historical fantasies. Katherine Kurtz lives in Ireland.

DEBORAH TURNER HARRIS is the author of the Mages of Garillon trilogy, and coauthor with Katherine Kurtz of the Adept series, including *The Templar Treasure*. Deborah Turner Harris lives in Scotland.

Also Available from Warner Aspect

KNIGHTS OF THE TEMPLE

An elite order of warrior-priests forged in the terror of the Crusades, the Knights Templar amassed knowledge and wealth enough to challenge the power of kings and popes. Seven hundred years after they were betrayed, mystery and wonder still surround the Templars' history.

The author of the classic Deryni series, Katherine Kurtz has gathered 20 stories into two volumes of original short fiction by the top talent of the fantastic—Poul Anderson, Elizabeth Moon, Deborah Turner Harris, Diane Duane, Andre Norton, and many more—to explore the most mystic and mysterious army ever.

✠✠ ✠✠ ✠✠

Tales of the Knights Templar

0-446-60-138-1, $5.99 U.S. (7.99 Can)

On Crusade: More Tales of the Knights Templar

0-446-67-339-0, $11.99 U.S. trade paperback, ($15.99 Can)

Also Available from Warner Aspect

KNIGHT OF THE TEMPLE

An elite order of warrior-priests forged in the terror of the Crusades, the Knights Templar amassed knowledge and wealth enough to challenge the power of kings and popes. Seven hundred years after they were betrayed, mystery and wonder still surround the Templars' history.

The author of the classic Deryni series, Katherine Kurtz has gathered 20 stories into two volumes of original short fiction by the top talent of the fantasy—Poul Anderson, Elizabeth Moon, Deborah Turner Harris, Diane Duane, Andre Norton, and many more—to explore the most mystic and mysterious army ever.

# # # # #

Tales of the Knights Templar

0-446-67238-1, $5.99 U.S. ($7.99 Can.)

On Crusade: More Tales of the
Knights Templar

0-446-67539-0, $11.99 U.S. trade paperback ($17.99 Can.)

558

VISIT WARNER ASPECT ONLINE!

THE WARNER ASPECT HOMEPAGE
You'll find us at: www.twbookmark.com then by clicking on Science Fiction and Fantasy.

NEW AND UPCOMING TITLES
Each month we feature our new titles and reader favorites.

AUTHOR INFO
Author bios, bibliographies and links to personal websites.

CONTESTS AND OTHER FUN STUFF
Advance galley giveaways, autographed copies, and more.

THE ASPECT BUZZ
What's new, hot and upcoming from Warner Aspect: awards news, best-sellers, movie tie-in information . . .

VISIT WARNER ASPECT ONLINE!

THE WARNER ASPECT HOMEPAGE
You'll find us at: www.twbookmark.com then by clicking on Science Fiction and Fantasy.

NEW AND UPCOMING TITLES
Each month we feature our new titles and reader favorites.

AUTHOR INFO
Author bios, bibliographies and links to personal websites.

CONTESTS AND OTHER FUN STUFF
Advance galley giveaways, autographed copies, and more.

THE ASPECT BUZZ
What's new, hot and upcoming from Warner Aspect: awards news, bestsellers, movie tie-in information ...